Murder, Mystery & Malone

CRAIG RICE
edited by Jeffrey A. Marks

Crippen & Landru Publishers
Norfolk, Virginia
2002

Crippen & Landru Publishers
P.O. Box 9315
Norfolk, VA 23505
USA

www.crippenlandru.com
CrippenL@pilot.infi.net

Contents

Introduction

Mystery writer Craig Rice never lived to see her short works collected into book form, but others have been busy on her behalf since her death in 1957. Shortly after she died, *The Name is Malone* appeared. The book took ten of her Malone stories from *Ellery Queen's Mystery Magazine* and *Manhunt*, among them her most popular and most frequently anthologized works. Three years later, *The People vs. Withers and Malone*, the collection of stories that combined her detective with Stuart Palmer's Hildegarde Withers, came out, thanks to Palmer's efforts to keep the characters alive. Still, that left a number of uncollected short works that still sparkle like hidden treasures after all these years. Having spent so much time with Craig Rice, I can honestly say that she'd be thrilled to have a new collection of her short stories published forty–five years after her death. While most of these stories haven't appeared in print in over forty years, their mirth and wit can still make the reader crack a smile at Craig's comic genius.

Craig loved the short story form, and the era in which she wrote allowed her to produce a number of works of short mystery fiction. Beginning in 1943, she wrote for friend Frederic Dannay's *Ellery Queen's Mystery Magazine*, and for Anthony Boucher at his various publishing enterprises. During her binge-drinking days in New York City in the early 1950's, she went to the offices of the Scott Meredith Agency every day to write short stories. The agent put her in a room where she was expected to write for eight hours. At the end of the day, Craig would be paid for her work. The first few stories showed the rust on her style, but she quickly recovered her form. Most of those stories appeared in *Manhunt*, a mystery magazine that was heavily supported by Scott Meredith's literary agency. Even when she was wracked up with neurological problems in Rachos Los Amigos, she continued to write short stories, focusing her efforts on twists and turns based on her knowledge of the genre and its taboos.

The form loved her in return as did her readers. She won *Ellery Queen*'s Readers Choice award for one of her first efforts, and she was nominated more times than she could count. Her name was usually billed first in whatever maga–zine her stories graced. One issue of *The Saint Mystery Magazine* listed her name prominently on the cover by itself. Editors knew that she sold magazines.

The kudos continued, but as she sank into depression and alcoholism, she was wont to write stories in order to buy another bottle. At times, she would bypass her agent in order to keep more of the money for herself. She wasn't above reselling the same story as new by just changing the first few lines of a story. All of this only added to the confusion surrounding Craig's body of work. By the time that *Who Was That Lady? Craig Rice: The Queen of Screwball Mysteries* was published in 2001, reviewers had actually attributed a fictitious anthology of stories to Craig. She would have had a good laugh over that. Craig was never one to let facts get in the way of a good story.

In putting together this collection, I chose the best uncollected stories from her career. Most of them are Malone stories, but the collection would be in—complete without a few of her other stories as well, so Melville Fairr is also represented. I hope that this collection showcases the consummate skill and the humor that made Craig Rice the cover person for *Time* magazine in January 1946.

Wry Highball

"You've got to believe me," the beautiful girl said. "I had nothing to do with it. I was just as surprised as Arthur — "

She produced a handkerchief from her purse and cried into it, softly. John J. Malone sat behind his desk feeling uncomfortable. "Now, now," he said. The girl went on sobbing. Malone said, "There, there."

"But it's terrible," the girl said at last. "Arthur is dead, and — " She went back to the handkerchief.

Malone sighed. "I'd like to help you," he said untruthfully, "but you'll have to tell me all about it. Now, let's start from the beginning. Your name is Sheila Manson."

The girl stopped sobbing as if someone had thrown a switch. She brushed hair the color of cornsilk away from her tear–stained face, looked up at Malone, and said, "But how did you know?"

Malone didn't think it was worthwhile telling Sheila Manson that a good description of her had been in every Chicago newspaper for the past forty–eight hours. "I have my methods," he said airily, trying to look mysterious.

"Then you must know about Arthur, too," Sheila Manson said.

"Suppose you tell me," Malone suggested diplomatically.

Sheila nodded. She put the handkerchief away in her purse and said, "He was my fiancé. Arthur Bent. We were going to be married next week."

"And now he's dead," Malone encouraged her sympathetically.

She nodded again. "And the police think I did it, but I didn't. You believe me, don't you, Mr. Malone?"

"Why do the police think you killed your fiancé?" Malone said, side–stepping neatly.

Sheila Manson shook her head. "I don't know why," she said. "But I can tell you who really did kill him."

There was a little silence. At last Malone prodded, "Who?"

"Mae Ammon," Sheila said. "She would murder anybody if she thought she could get something out of it."

"And what could she get out of murdering Arthur Bent?" Malone asked.

Sheila shrugged. She was beautiful even when she shrugged, Malone thought.

He decided he had to take the case — even if there wasn't any money in it. Even if he owed the telephone company, his landlord, the electric company, and three restaurants. They could wait, but Sheila Manson was the kind of vision that dropped into a man's office once in a lifetime.

"She was just jealous," Sheila said. "I was Arthur's fiancé, and she was jealous."

To Malone it sounded as if Mae Ammon had a better motive for murdering Sheila than for doing away with Arthur. However, this was no time for fine distinctions. "I'll do what I can for you," he said decisively.

"I can't pay you very much — "

"Don't you worry your pretty head about that," Malone said. "Just give me your address, so that I can get in touch with you — and then go home and try to relax."

"Mr. Malone," Sheila stood up. Her figure was slim and breathtaking. The last shreds of monetary regret disappeared from the little lawyer's thoughts. "If the police come — what shall I do?"

"Shoot it out," Malone said. Then he caught himself. "Sorry — I must have been thinking of someone else. If the come, just call me. I'll be right here, or else my secretary will find me. Now, you just relax and stop worrying."

"All right, Mr. Malone." She started for the door, under the lawyer's breathless scrutiny. At the door she turned. "Malone," she said, and her voice dropped an octave, "I'm — very grateful to you."

The door banged and she was gone.

After a minute Malone wiped the smile guiltily off his face, put on a businesslike frown, and told himself that precious time was passing.

He leaned back in his chair, closed his eyes, and tried hard to think about Arthur Bent.

Of course, he had read about it in the newspapers. Bent had been a rich man — and just recently rich, Malone reminded himself. On his twenty–fifth birthday he had become heir to the Bent fortune, as provided in his father's will. Two weeks later Arthur Bent was dead. He'd been poisoned with arsenic, placed in a rye–and–ginger–ale highball. He had taken this fatal drink in his own home, and no one else had been present except Sheila Manson and Mae Ammon.

But neither the bottle of ginger ale nor the bottle of expensive rye had been tampered with. The poison had been only in Bent's highball.

It certainly looked as if there were only two possible suspects: Sheila Manson and Mae Ammon. Well, he was working for Sheila Manson, Malone told himself; that meant he had to see Mae Ammon at once.

It was perfectly obvious, when you thought about it, that Mae Ammon had committed the murder. After all, Sheila was a beautiful young girl, and beautiful young girls just didn't do things like that. Or, at any rate, Malone was convinced this one hadn't done it.

Unfortunately for Malone's first theory, Mae Ammon was beautiful too.

Her address was, conveniently, in the Chicago telephone directory. Malone took a cab to the quiet brownstone, walked up the steps, and rang the bell.

The girl who answered the door had short black hair and a figure that made Malone almost stop breathing. She was not slim, like Sheila Manson, but Malone decided that he preferred curvaceous and cuddly brunettes. She wore a dark-green dress that clung to her figure like adhesive tape.

"I'm looking for Mae Ammon," Malone said. "But I'd rather be looking for you."

The girl smiled. "In that case," she said, "you're lucky. I'm Mae Ammon. Come in."

Malone followed her, in a daze, through a hallway and up one flight of dim stairs. "Most of the people who live here work during the day," she said as she pushed open the door of a large bright room. "I'm the only one here, so I answer the bell."

Malone said, "Ah," in an intelligent fashion, and followed her inside. The room was high-ceilinged and sunny. Magazines were scattered everywhere — on the blonde-wood coffee table, over the light-green couch and chairs, piled on the hi-fi and the television set. There was even a large bundle of them stacked on the yellow spread of the single daybed.

"So you're Mae Ammon," Malone said, for lack of anything else to say.

"That's right." She smiled again. "Just put some of the magazines on the floor and sit down. Who are you, by the way?"

Malone took a stack of *Lifes* and *Looks* from the couch and sat down. "I'm John J. Malone," he said.

"*The* John J. Malone?" Mae Ammon's face showed surprise.

Malone nodded. "The lawyer, anyway," he said with what he hoped was modesty.

"And you're here about poor Arthur," Mae said. Her smile disappeared. "I hope that woman gets the chair," she burst out. "Killing Arthur — and out of sheer jealousy, that's all it was — just because he was my fiancé — "

Malone said, "Stop."

Mae looked down at him. "Stop?"

"Did you say Arthur Bent was your fiancé?"

"That's right," the girl said.

Malone sighed. Things were getting a little complicated, he realized. "I'd heard that he was Sheila Manson's fiancé," he said cautiously.

"Sheila Manson!" Mae looked around the room suddenly, and saw a china dog lying on the floor. She picked it up and threw it against the wall. Malone ducked. The dog landed over his head with a sharp crash, and little pieces of china drifted down the back of his collar.

"*That's* what I think of Sheila Manson!" Mae said. "I hope she gets the chair! Arthur Bent was my fiancé, and I don't intend to forget it!"

Malone rose slowly. "I was only asking," he said mildly.

Mae came over to him and put a hand on his shoulder. "Oh, I wouldn't hurt you," she said. "I don't have anything against you. After all, you know I didn't kill Arthur. Why should I — we were going to be married week after next."

"Sure," Malone said. This didn't seem like the proper time to tell Mae Ammon that he was working for Sheila Manson. But Sheila had said she was going to marry Arthur Bent next week. That gave her a week's priority on Mae Ammon. Malone decided, in a hurry, that he'd better not mention that either.

"I just want to find out the truth," he said.

"Well, you know the truth," Mae said. "It was that hussy Sheila Manson, that's who it was. She slipped poison into his drink and he died. And now she's going to be caught and tried and convicted, and I hope she gets the chair — " She bent down and Malone ducked again. But she was only picking up a magazine. "They sometimes give women the chair," Mae said. "This magazine has some stories — but that's not important. I *want* Sheila Manson to get the chair."

Malone took a deep breath. "Suppose," he said gently, "that she didn't do it."

"But she did," Mae said. "I was there. I know."

"Did you see her actually put poison into his drink?"

"Well," Mae said, "not exactly. But I saw him mix the drink — take out the bottles and everything — take his own little stirrer out of the glass, and then drink it. And if *I* didn't kill him, then *she* must have! We were the only ones there."

Malone nodded. There was, he felt sure, another question he should ask, but he couldn't come up with it. "Was there ice in the drink?" he said at random.

"Of course there was," Mae said. "But the police checked the ice tray. There was no poison in it."

That, Malone thought, eliminated another possibility. But it had been a good idea. "Suppose Sheila Manson didn't murder your — suppose she didn't murder Arthur Bent," he said. "Who else might have had a motive?"

"Everybody loved Arthur," Mae said. "He was a wonderful man."

"Sure," Malone said. "But he was rich. Who's going to inherit his money?"

"I was his fiancée," Mae said. "I'm going to inherit."

"Did he make a will?"

Mae shrugged. She too was beautiful when she shrugged. "I don't know," she said with insouciance.

"How about any close relatives?" Malone said.

"He only had two cousins," Mae said. "Charlie Bent and J. O. Hanlon. They both live in Chicago. But they weren't even at Arthur's place. I tell you, I saw everything. He put in the ice, then the rye, then the ginger ale, then he stirred it all up and drank it — "

"I'll do what I can," Malone said diplomatically.

"I'm sure you will," Mae said. "By the way, why are you asking questions? Are you working with the police? Because I told them all this — "

"I'm just a friend," Malone lied smoothly. "I'm interested in Justice."

"So am I," Mae said. "And justice means giving that hussy the chair."

Well, Malone thought when he arrived at his own office again, there's still J.O. Hanlon and Charlie Bent.

He didn't feel much like seeing them, but somebody had to be the murderer. As things stood, the only suspects were a beautiful blonde and a beautiful brunette. Both, it seemed, had been fiancées of the dead man. And each was convinced the other had committed the murder — unless, Malone thought, they were both awfully good actresses.

But if neither girl had murdered Arthur Bent, Malone thought slowly, then how did he die? The arsenic was in his drink. It wasn't in the bottle of rye or in the bottle of ginger ale. It wasn't, according to Mae Ammon, in the ice cubes. So somebody had put it in the particular glass Arthur had used.

Unless he only used one particular glass — and somebody had painted the inside with arsenic beforehand. You could do that, Malone knew, if you used an arsenic–in–water solution. The poison would dry as a thin film, and dissolve again in any liquid.

Of course, it would make the glass look a little filmy...

Malone sighed and reached for the telephone.

Five minutes later he put it down. Von Flanagan had been exceptionally polite and courteous — for von Flanagan, that is. He'd actually told Malone what he wanted to know, and hadn't threatened even once to arrest the little criminal lawyer.

There was no arsenic residue in the glass above the level of the drink.

So the glass hadn't been painted with arsenic.

And that meant that either Mae or Sheila had murdered Arthur Bent.

The only trouble was that Malone was sure neither had.

Of course, the glass might have been painted only at the bottom. Malone wondered if von Flanagan had thought of that, and started to call him back before he realized it wouldn't have made any difference.

"It's a funny thing," von Flanagan had said. "Here's a guy who monograms everything he owns — got his own special monogrammed coasters, for instance. Nobody else uses his coaster. But he didn't monogram the glasses. So there'd be no way for anyone to tell in advance which glass he'd use."

And that, Malone thought, made the cheese even more binding.

He reached for the telephone again.

J. O. Hanlon, it developed, would be right over. He sounded on the telephone like the gruff and overbearing type, and Malone wondered if he were in for more trouble. Charlie Bent, unfortunately, couldn't be reached. His housekeeper said he'd been in Central Africa for the last six months on a safari.

And that's where I should be, Malone told himself sadly.

J. O. Hanlon charged into the office like a bull. Behind him the door slammed shut and rattled. "You wanted to see me?" he asked Malone in a voice that sounded as if it had come from the quarterdeck of the *Bounty*.

"Sit down," Malone said nervously. "And relax."

Hanlon dropped into a chair and stared belligerently across the desk. "What can I do for you?" he roared.

Malone winced. "I'm investigating the death of Arthur Bent — "

"I spoke to the police," Hanlon said. "Told 'em everything. You ask the police about it." He started to rise.

"I'd like to ask just a few questions," Malone said. "This won't take much of your time."

"All right," Hanlon said, and dropped back into the chair with a thud. "Ask away. I'm a fair and reasonable man. Willing to help if I can."

Malone cleared his throat, then said, "I understand you were Arthur's cousin."

"That's correct — mother's side of the family. My mother was Arthur's mother's sister."

Malone tried to work it out in his head and gave up. "Cousin" would have to do. "Do you know if Arthur Bent made a will?" Malone said.

"Told that to the police, too," Hanlon bellowed. "Charlie gets it all — good old Charlie."

"Charlie Bent?"

"Right," Hanlon shouted. "Charlie's in Africa now — hunting or some such foolishness. He'll find out when he gets back."

"Ah," Malone said. Hanlon, then, was motiveless. And that still left only two suspects — neither of whom, Malone assured himself dismally, was guilty. But maybe he could clear up a few of the cloudy points.

"I understand your cousin was engaged," he probed cautiously.

"Engaged?" Hanlon broke into gusts of laughter. Malone sat patiently, waiting for the outbursts to stop. At last Hanlon said, "Those two girls, right? Good game of Arthur's, poor man. Engaged to nobody — but he let the girls *think* he was engaged to them. That's why the three of them met up at his apartment that night — to compare notes."

"They had found out about each other?" Malone said.

"Oversight of Arthur's," Hanlon explained. "They both went to his apartment that night to talk things out with him."

Malone suddenly thought of another question. "How do you know about all this?"

"Me?" Hanlon said. "Been going with one of 'em myself — Arthur took her away. She told me all about it before she went to his apartment."

"Which one?" Malone leaned forward.

"Sheila," Hanlon said. "Good old Sheila. I'm sure she didn't do it. Must have been the other one — what's her name — Mae. Sheila wouldn't do a thing like that."

Malone closed his eyes for a long time. At last they opened. "My advice to you," he said, "is to hire a good lawyer. Me."

"Lawyer?"

"To defend you on a charge of murder," Malone said. "You see, I knew there was something — I knew I'd heard *something* that explained the whole killing. But I had to wait until now, when I saw a motive, to remember it and put all the pieces together."

"You're not making any sense," Hanlon said.

"Wait," Malone promised, "and I will. Hanlon, you murdered your cousin — so you could get your girl back."

"What?" Hanlon bounced up.

Malone said, "Relax. I'm going to defend you. Never lost a client yet."

"But I wasn't even there!" Hanlon exclaimed.

"You didn't have to be. Arthur Bent made the perfect victim — for a clever killer. Each of you had some kind of a motive — both girls, and you, and Charlie. But the girls didn't do it — they'd have killed each other first. And Charlie's in Africa. Arthur Bent monogrammed except — for some reason— drinking glasses."

"They were new — he hadn't got around to having the special monogram put on them," Hanlon said.

"And Mae kept talking about Arthur's own individual little stirrer."

Hanlon began to wilt.

"All right," he said at last, like a balloon gasping out its final breath. "I painted the arsenic on his stirrer... I had to get rid of him — so Sheila would come back to me."

"Don't worry about a thing," Malone said. "And admit nothing to the police. You were overwrought. You didn't know what you were doing."

"What?"

"Of course, my services come high," Malone went on persuasively.

"I'll take care of you, Malone," Hanlon said. "I've got some money of my own... "

Malone leaned back with satisfaction. Maybe, he thought, he'd get paid by everybody — each in his, or her, own fashion...

Most of Craig's novella length works were written when she lived at Rancho Los Amigos, precursors for what would later become novels. Because of the alcoholic break in her career, Craig had to prove herself a second time. She did that with a series of novellas that displayed her talents all over again. "The Frightened Millionaire" gives us an original novella length work by Craig, and a rare glimpse into the personal life of Maggie, Malone's long–suffering secretary. -JM

The Frightened Millionaire

John J. Malone didn't like it. All things considered — he didn't like it at all.

Maggie had never been late for work before. Always when the little criminal lawyer arrived at his office — which might be any time, depending on where he'd been the night before — she'd be there at her desk, making excuses over the telephone for his absence.

But on this particular morning, there was no Maggie. Malone's watch told him it was twenty to ten — a fair average for his own appearance — and there was no Maggie. Nothing, in fact, to indicate that there ever had been a Maggie, or even that she might have come in and gone out again. The mail, which he kicked aside, had been shoved through the slot in the door.

Incredibly, and against all precedent, Mary Margaret O'Leary was late to work. Black–haired, blue–eyed, a judicious mixture of explosive petulance and almost divine patience, Maggie was alternately the bane of Malone's existence, and it's mainstay. And on this particular morning he was counting on her to be the mainstay. At eleven Jake Charlotte, his best and most profitable client, was coming in, and words of great pith and moment would have to be put on paper.

When a client is suing a multi–millionaire for a cool million, he doesn't want a lawyer who doesn't have a secretary.

If he could only find *Maggie!*

Nothing to worry about, he told himself firmly. Maggie would never allow anything really disastrous to happen to him. He reached for the telephone and tried to decide whether to call the police, the hospitals or the morgue.

The telephone beat him to the punch.

"*Malone!*" It was Maggie's voice. "I've been calling and calling — "

"Maggie," Malone asked desperately. "Are you ill?"

"No," she gasped over the wire. "No, *no*, no. I feel fine. But Malone, grab a cab and come out to my house quick. There's six dollars in the emergency fund,

16

and the key to it is behind the Winston Dictionary on the second shelf of the bookcase in the outer office."

Right away Malone knew it was a real emergency. Never before had Maggie told him the location of the key.

"Don't get excited," the little lawyer said. "Keep calm. Don't worry about a thing. I'll be right there." Almost as an after–thought he added, "What happened?"

"Malone," Maggie said, "there's a dead sailor in Ronnie's bed." She hung up.

"I'll take care of the traffic tickets," Malone told a cab driver approximately sixty seconds later. He gave the Wrightwood Avenue address, and added, "Scoot!"

The cab moved out into the stream of traffic and quickly picked up speed. "What's the rush?" the driver growled.

"There's a dead sailor in my secretary's brother's bed, and shut up," Malone told him.

The O'Leary House didn't need a Welcome Doormat to say, "Come in." Wide, wooden, and desperately in need of paint, it was sandwiched in between massive apartment buildings — a hold–over from the lavender decade. If there had ever been a key to the front door, it had been lost a generation before. More than once Malone had parked witnesses there, and he had lost count of the times he had gorged himself on Aunt Aggie's cooking.

Malone walked up the worn wooden steps with worry in his eyes, and tension in the set of his jaw.

Maggie opened the door and said with a gasp of relief, "Praise be, you're here!"

The rest of the family was in the big, slightly shabby living room. The four O'Leary brothers — appropriately named Matthew, Mark, Luke, and John — were sprawled on the big, old–fashioned sofa. Ronnie sat self–consciously on a chair by himself. Katie, aged nine, reclined on her stomach on the floor, reading the *Herald–American* comics. Grandfather O'Leary sat in his wheel chair, as if ready to tell anybody at the drop of a hat about his extraordinary meeting with Big Jim Corbett in a Boston saloon. Aunt Aggie sat in her customary rocking chair with her usual bit of knitting.

The little lawyer managed an all–inclusive smile. "We can talk later," he said. "Maggie, where's the body?"

"In Ronnie's room," Maggie said in an amazingly small voice. "It's right off the kitchen. I'll show you — "

It was a dead sailor, all right.

"Anybody touched the body?" Malone asked.

She shook her head. "Malone, Ronnie works from twelve till eight. When he got home *it* was here? Or should I say, *this* was here? Or would *he* be better — "

"You shut up," Malone said, in a singularly gentle tone. "Shut up — and get out!"

A few minutes later he walked into the living room and said, "There's no identification on him. What is even more puzzling there are no visible marks of violence on his body. No bullet wounds, no stab wounds — "

Aunt Aggie looked up from her knitting with a severely disapproving frown. "Malone, *must* you use words like that? And in this house?"

"Why not?" Malone said imperturbably. "You've got a possibly murdered man in it."

He waited for the color to come back to her face. Stoical Irishwoman that she was, for a moment or two she'd been very close to chock.

He spoke quickly. "Suppose we start with the dead man. I just want to know whose friend he was, and how he got here. Somebody please talk, and let me do the worrying."

Everybody started talking at once, and Malone roared, "Hush!"

"Malone," Maggie said with pure desperation in her voice, "you'd better let me tell you. You know how it is in this house. People drift in and out. Some of them are friends of Matthew, Mark, Luke, and John. Others know Ronnie. They come in at any hour of the day or night, raid the ice–box and spend the night. A few weeks ago I came home late — the night I helped you at the office getting out that Beeble contract — and found six ten–year–old girls sleeping on the living room rug."

Katy lifted her head from the comic section long enough to explain: "They were all members of my club, and their folks told them they could stay. So there!"

"Quiet," Malone said.

Katy gave him a mean look, walked out to the kitchen, and came back with an apple. Sullenly she resumed her reading.

"Malone," Maggie said, "this stranger — Malone, what shall we call him?"

"Just call him the corpse," Malone advised grimly.

"All right — Mr. Corpse then. But he wasn't a corpse when he walked in here. He was walking, and talking. And he was alive — "

"Maggie," Malone said sternly, "if you become hysterical I'll get you a job in the police department. That's how mean I can be. *Calm down.*" He began to unwrap a cigar. "Now suppose we try to get the story straight."

"By virtue of age," Grandfather said, "I am the head of the house. Aggie, you be still. I was sitting right here in my chair, minding my own business and working on a crossword puzzle, when the sailor wandered in. He said he was looking for a friend."

"He found one," Malone commented dryly.

"I naturally thought he was a friend of one of my grandsons. I told him they were all out, but would be coming along presently. I told him there were four cans of beer in the icebox and to help himself."

"After one beer," Malone said, "he probably became a friend of yours too."

Mark got up — all six foot four of him — and said impatiently, "Maybe I can help. I came in a little after midnight. This sailor and Grandpop were sitting here guzzling beer — "

"*Drinking* beer," the old man interrupted, "and have more respect for your elders."

"All right *Grandfather*. You and he were *drinking* beer, and you were telling him how you could have beaten John L. Sullivan with her bare fists if you'd had the chance."

"Save your family fights till later," Malone admonished, chewing his cigar. "Who else saw him? Alive, that is."

Matthew, Luke and John had little of importance to contribute. They had each in turn seen the sailor alive. Matthew had assumed the silent visitor was waiting for Luke, and since Grandfather O'Leary had fallen asleep in his wheelchair he had, out of concern for his comfort, put him to bed.

Luke had come in a short while later, and found the visitor sitting by the window holding an empty beer can. He'd simply said he was waiting for somebody. John's story differed from the others in no important particular.

Everybody had assumed the reticent visitor was a friend of some other member of the family. Maggie and Katy? They'd both been asleep in bed at the time of the unfortunate man's arrival.

"I'd just like to know," Malone said vehemently, "who was the *last* person to see him alive."

"Malone," Aunt Aggie said, "it was myself. I should have told you before."

The little lawyer turned and looked at her admiringly. There were few people in the world he liked better. She was an old–maid aunt, and her aspect confirmed it. But no one else could have done a better job of rearing a family of orphaned O'Learys.

"I came downstairs sometime past midnight and found him here," she said. "He was very weary, poor fellow. He told me he was waiting for a friend. I felt sure it had to be Ronnie, because everybody else was in. So I led him to Ronnie's room and advised him to rest himself on the bed."

Ronnie lifted his head and said, "I never saw the guy before in my life. But when I came home from work, there he was parked on my bed. I shook him to wake him up and make him move over. I just thought he was a friend of — "

"I know," Malone said hastily. "Go on."

"Well, he didn't move, and I thought maybe he was sick. Maggie was coming down the stairs and I called her. It didn't take us long to find out he was dead. Then Maggie started calling you."

"Maggie," Malone said, "call a cab. Make it an Ajax. There's a stand a block from here."

While she was busy telephoning Malone issued a warning. "I want you all to stick to that story. It should not be difficult because you have nothing to conceal. A few slight deviations, however, will do no harm when the police get here.

Maggie left for work as usual. Ronnie — you didn't want to wake up a sleeping guest. You can discover the body, say thirty minutes from now. If the police give you any trouble — and they will — call me."

"Cab's on the way," Maggie said, returning into the room.

Malone nodded. "We've got to move. Remember, we're taking a statement on the Charlotte–Forstman case. And we've still got to get those witnesses."

He shook hands with Matthew, Mark, Luke and John, and gave Ronnie a pat on the shoulder, kissed Aunt Aggie, promised Grandfather O'Leary tickets to the next fight, pulled Katy's pigtails, and wound up with: "You've got your story straight, now stick to it."

He shoved Maggie through the doorway just as a *beep–beep* sounded from the cab outside.

II

Halfway downtown the little lawyer said, "Maggie, I don't like this. I don't like it at all. He was wearing green socks."

Maggie said, "*What?*"

"Sailors don't ordinarily wear green socks," Malone told her. "And don't worry me with questions."

Back in the office, Malone threw his hat in the general direction of the couch, plumped down behind his desk, and began scanning a folder of papers he already knew by heart.

"Maggie," he said at last, "I don't like the Charlotte case either. But a million bucks is a million bucks."

"That," Maggie said, "you can say again and again and again. Even if you do get only forty per cent."

"What can you do with money," Malone said gloomily, "except maybe spend it. And possibly we won't even get it — not without those two witnesses."

"We've advertised for them," Maggie reminded him.

Malone chewed savagely on his cigar, got up and began to pace restlessly up and down the room.

"One man was riding down the Outer Drive on a motorcycle. He didn't stop. But he must have seen the crash in every detail. The other witness, according to Jake Charlotte, was standing at a bus stop. Why did both of them have to vanish before the cops and the ambulance arrived?"

"The second witness," Maggie said gently, "could have been waiting for a bus."

Malone ground out his cigar. "Fine thing," he muttered. He started on another cigar and said, "Maggie!" He finally lit the cigar. "Five forty–seven in the morning and he was waiting for a bus!" He looked up. "Maggie, there wouldn't be any suit except that Arthur Forstman happens to have about half the money in this hemisphere. So at a very small hour of the morning he drives home drunk — "

Maggie interrupted him to say, "That will have to be proven in court, Malone."

The little lawyer shoved his half-smoked cigar viciously into an ashtray. "Don't worry, it will be. Drunk or sober, he runs head on into the car of a small-time fur dealer named Jake Charlotte — who, by the way, has promised you a nice bit of rabbit if we win. Question: What was Charlotte doing out at that hour? Deponent isn't saying. His wife's ankle was broken. His car was smashed. So he sues for a cool million."

"It's our case," Maggie said softly. "Don't let us talk ourselves out of it by finding for the opposition."

He smiled at her. "I always like to visualize the opposition's side. Here's my point. If Forstman hadn't long since lost count of his millions the entire affair would have been a simple little matter between insurance companies. Medical expenses, car repairs, et cetera. As it is — " He started on a new cigar. "Maggie, it must be hell to be rich!"

"I'd like to try it sometime," she said. "Malone — is everything going to be all right?"

"The sailor? Of course. All the O'Learys are in the clear — or soon will be." He hoped with all his heart that he was telling the truth. "Now go away and let me worry until Jake Charlotte comes in — or the cops come to tell me there's a dead sailor in your kid brother's bed."

Maggie managed a wan smile, went away, and came back fast.

"Malone," she said, "this was in the mail, along with a lot of bills you'd probably rather not see right at the moment. It might be important, and then again it might not be."

The little lawyer looked at the envelope. It was grimy, the stamp had been stuck on askew, and it was addressed in pencil. The name on the corner was HAROLD SPRUCE, and the return address was on North Clark Street. The note inside read as follows:

> *"Dear Sir, I saw your ad in the papers and I didn't go to the police account of I had a little trouble with the cops previous but I saw your ad and yes sir I was the man on the motorcycle."*

"Well, you've got one of the missing witnesses," Maggie said, elation in her voice.

John J. Malone mopped his brow and nodded. "I was pretty sure the ad would pay off," he said. "We'll contact him before he changes his mind and — "

The phone rang, and Maggie turned pale. Malone smiled at her with a reassurance he didn't feel and reached for the instrument himself. His eyes widened in swift surprise. Looking significantly at his secretary he said genially:

"Mr. Featherstone? Good to hear from you! Just a minute while I transfer this call to my private office — "

He laid the receiver gently on the desk, and whispered to Maggie, "Plug in the extension phone and bring it in here — with your notebook. I want to have every word of this. It's Orlo O. Featherstone."

As she started for the extension phone she whispered back, "Isn't he the lawyer who saw Lincoln buried?"

"According to my information," Malone whispered in reply, "he saw Lincoln born." He smiled into the receiver and said, "Featherstone? Sorry about the delay. How about lunch at the Republican Club tomorrow? Or a date at the Chez? Oh, nonsense. How do you do it? I could have *sworn* you weren't a day over fifty. Now what can I do for you besides telling you the story of your life?"

Maggie managed not to choke over that. Malone leaned back and lit his cigar. He listened for a moment in silence, nodding as the other talked.

"The Forstman case? Featherstone, you're backing the wrong Pullman train."

Featherstone immediately countered with a proposal for a settlement. All medical expenses and repairs to the car. After all, Arthur Forstman must have been driving with care, since he had been taking a girl home from a party. Malone made a gently remark about the hour he'd taken the girl home. Featherstone pointedly suggested that Malone must have been young once himself, and Malone winced.

Malone pointed out that Jake Charlotte's wife might never be able to walk again, and that the car had been damaged beyond repair. Furthermore the car was important to Mr. Charlotte's only means of livelihood, and there was such a thing as emotional shock — "

Mr. Featherstone said that his client would settle for all medical bills, a new car, and two thousand dollars in cash.

"Your client — "

Maggie caught Malone's eye just in time. Her lips said, "Watch yourself, my fine talkative friend!"

"Your client was driving through a red light," Malone went on. "Moreover, he was drunk. He had not had sufficient sleep. He struck Mr. Charlotte's car — thereby putting Mr. Charlotte out of business, and injuring Mrs. Charlotte for life." Malone paused for breath. "We will settle," he said, "for one million dollars. Plus, of course, medical expenses and repairs to the car. Not to mention court costs and — this is most important — legal fees."

Orlo O. Featherstone pointed out that it might take five years for the case to come to court. Malone said cheerfully that he expected to live that long. He then asked Orlo O. Featherstone how he was feeling, in a very solicitous voice, and reminded him of the luncheon engagement at the Republican Club, and hung up with a smug smile on his face.

Maggie put down the notebook and said, "But Malone, how do you know?"

"I don't," Malone said. "I'm bluffing." He relit his cigar. "So far at least I'm holding only the joker. But once we get those witnesses — "

There was a little silence.

"Malone," she said at last. "Are you sure?" About the sailor, I mean."

"A million buck lawsuit," Malone said, "and you worry me about dead sailors. I told you it would be all right. Switch all calls to my personal phone, and when Jake Charlotte turns up stall him in the office for a minute or two. Tell him I'm busy with an overseas call — and when I push the buzzer, send him in."

III

There was a sudden, quite alarmingly insistent pounding on the door. Maggie looked up, her face pale. "Malone, that's von Flanagan's knock! I'd recognize it through ear–muffs."

"Keep your thoughts to yourself," Malone said. "Go on taking dictation and let me do the worrying."

The pounding grew louder. Malone yelled, "Why don't you just open it? Don't break it down."

Von Flanagan came in like a red–faced hurricane, with two uniformed cops behind him. He motioned the pair to be quiet, and slammed the door shut.

"Malone, one of these days you're going to push me too far!" he said.

Malone smiled from behind his desk, and offered von Flanagan a cigar. "What's the beef?" he asked, his voice strangely gentle.

Von Flanagan sank down in the only easy chair in the office. He caught his breath, frowned at Malone, and refused the match Maggie offered him. "Thanks, I have a lighter." After a number of tries he accepted the match, and said, "Malone, we've been friends for a long time."

"Longer than that," Malone said. "You don't need to disrupt my morning's work to remind me, especially when I'm busy with an important lawsuit. Come on, what's the beef?"

"No beef," the big police officer said, breathing heavily. "I'm here to do a favor for Miss O'Leary, whom I have always looked upon as a friend." He nodded towards Maggie. "A guy turned up in her house dead. Dead as a doornail. Dead as a — "

"Never mind," Malone interrupted hastily. "Let's just say the man was dead."

"Just as you choose," von Flanagan said. "We were plenty thorough. We checked when he went in the house — and where he must have secured the poison."

Malone lifted a startled eyebrow.

"Chloral hydrate," von Flanagan said. "Chloral hydrate in a lethal dose. He seemed drunk when he strayed in, but actually he hadn't been drinking much. Maggie here is in the clear. Her whole clan is in the clear. That's according to the experts — and the time element."

He cleared his throat noisily. "But remember, Malone, I'm your friend. Once in a while I read newspapers too. We managed to identify the man."

Malone lifted the other eyebrow.

"His name," von Flanagan said, "was Harold Spruce."

Malone sat absolutely silent for what seemed to him like ten thousand years.

"Don't get up now," von Flanagan said gently. "Wait for the count of nine. What have you to lose?"

Malone considered a number of possibilities. One of them was jumping out the window. Another was shooting himself in front of the Tribune Tower, something he'd always wished someone would do. A third was to steal a small boat from the Navy Pier and steer for South America.

He threw his cigar butt inaccurately at the corner wastebasket and said, "Green socks."

"Malone," von Flanagan said anxiously. "I know this has been a great shock to you, and if you'd like a drink to steady your nerves — "

The little lawyer shook his head. "No," he said. "I'd like forty percent of a million dollars, but I'm afraid it's slipping away from me. Be that as it may, my immediate concern is centered in the late Harold Spruce. I don't especially want to look at him. I want to look at his clothes."

"Malone," von Flanagan said, "are you sure you feel all right?"

"I never felt better in my life," Malone assured him.

"If you really want a drink don't let my being here stand in the way — "

"Nonsense!" Malone said. He found his hat with a little difficulty and muttered, "Green socks. Green light."

Von Flanagan said, "I hope you know what you're doing. Remember, I trust you as far as I can throw the City Hall into Lake Michigan." He turned to Maggie and said, "As far as you and your family are concerned, we feel you're all in the clear."

She looked up at him and said earnestly, "This is the first time in my life I've ever *really* wanted to kiss a cop!"

"Don't!" von Flanagan said, and fled into the anteroom.

There was a slight rumpus going on there. Kluchetsky and Scanlin were standing by a furious little man who looked angrily at Malone and said, "Well, it's about time."

He was an ugly, unctuous little man, with very little that was commendable in his behavior and general aspect. His clothes had a conspicuously expensive look, but he wore them in such a way that they did nothing to enhance his dignity.

He gave Malone a smug smile and asked, "Well, how is our lawsuit coming?"

Malone gave him back the same smile and said, "Fine — just fine. I'm doing some important work on it now. I'll see you here in an hour, if you wish, and we can go over it in detail."

"Hold on, Mr. Malone!" The little man was angry. "I just want to know — "

Malone swallowed his rage and said, "Mr. Charlotte, if you want to transfer this case to another lawyer, you're entirely free to do so. I'll let you know when I need to talk to you."

He calmed down a little. After all, Jake Charlotte was his client, and a million dollars had a certain eloquence of its own.

He put a reluctant hand on his client's shoulder. "I'm on my way now to see one of your witness," he said. "Everything is proceeding satisfactorily. Go home, and don't worry."

Malone's voice has a soothing quality, and his expression carried conviction. Jake Charlotte relaxed and smiled.

"Then I'll hear from you, Mr. Malone," he said, and took his departure.

After a minute's silence, von Flanagan growled, "You might at least have told him the witness you're going to see is dead."

On the way downtown Malone finally summoned enough composure to ask, "How did you identify him so quickly?" He had been on the point of adding "When there was no identification on him," but he caught himself just in time.

"Pure luck," von Flanagan said. "Plus, of course, some smart police work." He coughed modestly. "The guy had a girl friend who was waiting for him at home. He told her he had to go out on some important business, and promised to be back before midnight. Around ten o'clock this morning when her alarm reached the acute stage she started calling hospitals. Finally, she called the cops. By that time, of course, we had the dead sailor. She identified him, and so did his landlady."

Malone was beginning to feel that this was one of the days he should have spent sleeping.

The conviction grew on him even more after his second look within twenty-four hours at the dead sailor. He had died at a tragically early age but at least he'd died quietly and without pain. A handsome young man — with the daredevil smile of a motorcycle driver still on his face.

"According to the medical examiner," von Flanagan said, "he swallowed the poison about three hours before he died. It gave him time to move around a little. But why did he pick the O'Leary house?"

"Maybe he just picked the first house he came to," Malone said.

Von Flanagan shook his head. "Malone, it was the only house on the street. The rest were all apartment buildings. I tell you, he was *aimed* at that house."

Malone said, "Let's get out of here." On the way out he demanded, "But who aimed him?"

The big policeman said nothing, in a nasty tone of silence.

"My missing witness," Malone mused out loud, "found dead in my secretary's house."

Von Flanagan's silence became almost profane.

"If you'll just let me take a look at those clothes," Malone said, "we'll remain friends."

This time von Flanagan gave him only a cold stare.

The expressive silence remained mutual all the way up to von Flanagan's office. The big police officer said a few terse words into the intercom and a moment later Scanlin came in with a bundle.

Malone looked over the contents, and made a swift inventory. A sailor suit. Underwear — not Navy issue. A pair of green socks. A crumpled handkerchief. Black shoes, newly polished.

He tossed the articles of clothing back on von Flanagan's desk. "Save these for me," he said.

The angry–faced police officer almost strangled on the single word, "*Why.*"

"Someday," Malone said, "I may want to give them to the Salvation Army. On the other hand, I might want to unravel them and knit them up into rugs. Or crochet a set of doilies... But how," he finished mildly, "did you know he was my missing witness?"

"Because," von Flanagan said, even more mildly, "he sent a little note to the police department mentioning you and saying that he'd decided to come forward. Now how about your other missing witness?"

"I hope the police find him," Malone said, "before the killer does."

IV

The instant Malone left the elevator in his office building he knew something was wrong. He went in through the door to his private office and buzzed for Maggie.

"Has anyone called?" he asked.

"Malone," she said in a very soft voice, "Mr. Forstman is here to see you. Mr. *Arthur Forstman.* The name should mean *something* to you."

Malone waited a full minute before coming to a decision. "Don't send him right in," he said. "Tell him I'm busy. I'll buzz you when I'm free."

"Malone," she whispered, "everything is all right, isn't it? About the — "

"It is," Malone said. "Now go away and don't worry."

He spent nearly ten minutes inaccurately working a crossword puzzle. Then he buzzed Maggie.

She ushered in Arthur Forstman. "Will you need me?" she asked and without waiting for Malone to shake his head, discreetly closed the door.

Malone rose from behind his desk, extended a cordial hand — it wasn't every day a multi–millionaire paid him a visit — and ushered his guest into the one comfortable chair.

"Sorry I had to keep you waiting," he said, "but I was on the long–distance phone. I was trying to get some information on this Harold Spruce person."

"Oh," Arthur Forstman said, fumbling for a cigarette.

The little lawyer gave him a close look. Forstman had the kind of face that should have been ruddy. Instead it was pale. His hands, that could so competently handle golf clubs, polo mallets, and racing cars, should have been steady. But Malone had to leap around the desk and hold a match to a cigarette held between shaking fingers.

He didn't bother to ask if the wealthy sportsman would care for a drink. He rinsed out a glass, opened the file drawer labeled EMERGENCY and pulled out the bottle of brandy he'd been saving for a chance meeting with Grace Kelly, or Marilyn Monroe.

Arthur Forstman downed it straight without batting even one eyelash. "Malone, I've got to talk to you about something I can't discuss with anyone else."

Malone listened, very quietly.

"I'm here to make you an offer," the tall slightly stopped man said. He slumped down in his chair.

Malone gave him six seconds, catfooted around the desk to refill his glass, and said, "Orlo Featherstone has already made me one, and I turned it down flat."

Arthur Forstman sat up straight. "That isn't what I mean," he said. "Sure, I'd fought with that slimy little crook. It would be worth it to get him off my neck. But, Malone, this is something else. That man who was found murdered this morning — "

There was a little silence, and then Malone said, "Yes?"

"He was one of the witnesses. Obviously I'm going to be accused of having him done in. I'll pay you a five thousand dollar fee if you can prove I had nothing to do with it."

Malone got up, walked to the window and looked out. The customary Indian Summer heat wave was sending little light shivers across the tops of the buildings. Sooner or later there would be rain.

"And one thousand dollars down," the voice said behind him, "as a retainer."

Malone argued with the voice of temptation for about thirty seconds. The emergency fund was cleaned out, he might need money for Maggie, and he wasn't sure how Joe the Angel would react to a touch.

He turned around and said, "Put your money in your pocket. Let's talk about more pleasant things. A cracked up car, and a badly injured woman — "

Forstman turned white and Malone reached for the brandy bottle again.

"We were driving home," Forstman said. "Sure it was late. We'd been to a party down the south side to celebrate our engagement."

"Where?" Malone asked wearily.

"At William Turner's. The broker, you know. She's May Turner, his niece. It got to be late. I was driving her home. She went to sleep on the way." Forstman relit his cigarette with hands that shook only a little now.

"It all happened so suddenly. The street ahead was empty. I'd had a few drinks at the party, but I wasn't drunk. I may have been exceeding the speed limit, but I don't think so."

"Wait a minute," Malone said. "I'm the opposition lawyer, remember? Save your confessions for the courtroom."

Forstman managed a thin smile. "I'm only trying to tell the truth. Suddenly this car came out of a sidestreet and smashed into us. The rest was all pretty much confusion. I know I was completely stunned for a minute, and I guess the Charlottes were too." He crushed out the cigarette and started on another one.

"It's none of my business," Malone said, wishing he didn't like Arthur Forstman so much, "and I shouldn't be asking you this, being on the other side. But how did you know there were two witnesses?"

"I saw one," Forstman said. "It was just before the crash. He was standing on the bus stop corner. I remember hoping he wouldn't try to cross the street. And then, at the moment of the crash, this man on a motorcycle raced by. That's all I remember for a few minutes."

He closed his eyes for a moment. "I tried to get out of the car. I wasn't hurt, but I was pinned in. I thanked God that May was all right. She'd waked up, a little frightened, but perfectly calm. We could hear Mrs. Charlotte screaming. May could get out on her side of the car, and she ran out to see how badly Mrs. Charlotte had been hurt. Then she ran down the road until she could flag down a car to send a call for the police. The rest you know."

"May," Malone commented, "sounds like a level-headed girl in an emergency."

Arthur Forstman's eyes lighted up as though someone had struck a match to them. "May," he said simply, "is wonderful."

After a long moment he went on: "About this lawsuit. I'd be willing to settle on generous terms, but I'm damned if I'll have people going around saying I arranged for a witness to be murdered in order to avoid a lawsuit."

Malone tapped the ash from his cigar and said, "Obviously I can't take you as a client, since Charlotte has already engaged me. Neither can I take your money. I will do my best to ascertain whether you were or were not guilty of arranging for the murder of Harold Spruce. If you didn't, you have nothing to worry about. You don't need me. If you did — " he paused, coughed delicately and said, "We can talk about that another time. It would alter the entire picture."

He rose, walked around the desk, smiled reassuringly and said, "There's always the possibility that the murder of Harold Spruce had nothing to do with your little mishap."

Arthur Forstman said hoarsely, "In that case, why was his body found in your secretary's house?"

Malone reflected that he'd like to know that himself. "It could be pure coincidence," he said. "Meantime, *don't worry!*"

Forstman's goodbye handshake was a solid one.

Maggie came in — after he had left — with her notebook and said, "I got every word of it down. But I thought you always saved that 'don't worry' line for clients and prospective clients."

"For all I know," Malone said gloomily, "he *is* a prospective client."

"Malone," she said in a sad little voice, "what do we do now?"

He managed a smile at her. "We don't worry. I can say that to you because you're also a client, and I may be my own client before this is over. You do three things. First you check with your blessed family as to what time the sailor got there. Next, you call Doctor Flamm and ask him how long it would take for a fatal dose of chloral hydrate to take effect. Third, you bring me the classified phone directory. I've got to call up every costumer in town."

Malone looked at the directory wearily. So far it had been a busy day, and promised to be even busier.

Maggie stuck her head around the corner of the door. "Malone," she said, "try Campbell's first."

"Maggie," he said happily, "an inspiration! In fact, I think I'll try it in person!"

Naturally, it had to be Campbell's! Why hadn't he thought of it himself!

He caught himself on the verge of telling the elevator man to drive faster, and went back to thinking about Campbell's. There were other costumer's in Chicago, and good ones. But the renting of the sailor suit was the job of someone who didn't ordinarily rent costumes.

With such a job in prospect Campbell's would naturally be the first place that came to mind. Almost everyone knew that Campbell's, highly listed in the Classified Directory, would rent anything — including, probably, a second-hand space ship, and certainly a sailor suit.

And if he were wrong, he reminded himself, he could still tackle the others.

That reminded him of something else. He felt in his pockets and found fifty-five cents left over from the emergency fund. It was no time to go back and talk to Maggie, with all the worries she had on her mind.

With a heavy sigh, he walked down the street to Joe the Angel's City Hall Bar.

Joe greeted him with all the heavy cordiality he would have given to the main exhibit at a wake. He slid a drink across the bar without being asked. "Malone," he said mournfully, "I *am* sorry."

"Don't worry," Malone said, "you know you'll get it back."

Joe the Angel's eyes widened. "You mean you need *money*? Why did you not say so? How much you need?"

The little lawyer caught his breath and said, "Just cab fare."

"Cab fare to where?" Joe the Angel demanded. "State and Madison, or Gary, Indiana?"

"I don't know yet," Malone said, wishing he were asleep.

After a brief discussion, they settled for ten, and Joe the Angel marked it up on Malone's bill.

"And Malone," he said sadly, "I am sorry that you lose the witness. I read it in the papers."

"Oh," Malone said quickly, "*that!* Nothing important." He relit his cigar. "I have another one. And besides, I had an offer of a settlement. Maggie has it all down on paper." He puffed at the cigar. "For a million dollars"

Joe the Angel turned pale. He broke a rule of the house and poured himself a drink, gulped it down, coughed and said, "But Malone! A million dollars — "

" — is a million dollars," Malone finished for him. He rose and started for the door.

"Wait, Malone," Joe the Angel gasped. He reached for the register. "Better you take another ten. And, one on the house, Malone!"

V

Campbell's in North State Street, was famous and fabulous. One window displayed sets of dueling pistols, another a suit of armor. A sign read WE BUY, SELL, OR RENT ANYTHING.

Malone made his way through the semi–darkness of the elderly building, ducked away from a cigar store Indian who had a mean look, glanced briefly at a display of a fortune's worth of antique jewelry, bypassed a table loaded with second–hand kitchen utensils labeled ANYTHING YOU SEE, FIVE CENTS, and finally, a shaken man, wound up at the costume rental department.

"I'd like to see a man about a sailor suit," he said.

The pleasant–faced young man said, "I doubt if we have anything to fit you, sir, but — "

"No," the little lawyer said. "*No!* I don't want to rent a sailor suit. I just want to *ask* about one."

The young man, not looking quite as pleasant, said "Yes, sir. Now if you will give me his size — "

"I don't know his size," Malone said explosively. "That's what I came to ask you!"

"Perhaps you'd like to talk to the manager?" the young man said anxiously.

"Perhaps I'd like to talk to you," Malone said. He lit a cigar and began to relax.

"If there's any complaint — " the young man said.

"I won't make it," Malone said warmly. "I'm just asking about the rental of a sailor suit, sometime yesterday, or maybe the day before. Who rented it and when."

"I'll check the books, sir," the young man said. "And you are —?"

"Malone," the little lawyer said grimly. "John J. Malone."

"*That* Malone!" A light came in the young man's eyes. "I'll check for you, right away."

He came back in an amazingly short time, with the records. The suit had been rented the day before, at 6:00 p.m., just before closing time. A deposit had been left. The renter had signed for it as Jack Johnson, address 3145 East Huron Street.

Malone reflected unhappily that not only did the name Jack Johnson show a shocking lack of originality, but that 3145 East Huron Street would be halfway across Lake Michigan. He said gently, "And what did he look like?"

"I don't know sir. *Mister* Malone, I mean. I didn't see him, because I wasn't here. You see, I'm a substitute. Usually, I'm in stuffed birds. The regular man here left on his two weeks vacation early this morning."

Malone said a very bad word under his breath, and asked, "Where was he going?"

The young man looked even more unhappy, shook his head and said, "Maybe the assistant manager would know."

The assistant manager looked at Malone as though he suspected him of attempting to shop–lift a suit of antique armor.

"This gentleman," the young man said breathlessly, "is trying to locate Walter — "

"I'm a lawyer," Malone said quickly. He handed out one of the business cards Maggie had insisted on having printed. "Walter may be the key man in a million dollar lawsuit. If I can locate him — "

The assistant manager's eyes softened. "I wish I could help you. A million dollars is a lot of money, isn't it? But Walter left this morning on a fishing trip. He himself didn't know where he was going. He'll be back in two weeks." He accepted the cigar Malone offered him. "Tell you what I'll do. He's bound to send postcards or souvenirs. The minute we hear from him, I'll telephone you."

"More than fair enough," Malone said.

"Sir," the young man said, after the assistant manager had gone, "there's a chance someone in the store might have noticed him. Would you like me to ask around?"

"I would," Malone said. He leaned on the counter, and concentrated his gaze on a glass–encased bull–fighter's costume. He had about decided he would look well in it when the young man came back.

"I'm sorry, sir," he said. "Nobody noticed anything or anybody. That's a busy time of day. People are always coming in and out."

"It's all right," Malone said. "You did the best you could." He fumbled through his pockets. "Do you and your girl–friend like the fights?"

The young eyes brightened. "How did you know I had a girl–friend?"

"You looked as though you would," Malone said. He handed them the fight tickets he'd planned to give to von Flanagan. "Thanks for everything, and have fun," he said and again fought his way through the maze.

In a state of utter despondency, he ignored an available cab, and rode the streetcar to his office.

So far, everything had gone wrong, and what would happen next he didn't know and didn't want to guess.

He snarled at the elevator man, a friend of many years standing, strode into his private office, slammed his door, threw his hat in the general direction of the couch, glared through the window at a sky that was already beginning to cloud, and finally slumped down in the chair behind his desk and yelled for Maggie.

She arrived as though she'd been jet–propelled.

He lit a cigar and glared at it.

"Nothing," he said hoarsely. "Absolutely nothing." He added the details. "The chances are that if this clerk does turn up — it'll turn out that the man who rented the sailor suit was Harold Spruce himself."

"Malone," Maggie said, "don't be discouraged."

"I'll be discouraged if I want to," Malone said.

"There are a couple of women waiting to see you," Maggie said. "One, blonde."

"I don't care," the little lawyer growled, "if the whole Chez Paree chorus is waiting in the outer office. What did *you* find out?" He looked at her hopefully.

Her face clouded. "Malone," she said gravely, "a little less than nothing. I checked with Dr. Flamm. The sailor must have gotten the drink less than a few minutes — say, ten — before he got to our house. I checked with the family as to when he came in. And I called Matthew about bars. There isn't one within half an hour's walking distance. And since he had no car, he must have walked. Malone," — her face whitened — "does that mean he got it after he came in our house?"

"No," Malone said, "no, no, no, *no*." He got up, kicked the wastebasket savagely and began pacing the floor. "Somebody drove him to, or near your door. The same somebody probably offered him a drink from a loaded bottle. *Why?* I don't know. *Who?*" He paused in his pacing. "I don't know that yet either."

Malone looked through his window at the Chicago rooftops. The dreary gray rain was beginning. Why was it, he wondered, that important crimes always happened during a record–breaking heat–wave, a blizzard, or the rainy season!

"Maggie," he said quietly, "I begin to feel as though I were hitting my head with a brick wall."

"You mean — " she began.

"I know exactly what I mean," he said.

"The word for it," Maggie said acidly, "is frustrated. And you have two people waiting — mother and child."

Malone managed a wan smile and said, "Bring on the dancing girls."

VI

The girl was a very young, very blonde, very pretty, and right now, very tearful. Her mother looked as though her face should be carved into the side of a mountain.

"It's about Harold," the girl said. "Harold Spruce."

Malone bounded to his feet and ushered them into the best chairs as though they were visiting royalty. He caught himself on the verge of offering cigars.

He excused himself, whipped into the outer office, and said to Maggie, "Phone the drug store and have them send up a quart of ice cream — strawberry — and rush. With dishes and spoons. And, you take down every *word* of what they say."

He slowed down at the door.

"Sorry for the interruption," he apologized. "And very sorry I kept you waiting so long." He gave the girl his most reassuring smile and said, "Now, my dear — ?"

She gave back a very small smile. "Mr. Malone, my name is Dawn O'Day — "

"Emmaline," her mother said, in a voice as cold as an Eskimo's icebox, "tell the man the truth."

Her blue eyes freshened with a promise of new tears. "All right, Mr. Malone, my name is Emmaline Biggers. But I'm studying to be a model, and you can't get far with a name like that. And Ma — "

Ma said, "My name is Mrs. Emma Biggers, and I've gotten along fine with it for years."

Malone smiled impartially at them both. "Never mind the names," he said. "How about Harold Spruce?"

"Ma said I should talk to you. Harold wouldn't want me to tell you this. I mean, he wouldn't *have* wanted to tell you this. But now he can't be hurt — "

The tears started again. Malone grabbed for his handkerchief, but Ma Emma beat him to it with a wad of Kleenex.

Providentially, the ice cream arrived at that moment.

"Don't cry into it," Malone ordered. "It doesn't taste good with salt."

The tears began to dry. Ma Emma looked as though a smile might appear on the great stone face.

"I really wanted to be a stenographer," Emmaline said, "like Ma wanted me to, and I went to a business school. But seemed like I couldn't learn to type, and my spelling isn't so good. Seems like I'm dumb." She gulped down another spoonful of ice cream.

Malone looked at her, at the face, the hair, the figure, and decided she could afford to be dumb. He said gently, "Now that I've heard the story of your life, tell me about Harold Spruce. And *don't cry!*"

"Emmaline," Ma Emma said, for the third time, "tell the truth."

"Come on, Dawn," Malone said warmly. "He'd want you to tell me." He gave her the best smile he had at the moment. "You know he should have stopped at the scene of the accident."

She took another gulp of ice cream. "He couldn't stop," she said, "because of the motorcycle."

"You mean, the motorcycle wouldn't stop?"

"No. But he couldn't stop because it wasn't *his* motorcycle."

Malone counted to ten, slowly. "You mean he stole it?"

"He borrowed it," Emmaline said miserably. "It belonged to the owner of the gas station where he worked. He'd borrowed it a lot of times. But if the owner found out, Harold would have lost his job. He saw the wreck, but of course he couldn't stop. Maybe he should have stopped. He might have lost his job but he wouldn't have lost his *life!*"

"Now, Emmaline!" Ma Emma said. She reached for more Kleenex, just in case.

"Finish your ice cream before it melts, Dawn," Malone said gently.

"Well, then there was the lawsuit. It was in the papers. He said he was going to make so much from it that he wouldn't care about the job. He called up those people — I mean both of them — and told them he would be available as a witness."

"Tell the truth," Ma Emma said.

"Well, I mean he said he could — well, he could, for a price — " She gulped, wiped her eyes, finished the ice cream and licked the spoon. "He was offered five thousand dollars. Then he was offered a cut of the take."

"Emmaline!" Ma Emma said.

"Well, that's exactly the way he said it. And then one of the gentlemen got to be very friendly. He gave Harold a little money from time to time. And then yesterday Harold stopped by on his way from work."

She paused, blew her nose, and said, *"Ma!"*

Ma Emma passed over the rest of the ice cream.

The little blonde took a spoonful, looked at Malone and said, "He was very happy. His new friend had asked him to play a practical joke on someone. It was some kind of a birthday joke, Harold said. And Harold loved jokes. He was going to be paid for it."

Ma Emma said, "Tell the truth. Harold loved money even more than he loved jokes."

"Ma, please!"

"Don't bleat at me," Ma Emma said grimly. "Harold was a boy of no character. He loved money. He had a good job, but he came to the house almost every night. Not to see Emmaline, like she thought, but because he'd get a free meal."

"Ma!"

"Shut up," Ma Emma said. "I'm telling the truth. The only other thing he cared about was moving fast. That's why he borrowed his boss's motorcycle. He was saving his money to buy a racing car. That's why he was willing to take a bribe. And besides," she added disapprovingly, "he drank."

Malone thanked his lucky stars he hadn't offered Ma Emma gin instead of ice cream. "Now, Dawn, don't cry anymore," he said soothingly. "Just tell me the rest of the joke."

"Well," she said miserably, "he was supposed to rent some kind of costume, and meet his friend and go to this house, and pretend to be a friend of the family."

"One thing more," Malone said. "Harold did see the accident, that we know. He must have described it to you." He wished for luck and said, "Did he tell you if the stop–light was green or red?"

"He didn't tell me," she said. "I guess because I didn't ask him."

The little lawyer counted to ten silently.

"That's all I know," she said. "That's all. Except that he's dead." She grabbed at the Kleenex again.

"Now, Emmaline," Ma Emma said, in a voice that was actually gentle. "Mr. Malone, we'll be going now. And thank you for the ice cream."

Malone bowed them to the door as though they'd been a pair of visiting Hollywood stars, and turned to Maggie. "How many of your brothers were in the Navy?"

"All of them" she said in an unhappy voice. Her face was pale. "Ronnie only two years."

"Therefore," Malone growled, lighting a fresh cigar, "your whole family would have been definitely receptive to a young man who turned up dressed as a sailor, looking for a friend. That explains the rented suit, and the green sox." He sighed deeply. "But we will seem to get right back to where we started."

"Find the other witness," Maggie said acidly.

"According to the latest census," Malone said just as acidly, "there are three and a half million people in Chicago. And no one, including Jake Charlotte, can give us a description of him. Just a shadowy figure at a bus stop, in the gray pre–dawn mist."

"Malone," Maggie said, "you'll never be a poet. Have any of you geniuses in this case thought of talking to the bus driver?" As Malone stared at her, she went on, "Your missing witness was waiting at a bus stop. Obviously, he was waiting for a bus. Obviously a bus must have come along. Obviously, there must have been a bus driver. There's less than a three–and–a–half–millionth chance you'll learn anything, but it's worth a try."

"Maggie," Malone said happily, "*you* are the genius in this case! Get me an address of the bus company!"

She grinned at him. "And incidentally, the exact census figure is three million, six hundred and twenty thousand, nine hundred and sixty–two."

"Now minus one," Malone said. "Hurry up, genius, get me that address."

VII

For the first time that day Malone began to feel that life could be made worth living. The taxi he took to the bus office seemed to be a jet–propelled cloud.

The Head Dispatcher turned out to be a long–faced man with a definitely pessimistic disposition and, Malone suspected, ulcers. He looked even gloomier as Malone explained the situation.

"I'll look it up in the records," he said in a voice like a radio announcer advertizing cut–rate funerals. He came back in a few minutes. "It was Melrose," he said. "Bill Melrose. But he can't help you, Mr. Malone. He didn't see the accident. By his schedule, he must have gone by the corner just before it happened."

The little lawyer scowled. "Are you sure?" he said.

The Head Dispatcher looked at Malone as though he were an unwanted idiot child. He said patiently, "Because if he'd seen the accident, he would have stopped to see if he could offer emergency assistance. Then he would have reported it to the police, and put it in his own daily report here. Those are strict rules, and we enforce them."

Malone thought about the still unknown witness who had been waiting for a chance. If the bus had just gone by, he wouldn't have been there.

"Just the same," he said stubbornly, "I'd like to talk with him."

The Head Dispatcher sighed again. "I'll see if I can find him for you. He's just gone off duty, but he may still be around."

He went away again and came back with a man with a friendly grin and built along the general lines of a top league basketball star. "Just luck he was still here," he said gloomily, "but he can't do you no good."

"That's right," Bill Melrose said. "I'm sorry, but I must have gone through that crossing about one minute before it happened. The papers say it happened at 5:47 a.m. because that's what both the dashboard clocks stopped at when the crash came. So according to my schedule, I must've gone past about 5:45 or 5:46."

Malone shook his head sadly. "Well, I had to check everything. Too bad you weren't a few minutes late that morning."

He turned on one of one of his best smiles and said to the Head Dispatcher, "Thanks for all your trouble. May I buy you a beer?"

"I'm still on duty!" the Dispatcher said, as though he were prophesying the end of the world.

Malone turned the same smile on Bill Melrose. "Why, yes, thanks very much," he said.

There was, as always, a little place across the street, which, though not the best in the world, was at least, the nearest. Comfortably settled in a secluded booth, Malone suggested that his guest might like something better than beer.

Bill Melrose again said, "Thank you very much," and ordered a gin and coke.

Malone winced, ordered rye with a beer chaser, and then quoted Ma Emma by saying, "Tell the truth, Bill," in his best courtroom manner.

Bill Melrose turned pale and started to say, "I am — " as Malone expected he would, turned even more pale and said, "Well, you see — " as Malone had also expected he would. He'd intimidated far tougher witnesses than Bill Melrose.

"I've got a wife and kids." They always had, the little lawyer reflected. "I've also got an accident record. I know I should have stopped. But I see this pile–up ahead of me and I lose my head. Maybe they figure I'm somehow involved. And I've been warned, one more and I lose my job. The bus is empty, so it's just a matter of driving by fast."

He took a big gulp of his drink. "But I see this guy on the corner. He's one of my regulars. I think fast. I stop quick, open the door, grab him in. He seemed dazed. We was eight blocks up the street before he really comes to. I explain my situation. He understands it. He's been riding with me a long time. There aren't many passengers that early in the run, and we talk about this and that, and get to be good friends. So he agrees to keep his trap shut."

Malone waved for another round.

"Now," Bill Melrose said wretchedly, "I suppose I got us both in trouble and I suppose I'll lose my job." He took half his drink in one gulp, and said automatically, "Thanks very much." Then he added, "And me with a wife and five kids."

"Bless you, Bill Melrose," Malone said, downing his own drink, "and bless the wife and five kids, too. You are not going to lose your job. Neither you nor your friend are going to get into any trouble. Just tell me where I can find this guy."

The grin and the color began to come back to the bus driver's face. "Why sure," he said. "His name's Don Cass. I don't know where he lives, but I know where he works." He looked almost cheerful. "The fact is, my car's right here, and I'll drive you there."

This time it was Malone who said, "Thanks very much." Joe the Angel's investment was dwindling rapidly. He was halfway in the car before he remembered his new friend's accident record.

His worst suspicions were immediately verified. Bill Melrose drove like an inspired madman in a hurry. Malone tried to keep his eyes closed and hoped that in time he would be able to forget.

They came to a squealing stop in front of a very small novelty store, one of the many selling cigars, cigarettes, candy and a few comic magazines. Malone had talked to the owners of enough of them to know that total sales from merchandise would probably not be sufficient to pay the light bill.

The fat faced woman behind the counter informed Malone that Don Cass had gone for the day. She looked at him suspiciously and added, "You can see him tomorrow. He's here any time after six–thirty."

Just in time, Malone thought, to get the early dope from the eastern tracks.

"I'm sorry," he said smoothly, "but it's urgent. I've got to see him today." He tried turning on a little charm and realized right away it wouldn't work.

Her hard eyes narrowed and she said sharply, "He isn't in any trouble, is he?"

"No," Malone said. "No, no, no, *no!*" He handed one of his cards. "He's wanted as a witness in a lawsuit. A million dollar lawsuit." He saw her eyes widen, and added quickly, "He'll probably make a good thing of it himself." It was amazing he told himself, and sometimes heartbreaking — the effect that the magic words "a million dollars" had on practically everyone.

"That's a lot of money," she said dreamily. She was silent for a moment, and Malone could almost hear what was going on in her mind. Finally she said, a little warily, "I'll give you his address. But mind you don't get him into no trouble."

She pulled out a notepad, wrote quickly, and came up with a smile that cracked her pancake makeup almost from ear to ear. "And since you're here, I've got a very good thing for tomorrow. Mr. Bat, in the fifth."

VIII

It was well worth the two dollars, Malone decided, as he walked out the door after a very cordial goodbye. And besides, Mr. Bat might win.

Bill Melrose opened the car door and automatically Malone got in.

"She gave me his address," Malone said, and handed over the paper.

"Fine," Bill Melrose said. "Fine, fine." He reached over and slammed the door. "I'll drive you there," he said.

The little lawyer shuddered. Then he remembered that the way to stay young was to live dangerously, and hoped for the best.

The rain had turned to an unpleasant nasty drizzle. It had also turned the streets into something resembling a newly waxed floor.

"Y'know, Malone," Bill Melrose said, "I was a race track driver for a coupla years when I was a kid." Suddenly he scooted around a delivery truck, narrowly missing a car coming in the opposite direction. He said cheerfully, "Better to go around 'em than hit 'em. It saves time.

"As I was saying, Malone, I worked six years in New York, cabbing. One year, ambulance driving. Then I got married. Her folks live in Chicago so we came out here. Being a married man, I figured I'd get into something safe."

Passing a streetcar on the left, causing a momentary traffic tangle from which he emerged miraculously unscathed, he went right on, "So now I pilot a bus."

Malone said weakly, "Do you ever ride a bicycle? Or a horse?"

Bill Melrose took his hands off the wheel for a split second, glanced at Malone at the same time. "*Me?*" he said. "You think I'm crazy? Those things are dangerous!"

There was an immediate tangle with the driver of an opposition car, and an exchange of dialogue which included nouns, verbs and adjectives that even Malone had never heard before.

"See?" Bill Melrose said, still indignant. "Guys like that never heard of no safe driving." He muttered a few more words under his breath, and Malone hoped he could remember them. "Well, hang on, Malone. We're here."

He managed a completely illegal but successful U–turn, disregarding a symphony of indignantly honking horns, and stopped in front of a No–Parking sign in front of one of Chicago's better remodeled old mansions on the near north side. This time, the car didn't squeal to a stop. It only shivered. There was an echo from Malone.

"I'll go up with you," Bill Malone said cheerfully, "and acquaint you with him, so he'll know you're all right. Then, on account of you might like to talk private, I'll exit. I gotta check these brakes anyway, on account of they don't work right. I've been putting it off too long."

For one of the few times in his life, Malone was close to fainting.

In the glassed–in vestibule at the top of the weathered brownstone steps was the usual list of tenants, and apartment numbers, some typed, some clipped from business cards, and some lettered in ink. Bill Melrose pushed the button opposite *Cass.*

It was almost a matter of seconds before a buzz sounded, and Bill Melrose shoved open the door.

The first door on the right opened, and a small figure appeared in the doorway. In the half dusk of the hallway Malone suddenly remembered the prophetic description he'd given Maggie. "A shadowy figure... in the gray pre–dawn mist."

The figure was shadowy, all right, the more so in the dimlighted hallway. Gray suit, light gray shirt, dark gray tie, gray hair. Gray eyes, too.

"This is a good friend of mine, Don," Bill Melrose said. "You can trust him. He's going to tell you how to make a lot of money, fast. Name's Malone. John J. Malone." He caught his breath and added, "I'll go fix them brakes, Malone." And vanished.

Don Cass said, in what might have passed for cordiality in an ice–cube tray, "Pleased to meet you." Then fixing Malone with eyes that might have been those of an alligator left overnight in a deep freeze, he demanded, "What's the pitch?"

Malone said, "It's just a little piece of business for a client. There might be some money in it for you."

The alligator eyes thawed out just a trifle, and by the time Malone had explained the purpose of his visit they were, if not friendly, at least candid.

"It was early in the morning. I was a bit sleepy, I guess. Anyway, when my pal Melrose came along I hopped into the bus. Sure, I saw the accident, but Melrose asked me to keep my mouth shut. He didn't want to lose his job. I guess anybody'd do that much for a pal."

Malone said, "Did you notice whether the traffic light was green or red?"

"I didn't notice nothin'," Don Cass told him. "I told you, it was early in the morning. I was sleepy. I just hopped in and we was off before anyone could say — "

"Jackie Robinson," Malone prompted.

"Jackie who?"

"Never mind," Malone said. He had a hunch Don Cass was telling the truth about the lights, and decided to try another tack. "Okay, forget the lights. There was another accident. You're a material witness. Of course you could be subpoenaed — "

The eyes froze up again. "I ain't tanglin' with the law. Not me. Not for nobody."

"You don't have to," Malone told him. "Not if you follow my advice." He assumed his best cell-side manner. "I'm your friend, Mr. Cass. I promise you that neither you nor Mr. Melrose will be in any trouble. All you need to do is call up Mr. Jake Charlotte and tell him you're the missing witness. Tell him you're ready to talk — at a price, of course."

He scribbled a telephone number and handed it to Cass. "Tell him to meet you here at eight o'clock tonight."

Don Cass looked down at the piece of paper Malone had handed him. "Are you sure it's — " he began, and dropped the question. "Is that all I got to do?" he asked instead.

"Just one more thing," Malone said. He scribbled another telephone number and handed it to Cass, saying, "When you've finished calling Mr. Charlotte, call this number and ask for Mr. Arthur Forstman. Tell him you're the missing witness and you're willing to talk — at a price, of course."

Just the faintest crinkle of a smile played around the corners of Don Cass's steel gray eyes. "I see," he said. "Both ends against the middle. Pretty smart."

"Let's just say, playing it fair," Malone said. "Tell Mr. Forstman to meet you here tonight at eight o'clock sharp."

"Wait a minute! What are you trying to do, get me surrounded?"

Malone reassured him. "There will be protection. I'll see to it myself. And there'll be money in it for you — cash money. If you play your cards right, understand?"

"I don't know nothin' about cards," Cass said. "Cards ain't my racket." He rose and followed Malone to the door. "But I can tip you off to a good one in the fifth at Hialeah. Black Jet."

Malone parted reluctantly with two of the three dollars he had left and took the streetcar back to the office.

"I drew a blank," Malone told Maggie as he tossed his hat on the rack and sank into his swivel chair. "Cass doesn't remember if the traffic light was red or green. I think he's telling the truth."

"The light was red," Maggie said.

Malone unwrapped a cigar in a slow double take, reached for the desk lighter and froze in shocking fashion just as he was about to light up. "What did you say?"

"The light was red," Maggie repeated, perfectly dead pan.

Malone just gaped at her, waiting for her to go on.

"Don't look at me as if *I* was the missing witness," Maggie continued. "It just occurred to me to ask them, that's all."

"Ask who?"

"Ask *whom*," Maggie corrected him. "Why, the traffic department, of course. I called them up and asked them to check on it. Those lights are clocked, timed to the split second. At five forty–seven a.m. the light was red. Forstman was driving through a red light. That means Jake Charlotte was driving through a green light. It's as simple as that."

Malone said, "Remind me to raise your salary five dollars. No, make it ten. Which reminds me — you couldn't spare a couple of bucks cash, could you? And get me von Flanagan."

Maggie produced two tired, crumpled dollar bills from her purse. Then she dialed police headquarters and got the chief of homicide on the phone.

"Meet me at one thousand and twelve Goethe Street at eight o'clock tonight." Malone told von Flanagan. "Be there with friends. We've got a date to meet the man who murdered the sailor." He hung up.

Maggie said, "I hope you know what you're doing."

"If I don't, you'll read about it in the obituary column in the morning paper," Malone said.

IX

Early that evening at Joe the Angel's City Hall Bar the little lawyer, waiting for the appointed hour of the meeting at Don Cass's apartment, brooded over his drink while Joe nodded sympathetically, polishing glasses.

"A million dollars riding on the turn of a red or green traffic light, a dead sailor turns up in Maggie's apartment, and who is he? No friend of Maggie's, or of Matthew, Mark, Luke or John." Joe nodded, puzzled but pious at the mention of the apostles, and went on polishing his glasses. So what happens? It turns out he's wearing green socks."

"Sailors don't wear green socks," Joe said helpfully.

"Right," Malone said. "So it turns out he's Harold Spruce, the missing witness in the million dollar damage suit — dead."

Joe the Angel shook his head in genuine, if uncomprehending, sympathy.

"And so it goes," Malone said dolefully. "The guy saw the accident but he couldn't talk because he was driving a motorcycle that didn't belong to him and he had no business being out with. The bus driver saw the accident but he can't talk because he failed to stop. He had an accident record he concealed from the company when he got the job, so he was afraid of getting mixed up in the affair. Then there's the passenger who can't talk because he's afraid of getting his friend the bus driver in trouble. And everybody holding out till he sees how much there's in it for him."

Joe the Angel shrugged. "A million dollars is a million dollars," he said.

"So I've heard tell," Malone said sourly. He was beginning to wish he'd *never* heard it. He looked at his watch. It was time to be off for Don Cass's apartment. He looked across the bar at Joe.

"Speaking of a million dollars," Malone said, "you couldn't spare a five spot, could you? For cab fare. It costs money to make money, you know.

Joe the Angel rang up *No Sale* on the register and handed five singles across the bar to Malone.

"Thanks," Malone said, "you are the one man in a million, Joe."

He went out to find a cab. It was beginning to rain, and before he succeeded in flagging down a vacant cab it was coming down in buckets and Malone was drenched.

"Pity poor sailors on a night like this," the driver sang out cheerfully as Malone stepped into the cab and gave him the address.

"This poor sailor's been busted for good," Malone came back.

"What for?" asked the driver.

Malone said, "For wearing green socks, I guess."

"Happens all the time," the cabby replied, and stepped on the gas.

Malone found von Flanagan waiting for him in the foyer. "Well," snapped the chief of homicide, "where is he? I've got the joint staked out. What's the set-up?"

Malone looked at his watch. "By now," he said, "either Jake Charlotte or Arthur Forstman should be showing up at Cass's apartment, whichever one is most anxious to buy off the missing witness. Whoever killed Harold Spruce because he was a witness to the accident will have just as much reason to try and buy off Don Cass."

"Or *bump* him off," von Flanagan put in.

"That's what you're here for," Malone replied. "To put the arm on him before he tries it. We'd better hide out now before he gets here."

"Wait a minute, Malone. I thought you said there were two, Jake Charlotte and this other guy — whom did you say it was? Forstman?" He paused and stared at Malone, the name ringing a bell in his mind for the first time. "Say, you don't mean Forstman! The millionaire, *Arthur* Forstman! Are you crazy, Malone? How does *he* figure in this?"

Malone gave von Flanagan a fast briefing on the case. "And now," he said, "we'd better get out of sight before they get here."

Kluchetsky and Scanlin were waiting in the chief's unofficial–looking car down the street. Malone piled in and they sat down to wait keeping an eye on the apartment house entrance for the arrival of Charlotte, Forstman — or both. Eight o'clock came, and passed. Eight five. Eight ten. Eight fifteen.

"Okay," Malone said, "maybe it didn't work. Let's go and have a look."

"Either you're pulling something," von Flanagan growled, "or Don Cass has run out on you."

"We'll see," Malone said.

They went back to the apartment house and rang Don Cass's doorbell. No answer. Malone punched at the bell till the landlady came out.

"Looking for Mr. Cass?" she asked. She was as thin as a Saturday newspaper, and must have been born with a worried look, Malone reflected. "He must be in. I didn't hear him go out." She glanced at von Flanagan, who had never been able to shed his official look.

"No trouble at all," Malone said. "Mr. Cass may be able to give us important details in an accident case. I assure you, Mrs. — ?"

"Sheldon," the landlady said. She had relaxed a little. "Come on in. I'll show you his door."

Repeated knocking on the door brought no response. At a sign from von Flanagan, Kluchetsky applied two hundred pounds of policeman to the door and it caved in. On the floor in a pool of blood they found Don Cass, his eyes vacantly staring.

Von Flanagan examined the body. "Dead as a doornail," he said. "Dead as a mackerel, dead as a — "

"Let's just say he's dead," Malone said. He turned to Mrs. Sheldon who was wringing her hands and seemed on the point of hysterics. "Pull yourself together, Mrs. Sheldon," he said, consolingly. "We know you didn't do it. Was anybody here to see Mr. Cass today?"

"He — he made a couple of phone calls," she replied weakly, pointing to the phone out in the hall. "I heard him. Then a man came to see him — an hour ago, maybe a little more."

Further questioning brought out no more than the fact that she had heard a man going up but that when she had stepped out into the hall he was already up the stairs and around the landing. She hadn't seen him, but apparently he had knocked on Don Cass's door, for Mr. Cass had let him in. She had heard Mr. Cass saying hello to the visitor. And that was all. She didn't hear the man go and assumed he was still there.

By this time Kluchetsky had the place practically apart, looking for clues. Scanlin was peeping into closets and desk drawers as if he expected the killer to be hiding in one of them.

Von Flanagan, after a brief examination pronounced the victim dead for the second time, this time adding insult to injury by making the enlightening observation that the deceased had been killed with the traditional blunt instrument.

Malone said, "Okay, that makes it official. Now — who was it? Jake Charlotte or Arthur Forstman? Or somebody who lost two bucks on Black Jet in the fifth at Hialeah."

"Black Jet came in and paid nineteen dollars," von Flanagan told him. "He's got the book on him and if he wasn't a dead bookie now I'd have to take him in on a gambling charge. It wasn't a grudge killing and it wasn't a burglary." He held up the wallet he had taken from the victim's pocket, his lips set in tight lines.

Malone could see it was stuffed with bills to pay off the winning betters. Nineteen dollars of it would have gone to him, he reflected ruefully, and wondered if he could legally claim it, or just charge it up to expenses.

"One of them guys must have done it," von Flanagan went on. "Charlotte or Forstman. I'd better start checking on both of 'em right now."

An hour later, in von Flanagan's office, Malone heard the results of a police check–up. Arthur Forstman had been addressing a civic banquet at the time of Don Cass's murder. Three hundred alibis. So Forstman was in the clear. That left Jake Charlotte.

Malone rose and shook the cigar ashes off his vest.

"If you promise me you won't send your blundering flatfoot cops after him, and that you'll keep it out of the papers that Jake Charlotte is a suspect in the murder of Don Cass," he told von Flanagan, "I'll have the suspect in your hands by noon tomorrow." He made for the door without waiting for an answer.

X

A call to Jake Charlotte's home brought Mrs. Charlotte hobbling to the telephone. She was still in a cast as a result of the accident. Mr. Charlotte, she told him, had left the house directly after dinner and hadn't returned yet. Was it something important? A settlement of the lawsuit? And if so, how much?

"Mr. Forstman hasn't named a figure yet," Malone told her, "but I've got a hunch the case is coming to a head and I've got to talk it over with Mr. Charlotte right away — tonight. When he gets in tell him to wait up for me. I'm coming right over."

It took the last of Joe the Angel's five dollars to pay off the cab driver at Jake Charlotte's door. It was an old frame house with a "modernized" pink stucco front that was already beginning to crack and blister. In the light of the street lamp it looked like something out of Dali in one of his most nightmarish moods. The living room light was on. Malone rang the doorbell.

Mrs. Charlotte's voice called out to him, "Come in, the door is open."

"I'm so worried about Jake," were the first words with which she greeted Malone. "It isn't like him to go off like this directly after dinner and not tell me what his plans are. And it's not like him to stay out so late. He is a homebody,

Jake is. Besides, he missed his favorite television program.

She was a matronly woman with the harried but still hopeful look that one finds at the cosmetics counter at a drugstore *One Cent Sale*. Her injuries were evidently quite as extensive as the insurance investigators had reported. But she had managed to give her hair a few hurried touches and make up her face for the visitor with her one good arm.

"I'm sure Jake will be along any minute now," she went on, to reassure Malone. "He *never* stays out this late. Can I offer you a cup of tea?"

Malone felt his gullet take a nose–dive into his solar plexus. His throat was acutely parched — like a camel's after a non–stop journey across the Sahara.

"No, thank you," he said politely. "Tea aggravates my neuritis. I could stand a drop of rye, though — or anything else you might have in the house," he added quickly.

Mrs. Charlotte looked over at him archly. "Well," she said, "if you promise not to tell Jake. He disapproves of liquor in the house. But I've got a bottle stashed away — if you don't mind getting it yourself. It's in the linen closet there, under the guest towels."

Malone made a beeline for the linen closet but before he was half way across the room there was a sound of the front door opening and he was barely back in his chair before Jake Charlotte entered the room.

Jake Charlotte looked, if anything, uglier and more unprepossessing than he had looked on his recent harried visit to Malone's office. If he was alarmed at finding John J. Malone in his living room he was trying not to show it.

He greeted the little lawyer with, "Well, well, it's nice seeing you again, Mr. Malone. You have some news about our lawsuit, of course. How much is he willing to settle for?"

But before Malone could answer Jake Charlotte had turned to his wife. "You shouldn't have stayed up so late," he told her. "You know it isn't good for you to lose sleep like this. Come now, I'll help you to your room. Mr. Malone, will excuse you, won't you Mr. Malone?"

By sheer force but with an outward show of gentleness he got his wife out of the chair and limpingly into the bedroom — very much as one would half–drag and half–coax a reluctant but submissive child. Two minutes later he was back, closing the bedroom door carefully behind him and winking at Malone as if to say, "There, that's done. Now we can talk freely."

Meanwhile Malone had been doing some fast thinking. If Charlotte was guilty, and had given the sailor the lethal dose of chloral hydrate, and then had gone to Don Cass's house an hour before the appointment and murdered him with a blunt instrument to remove a second witness, then what would he not be prepared to do now? What would he not be prepared to do if he got wind of the fact that he was suspected of the crimes and that Malone had come at this late hour to deliver him over to the police for questioning?

Malone was beginning to wish he had told von Flanagan to let his cops make the arrest themselves. But after all, he reminded himself, there was still no direct evidence linking Jake Charlotte to either crime. Besides, the man was still his client and entitled to any legal protection he could give him.

Just the same he should have stopped off at Joe the Angel's City Hall Bar and borrowed Joe's gun, or at the very least fortified himself with a double shot of rye. His throat by this time was feeling like the last days of a California drought and a dangerous fire hazard.

"My wife is the worrying kind," Charlotte said. "And she hasn't got any kind of a head for business. You know how women are."

"The kind I've known have a good head for business, all right," Malone said. "And the only worrying they do is where the next mink coat is coming from. I just dropped in to talk over the case with you." He was sparring for time, trying to decide just what line of questioning to take with Charlotte in order to smoke out the facts.

"I thought it might help to make a better settlement with Mr. Forstman if I could spring at least one good witness on him for our side," he went on quickly. "Do you think you could identify a witness if I produced one?"

Charlotte gave Malone a sly look, in which there was just the faintest trace of suspicion. "I guess I could identify a witness," he said, "if he was on our side. Who did you have in mind — and how much is it going to cost?"

"I don't know yet," Malone said. "I got a note in the mail a few days ago from somebody on North Clark Street, but I haven't been able to contact him. He left the house and hasn't been back since. I thought you might be able to give me a line on him. His name's Harold Spruce."

He saw Charlotte's face blanch and his hands flutter in a moment of panic. But only for a moment.

"The name don't mean a thing to me," Charlotte said, shaking his head. "I'd have to see the man. When you catch up with him let me know and I'll come over to the office — " He paused. "It's getting cold in here. I could stand a little nip of something."

He rose and went over to a desk in the corner of the room and unlocked one of the lower drawers. "I've got to take it on the q.t.," he said, lowering his voice to a conspiratorial whisper. "My wife disapproves of liquor." He disappeared into the kitchen where Malone heard him fiddling with ice cubes. "How will you have yours?" he asked, poking his head out of the kitchen door.

Malone's heart sank. "Thanks, but I don't ever touch the stuff," he said, remembering the sailor and the chloral hydrate. But when Charlotte returned he had a glass in his hand and another which he offered to Malone.

"You're kidding," he said. "Everybody knows John J. Malone never passed up a drink. Here, drink up."

Malone took the glass and set it down on the end table beside his chair. "Well, just a drop," he said, "when we've finished talking business. I've been tipped off that there's another witness — somebody who was waiting for a bus on the corner when the accident occurred." Malone was watching Charlotte narrowly as he spoke. "Somebody by the name of Cass — Don Cass."

The glass trembled in Charlotte's hand. He set it down and sank into a chair. There was a wary look in his eyes now. A hunted look. Malone decided to give it to him straight and braced himself for the next move.

"Don Cass is dead," he said. "And so is Harold Spruce. Somebody is bent on murdering all our witnesses. You wouldn't know who it is, would you, Mr. Charlotte?"

The words were barely out of his mouth before Charlotte was out of his chair and making for him with a knife he had picked up in the kitchen and concealed in his breast pocket.

Knife fighting was not in Malone's line. He had dealt in his time with guns, blunt instruments, and broken whiskey bottles. But a knife was something else again. Instinctively he dived for Charlotte's weapon hand, dodging the blow as he did so. But he missed and both men came down in a heap on the floor. Malone managed to kick out at the knife hand and this time the weapon went clattering across the floor.

He was up and on top of Charlotte before the latter could recover the weapon. But a vicious blow to the jaw made his head reel and he found himself pinned down under a rain of blows from Charlotte, who was fighting like a madman now.

Mrs. Charlotte had come hobbling out of the bedroom, and was screaming blue murder. Bells were ringing somewhere, but whether they were doorbells, telephone bells or bells in his belfry Malone couldn't tell at the moment.

He had a firm grip on his assailant now, probably on the jugular, but he couldn't tell exactly. All he knew for certain was that he had to hold on because if he ever let go — Then there was a flash of fireworks in his head and suddenly everything went black.

When he came to again it was the face of Captain Daniel von Flanagan that swam into focus above him.

"Just take it easy," von Flanagan was saying, "all you need now is a stiff drink." He picked up the glass Malone had set down on the end table and held it out to the little lawyer.

Malone shook his head. "Take it away," he said, "and mark it exhibit A."

The Chief of Homicide turned to officer Kluchetsky. "You're a witness," he said. "This is the first time John J. Malone ever refused a drink. Remember that when the sanity hearing comes up."

The next day at the office, Maggie, between cold towels on his multiple swellings, bruises and contusions, plied the little lawyer with questions.

"Tell me this, Malone. If Harold Spruce was dickering with Arthur Forstman and Jake Charlotte, trying to sell his testimony as a witness to the highest bidder, why did he send a note to the police department offering to come forward and testify?"

"Harold Spruce was trying to bring pressure on both bidders," Malone said. "He figured that if they knew he had offered to talk they'd both get scared and up the ante. Jake Charlotte was up against it. He knew he couldn't compete with Forstman's millions, so he slipped Harold Spruce a lethal dose of chloral hydrate to get him out of the way. Which reminds me, is there anything in the emergency file?"

Maggie went to the filing cabinet and brought out a bottle of rye. "Joe the Angel sent this over when he heard you had met with — an accident," she said. "It's for internal use only."

"I can use it," Malone said, pouring himself a drink. "Have you heard from the police lab yet about that drink Jake Charlotte offered me last night?"

Maggie said, "Von Flanagan called up just before you got in. He said to tell you it was spiked with chloral hydrate. Enough to kill even a lawyer — and what he said about that I didn't wait to hear. I hung up. Anyway, it was a good thing he was having you shadowed and got there on time to save you from Charlotte, or — I don't even want to think what might have happened."

"I would have had him hog-tied and ready for delivery," Malone said, "if his wife hadn't conked me on the head with the table lamp." He laid aside the cold towels and got up to go. "I've got some unfinished business to attend to," he said. "If von Flanagan calls up again tell him I'll be over later to confer with my client."

Maggie gave him a sharp look. "Your client?"

At the door Malone turned. "Mr. Jake Charlotte," he said. "He's still my client, isn't he? And remember, I never lost a client yet."

"No," Maggie said, "but this time your client nearly lost you."

XI

At Joe the Angel's City Hall Bar, Malone sat staring glumly into his drink and turning the situation over in his mind. The million dollar suit had gone glimmering, of course. All the money he could expect for defending Jake Charlotte probably wouldn't pay for the drink in front of him, let alone what he already owed Joe the Angel. And the rent was due. And Maggie's back pay, to say nothing of what he owed her in cash loans. Things had never looked so black before.

Joe was morose, but sympathetic. "Why did the guy have to go do things like that?" he said, shaking his head sadly. "And a mickey finn yet! It gives the saloon business a bad name."

"A million dollars," Malone brooded. "A cool million bucks — right out the window."

He was still brooding when he felt a tap on his shoulder and turned to find Arthur Forstman seating himself on the stool beside him.

"Your secretary told me I'd find you here," Forstman said. He took out his wallet, extracted five one thousand dollar bills, and laid them on the bar. "I promised to pay you five thousand to prove I was not the murderer," he said. "Here's your money. I'm sorry you got roughed up doing it."

Malone looked at the crisp thousand dollar bills. Joe the Angel was watching him, with a grin a mile wide, a grin that changed to a puzzled frown as Malone continued to stare at the bar. When Malone's hand went out to the money the grin returned to Joe's face, but only for an instant, for Malone was shoving the bills back to Forstman.

"I can't take it," he said. "I've already got a client, and I can't have two clients at one time."

Joe looked as if he was going to burst into tears.

"But I'll tell you what I *can* do," Malone said to Forstman. "I can steer you on to a hell of a good investment, and maybe we can both make some money. Just maybe."

"That would be just fine with me," Forstman said. "I'm always open to a good business proposition."

"Then wait for me out in the car," Malone said, "and I'll join you in a few minutes."

When Forstman had gone Malone said to Joe the Angel, "Joe, I'm cutting you in on the investment, too. All you need to invest is ten bucks."

"What kind investment," Joe asked suspiciously. But at the same time he handed over the money.

Malone said, "I'm taking Arthur Forstman out to a floating crap game on upper Wabash Avenue. You'll get your money back. Besides, it'll be good to be among honest men again."

"Shot in the Dark" is the archetypal Malone story. Malone is trying to woo the beautiful Dolly Dove when murder intervenes. Daniel von Flanagan shows up complaining about his job, and effectively ruins the date. Of course, Malone solves all before the last page, except how to get his evening with Dolly Dove back on track. -JM

Shot in the Dark

John J. Malone looked affectionately at his newest currently favorite blonde and said, "Let's stop here for a minute. There's a view I want to see."

Dolly Dove, recently voted Chicago's favorite model, obediently braked her car to a stop. A date with Chicago's most infamous criminal lawyer was something to put in her memory book. Besides, she thought she really liked the little guy.

Malone sighed happily. He had plans. Some of them had been carried out. A perfect dinner in a special little roadhouse. The drive back to town. For later, reservations were waiting at the Chez Paree, and after that — heaven only knew, and probably wouldn't tell.

But the view itself was worth the stop. There were trees and flowering bushes against a nicely moonlit springtime sky. He could almost have sworn he heard a cricket.

Suddenly he heard more than that. He heard shouting, and a man came plunging up through the bushes on the side of the road.

Dolly Dove grabbed his arm and said, "Malone!"

"Stay here," the little lawyer told her, reaching for the door handle.

Just then the man reached the car, running, as if he'd been shot out of a cannon. He half–collapsed against Dolly's lime–green convertible, and gasped, "Violet! She's dead! He killed her!"

Malone grabbed his arm with one hand. With the other he reached for the brandy bottle in the glove compartment. "Hold still," he said sternly.

For a moment it was a question whether the frightened man would calm down, completely collapse, or drop dead. To Malone's intense relief, the man calmed down.

"Thanks," the frightened stranger said, catching his breath. He seemed to be mentally counting to ten before he said, "She's down there. What can we do?" Apparently he counted another ten before he said, "What can we *do?*"

"Take it easy," Malone said. Instinctively he added, "Don't worry."

He took a quick look at the stranger. A medium–sized man, probably average height, average weight, brown hair turning grey, eyes that were just plain eye–color, a few scratches on his face.

"You stay here," Malone said. He managed to get the still shaking man into the convertible, and said, "Now sit there, and keep quiet."

Dolly Dove handed him a flashlight from the glove compartment. Malone thanked her with his eyes. This was the time to catch his own breath. He leaned against the side of the car for a few seconds.

"Dolly," he said, "I've got to go down there. Will you be safe here, with him?"

By way of an answer she held up a tire iron in one hand and the brandy bottle in the other.

The little lawyer smiled for the first time in the past five minutes, and whispered, "But will he be safe with you?"

She said a very rude word, made a mock pass at him with the tire iron and said, "But hurry, Malone!"

Malone hurried, through sweet–scented bushes whose soft leaves caressed his face. He wished he could bottle their perfume and send it as a gift to Dolly Dove. He wished too that the carefully planned evening would turn out all right, but in his heart he knew it would not.

He finally reached the side road and searched around with his flashlight.

Violet X was dead, there was no doubt about that. In spite of her still–bleeding bullet wounds he could see that earlier in life she had been beautiful. Her well–dyed hair was dark and soft as the shadows cast by the moon behind the trees. Even with only the flashlight and the half–hidden moonlight, he could see that her face was not young, but had been carefully and expensively made up.

She was sprawled on the pavement as though she'd been thrown from a car. A black moleskin handbag hung from her wrist by its strap. Malone was tempted to open it for identification, and resisted it as he had never resisted temptation before. An alligator hide jewel case lay beside her. The little lawyer resisted that temptation too.

He'd seen enough for now. He plunged back up the sweet–scented hill, following the trail the frightened stranger had blazed for him.

Dolly was still behind the wheel, one hand on the tire iron, the other on the brandy bottle, and a wary eye on the unwelcome stranger.

"We've got to stay here," Malone said hoarsely. "We're witnesses. But somebody's got to call the police."

As though Providence had been listening in, headlights appeared over the hill ahead of them. Hastily the little lawyer turned on the flashlight and signaled it to stop. An ancient and noisy sedan slowed and stopped with a jolt that was probably recorded on seismographs halfway around the world.

A scared middle–aged face looked out and a worried voice said, "We were only going twenty–five. I'm Mr. Edgar Osterhout and this is Mrs. Osterhout. I'll show you my license — "

"Never mind your license," Malone said. "See if you can make forty–five. Or even fifty–five. There's been a murder here."

The plump, blondined Mrs. Osterhout gave a frightened yelp.

Malone said quickly, "Find the nearest phone. Call the police and ask for Homicide, Inspector von Flanagan."

"Young man," the white–haired Edgar Osterhout said, thereby giving Malone the happiest moment he'd had in years, "I am a private teacher of mnemonics, I remember everything. Take one of my pamphlets." He shoved a paper into Malone's hand, reached for the gear shift and said, "It will be a matter of minutes."

The white–haired, memory course teacher stepped on the gas and the old sedan moaned, groaned, and finally took off with a roar that would have raised envy in a jet plane.

Again Malone leaned against the lime–green convertible. Dolly's warm hand reached out and held his. With her free hand she reached for the brandy bottle. Both of them made him feel a little better, but not much.

"Malone," she whispered, "Everything is going to be all right, isn't it?"

"Of course," he reassured her, and hoped he was telling the truth. He nodded toward the stranger. "Has he said anything?"

"He said 'Boo!' once, but I don't think be meant it."

The little lawyer sighed, handed her the pamphlet and said, "While we wait for the cops, read it. Out loud."

This time Dolly sighed. "I'm your gal, Malone. The title is 'You Too Can Remember.' "

"There are times," Malone said, "when I'd rather forget. But go on." He reached for a cigar and said, "but I do remember a few things — "

Dolly said, "Shut up," but in a very soft voice. "This is the first lesson in a memory course. You memorize these words first and you can remember anything."

"Shoot," the little lawyer said. He was beginning to wish he had died in his cradle.

"Bat," Dolly read out loud.

"Bat," Malone repeated dutifully.

"Hen."

"Hen."

"Bug."

"Bug," Malone repeated and added, "Where's the brandy?"

Dolly handed it to him, and said, "Hill."

Malone came back with "Hell," and Dolly said that was no language to use in the presence of the witness to a murder.

It took a few minutes, and a sip from the brandy bottle, but Malone made it.

"Bat, Hen, Bug, Hill, Shoe, Hat, Cow, Ape, Woods, Dog," he recited triumphantly. He tried it again. "Dolly, this should be set to music. I know an orchestra leader in Los Angeles named Spade Cooley." He tried on a tune for size, and was advised by Dolly that he'd better stay with the legal profession.

"Not that I don't have faith in this memory course," she said encouragingly.

The stranger suddenly sat up and said, "Violet!"

"See?" Dolly said. "It's even making him remember."

"Olive!" the stranger said. "*Olive!*" He lapsed back into his white–faced silence.

"He probably wants a martini," Malone growled.

II

It wasn't long before the sirens sounded. Dolly clutched his hand.

"Don't worry," Malone said. "It's only a murder."

It was von Flanagan who got out of the police car. He stormed over to the convertible and gave Malone one of the dirtiest looks in history.

"I might have known it," he said unhappily. "But how did you get here so fast?"

"Believe me," the little lawyer said, in his most conciliating voice, "we were here first. Miss Dove and I had stopped to admire the view."

The big police officer caught himself on the verge of a very rude remark about the view. Dolly Dove was a view anybody would stop to admire.

"We heard the shots," Malone went on smoothly. "This man came running up through the bushes. He said there had been a murder. Frankly, I think he's in a state of shock."

"Stick to the story," von Flanagan said, "and skip the comments."

"Naturally," the little lawyer went on, "I went down to investigate."

Von Flanagan said in a nasty voice, "Naturally, you would."

"You have three witnesses," Malone said. "And you have a corpse. What more do you want?"

At that moment the Osterhouts's well–used sedan came around the bend with a noise like an old garbage pail, filled with nuts and bolts, being shaken to and fro in a Nevada earthquake.

Edgar Osterhout's pink face peered through the window. He said, "Can I be of any more help?"

Malone muttered under his breath, "You've been too much help already." He went on hastily to von Flanagan, "After we heard the shots, and I went down and discovered the body, I came back up here and flagged the first car that came along. It happened to be this one. This gentleman was kind enough to telephone the police."

"It was no trouble," the professor said. "Do you wish us to stay here?"

Von Flanagan groaned. "As it is, we'll probably have traffic tied up from Gary, Indiana to Milwaukee, Wisconsin. You'd better get on home and let me know where to reach you."

"Gladly," Edgar Osterhout said. "My card. It has my home address, my business address, and a day–or–night telephone number." He added proudly, "I am a professor of mnemonics." The sedan moved away with a visible shudder.

Von Flanagan looked at the card, glared at Malone and growled. "Fine. A name I can't pronounce, and a job I can't even spell."

"Mnemonics," Malone said. "Memory. He teaches you how to remember everything."

At that the white–faced eye–witness half opened his eyes and began reciting, "Dog, Woods, Ape, Cow — "

"Gosh," Dolly said. "He's got it, but he's doing it backwards!"

The big policeman said slowly, and very patiently, "For years I have been planning to retire from the force. I am going to do so tomorrow. One eye–witness, who is either drunk, crazy or both. And you, Malone — " He paused, and said wearily, "Well, let's go look at this corpse."

He raised his voice and called, "Danaher!"

A young blond policeman who could have posed for Mr. America, Apollo, or both, popped out of the car.

"Danaher," von Flanagan said, "stay by this car. Don't take your eyes off either of these people."

Danaher took one quick look at Dolly Dove and said, "Yes, sir!"

Von Flanagan growled something under his breath and yelled, "Klutchesky! You and Patapoff stay with the car." He turned to Malone. "All right, where is it?"

Malone pointed and said, "Down there." He added, "It's the old road and, before this masterpiece was opened, it was the boulevard. Turns off about a block below here. We can walk back and come in that way, or we can go through the bushes."

Von Flanagan headed for the bushes and said, "If they keep working on the boulevard system, you'll need a compass to drive through Lincoln Park."

At the end of the bushes, Malone said, "There's probably tire marks."

"Twenty–four years on the force," von Flanagan growled, "and you tell me about tire marks!" He pushed on through the bushes and snapped on his flashlight. Then he walked carefully along the edge of the road.

He surveyed the scene, the dead woman, the purse, the alligator–hide case. Gingerly, he moved in a little closer.

"Malone, looks to me like five bullet wounds, and any one could of done it. Guy wants to kill her, why not stop with one shot?" He sighed and said, "All that's got to wait until the experts get here." He said *"experts"* as if it was a word that shouldn't be said within five blocks of a public school, church, or polling place.

Suddenly he yelled, "Klutchesky!"

There was an answering hail.

"Come down here." He added, "Come through the bushes and don't step on the road. Could be tire marks."

Malone maintained the most discreet silence in a fairly long lifetime of discreet silences.

Two hundred and ten pounds of Klutchesky plunged down the little hillside, walked carefully alongside of the road, surveyed the scene and said, "Looks dead."

Malone knew the procedure. The expensive black moleskin handbag had to be opened. The alligator–hide jewel case had to be opened. Someone, this time Klutchesky, had to be present.

The handbag revealed the usual female paraphernalia: compact, two lipsticks, pancake makeup, a tube of stick cologne, a few old ticket stubs, a half–used package of cigarettes, two sticks of chewing gum, a handful of Kleenex, and a wallet.

Before touching the wallet, von Flanagan turned to Malone and Klutchesky. "You're witnesses. I just want you to make sure I didn't swipe a dime."

The bill compartment of the wallet contained $417 in assorted bills. The change compartment contained three quarters and a nickel. Klutchesky made a note of the total amount, which Klutchesky and von Flanagan signed, and Malone initialed.

The other compartment of the wallet contained a membership card in an exclusive women's club, a business card giving a home address in an expensive building on the Drive, and a driver's license.

What it all added up to was that the dead woman's name was Violet Castleberry, that she was in the real estate business, and that she lived well.

"No keys," Klutchesky grunted.

"Naturally," von Flanagan said. "They'd be in the car over there." He looked at the alligator hide jewel case. It had a lock on it, but experimentally, he pushed the catch.

Surprisingly the lid flew open.

A dazzling array of diamonds blazed at them from necklaces, bracelets, rings, earrings and clips.

Von Flanagan said one word, but he said it reverently.

He slammed the lid shut. "This has to be sealed and taken to Headquarters."

III

A rapid inspection of the car, a late model Cadillac, revealed no bloodstains, and no trace of the murder weapon.

Malone looked at his watch. Yes, it was nine–fifteen. Still time, with good luck, to make that reservation at the Chez. There was always a chance the Chez would hold it for him.

Von Flanagan glanced back at the jewel case. "If I owned a tenth of what that's probably worth," he said a little wistfully, "I'd retire to California and raise chinchillas. I understand that — " He got his mind back on his work and said, "Well, it wasn't robbery."

Malone decided it was safer not to say anything.

"I'm going to retire anyway," the big policeman said, his voice beginning to rise ominously. "A nice simple little murder, I can understand. But this — " He glared at Malone as though the whole thing was his fault.

Malone said smoothly, "I didn't invite myself to this murder."

Von Flanagan turned to Klutchesky. "The experts will be along any minute." Again his tone of voice indicated what he thought of experts. "You take over. Get that stuff — " he glanced again at the jewel case, "downtown as soon as you can. Come along, Malone."

"I will," the little lawyer said, "and quietly."

As they neared the lime–green convertible, they could hear what seemed to be a chant. The handsome Danaher was leaning against the door, gazing adoringly at Dolly Dove, and reciting "Bat. Hen. Bug. Hill. Shoe."

"*Danaher!*" von Flanagan roared. He groaned. "Now one of my best cops goes crazy."

Danaher blushed. "It's a memory course, sir," he explained apologetically. "It teaches you how to remember everything."

"There are times," von Flanagan growled, "when I'd be satisfied if you remembered *anything.*"

"It's really wonderful, Inspector," Dolly Dove said softly. She handed him the pamphlet.

Von Flanagan glanced at it, turned to Malone, and asked, "Do you suppose there is anything to this stuff?"

"If there is," Malone said acidly, "you ought to have it made required reading for the whole police force."

Von Flanagan opened it, looked at it. He began to read aloud, "Bat. Hen. Bug." Suddenly be hurled the pamphlet into the convertible, and, forgetting Dolly Dove's presence, said a very rude word.

"Danaher," he said. "You and Patapoff stay up here with the car. When the experts get here, direct them to go down through the bushes and walk on the grass. Tire marks."

Again Malone was tactfully silent.

Danaher said, "Yes *sir!*" took a wistful look at Dolly Dove and went away. Sirens were beginning to sound in the distance.

"And now," von Flanagan said grimly, "we'll see what *he* remembers." He walked around the car and said in what was, for him, a gentle voice. "I'm von Flanagan of the police department. I just want to ask a few questions."

"I'm Alvin Orvell," the frightened stranger said. He seemed a little more calm, a little less pale. "Violet was murdered, wasn't she? He did kill her, didn't he? I didn't imagine it?" He looked at Malone for reassurance.

"Yes," Malone said soothingly. "but who was *he*?"

"I don't know. You see, we'd never seen him before." He paused for breath. "I mean we didn't know him. He answered Violet's advertisement. Violet is my fiancée. We're going to be married." He paused again, began to sob, and said, "I mean, we were."

Dolly Dove automatically handed him the brandy bottle and said, "Hold everything, chum."

Alvin Orvell gulped, said, "Thanks," and blew his nose. Von Flanagan muttered something about getting his one eye–witness drunk.

"Olive can tell you more about it. Please, who's going to tell Olive? She is — I mean, she was — Violet's step–daughter. They are — were — more like sisters. She knows a lot about Violet's affairs. It was all about the jewelry. Olive can explain. She lived with Violet. If it hadn't been for the jewelry and the investment and the advertisement, this wouldn't have happened." He closed his eyes and was silent.

"It's none of my business," Malone said softly, "but I have a hunch we'll get more sense out of this if we have Olive present."

Von Flanagan gave him a look.

Cars were beginning to arrive. Von Flanagan bellowed "Danaher!" The handsome young cop raced over as though he were trying to break Bannister's track record.

"I've decided we'd better go to Mrs. Castleberry's apartment," von Flanagan said. "Klutchesky has the address and phone number. He's in charge, and the experts know what to do. You stay here with the car and remember, tell those guys to go down through the bushes." He paused, scowled, and said, "Hell, you've got to keep the car here, and — "

"Deputize me," Dolly Dove said sweetly, "and I'll drive you."

The big policeman managed a grateful smile, and went on giving orders to Danaher. "Send Gadenski over here, he's going with us." He turned to Alvin Orvell. "Whose car is it?"

"It was her car," Orvell said. He blinked his eyes as though trying to remember. "She was driving."

"Okay, let's get moving," von Flanagan said.

Danaher moved, and, in a matter of seconds, so did everybody else. The tall, lanky figure of Gadenski started moving fast toward the lime–green convertible. Members of the Homicide Squad, carrying their equipment, started moving fast through the bushes.

"If this keeps up," Malone commented, "they'll beat a path that will be discovered by the Park Department, which will promptly start to build a new boulevard."

Von Flanagan ignored that, said hoarsely, "Get in back with this guy, Gadenski, and let's get out of here before the reporters come around the bend." He smiled at Dolly Dove and said, "How fast can you drive, young lady?"

"Don't tell him," Malone said. "He'd use it against you the next time you're arrested for speeding."

"I'm a deputy now," Dolly Dove said, and stepped on the gas.

IV

Approximately twelve minutes later the convertible came to a screeching stop in front of the impressive address on Lake Shore Drive.

"Young lady," von Flanagan said breathlessly, "I'd back you in the Memorial Day Race any time."

She smiled her thanks and said, "I'll wait for you here."

"You will not," Malone said in a stern voice. "You're coming with us. There's a killer loose, and after all, you're more–or–less of a witness."

It was a small, modest, and probably, Malone reflected, incredibly expensive apartment building. One apartment to a floor, as he discovered when the self–service elevator let them out at the second floor into a small but perfectly decorated foyer.

The woman who answered their ring almost made Malone wish he didn't prefer blondes, but not quite. Beautiful, he decided quickly, was not quite the word for her. Breathtaking might be better. Her hair was very dark, smooth and shining, and swept into a coil on the back of her neck, and her skin was the exact color of the cream he liked on strawberries. Her eyes were a shade somewhere between grey, green and brown, and right now they were wide with startled surprise.

"Olive!" Alvin Orvell gasped. He stumbled past her into the room.

Malone and the others followed. Von Flanagan kicked the door shut behind them.

"Alvin!" the lovely girl said, and Malone couldn't decide whether it was anger or amazement in her voice, "Alvin, you're drunk! And who are all these people?"

Alvin shook his head, said nothing, sank down into a chair that was an interior decorator's dream of glory, and buried his face in his hands.

Von Flanagan cleared his throat and said, "Miss — "

"Castleberry," she told him coldly as though he should have known it all the time.

The big policeman introduced himself and Gadenski as " — both from Homicide," Malone as " — criminal lawyer," and Dolly Dove without comment.

Olive Castleberry stared at him and then, as though she might have been ordering the band to keep on playing on a sinking ship, said, "Won't you sit down?" Then she said, in an anxious voice, "Is Alvin in any trouble?"

Von Flanagan was never one to break news gently, with such phrases as, "There's been a little accident," or, "Just a little trouble." He told her, simply and bluntly, "Your step–mother has been murdered."

And then Olive Castleberry sat down. "That man!" she said.

"All right," von Flanagan said, "Tell me about that man. Gadenski, take this down." He looked admiringly at her. He liked women who didn't fly into hysterics and have to be calmed before they could get out a coherent word.

Gadenski obediently got out his notebook and looked expectant. Malone just opened his ears and wished he'd met Professor Osterhout a few years before. Dolly Dove yawned and lit a cigarette.

"And start from scratch," von Flanagan said.

V

"My father," she said quietly, "married Violet a little over five years ago. He'd been a widower. Violet was just a few years older than I — and I liked her right from the beginning. They wanted me to stay here with them, and I wanted to. Then my father died a few years ago."

She paused for a minute, and no one broke the silence.

"Alvin — was almost one of the family. When my father died, he was wonderful to us. I don't know what we'd have done without him. Then he fell in love with Violet. I wasn't surprised. Everybody who knew Violet loved her. I was so happy for them both — "

For the first time her calm, low–pitched voice almost broke. Alvin Orvell moaned softly and kept his face in his hands.

"My father was in real estate. That's how he and Violet met. He never made a great deal of money. But he used to say of her that she had the greatest gift of turning money into more money that he'd ever seen."

She looked at the big policeman as though asking what more he needed to know.

"About tonight — " von Flanagan began.

Alvin Orvell sat up suddenly and said, "The jewelry. The advertisement. The investment." Then he sank back and put his face in his hands again.

Olive Castleberry frowned. "I don't know how much money Violet had, but I do know it was all tied up in properties she couldn't touch without a terrific loss. This opportunity came up — to invest in a new project. She couldn't turn it down, not Violet. So she decided to sell some of her jewels. She never wore them anyway, not since my father died. She put an advertisement in the *Tribune* offering them for sale. This man telephoned and made an appointment for this evening."

Now, Malone thought, we're getting somewhere, but with the speed of a lamed turtle. He'd already crossed off all hopes of the Chez, and he suspected Dolly Dove had fallen asleep.

"I let him in, and called Violet," Olive Castleberry went on. "Alvin was here. Violet brought out the jewel case and they went through it. He said he wanted to buy it as a gift for his wife. They agreed on the price. Twenty–five thousand dollars."

Malone thought about all the things he could buy with twenty-five thousand dollars, besides jewelry. He glanced at Dolly Dove and saw that she'd suddenly sprung awake just at the sound of those words.

"But," Olive Castleberry said, "he wanted his wife to see and approve the jewelry first. His wife couldn't come here because she's a semi–invalid. He asked Violet if she'd bring the jewelry to his home, for her to see. Violet agreed. After all, she was terribly anxious to make the sale. He was going to call a taxi — he said he'd come in one — and she suggested that they use her car. That's all I know. Except that Alvin went along to protect Violet."

Malone took another look at Alvin and decided that he couldn't protect an agile mouse from a lazy and overfed cat.

Von Flanagan looked at Alvin and said expectantly, "Well?"

Alvin looked up. "It was like this. All my fault, I guess. Leaving Violet alone with that man. And with all that jewelry in the car."

He paused to blow his nose. Loudly.

"Violet was driving, naturally. He was sitting between us, giving directions. He said it wasn't far from here. But going through the park he seemed to get lost. Then we ran out of gas. Violet told me to walk back to the highway and try to flag down a car, maybe borrow some gas or get a lift to the nearest filling station. I shouldn't have left her alone with that man."

He paused again and put his face back in his hands.

Olive Castleberry leaped up, made a quick run to the sideboard, came back with a glass that she handed to the white–faced man, and said sternly, "Here. And don't try to tell it so fast. Nobody's in any hurry."

Except me, Malone thought, looking at Dolly Dove.

VI

A little more color came into Alvin Orvell's face.
"I don't know how many cars passed by. Nobody would stop for me. Then I heard her scream. When I ran back to the car she was lying on the ground. Dead. There was no sign of the — the murderer. Then I ran back up to the highway. The bushes scratched my face but I kept on running. I think I fell once or twice. I was frightened. Then I found these people, or they found me." The color began to recede from his face again. "That's all I remember. That's all . . . that's all... "

He slid from the chair like a puppet with the strings suddenly cut, to land supine on the floor.

Everybody jumped up except Malone, who said, "Only a faint. Leave him alone. Miss Castleberry, could you get a blanket and throw it over him?"

Dolly Dove said weakly, "He might have a bad heart."

"If he had," Malone said, "he'd have fallen down long before this." And, "Miss Castleberry, that's fine, but don't put the pillow under his head. Put it under his back."

Von Flanagan said coldly, "And since when have you been a combination of the Red Cross, the Emergency Service, and the Visiting Nurses Association?"

"Since," Malone said, just as coldly, "I had to wash the sand out of your eye back in third grade, after a kindergartner knocked you down in the play–yard." He took Olive Castleberry by the arm and said, "There's nothing to worry about. He's had a terrific shock tonight and it's small wonder he fainted after telling about what happened. Meantime, suppose you go on with more details, and don't you faint."

She gave him a wan smile and sat down.

Von Flanagan gave Malone a look that, under other circumstances, would have passed for gratitude, and said, "Miss Castleberry, I know this is all very painful, for you." It was the voice and manner, Malone recognized, that the big policeman used in emergency occasions among the upper–income brackets.

"I understand," she said in her coot smooth voice. "I'll tell you anything you need to know, if I can."

Gadenski immediately reached for a fresh pencil and looked as hopeful and expectant as if he were one of a pack of hound dogs waiting at the foot of a tree in Tennessee, watching a treed coon.

"A little more information about this man," von Flanagan said. "His name. He must have given you his name."

"His name was Otto Bergholtz. I mean, he said that was his name. He said he was a poultry dealer."

"Address?"

"He didn't say. He just said it wasn't very far from here. Maybe he told it to Alvin, I don't know."

Malone murmured, "There can't be many poultry dealers named Otto Bergholtz in the telephone book."

"You mind your business," von Flanagan said, "and I'll mind mine." He turned back to Olive Castleberry and said, "Now, if you'll just describe him."

"Well — " For a moment puzzled lines appeared between her lovely eye brows. "He seemed sort of middle aged. Maybe thirty, forty, fifty, sixty. Medium high. Not fat, and not really thin, either. Sort of brown hair. Just hair– color hair. I didn't notice the color of his eyes. He had on a suit. I think it was grey… " She added, "I really didn't pay too much attention to him."

The little lawyer said nothing, closed his eyes, and reflected that this was the kind of description that drove policemen into resigning and going to California to raise chinchillas. "He had on a suit." What would she have expected him to wear, an embroidered Zambezi robe, or a pair of Hollywood shorts? It was a description that would have fitted half the males in the Western hemisphere, and probably a goodsized number in the Eastern. He knew from von Flanagan's breathing and wordlessness that he was thinking the same thing.

She added one helpful note. "And he wore horn–rimmed glasses."

So, Malone told himself, did a fair percentage of American men who would never even hurt a mouse.

He heard von Flanagan say, in a weary voice, "Thank you, Miss Castleberry. You've been very helpful." From the sound of his voice, Malone knew that before the night was over he would hear a lamentation from von Flanagan dealing with the fact he had never wanted to be a cop, the reasons why he had become a cop, and what he was going to do when he retired. From the way he heard the notebook slam shut, he knew Gadenski was thinking the same thing.

Alvin Orvell moaned and sat up.

"Get him to a hospital," Malone said quickly.

Olive Castleberry frowned. "He can't be that sick. And he doesn't have a bad heart. You said yourself it was the shock."

"True," the little lawyer told her, "but he will have a bad heart if somebody puts a shot through it. And it will be a lot easier to guard him in a hospital."

Her eyes widened.

"He saw the killer," Malone went on quickly before von Flanagan could steal the scene. "He can identify him. And the same goes for you, Miss Castleberry. As far as you know, did anyone else get a look at him?"

She shook her head. "There's no elevator man. And the maid had gone to bed."

Von Flanagan muttered crossly, "Why do I need the Chicago police force, when I have a lawyer for a friend!" He snapped at Gadenski, "Get the phone. Twenty–four–hour protection for Miss Castleberry. Put him in Wesley Memorial, it's the closest hospital to here. Round the clock for him too. Stay here until her guard arrives. And move fast, because this place will be lousy with reporters any minute now." He rose and put on his hat.

Dolly Dove smiled and said, "I'll be more than glad to drive you anywhere you're going."

Malone glanced at his watch, and sighed. The last show would be going on any minute now at the Chez. Why couldn't this particular murder have picked any other night in history to happen?

<h1 style="text-align:center">VII</h1>

He sighed again when the lime–green convertible stopped in front of Headquarters, and Dolly Dove said sweetly, "Unless you boys need me for anything more, good night."

The little lawyer laid a hand on the wheel. "Not so fast," he said. "Remember, you're a material witness. Von Flanagan, tell her she can't go yet." He added, "If she goes then I have to go too. Can't let a girl go home alone — with a killer prowling the streets."

"That's right, miss," von Flanagan said, "With Mr. Malone here to help us it shouldn't take long to wind up this case." He gave Malone a dirty look.

Reporters were waiting in the anteroom of von Flanagan's office. The big policeman shouldered his way through them, Malone in his wake.

At the door von Flanagan paused long enough to recite, "We have a definite suspect and an arrest is expected shortly." He slammed the door shut fast.

He plopped down behind his desk without saying a word, reached for the classified directory and began pawing through it. Suddenly he looked up at Malone, wonder in his eyes.

"There is a poultry dealer named Otto Bergholtz."

"Naturally," Malone said, lighting a cigar. "Nobody would make up a name like that on purpose." He added, "Maybe an arrest is expected shortly. Maybe for once you told the reporters the truth."

Von Flanagan pushed the switch on the intercom and barked out orders. "Look up his home address. Have him picked up and brought down. And *now!*" He looked at Malone and said, "And I hope he doesn't live in Maywood or South Chicago. Because I'm holding you as a witness."

"Nonsense," Malone told him. "You just want company."

The buzzer sounded. Von Flanagan flipped the switch and listened.

The first report had come in. A .38 revolver had been found near the scene of the crime.

Von Flanagan growled, "It took you guys long enough to find it."

"I think," Malone said, crushing out his cigar and reaching for a new one, "you can safely tell the gentlemen of the press that five .38 caliber slugs will be found in the late Mrs. Castleberry."

"By now," von Flanagan said, "those bums will have taken enough pictures of the car to fill a Sunday supplement."

The second report arrived in person, from Gadenski. Alvin Orvell was safely tucked away in the hospital. Guard had been posted there and at the Castleberry apartment. Half the reporters and photographers in the city of Chicago had tried to get in and failed. And he was very tired and would like to go home.

The third report arrived, from Klutchesky. The jewelry, purse, and cheap wrist watch had been properly put away. The body had been removed. The experts had come and gone. Curious spectators had tied up traffic in four directions. The other half of the reporters and photographers in the city of Chicago had littered the area with used flashbulbs and cigarette butts. Danaher had been left at the scene and was not too happy about it. Finucane would relieve him. And he, Klutchesky, was very tired and would like to go home.

After they had gone, Malone said lazily, "Let's all go home and go to bed."

Von Flanagan gave him a long, sorrowful look. "Malone, I never wanted to be a cop. I wanted to be an undertaker."

Here it comes, Malone told himself. He half closed his eyes, and dozed. A few phrases came to him through beautiful dreams of Dolly Dove.

" — if the alderman hadn't owed my old man money —

" — never asked for a promotion. Especially not to Homicide — "

Malone visioned Dolly Dove floating on a rosy pink cloud, in a spring wind.

" — murderers seem to go out of their way to make life hard for me —

" — and they say there's a fortune in chinchilla. You just buy two of them —

" — now a maniac killer — "

Malone looked at Dolly Dove. She was yawning. He reached for a cigar, and said sleepily, "I think you hit yourself on the head with a nail that time." He paused, blinked and said, "I mean you hit the hammer with a nail."

"Never mind," von Flanagan said, "I know what you mean. Sure, this poultry dealer is nuts. He answers an ad to sell jewelry. He arrives, agrees on a price, wants to show the jewelry to his wife. It's a lot of money." He scowled. "I guess there is a lot of money in hens and chickens at that. Maybe when I retire — "

"As you were saying," Malone said quickly.

"So he shoots her five times, when one would of done it," the big policeman growled. "The little guy, this Alvin what's–his–name, he's gone after a can of gas. This poultry dealer takes it on the lam. But why doesn't he pick up the jewelry? Or her purse?"

"Ask him when he gets here," Malone said. He was very tired now.

VIII

Another report came in. No fingerprints on anything, not on the car, the jewel case, the gun, except the legitimate ones of Violet Castleberry, Olive Castleberry, Alvin Orvell, and a few cops that von Flanagan stated he would deal with personally in the morning.

"In these days," von Flanagan said furiously as he switched off the intercom, "nobody wears gloves. And two people saw him. If he'd of had gloves on, it would of been noticed."

"Maybe," Malone suggested coyly, "no hands." He went on very fast. "You don't need to worry. You've got the guy's name and address, and he's probably on his way down here right now. He'll probably talk your ears off."

"And you'll probably get him for a client," von Flanagan said bitterly.

Malone said, "You've skipped something. Fingerprints in the Castleberry apartment. He was there quite a while, and he must have touched something. And Olive Castleberry would have noticed if he'd worn gloves."

Von Flanagan swore softly under his breath, and gave more orders over the intercom.

A moment. later the intercom spoke back to him. "They brought Bergholtz in."

"Send him here," von Flanagan said, and immediately regretted it. From the sound effects in the corridor, a minor riot was going on. Then came the popping flashbulbs and the sound of voices from the anteroom. Finally the door was kicked open, two perspiring squad car officers shoved their loudly protesting prisoner into the office, slammed the door shut behind them, and said, "Here you are."

Otto Bergholtz, poultry dealer, was, roughly, somewhere between five foot two and five foot three, and very much on the chubby side. He had a round, pink face, bright blue eyes, a white moustache that matched a fringe of white hair surrounding a round, pink bald head. At the moment, he was probably the angriest man in the state of Illinois.

"What kind of outrage is this?" he wanted to know. "I want to buy a nice present for my little woman, my Bertha. It's our twenty–fifth wedding anniversary. I see this advertisement in the paper. I go there and it looks all right, nice jewelry. Fine. Only mamma — she should see it first. I never buy anything without mamma sees it first. So we go in the car, and the car runs out of gas. This young man, he says, you go get some gas, please, and we wait here. I get out of the car and I start walking. A block away I hear the motor starting and the car driving away — back. When I come home I tell mamma, she thinks I'm crazy. Then policemen come — "

Von Flanagan looked at Malone, then he looked at Mr. Bergholtz. "You say *you* got out of the car? *You* went for the gas?"

"Sure. Why do you ask me questions? Am I arrested? What happened? All I wanted to do — "

Malone spoke up. "Did anybody see you get out of the car, Mr. Bergholtz? Anybody, that is, except Mrs. Violet Castleberry and Alvin Orvell?"

"Sure," said Mr. Bergholtz. "They saw me get out of the car. You ask them, they will tell you."

"Did anybody *else* see you there?" Malone asked patiently. "Any passing car — "

"No," said Bergholtz.

"How did you get home?" asked von Flanagan.

"I walked to the filling station at Milwaukee crossing, I called up for a cab and I went home. What is the matter? Did — did anything happen?"

"Oh, nothing at all," von Flanagan replied. "Nothing at all." He turned to the little lawyer. "Malone, what do you make of it?"

Malone said, "Looks like we've hit a detour. You know the procedure. Hold the suspect while you check his story. It shouldn't be hard to find the gas station attendant, and the cab driver. If his story holds up you've still got Alvin Orvell —

or would you rather hang it on me? Or Miss Dolly Dove? After all, it's only a slight case of murder."

"Murder!" It was Mr. Bergholtz, and it sounded more like a shriek than a question.

"Yes, murder," von Flanagan said. "I'm holding you — only on suspicion, mind you — until we check your story — for the murder of Mrs. Violet Castleberry."

IX

If he had been made of inflated rubber and someone had pricked him with a pin Otto Bergholtz couldn't have gone limper than he did that instant. After a glass of water he revived enough to gasp, "Murder? How could it be? They weren't supposed to — " He caught himself, took another sip of water, and looked around him miserably.

"Who wasn't supposed to what?" Malone asked. "Was there somebody else?"

Otto Bergholtz looked down at the floor. "I'm not saying any more," he said. "I want a lawyer."

Malone stepped forward. "At your service," he said, handing Mr. Bergboltz his card. "John J. Malone, attorney at law." He turned to von Flanagan. "Would you mind leaving me alone with my client for a few minutes?"

Von Flanagan's reply to this request was an elaborate and profane no, with apologies to Miss Dolly Dove. "Not till *I'm* through with him," the chief of homicide continued more moderately. He turned back to the poultry dealer. "You were saying, Mr. Bergholtz — they weren't supposed to — what? Murder the victim? What *were* they supposed to do? And who were *they*? Your accomplices?"

Otto Bergholtz looked at Malone questioningly.

"It's all right," Malone said. "If you're innocent you have nothing to fear, Mr. Bergholtz. Tell us what happened."

The poultry man looked at Malone, nodded, and turned to von Flanagan.

"I don't know what happened," he said. "All I know — these men, they come to me in my store. Two men. We want to buy some jewelry, they say. They show me the advertisement in the paper. They are diamond merchants, they tell me, but they don't want to buy direct. They want I should be their agent. Something about income tax. I don't know. Anyway, you can buy cheaper, they tell me. You're a private party. Tell the lady you want the jewels for your wife, for a wedding anniversary present. Tell her you have to show them to your wife first. We will be in your house when you come home and you can say we are friends. You want us to look at the jewels for you, give you advice. If everything is okay we give you the money to pay, and we give you also ten percent for being agent."

"And when you got home tonight," Malone prompted him, "they were waiting for you to look at the jewels?"

Otto Bergholtz shook his head. "No, nobody was waiting for me. I don't understand."

Von Flanagan gave out with an incredulous grunt and a scowl that he divided equally between the suspect and his lawyer. "So you come here and tell a cock and bull story," he said, "about getting out of the car to go for gas and the car driving away — "

"My client hasn't finished his story," Malone said icily. "And now, Mr. Bergholtz. Since you are only an innocent victim in this case, you won't mind telling us, will you — who were these two men? What were their names?"

"Names?" the poultry dealer turned a perplexed look on Malone, then on von Flanagan. "They didn't tell me their names," he said. "It was all very — uh — confidential, you understand."

"Yes, I understand," von Flanagan said. He turned to Malone. "Your client is innocent," he said with a smile that looked like the calm before a storm. "Your client is the injured party, Malone. Take him home to mama and let me know where to send my apologies." His voice took on the sound of low thunder. "Two men drop down from Mars, in a flying saucer. They set up this guy for a heist, murder the victim, leave the loot at the scene of the crime, and skedaddle back to their flying saucer. Is that the story you want me to tell the reporters?"

Malone said, "You forget the gas station attendant. And the cab driver. How do you know his story isn't going to stand up?" He turned to the poultry dealer again. "These men you mentioned — since you don't know their names, could you describe them for us?"

Mr. Bergholtz nodded. "One was tall, and he had a grey suit on — "

"And the other one was short and he had a brown suit on," von Flanagan said.

Mr. Bergholtz beamed. "That is right," he said. "You know them, maybe?"

"Yes, I know them maybe," von Flanagan shot back. "They're old friends of mine. We used to shoot pool together." He barked into the intercom and Gadenski came in. "Put this joker in the lock-up until we can check his story," he told the officer. "And as for you, Malone, I'd lock you up *with* him if the law allowed. Why does everything have to get complicated for me the minute *you* turn up on a case?"

"Why should you worry?" were Malone's parting words. "You've got the case on ice."

Out on the street again Malone looked at his watch. "We can just make the finale of the last show," he said to Dolly Dove. "A couple of drinks is what we need, and then, well, the night is still young."

"I've got an early morning modeling date," Dolly Dove said, "but maybe just one, and then I've got to get my beauty rest."

"Then let's not lose any more time," Malone said as they got into the green convertible.

"Am I still deputized?" Dolly Dove asked as they sped away.

"As far as I'm concerned you're chief of police," Malone replied, "so don't spare the horses."

X

The head waiter at the Chez greeted them as they walked in. "Mr. Malone," he said, "you're wanted on the telephone. The party said he'd hold the phone till you got here."

"Sit down and order a double rye for me," Malone told Dolly Dove. "I'll be right with you."

He went to the booth and picked up the receiver. It was von Flanagan.

"Malone," said the chief of homicide in a sepulchral voice, "I've got news for you. That jewelry the Castleberry woman was going to sell for twenty–five grand. The lab has just reported on it. It's fake, nothing but glass. The settings are genuine, but the stones are phoney. And another thing, the gun. We've traced it. It belongs to Violet Castleberry."

Malone tried to conceal his surprise. "So what do you want me to do about it?"

"Look here, Malone," the voice on the phone exploded. "You got me into this. You and your half–witted poultry dealer. How do you suppose I'll look to the reporters if I tell them — "

"Tell them nothing," Malone said. "Do nothing till you hear from me. I've got a hunch, and I think I can wind this thing up for you before morning." He hung up.

Back at the table he drank his double rye and ordered another. The last show was over and the waiters were beginning to look their way impatiently. "Let's go," Malone said to Dolly Dove. "It's been a lovely evening."

When they were seated in the green convertible again he broke the news to Dolly. "We're not going home," he said. "Not just yet."

She started to protest but Malone ignored her. "If you were a jewelry faker and you wanted to hide the *real* jewels, where would you hide them?" Malone asked her.

"Who's a jewelry faker?" Dolly said, showing sudden interest. "Mr. Bergholtz? Violet? Olive? Or Alvin Orvell?"

"I don't know yet," Malone said, "but I'm going to find out. If you turn off here and head up the drive we should be able to get to the Castleberry apartment in about five minutes flat."

He identified himself to the policeman on guard at the door, and rang the bell. Olive Castleberry answered the door. She was in negligee but it was plain that she hadn't slept. In a few words he told her the latest developments in the case. "I know you'll want to help," be said. "Did Violet ever say anything to you about having the gems copied, and reset?"

Olive said, "No, but she didn't tell me everything she did. Not about business matters."

"Then you won't mind if we have a look around," Malone said hopefully.

"Not at all," Olive said. "I'll help you. You think the real jewels might be somewhere in the house?"

"I don't know where else they'd be," Malone said. He paused. "Do you suppose she might have asked Alvin to have the gems copied for her?"

Olive gave a start. "I — don't know why she should. He would have said something about it if he knew. He — he's like one of the family — like a brother to me. It's been such a shock to him."

"I know," Malone said soothingly. "I know. Well let's have a look around. Miss Dove here will give us a hand."

In no time at all they had the place turned inside out — drawers, closets, desks, and no sign of the missing jewels.

"While you girls keep looking I'll go to the kitchen and fix us some drinks, Malone said. "I'm sure we could all do with a bit of liquid refreshment."

He found the makings and as he filled the glasses and dropped in the ice cubes he turned the case over in his mind. Presently he returned to the living room and set the loaded tray down on the cocktail table. A discerning glance would have revealed that his hand shook a little as he did so, but if he had come to any startling conclusions about the case his face did not betray them.

Dolly Dove glanced at the array on the tray. "You don't expect us to drink all that," she said. "You must be expecting company."

"I am," Malone said. He went to the telephone and got von Flanagan on the wire. "Get over here right away," he told the chief of homicide, "and bring Bergholtz with you. And Alvin Orvell. The men from Mars have landed."

And he hung up.

XI

When everybody was assembled in the living room the little lawyer lighted a fresh cigar and turned his attention first to Olive Castleberry. "You knew, did you not, Miss Castleberry, that you are in a direct line to inherit your step–mother's fortune?" Olive nodded. "And you knew that if Violet married Alvin Orvell — "

"You leave Olive out of this," Alvin Orvell spoke up. His brief hospitalization seemed to have revived him remarkably and, despite the late hour, he was alert and easily the most wide–awake person in the room. "Olive had nothing to do with it," he said flatly. "You're not accusing her of — " He paused.

"Of what?" Malone asked. "Of the murder? Certainty not. We all know Miss Castleberry was not present at the scene of the crime. But the science of criminology knows of such things as intermediaries, accomplices, agents, innocent and criminal — "

"Never mind the lecture," von Flanagan broke in. "You didn't get us all up here at this god–awful hour to hear a lecture on criminology. Are you hinting that Olive Castleberry hired those men from Mars to come down in a flying saucer and murder her step–mother?"

Alvin Orvell put his hand to his forehead and for a minute it looked as if he was going to do a collapsing act again. "Flying saucers? Men from Mars?" he muttered. "Is everybody going crazy?"

"I'm not hinting anything," Malone said smoothly. "I'm only trying to establish the facts. If Olive stood to inherit, she had a motive. If she had no taste for becoming the stepdaughter, or the ward, of Alvin Orvell, she had a double motive."

Olive Castleberry spoke up angrily. "I don't know what you're driving at, Mr. Malone, but I have nothing to hide." Her eyes flashed. They were more green now than grey or brown. "If it's me and Alvin you're hinting at, Mr. Malone, I'll confess that I'm fond of Alvin. After all, he's like a member of the family."

"Olive!" It was Alvin Orvell, and his face was flushed. "Don't say another word, Olive. It's nobody's business how we feel about each other. It hasn't got anything to do with this case, anyway." He turned to Malone. "What is it you're driving at, Malone? We've told you everything."

"Not quite," Malone said. "For instance, about the jewels. Did Mrs. Castleberry have them copied and reset, or did you take it upon yourself to do it?"

The flush vanished from Alvin's face and gave place to an ashen white. It was a full minute before he was able to answer, in a low voice. "She asked me to have it done for her. Said she was afraid to show them to prospective buyers for fear of theft. She'd heard that jewel thieves answer newspaper ads and then come back and burglarize the house. She didn't mean to offer fake jewels. The buyer would get the real ones when the sale was made. Is there anything wrong in that?"

"That figures," von Flanagan spoke up. "If Bergholtz's accomplices got a look at those phony jewels — " He looked hard at Alvin Orvell. "You said you got out of the car and went to find some gas, is that right?"

Bergholtz shot up out of his chair. "It's a lie!" he shouted. "Me — he sent *me* for the gas. First they try to sell me fake jewelry, and now they say *he* went for the gas." It was all the officers could do to keep him from pouncing on the pale and frightened Alvin Orvell.

"I don't know who's trying to frame who or who's protecting who," von Flanagan said, "but if Bergholtz's story isn't a flying saucers yarn, it looks like a plain case of the old jewel-hijacking racket. They get this poultry dealer to lure the victim out of the house with the jewels, they follow them in the car and then pull a stick–up. The way I see it, if Mr. Orvell here wasn't in on the stick–up why did he have to lie about getting out of the car to go for the gas? As far as I'm concerned, I'm holding them *both* for the crime. When we find their accomplices we'll have an air–tight case against the whole mob."

"Not so fast, Chief," Malone said. "You forget there was a murder committed."

"Before we go any further," Malone said. "Let's all have a drink before all the ice melts in those glasses. Here, let me play host, since I mixed the drinks."

He picked up the tray and passed it around. When he came to Alvin Orvell he handed him a glass himself, saying, "I mixed this one especially for you. Those scratches on your face, Mr. Orvell. You say you got them coming up through the bushes. Von Flanagan, you went through those bushes. Did you get any scratches on your face?"

"Not I" von Flanagan said.

"Neither did I," Malone said. "Are you sure, Mr. Orvell, that you didn't get those scratches from a lady's fingernails? Mrs. Castleberry's for instance?"

Alvin Orvell was silent, staring down into his glass, his eyes fixed and glassy, like a marmoset hypnotized by a snake. Suddenly he flung the glass from him. The all but melted ice cubes scattered on the floor. As he made wildly for the door von Flanagan's cops grabbed him.

Malone picked up the scattered ice cubes and laid them on the cocktail table. There in plain view, bedded in the remaining pieces of ice, lay the missing diamonds.

"There is your missing evidence," Malone said to von Flanagan. "Hot ice."

"Then you didn't gang up with those jewel thieves?" von Flanagan asked Orvell.

"I don't know anything about any jewel thieves," Orvell said. "I fixed the tank so we'd run out of gas. I sent Bergholtz for the gas, figuring I could frame him for the murder. It was only his word against mine. I was going to strangle Violet. I didn't know she had a gun in the glove compartment. She jumped out of the car. I struggled with her. Then — I lost my head, I guess. I forgot about the jewels — the fake jewels. I didn't want to take a chance with the real ones in the car with Bergholtz, that's why I had copies made. I guess I bungled everything. All my life… everything I ever tried to do… "

He let out a low moan and folded up in the arms of the policeman.

"Well, there's your case, chief," Malone said.

"Here I am," Dotty Dove said. She looked groggy, but whether sleepy or drunk Malone couldn't tell.

"Let's go," he said. "If we drive fast we can just make it in time to see sunrise on Starved Rock. I've always wanted to see sunrise on Starved Rock. We'll just pull up by the side of the road and admire the view… moonlight… springtime… "

"And a scream from the bushes," Dolly Dove said. "And a dead body beside a car in the road. Okay, here we go again."

Using one of her most ingenious murder methods, Craig wove a story around an office plant as Malone tries to escape the dreary Chicago climes for Havana. In having Malone try to guess the first name of his blonde client, Craig plays a familiar trick by including inside jokes in the story. She lists her own given first name as one of the guesses. -JM

Say It With Flowers

"You wouldn't refuse to help poor little me?" the beautiful blonde said. She leaned over the desk and fluttered her eyelashes at John J. Malone.

Malone sighed and looked away. He gazed, apparently fascinated, at the row of filing cabinets that lined one wall of his office. Turning his head slightly, he stared with the same fixity of expression at the tiny shelf which Maggie had put up against the adjoining wall. It held a small potted plant which was beginning to overflow its pot and creep down the dingy wall, a miniature brass teapot and a particularly repulsive porcelain rabbit. "Cheer up the place," Malone muttered to his cigar. "Add a little atmosphere." He sighed again, bitterly this time.

"What?" said the beautiful blonde.

Malone waved negligently at the shelf. "What do you think of it?" he asked. "Do you think it adds a cheery atmosphere?"

The blonde stared for a second. "I think it's horrible," she said decisively. "But, listen, Malone, I didn't come here to talk about decorations. I want you to — "

"I know," Malone said. "You told me. Your uncle Jasper McIlhenny — "

"Jabez," the blonde murmured."

"It doesn't matter," Malone said grandly. "Your uncle has disappeared, and you want me to find him."

"Yes, Malone," the girl said. "And you will do it, won't you? For me, Malone?" She batted her eyelashes again. Malone turned resolutely away and tried to think of something else.

"I don't need money," he said at last, expansively. "I'm on my way to Havana. Havana, Cuba," he added, in case there had been a misunderstanding. "And, besides, what can I do that the police force of Chicago can't do better?" He hoped that Miss McIlhenny didn't know the answer to that one.

"It's been two weeks, Malone," she said. "I went to the Missing Persons Bureau and they say they're working on it, but two weeks is a long time. I've heard about you, and I just know you can find Uncle Jabez, if anyone can."

"The fact remains," Malone began, and wondered what else he had been going to say. "The fact remains. And moreover, I am on my way to Havana, Cuba. If I see your uncle there I'll give him a message from you. I can't be fairer than that, can I?"

"Malone," the girl said, "you are heartless. Absolutely heartless." She stepped back to give the rumpled little lawyer the full benefit of her gaze. It was a gaze that spelled murder, Malone thought. It spelled several other things, too. Reluctantly, Malone removed his mind from the brink of temptation.

"Miss McIlhenny," he began, in what he hoped was a fatherly tone, "I'm sure that — if you have a little patience — the police will be able to find your uncle. I really couldn't do a thing except send you bills. Exorbitant bills."

"Money doesn't matter," the girl said. "We have plenty of money." She dug into a black leather handbag and produced a sheaf of bills. She removed three of them and placed them carefully on Malone's brown desk. "Will that do for a retainer?"

Malone stared at the three one–hundred–dollar bills. "It would be fine," he said sadly. "But I have tickets. My boat leaves Friday. This is Thursday morning — early Thursday morning," he amended. "I just can't do a thing. I'm very sorry."

"Ha," the girl said. She picked up the money with one sweeping motion, and went to the door. She opened it, turned and said: "Heartless. Absolutely heartless." She banged the door behind her and went out.

Malone sat behind his desk. Missing Persons would turn up Uncle Jabez, he told himself. So, it was obvious that there was no use in thinking about the blonde Miss McIlhenny any more. He might as well pretend she had never existed. Instead, he could think about the poker game, the wonderful poker game to which Judge Touralchuck had invited him the night before. The game had given him enough money to buy tickets for a Havana cruise, and assure himself of a couple of weeks of fairly riotous living — and no girl was going to take all that away from him, even if she was beautiful, and seemed so lost, and murmured at him.

Perhaps thinking about the poker game wasn't such a good idea. He would stare at the shelf. The porcelain rabbit stared back unwinkingly. That was one good thing about the shelf, Malone thought vaguely; it gave a person something to think about when times were rough. Just because a beautiful blonde came to your office early Thursday morning and begged you to help her, that didn't mean...

Malone sighed.

I am going to forget all about her, he told himself firmly. "She wasn't even here," he said, and listened to his voice echoing in the room. It had a very satisfactory sound, a firm, no–nonsense tone to it that appealed to him.

"She wasn't even here," he said again. "Ladies and gentlemen of the jury, I defy you to prove that my client ever knew this woman. I defy you to prove that she ever came to his office."

The office door opened and Malone looked up guiltily. But the girl standing on his threshold was raven–haired and petite. "Now, Malone," she said. "What are you practicing for? You should take it easy. You're going to Havana for a nice rest."

"That's exactly where I'm going, Maggie," John J. Malone said in his firmest voice. "And not even all the blondes in Chicago — not even all the blondes in the United States" — he added recklessly — "are going to stop me."

II

"So you're leaving for Havana," Joe the Angel said, a little while later. He put a double rye in front of the little lawyer.

Malone looked around the musty precincts of Joe the Angel's City Hall Bar. Only the City Hall janitor inhabited the room, and he sat silently at the other end of the bar, nursing his beer. Malone picked up his glass and looked at it reflectively.

"Havana, Cuba," he said. "And when I'm nice and warm there, just lying on the beach with nothing to do, I'll think of you, Joe. By the way," he added anxiously, "do I owe you anything?"

"Just a couple of bucks on the bill, Malone," Joe the Angel said. "It'll keep until you get back."

"I'll pay you now," Malone said. He dug into his pocket and fished out a collection of crumpled bills. Carefully unwrapping two of them, he laid them on the bar. "Now we're all square," he said. He looked around the empty room. "This deserves a celebration."

Joe the Angel hesitated only a second. "Have one the house, Malone," he said grandly. Malone downed his first drink and Joe poured again. "We're going to miss you around here," he said.

"I'm not going to miss Chicago," Malone announced. "People always coming to you with problems they won't let you not solve or... " He considered for a minute and drank deeply. "Anyhow, I won't miss it. It's all water under a burning bridge. Or walking on water before you come to it."

"Sure, Malone," Joe the Angel said sadly.

"Listen," Malone went on, "when I get to Havana, the first thing I'm going to do... "

The telephone rang. In a dark corner of the bar the parrot screamed: "Ring! Ring!"

"Excuse me, Malone," Joe the Angel said. He went to the telephone, turned and scowled fiercely at the bar parrot. It shut its beak and looked at Malone disapprovingly. Malone stared back belligerently.

"Okay," Joe the Angel was saying. "Yes, sure he's here. You just wait a minute, he'll talk to you." He cupped the receiver against his chest and shouted: "Malone!"

"I'm not here," Malone said without taking his eyes off the parrot. "I went home hours ago."

"It's Captain von Flanagan," Joe the Angel said. "He sounds pretty mad."

Malone almost said: "I don't care how mad he sounds." He reconsidered just in time. After all, von Flanagan was an old friend.

"Hello?" he said tentatively.

A torrent of profane abuse scorched his ear. Malone held the receiver a little away from him and heard von Flanagan's voice screaming: " ...Just because you're too busy to help, I've got to talk to the Commissioner! He wants to see me now, and what am I going to tell him, Malone? This is what I get for helping you all these years... "

"Wait a minute," Malone said. "Wait a minute. Suppose you tell me what you're talking about?"

"Don't pretend you don't know," von Flanagan said. "Don't play innocent with me this time. I've got you dead to rights and you're going to wish you'd never been born. The next parking ticket you come to me with... "

"Von Flanagan." Malone's reasonable tone seemed to enrage the police officer even further, but after another shriek or two he subsided, muttering. "Now," Malone said, "what are you talking about? What did I do to you?"

"McIlhenny," von Flanagan moaned. "The Commissioner's own niece by marriage."

A horrible light began to dawn on Malone. "You mean that blonde," he said.

"That blonde. She can't find her uncle, and we're working on it. Malone, you know we're working on it." Von Flanagan's voice was breaking.

"Of course you are," Malone said. "That's what I told her."

"But she wants a report every five minutes," von Flanagan said. "I can't do any work with her bothering me every time I turn around. Malone, I swear to you, I suggested your name in all innocence. Not that you could do anything we can't... "

Malone thought of a number of things, and said none of them.

"...but if she'll pay you for being bothered, and then she'll come to you and we can get some work done."

"Why not just tell her you're working?" Malone suggested. "I've seen you brush people off before."

"*Malone,*" von Flanagan sobbed. "*The Commissioner's niece by marriage.*"

"Oh," the lawyer said. "I see."

"And then you refuse to help her. You tell her you're going away, some wild story like that. Malone, I swear to you, the next time there's an unsolved murder in Chicago, I'm going to pin it on you. I'm going to fake evidence if I have to, and bribe witnesses. I don't care. When you refuse to help an old friend… "

Malone thought quickly. On the one hand, he *was* going away, where von Flanagan couldn't reach him. On the other hand, he might want to come back some day, even if he couldn't imagine why. And von Flanagan was an old friend, after all, regardless of how he treated Malone.

And besides, his boat didn't leave until Friday, and it was only Thursday afternoon. That left almost one whole day.

"All right, von Flanagan," Malone said. "But this is the last time… "

The voice on the other end became silk–smooth. "Anything you want, Malone. Just ask me."

"Don't worry," the little lawyer said. "I will."

III

Malone went back to his office, humming *St. James Infirmary* under his breath. He got Maggie busy finding a Miss McIlhenny in the telephone book, relaxed, lit a fresh cigar, and thought about the situation.

There wasn't much to think about, he discovered. He had reached a point of deciding to look for Jabez McIlhenny in Havana, where any man with enough money and a little common sense would prefer to be found, when Maggie announced that a Miss McIlhenny was on the line.

Malone picked up the receiver and said in his most official tone: "This is Malone."

"I hoped you'd call," said the sultry voice he remembered. "You will look for Uncle Jabez, won't you? And I'm sure you'll do ever so much better than those old police… "

"I'll take your case," Malone said sternly. "The retainer will be… ah… " He paused for thought.

"If three hundred isn't enough," the voice said, "we'll make it five. You darling man, you!"

A little had been attractive, Malone decided, listening to the cooing of his new client, but too much was definitely enough. He wondered briefly exactly what he meant by that, decided to forget it, and said instead:

"Five hundred will be fine. But I'll have to talk to you… "

"Clues," said the voice. "I'll be down right away."

There was a dull click. Malone held the receiver in his hand, shrugged, and went back to puffing at his cigar.

He put in fifteen minutes staring at the china rabbit on his new shelf before Maggie entered. "A Miss McIlhenny to see you, Mr. Malone," she said.

"Can't you see I'm busy with these papers?" Malone growled. He grabbed a few papers from his desk and rustled them, convincingly, he hoped. "Oh, all right," he said, "send her in."

The beautiful blonde swayed in and sat, without invitation, on the chair next to Malone's desk.

"I had to make a check," she said. "I hope you don't mind." She put a folded up piece of paper on the desktop. Malone did not pick it up.

"I'll have to ask you a lot of questions," he said.

"All right," she said.

"You may not like some of them."

"If they'll help you find Uncle Jabez... " She blinked back a sob. "I don't mind." She looked like a brave little girl. Malone refrained from patting her hand, and wondered just how much of her was play-acting. All of her, he decided savagely.

"Did your uncle have any enemies, that you know of?" he said after a second.

Miss McIlhenny thought. "Everybody liked Uncle Jabez. He was such a sweet old man."

"Was?" Malone said.

"I mean... well, he still is, I suppose."

"He might be dead," Malone pointed out, and watched the blonde's face for a reaction.

Her expression didn't change. She took a handkerchief from her black handbag and held it near her eyes without using it. Then she put it down on the desk. "If he's dead, I'd like to know about it," she said. "The police can't find out anything... "

"I know," Malone said. "You told me. They're doing the best they can."

He thought for a minute and went on:

"When did you see him last?"

"He was just leaving the house, early Tuesday morning. Two weeks and two days ago. He lives in the big McIlhenny — well, I suppose you'd call it a mansion — near the Drive. I live with him."

"Anyone else in the house?" Malone asked. He remember the place: a turreted pile of stone with Gothic windows and a general air of crumbling decay. It sat alone near the Lakefront, brooding out on the water. The place had always given Malone cold shivers. He didn't like the idea of going there.

"Only the servants," the blonde said. "And when he left the house I asked... "

"Servants," Malone said. "Who are they?"

"Oh, a man named Paul Finn," the blonde said. Servants, Malone imagined, were beneath her dignity. One never mentioned servants. "He's Uncle's secretary. And my maid Rose. Rose Billington."

"Were they both in the house?"

"When Uncle left? Oh, no. Tuesday is their day off. I suppose they were out somewhere — smooching."

Malone tried to remember the last time he'd heard that word, and failed. He marked the fact down in his mind. The male secretary and the maid were having a romance. It sounded important. The lawyer didn't know why, and he told himself he might just as well be wrong.

"What did you say?" he asked, discovering that the blonde had gone right on with her paragraph.

She looked a little startled. "I said that I was all alone. I asked Uncle where he was going, and he said he had to see someone on business."

"What kind of business?"

"I don't know," she said. "I just didn't think about it at the time — you know the way a sentence just doesn't register on your mind — but when the police asked me I realized how strange it was. Uncle inherited a great deal of money, and it's been invested in very safe bonds. There's really — no business at all he'd have to attend to."

"He didn't say anything else?" Malone asked.

"He walked down to the corner and I went back in the house."

"Walked?"

"Uncle liked to walk," the blonde said. "He said it was good exercise for him."

"Where did he usually go when he went for a walk?" Malone asked.

The blonde thought. "Sometimes he went down to Eve's," she said. "And then there was Martine. Oh, yes, Martine."

The little lawyer began to feel confused. The conversation seemed to be traveling in a fog. "Eve and Martine," he said. "Girls he knew?"

"Well," the blonde said, "Martine was, anyhow. A girl. A — chorine? But he certainly wouldn't go to see her on *business*. Oh, goodness, no."

"I see," Malone said.

"Eve — that's Eve Washington — you've heard of her."

Malone considered. "No," he said at last.

The blonde shook her head. "Chicago's best known ceramicist," she said, "and you say you've never heard... "

"Miss McIlhenny," Malone said softly. "I'm a lawyer and I spend a lot of time in court. Sometimes I don't read the science page in the newspaper. You're going to have to tell me what a ceramicist is."

"Really," the blonde said. "Now you're just fooling little old me."

"No," Malone said.

"Oh." The blonde appeared to consider carefully, and Malone hoped for some reason that she wouldn't take the folded check from the desk, put it in her bag and leave. He would feel insulted. It wasn't a criminal offense not to know what a ceramicist was, he thought. He couldn't help it if he didn't know everything.

"Clay," the girl said. "She makes clay objects."

"Like mud pies," Malone said thoughtfully.

"More or — less," said the girl slowly. "She's very well–known and very expensive." She turned her head and seemed, for the first time, to catch sight of the brooding porcelain rabbit. "She might have made that," she said. "Though she wouldn't, of course?"

"Doesn't like rabbits?" Malone suggested.

"It's too cheap, mass–produced. Not at all her type of thing."

"But," said Malone delicately, "Jabez McIlhenny was her type of thing?"

"Not the way you're thinking," the girl said. "Uncle Jabez likes clay sculpture. He bought pieces from Eve every so often. They were — just good friends."

"Maybe that's what he meant by business," Malone said. "You go home. I'll call you later."

"What are you going to *do?*" the blonde said.

"I'm going to start earning that money," Malone said. He reached for the check and unfolded it.

"All right," the blonde said. She was out the door by the time Malone had read the first line on the check that read: "Five Hundred and 00/100 Dollars," and long before he drew his gaze down to the bottom line, where her name was signed:

"G. G. G. McIlhenny."

Malone realized he didn't know his client's first name. He didn't know any of her first names. The bank must, though, he told himself cheerfully as he pocketed the check, stood up, and left his office.

IV

The sign outside the door read, in a curlicued script: *Eve Washington: Ceramics.* There was a tiny buzzer underneath.

Malone pressed it. He wondered briefly what a mud-pie maker was doing on the tenth floor of Chicago's most exclusive set of apartments, but decided that there must be more to the business than met the eye. He was congratulating himself on his fairness when there was a click and the door swung open.

Malone stepped into a room which reminded him of some of the worst scenes from *Bertha, The Sewing Machine Girl*, the scenes that showed Bertha's life in her poverty–ridden home. Old grey jugs and shapes were everywhere, along with a fantastic litter composed of straw, sawdust, wood shavings and ancient yellow newspapers. Over everything hung a cloud of dust.

From a long way off Malone heard a whirring sound which reminded him of a sawmill. He called tentatively: "Hello?"

"Just a minute," a voice called back. Malone stared around him at the mess, and waited. When the minute was up, and had taken two or three more with it, a very dusty woman in an old smock appeared at the inner entrance of the room. "Yes?" she said.

"I've come to see Miss Washington," Malone said. "My name is John J.

Malone."

"You'd like to buy something?" the dusty woman said. She was only a little shorter than the little lawyer; her face was heart–shaped and her hair, as much of it as wasn't covered by dust, was a very dark brown. She might have been, Malone thought, twenty–eight.

"I'd like to see Miss Washington," he said. "I've got a few questions for her."

"I'm Eve Washington," the woman said. "But I'm quite busy now, I'm afraid. I really don't have time for interviews… "

"It's about Jabez McIlhenny," Malone said.

The woman stepped back. "You're with the police?"

Malone shook his head. "Just a friend," he said. "I understand he's dis–appeared, and I'd like to ask a few questions."

"I told the police everything," Eve Washington said. "Why don't you ask them?"

"This will only take a minute," Malone said. "Besides, I might be a customer. You never know."

"So you might." Surprisingly, Eve Washington laughed. The sound, like her voice, came from low in her throat. "Come in to my studio. McIlhenny was the only man I allowed back there, but you're a friend of his. Besides, you look as crazy as I am." She turned and went through the entrance again. Malone followed her.

They went through a long hall, and came out into a large airy room which seemed even more cluttered than the entrance room. Malone noticed four ashtrays, all made of baked clay, piled on a littered couch which, he estimated, had originally cost something over a thousand dollars. One of the ashtrays had three lipsticked cigarettes and a dusty cigar butt in it. The others were empty, but filmed with powdery dust. Malone felt as if he needed a bath.

In one corner a square box sat and whirred to itself quietly. "Kiln," Eve Washington said, noticing Malone's stare. "It bakes clay. Up to three thousand degrees in that furnace, so I wouldn't get too close if I were you."

Malone backed even farther away from the box. "Jabez McIlhenny disappeared just over two weeks ago," he said. "On a Tuesday." Somehow, that approach didn't sound right. "He was coming to see you when he left home, and his niece hasn't seen him since," he said after a pause.

The dusty woman waited, and finally said: "Yes?"

"When did he leave here?" Malone asked.

"He never arrived here," she said. "You say he was coming to see me?"

"That's right."

"He always called me in advance," Eve Washington said. "Every few weeks he would call, and I'd have a new piece ready for him to look at. He had fine taste, Mr. Malone. He always knew just what he wanted — and let me tell you, after some of the batty old ladies who come up and want little presents for their nephews... "

"I'm sure," Malone said sympathetically. "But this Tuesday — the day he disappeared — he didn't call?"

"No," she said. "I was expecting him to call me — it was about time, you know — and I had this all ready for him." She produced an object from the litter. Malone stared at a light–green vase about a foot and a half tall. "I've still got it, in case he does show up, you know. He'd want to have this." She patted the vase fondly. "And a real bargain, too," she said. "Only three hundred dollars."

Malone nodded absently. "Miss Washington," he said. "Do you know of any enemies Mr. McIlhenny had?"

"Had?" she said. "You mean he's dead?"

Malone thought it over. There seemed no harm in admitting the truth. "He's been missing for two weeks," he said, "and his niece hasn't gotten any ransom notes, or any word from him. He's probably dead. I'm looking for the person who killed him."

"Maybe he just got tired and went away," the woman said. Under the smock, Malone noticed, she was really very pretty. Maybe the vase was worth three hundred dollars. After all, Malone thought, he was no judge of vases. Three hundred dollars might even be a bargain. Maybe he could take Eve Washington out to dinner, and they could talk it over.

He reminded himself sternly that he was investigating what was almost certainly a murder, and that he had to leave Chicago the next day anyhow.

"People don't get tired and go away," he said. "Not without leaving some kind of note."

"Maybe the note hasn't been found yet," Eve Washington said.

Malone looked around the room. If the McIlhenny home looked anything like the Eve Washington Ceramics Studio, the note might not be found for months. But he doubted it.

"Did he have any enemies?" Malone asked again.

"Not that I know of," Eve Washington said. "He was such a sweet old man."

"I know," Malone said.

"He discovered me, you know. I was just another ceramicist, struggling to get along — you know how it is."

Malone tried to imagine a struggling ceramicist, but the image wouldn't come. He couldn't even pronounce the phrase, let alone go any farther.

"Well," she was saying, "I showed some of my work at a small gallery, and Mr. McIlhenny dropped in one afternoon — and that was that. He bought several pieces, and word got around, you know. I feel quite grateful to him. I'd be terribly broken up if anything happened to him."

"You haven't — heard from him since the Tuesday he disappeared?" Malone said.

"Of course not," she said. "I still have the vase, don't I?" She seemed to realize that she was still holding it, and suddenly smiled dazzingly at Malone. "Here," she said. "You take it. I can't hold a piece forever, you know. People might see it and want it. But if you see Mr. McIlhenny, you can give it to him."

Malone refrained from pointing out, again, that her client was probably beyond any interest in green vases. He didn't, he told himself, want to see Eve Washington all broken up, even though it would be nice to hold her head on his shoulder and dry her tears. He had, he thought sternly, too much to do, and almost no time to do it in.

He took the vase. "If I see him," he said.

"He'll pay me, of course," Eve Washington said. "You don't even have to mention money to him. He'll call me right up and send me a check."

The vase weighed a little over two pounds. Malone decided he'd better put it in his office safe before going on to his next suspect. Martine would just have to wait, he thought.

Somehow, he managed to get to the street with the green vase clutched firmly in his arms. He hailed a cab with difficulty, gave the driver directions to his office, and sat back in the leather seat. The vase was propped next to him.

Maybe I can put it on the shelf, Malone thought. Next to the rabbit. It might go nicely.

V

Back in his office, Malone admired the vase some more. It really was nice, he thought. It gave dignity to his office, right up there on the shelf. He could put it in the safe, but it was too pretty to be in a safe. And the cleaning woman wouldn't knock it over. He'd warn her about it.

On second thought, if he mentioned it she'd be self–conscious about it and knock it over trying to be extra–careful. He'd just have to let nature take its course.

Now, he told himself, for Martine.

It was at that point that he discovered he didn't know Martine's last name. He called a friendly night–club owner hurriedly.

"Girls named Martine?" the club–owner said. "Malone, they're all named Martine, or Sybil, or Fritzi. You find me a nice chorus girl named Bella, Malone, it'll be a big relief to me. Always Sybil or Martine or Fritzi. I mean it, Malone."

"You don't know a particular Martine who was friendly with Jabez McIlhenny?"

"None of them are particular, Malone. They're slobs. A bunch of slobs. I tell you, for one chorus–girl named Bella — she doesn't even have to dance, I'll just keep her around the club to tell people about. Look, Malone... "

With difficulty, Malone sidestepped an invitation to a "friendly little party" after hours. He promised the owner: "I'll do the same for you some time," and hung up.

He could, of course, ask von Flanagan. But somehow, he told himself, he didn't want to go to the police. They'd given him the case and he was going to solve it for them and show them. Vaguely, he wondered just what he was going to show them, but didn't get very far with the idea.

He remembered the servants. Paul Finn and Rose Billington. If he went to the McIlhenny home now, the servants would be there and he could talk to them, and find out Martine's last name from Miss McIlhenny at the same time. Maybe Miss McIlhenny's first name was Georgette. Georgette Georgina — er — Georgie McIlhenny. It had a nice ring to it, Malone thought.

The servants were having a romance, he remembered suddenly. That had sounded important, but it probably wasn't. He had the impression that he'd heard something that hadn't sounded important, but really had been. He tried to think of it, without success. Maybe, he told himself, it had been something he'd seen, and not something he'd heard at all.

When he found himself muttering: "Servants should be seen and not heard," he gave up. On the way out of the office he told Maggie: "Put some flowers in the vase. And don't wait up for me. Just leave a light burning in the window."

"You take care of yourself, Malone," Maggie told him.

He thought of the crumbling McIlhenny mansion, and shivered. Then he told himself not to be silly.

And he wondered what was silly about being afraid of a house which almost certainly had ghosts — and one ghost, in particular, who'd just joined the crowd in the last two weeks or so.

The cabbie looked up at the stone steps winding up to the mansion. "Some rich place," he said.

"Some people think it's pretty," Malone said defensively.

"Me," said the cabbie, "I think it's haunted."

Malone paid him with trembling hands. "Everybody to his own opinion," he said. He started up the steps, feeling as if ominous organ music followed him at every turn. Far, far below him, he heard the cab clash its gears and speed away, and he felt very lonely.

He climbed grimly to the top of the steps and faced the old oaken door. There was a silver knocker projecting from its center. Malone reached out, pulled his hand back, told himself not to be silly, and knocked once, timidly.

After a minute he tried again, a little louder.

The door opened with a creak, and Malone paled. A cadaverous face looked out at him. The face had eyes that burned right through Malone, and bushy black eyebrows. The eyebrows raised, slowly.

"Yes?" the face said.

Malone said: "I'm here to see Miss McIlhenny." He congratulated himself on remaining so calm.

"Whom shall I say is calling?" said the face in sepulchral tones.

"Me," Malone said. "I."

"Your name?" said the face.

Malone gave it, hurriedly. The door banged shut again.

Many years passed before it opened again. Malone was sure that his hair was white, if he had any hair left at all. He passed an experimental hand over his scalp and felt, but he couldn't tell the color. He chewed on his cigar, nervously.

Finally the door swung slowly open, and a familiar face peered out. "Oh, Malone," the blonde said. "Come in. Paul didn't know — I didn't mention your name to him when I went out... " Malone entered.

"That was Paul Finn," Malone said in the hall. "The — man who opened the door." He was beginning to feel better. The blonde had offered to mix him a drink, and he lit a fresh cigar. He really hadn't been afraid at all, he told himself. All that was just silliness.

"Of course," she said. "A friend of yours is here."

"Really?" Malone said.

"A policeman. I told him there was no need for him to do anything at all, now that you've agreed to take over, but he insisted on being here when you arrived. He said he wanted to ask you some questions."

Malone felt a cold knot in his stomach. "Von Flanagan," he said.

"He said that was his name, Malone. He's waiting in the living room. Come on, and you'll have that drink, and we can talk." She paused. "Have you found out anything yet?"

"I've found out your uncle had an enemy," Malone said savagely. He thought of von Flanagan, and Eve Washington, and his ship tickets, and wondered why he had ever let himself get involved in the case.

"Who was his enemy, Malone?" the blonde said anxiously.

"Me," the lawyer snapped, and marched past her into the living room.

VI

The blonde (Georgina? Malone thought. Gertrude? Gwendolyn?) went off to see about the drinks, and Malone and the police captain were left alone.

"It's murder, you know, Malone," von Flanagan said.

"I thought it was," Malone said. "Two weeks is a long time."

"He didn't have any motive to disappear. Everything was going fine for him, just the usual way. Only he didn't have any enemies."

"That's what I found out," Malone said.

"Every rich man has enemies," von Flanagan said sagely. "Even I have enemies, and what have I got?"

"Enemies," Malone suggested.

"I mean money. If I have enemies, Jabez McIlhenny had enemies. Somebody killed him, after all."

"Maybe it was an accident," Malone said. "Maybe he walked into the path of a car."

"We've checked every hospital and morgue record for the last two weeks," von Flanagan said sourly. "Somebody managed to dispose of his body perfectly. That was no accident."

"Maybe he jumped in the river."

"In this weather?" von Flanagan said. "It's cold out. He'd have to be crazy — and he wasn't any crazier than usual."

"How do you know?"

"Questioning the niece," von Flanagan said. "Unless she knocked off the old man... she could lie about it, I suppose, just to make things tough for me."

Miss McIlhenny returned with the drinks, and there were several minutes of meaningless conversation before von Flanagan said: "Look, Miss, I'd like to talk to Malone privately. Can we... "

"Of course," she said. "You stay right there. I've got work to do in the kitchen, anyhow."

When she was gone, Malone said: "What motive would she have for killing her uncle?"

"That's what I can't figure out," von Flanagan admitted. "The old guy left his money to an animal home. He never had any pets, and he felt guilty about it. He left a couple of thousand apiece to the servants, but nothing at all to his niece except a fund that would bring her about ten grand a year. She was getting more than that when he was alive."

"Maybe he threatened to stop giving her any money," Malone said.

"I talked to the servants myself," von Flanagan said. "They didn't hear anything like that. Everything was peaceful."

Malone said: "She didn't do it. She's my client."

"Now, Malone... "

"I know she didn't. I don't know why I know, but I know. Does that make sense?"

"No," von Flanagan said. "And you couldn't take it into court."

"She mentioned a chorus girl named Martine," Malone said.

"Martine Vignette," von Flanagan said. "That's her name. We talked to her. It seems she and old McIlhenny were just good friends. Sure. She's got kind of a temper, Malone. Maybe she got mad one night and bashed his head in."

"And made him disappear like a ghost," Malone suggested. "You searched her home, and the night club she works at, didn't you?"

"Sure we did," the police captain said bitterly. "People just go out of their way to make things tough for me, Malone. I never wanted to be a cop... "

Malone sat back, closed his eyes and waited until von Flanagan was finished with his complaint. Then he said: "How about somebody else?"

"There isn't anybody else," von Flanagan said. "Some crazy sculptor, this Martine Vignette, and the niece herself."

"Von Flanagan," Malone said. "What's her name?"

"The niece?"

"That's right."

"McIlhenny," von Flanagan said.

"I mean her first name."

A blank look passed over the police captain's face. "You know," he said, "I never asked."

"Neither did I," Malone said.

"I only waited for you, Malone, because I wanted to talk to you before we pulled the niece in. Just in case. Not that I think you have anything... I mean, you can't go up against the Chicago police force... but... "

"Wait a minute, von Flanagan."

"I called your office and that girl of yours said you were on your way down here. Malone, can you think of one reason why we shouldn't take her in?"

"She didn't do it," Malone said. "I saw something — or heard something — "

"What, Malone?"

"I don't know," the little lawyer admitted. He sighed deeply. "I'll find out, though, sooner or later."

"I can't sit on my hands forever," von Flanagan said. "The Commissioner... "

"Give me an hour," Malone said. "Just one hour."

"Malone, it's illegal... "

"One hour, von Flanagan, or I'll... tell your wife about that poker game."

"One hour," the officer said sadly. "Malone, I don't like this any more than you do. The Commissioner's niece by marriage... "

"Don't worry, von Flanagan," Malone said grandly. "I'll get you out of the fix."

The police captain's voice turned a violent purple. "Look here, Malone... "

"One hour," Malone said. "You promised."

Rose Billington's story was a simple one. Malone looked at her long, sad, horselike face and thought what a perfect match she and the cadaverous Paul Finn would make. They looked like two Charles Addams creations, he thought. He cocked a sympathetic ear.

"I told the story already three times, to the police. Now you want me to tell it all over again. I wasn't even here, me and Paul went out. We went to the movies. I told the police already three times what we saw."

"Did you notice anything unusual when you left the house?"

"It was just like always," Rose said. "Old Mr. McIlhenny, he was dressing up to go out, but he didn't say where, so don't ask me."

"I won't," Malone said.

"Miss McIlhenny, she was sleeping, like sometimes she sleeps late. Me and Paul, we went to a movie. You want to know what we saw?"

"No," Malone said, "that won't be necessary." He wished he had another drink. "Mr. McIlhenny's will leaves you each a little money. Enough to get married on."

"Oh, we don't want to get married," Rose said.

"You don't?"

"Paul, he's married already, so we don't want to break the law or anything. He married some woman in New York, and he can't get a divorce of anything because that would make her feel he didn't want her any more and that's bad for you, Paul says. He reads psychology."

"Doesn't she... doesn't she feel he doesn't want her any more now that he's in Chicago?"

"That's different, Paul says. He reads a lot. So we just go out like to the movies. I could tell you all about the movie, what we saw."

Malone felt his head whirling rapidly. "I don't need to know," he said. "As a matter of fact, I don't want to know. It would spoil things."

"It was a pretty good movie," Rose said.

"I'm sure," Malone said.

Paul's story backed up the maid's. "We went to see a film," was the way he put it. Malone refrained from asking about the first Mrs. Finn. There was no sense in complicating things any further.

That left only Martine Vignette. But von Flanagan had searched for McIlhenny's body and found nothing at all. You could trust von Flanagan to conduct a search like that, Malone thought.

All the same, G. G. G. McIlhenny hadn't committed any murders.

But if she hadn't, who had?

Or had her Uncle Jabez just gotten tired and gone away, the way Eve Washington had suggested?

That didn't sound right, either.

The whole thing was a mess, Malone thought.

A mess.

Suddenly his head came up and he marched to the living room. Von Flanagan was sitting in an overstuffed chair, looking uncomfortable.

"I'll be right back," Malone said. "Don't go away."

"Where are you going?" the police captain asked.

Malone chewed on his cigar with satisfaction. "To bring you back a killer," he said. "Now don't go away."

"Malone... " von Flanagan began, but the little lawyer was out of the front door and running down the steps as if he didn't even care about breaking his neck.

Von Flanagan sighed and settled back in the chair.

VII

"All right," the killer said, a half–hour later in von Flanagan's office. "I did it. He deserved to die!"

Gadenski took the murderer away. Von Flanagan tipped his feet up on the desk and said to Malone: "I was sure it was the niece."

"It had to be somebody else," Malone said. "If she'd killed her uncle, she wouldn't have come to me to find him. I've got a reputation, after all."

"But why... "

"Well, I found this note in her couch, slipped under the cushions. Probably fell there by accident. The trouble with Eve Washington was, she never cleaned house."

"You didn't know about the note when you went there."

"No, but it gives you a motive," Malone said. "It's from McIlhenny, and it tells her he's not going to marry her. It seems they were a little more than good friends after all — and when he came over to tell her in person she blew up and hit him with whatever was handy. That studio of hers has lots of things to hit a man with."

"But... " von Flanagan shook his head.

"The cigar butt in the ashtray," Malone said. "I saw it there the first time I came to her house. And she said nobody but McIlhenny ever came to her studio. I didn't think she would smoke cigars. So, she must have been lying. If she'd ever cleaned up that studio of hers, she might have been safe forever."

"They always slip up somewhere," von Flanagan said gravely. "But how did she dispose of how'd she get rid of him?"

Malone lit a fresh cigar and blew a cloud of smoke. "She's confessed, and I'm not going to take her case, because I'm going to Havana," he said. "So you don't need to know how she got rid of Jabez McIlhenny, and that'll just be our little secret."

"Malone!"

"I've got good reasons," the little lawyer said. "I'd think you could trust me by this time. After I've solved a case for you."

"You solved it?" von Flanagan said. "She confessed here. Right in this office."

"Listen, von Flanagan," Malone said. "One more word out of you, and I — I won't even send you a card from Havana."

"You listen to me, Malone," the officer began, but the little lawyer was gone.

At the bank, he cashed G. G. G. McIlhenny's check. "Incidentally," he asked a teller, "what do the initials stand for?"

"You mean you don't know?" the teller said.

"That's right," Malone said.

"You ask her," the teller said. "She gave you a check, you must know her."

Malone hunted up a phone booth and put in a call.

"Oh, you darling man, I knew you could solve it... " the blonde cooed at him from the other end of the wire.

Malone decided that too much was, very definitely, even more than enough. "Your uncle's dead," he said sternly.

"Oh, Malone, I can't even think of Uncle Jabez now that I know you're so handsome and clever... "

Malone muttered something impolite. "Miss McIlhenny, I have a question to ask you."

"Oh," she said. "Oh. The answer is — yes, Malone. Yes."

"The question," he said grimly, "is: what do the initials stand for?"

There was a long silence on the other end of the wire. "My friends call me G–G," she said. "Like the French name."

Malone waited.

"Well," she said, "father and mother both wanted a boy, but they were resigned to God's will. So when I arrived I was christened God Giveth Girls. God Giveth Girls McIlhenny."

"Oh," said Malone. Very slowly, he hung up. Then he picked up the receiver again and dialed his office.

Maggie answered at once. "Malone, there's a man here with a bill for the telephone, and... "

"I'll be there in the morning," Malone said. "I'll pay everything before I leave. Oh, and Maggie... " He thought for a second of the square humming box in Eve Washington's studio, and of the kiln that could heat up to three thousand degrees. It could reduce a body to nothing but ash, and you could mix the ash with clay and never worry that anyone would find traces of the man you'd killed...

"Yes, Malone?" Maggie said.

"Don't forget to put some fresh flowers in Mr. McIlhenny before you leave."

He hung up. After all, he told himself consolingly, it was a very pretty vase...

This is the only true Melville Fairr story (i.e. appeared under the Michael Venning pseudonym); Craig became convinced that Fred Dannay of Ellery Queen's Mystery Magazine *preferred the Malone short stories to her other efforts. Rice selected the pen name from one of the characters in her Malone series. When* Who's Who *came to photograph Venning for their annual book, she dressed up in husband Larry's garb and let herself be shot as her alter ego. Sadly, the three Venning novels were never sold to a paperback house or reprinted.*

The reference to Ophelia is, of course, from Hamlet — *another sign that this is not a typical Malone story, but rather the more literary persona of Michael Venning. -JM*

How Now, Ophelia *(by Michael Venning)*

Late afternoon sunlight poured over the well–kept lawn like honey over a warm griddle–cake. The trees made a weary pretense of rustling in the faint breeze and relaxed again, their leaves drooping. One crisp brown leaf detached itself from its twig and fell, slowly, gracefully, carelessly, rattling against limb and branch with a small sound suddenly made loud by the surrounding silence.

On the terrace in front of the pleasant, sprawling farmhouse, a small man in a gray suit sat on the edge of a reclining chair. The chair was upholstered in lime–green and flame; against the colors the man seemed like a colorless little sparrow which had perched there for one moment only. His hair, his eyes, even his eyebrows were gray, and his friendly face had the grayish tinge that comes from too many years spent in sunless city streets. He was a private detective, and his name was Mr. Melville Fairr.

A tall, rangy, middle–aged man sprawled on the adjoining chair. His eyes were almost too bright a blue, his heavy dark hair was whitening a little at the temples. His handsome, sensitive face was deeply tanned. Every movement he made seemed calculated, planned in advance; even his relaxed pose on the reclining chair appeared to have been carefully studied.

"Mr. Cattermole," Mr. Melville Fairr said earnestly, "I tried to make it plain to you over the telephone. I'm not a psychiatrist. I'm only a private detective. It's been very pleasant, coming out here, but — "

He paused. The great Jesse Cattermole was paying no attention to him. With a little sigh Mr. Melville Fairr leaned back in his chair.

It *had* been pleasant, coming out here. It was still pleasant, being here. Indian Summer had turned New York into a coppery furnace and for once Mr. Melville

Fairr did not long for its streets and alleys. A clump of willows growing by a brook, a wide, sweet lawn, and a house —

A house of madness.

"I'm sorry," Mr. Melville Fairr said. "I'd like to help you, if I could. But — "

"Wait," Jesse Cattermole told him softly. The girl who emerged from behind the willows seemed like a pale shadow against their dark green foliage. She wore a white tennis dress, and her arms were filled with wild flowers.

"There with fantastic garlands did she come," Jesse Cattermole quoted, half under his breath. He turned to Melville Fairr and said earnestly, "You'll under-stand. She's — oh, dash it, say she's — not herself. But she's my stepdaughter and — " His voice broke off.

Melville Fairr watched the slender girl as she crossed the wide lawn, her fantastic garland of wild flowers clutched to her. She was strangely lovely. Her hair was brown and smooth, left loose over her shoulders, and brushed till it shone. Her pointed face was delicately, almost luminously pale. Her dark eyes, set in an almost fixed stare, had a look of helpless desperation behind them. Her sweet pink lips wore a rather silly smile.

"You're afraid she may go violently mad — and murder her husband," Mr. Melville Fairr said in a very quiet voice.

"I know she will. I can see it coming." The great Shakespearean actor — now retired — stirred uneasily in his chair. "I'm not one of these psychologist fellows, but I know. And dammit, Fairr, I love the girl as if she were my own daughter. After all, she was a year old when I married her mother, and only three when her mother died. I brought her up myself. This marriage — " He paused. "Someone recommended you. And if *you* can't help — "

Little Mr. Melville Fairr kept his eyes on the girl who was coming, so slowly and gracefully, across the shadow–dappled lawn. He said, "So you called me in to prevent a murder."

"That's it. That's exactly it. Confound it, I don't care if the fellow is killed. Frankly, I'd like to see it happen. He's a drunken brute and he's driving her insane. But — " He paused to light a fresh cigarette.

"As I see it," Melville Fairr told him, "You have several courses of action open to you. Call in the police, and tell them what you've just told me. Or, better, call in a competent psychiatrist and let him take her away for treatment. Or even," — a frown crossed his friendly face — "why doesn't she divorce him?"

Jesse Cattermole stood up. "She hasn't any money, and neither have I. Just to pay your fee, I've had to sell some old books. Not that I begrudge them. Not for her. *He* has the money. Everything here belongs to him. The chair you're sitting on, the tea we've been drinking, the dress she's wearing, the pathetic armful of flowers she's gathered, even this cigarette I'm smoking." He took a last puff on it and flipped it away from him in a wide, graceful arc. His face went back to his normal pleasantness and he called, "Hello there, Lucia!"

She laughed, a lovely, silvery, almost tinkling little laugh that made a cold chill run down Melville Fairr's spine. She half–ran gracefully the last few feet across the lawn.

"I picked these because they were so lovely. But now I don't know what to do with them." Her voice was clear and childlike. "I thought they'd look beautiful on mother's grave. Then I remembered — she doesn't have a grave, does she, Jesse?"

"No, dear child," Jesse Cattermole said. "She was buried at sea."

"That's right. So I might as well throw them away." She tossed the armful of limp, wet flowers away from her, carelessly. They scattered on the grass.

"Lucia," Jesse Cattermole said, as she came up the steps, "This is Mr. Fairr. Mr. Melville Fairr."

"How do you do." Her big dark eyes were friendly. "So nice to see you again." A faint shadow of a frown crossed her brow. "Or have I met you before? I have a very bad memory. Bart keeps telling me that, and he must be right."

"A bad memory can be a good thing," Melville Fairr said, "just as a gift of prophecy can be a bad thing."

She smiled at him, that sweet, silly, limpid smile, and sat down on the terrace steps. "But I do remember mother being buried at sea. I can remember more than that, when I try. The gray glassy surface of the sea, and the birds flying overhead. And flowers, floating on the water."

"Lucia darling," Jesse Cattermole said affectionately, "you weren't even there. And it wasn't that way at all."

"You see?" She lifted her lovely, very pale shoulders. "I always remember the wrong things. And forget the important ones." This time her smile wasn't silly — as though she shared a delightful secret with Melville Fairr.

"That may be the secret of happiness," Melville Fairr murmured. "To forget all the important things."

The great Jesse Cattermole cleared his throat quietly. "Stay right there and rest, Lucia," he said. "I'll bring you your tea." He vanished into the house.

Little Mr. Melville Fairr sighed. This seemed too plotted, too planned, his being left alone with the girl. He suspected that Jesse Cattermole would not return with tea. He was right.

The girl looked up at him. "Jesse is always so good to me. I can't tell you how very fond of him I am. I was a baby when my mother died. She was an actress, you know. Jesse isn't my father, he's my stepfather, but he's done so much for me. I thought it would be — *nice* for him, my marrying Bart. But it hasn't turned out that way at all."

"What do you mean, for *him*?" Melville Fairr asked. "Why shouldn't your marriage just have been" — he hesitated at the word — "nice for you?"

"Jesse isn't young any more." She paused. Suddenly, in talking about Jesse Cattermole, she had ceased to be a sweet, silly, and quite possibly insane girl, and became a young woman, with warmth, affection, and even understanding. "I'd seen so many old actors — some of them who'd been famous — "

Melville Fairr nodded sympathetically. So had he. But he murmured something about other actors, even older than Jesse Cattermole, who'd gone on to new and greater successes. He was naming names and describing circumstances, when he heard her laugh.

It wasn't the silvery, cold, frightening laughter he'd heard before. It was pleasant, friendly laughter. She said, "Mr. Fairr, Jesse never was a great actor. He made a wonderful matinee idol, years ago, but just between us, he was a terrible ham."

Melville Fairr didn't answer that. He knew too well that it was true. He said gently, "And so you married Bartley Cannon who had a great deal of money, and it hasn't turned out successfully."

Her pale face twisted with worry. It wasn't, he observed, an adult kind of worry. It was childlike, and curiously frightened. When she spoke, it was again in that clear, limpid voice.

"It's my fault, really. Probably because I was too young to marry. When Jesse introduced Bart to me, I believe Bart thought I was a lot older than sixteen, because Jesse was so much older. Does that make sense? I hope so, because I know what I mean. I'd had one little part on the stage, you know, but I wasn't very good. It seemed like such a wise idea to marry Bart. Only I seem to do everything wrong. I forget things. Worse than that, I remember things."

Suddenly she rose and stood looking intently at him. Her white, nervous fingers picked a leaf from the nearby trellis and twisted it into tortured shapes.

"Mr. Fairr, tell me the truth. Are you another doctor?"

Little Mr. Melville Fairr lifted his gray eyebrows just a fraction of an inch. "*Another?*"

She nodded. "Jesse brought one here. He was supposed to be a friend of the family, visiting. But I knew what he was. He asked me a lot of silly questions. He wanted to take me to a hospital. But I cried, and anyway Jesse couldn't let him because Bart didn't know, not even about his being here. If only it weren't for Bart — "

Melville Fairr steeled himself to ask her, very coolly and quietly, if she was afraid she might go mad and murder her husband, when there was a sudden and noisy interruption.

"Lucia! Lucia, where the hell are you?" It was a thick and angry voice, coming from the house.

She turned, walked a few feet nearer the wide front door and stood leaning against one of the pillars. Melville Fairr could see her small fingers closing into fists, then opening again.

The screen door burst open and banged shut. Bart Cannon, a big, red-faced, and at the moment, very drunken man, came out on the terrace and glared at his wife.

"What was the idea of breaking our date with the Forresters for tonight?"

Lucia stared at him, her eyes blank and frightened. "I didn't!"

"Yes, you did! You called Milly Forrester and told her we couldn't go. What's the idea? Do you think I want to spend all my days and nights in this dreary rat's nest?"

Melville Fairr sighed again, and looked away in the direction of the sunlit lawn, the beautifully tended gardens, the tall and graceful trees.

"I'm sorry, Bart. I — don't remember."

"You never remember anything!" He noticed the little man in gray. "Who the hell's this?"

"He's — I don't know. A friend of father's."

The little man in gray rose and said pleasantly, "My name is Melville Fairr." He looked closely at his host. Bart Cannon was tall, wide–shouldered, and gone to flesh. His hair was a muddy brown, and his pale blue eyes bulged. He wore riding pants and a sweat shirt

"How d'ya do. I'm Bart Cannon. What are you doing here?"

Melville Fairr, who couldn't have been intimidated by the devil himself, sat down and said, rather primly, "I came to interview Mr. Cattermole."

"Then why in blazes don't you interview him instead of annoying my wife?" He turned to her and said, "Lucia, come into the house. I want to talk to you."

She shook her head wildly. Her tiny fingernails seemed to be digging into the wooden pillar she was leaning against. Bart Cannon slapped her, not too hard.

Melville Fairr started to rise, then sank back into his chair. He watched, while Bart Cannon half–led, half–dragged his wife into the house, his thick muscular fingers digging into her pale thin arms. He heard her faint whimper as she went into the hall, and the sound of another slap.

Little Melville Fairr sighed deeply. He liked people — good, bad, and all the stages in between; and he disliked seeing the many unkindnesses they did to each other. Down on the lawn below the terrace the flowers Lucia had carried from the fields were rapidly changing into ugly wisps of weeds, and Melville Fairr turned his eyes away from them. He wished that he had never seen them. He wished that he were back in the hot, dirty, smelly streets of New York. He wished most of all that Jesse Cattermole would come back to the terrace so that he could tell him he had decided to stay until this ugly affair was straightened one way or another — either by murder or by madness.

The house had suddenly become still. Much too still, Melville Fairr thought. And as though the emotions of a house could be sensed by its surroundings, the trees and gardens and the very air itself had likewise become still. Melville Fairr sat uncomfortably on the edge of his chair and wished uneasily that just one leaf would fall or one blade of grass would stir.

In that tremendous stillness the little gray man heard footsteps meant to be silent ones, hardly more than whispers on the soft lawn. It seemed to him as he listened that his ears must be twitching like a cat's. The steps came closer, paused, sounded again, and paused again. With all his heart Melville Fairr longed to turn his head and see who was approaching so stealthily along the side of house — not that it was any of his business, but he was, by nature, a curious man.

There was a very long silence while Melville Fairr waited breathlessly. And then a whisper, "Lucia — ?"

"She isn't here," Melville Fairr whispered back, "but I'm her friend. You can trust me." A full minute later he felt that it was safe to turn around.

He saw then that one reason for the softness of the footsteps was that the young man who made them was barefoot. He saw a tall young man with wiry muscles and a deep tan, dressed in nothing but a pair of faded dungarees. His short blond hair had been bleached pale by the sun; his eyes were a surprisingly bright blue. His browned face was at the same time friendly and wary, like a half-tamed woodland creature. It became more friendly as he stood surveying Melville Fairr with his quick bright eyes.

Melville Fairr had that effect on frightened people, children, dogs, cats, and the squirrels in Central Park. Perhaps it was because he was quiet and small, and gray as a shadow, because he was so soft-spoken and moved so very gently. He spoke very softly now, and moved with particular gentleness as he rose from his chair.

"Lucia's in the house." He paused and added, "with her husband." He stepped down from the terrace and said, "I should very much like to walk about the grounds. Perhaps you would be kind enough to guide me?"

The young man grinned at him and said, "Delighted." They took a few steps away from the terrace and he said, "Acting as your guide, perhaps I should point out to you that the yew trees beyond the formal garden were imported from England by Bartley Cannon's father. He bought them, I understand, at a steal. And the sundial in the center of the garden was a little item he picked up cheaply in Rome. Frankly, I've always thought it was in rather bad taste — and now that we're beyond earshot of the house, would you mind telling me just who the devil you are and how you fit into this mess?"

"I'm Melville Fairr," the little man in gray told him. "I'm a private detective from New York and to be perfectly frank with you I don't know how I fit into 'this mess' as you call it."

They were walking in the direction of the Woods. Melville Fairr waited a moment and then said, "I trust you won't mind if I ask you the same questions." He added, "And for the same reasons."

"My name is Tony Gay," the young man said, "and I'm a farmer. Nothing fancy, just an ordinary dirt farmer with one hired man, a small herd of Guernsey cows, a promising orchard, and a degree from the State Agricultural College. I fit in this mess because I lease my farm from Bart Cannon and he's threatening to cancel the lease."

"Why?" Melville Fairr asked.

"Because," Tony Gay said, "I'm in love with his wife and he knows it. And I think she's in love with me." He stopped suddenly, like a young deer startled motionless by some scent of unfamiliar danger. "Mr. Fairr, you're a guest at the house. You've talked to her. *What's* driving her crazy? If it's Bart Cannon, I'll kill him. I should have killed him long ago, anyway."

He turned around and looked back at the expanse of lawn and the architecturally perfect yet somehow incongruous house that Bart Cannon's father had had built for him.

"All that used to be part of our farm," Tony Gay went on. "Now, I rent my farm from him."

At exactly that moment there was a cry from the direction of the house. Melville Fairr recognized the voice as belonging to Lucia Cannon. Obviously, Tony Gay also recognized it. Melville Fairr reflected, as he watched the young man sprint across the lawn, that it had been many years since he himself could run so fast.

He reminded himself, as he walked across the lawn, that he was not, after all, a man of action. That reminder kept him from breaking into a sprint. Besides, it was Lucia who had screamed.

The house seemed very quiet and normal as he approached it. The scene on the terrace as he came around the corner was not quiet but he had a feeling that it was normal. Lucia was there, a bit more pale than she had been before, her eyes blank, her face bewildered. Bart Cannon was there, his broad face dark with anger, muttering something about his right to defend himself. Jesse Cattermole was there looking distressed, and somehow helpless.

Young Tony Gay stood at the foot of the terrace steps as though deciding what to do.

Catching sight of Melville Fairr, Jesse Cattermole said, with sudden suavity, "Something alarmed Lucia." He turned to her. "What was it, my dear — a mouse?"

She looked at him blankly.

"That's what I thought," Jesse Cattermole said briskly and cheerfully, like a doctor speaking to a difficult patient. "Perhaps you'd better lie down a bit before dinner. Yes, that's the thing to do."

She frowned slightly, then her pink lips curled into that sweet silly smile. "Very well, Jesse, but I don't *remember* a mouse." She walked over to Melville Fairr and he saw that she had been concealing something in her hand, under the folds of her skirt. She handed it to him and said, "Will you keep this for me while I lie down and rest?" and vanished into the house.

It was a tiny letter–opener, not big enough to harm a newborn kitten, but its point was darkened by a small smear of blood.

Jesse Cattermole stared at it as it lay in Melville Fairr's hand. "Is this a dagger?" he began, almost automatically.

"That's from *Macbeth*," Melville Fairr snapped, almost irritably, "not *Hamlet*."

Jesse Cattermole turned abruptly and followed his stepdaughter into the house.

Bart Cannon stared at the little letter–knife with hurt bewilderment on his broad red face. "She tried to kill me," he said. There was a kind of comic surprise in his voice, "My wife tried to kill me."

He seemed dazed and confused, rather than angered. Then suddenly he caught sight of Tony Gay standing at the foot of the steps. "Damn it!" he roared, "how many times do I have to tell you to keep off my property? If you're caught trespassing here again, I'll have one of the gardeners chase you off with a load of buckshot."

Tony Gay stared at him for an instant with mockery in his bright blue eyes, a deliberately insulting reminder that he had once owned this land himself. Then he turned and walked across the lawn with slow dignity and a kind of faunlike grace.

Bert Cannon sat down heavily in the nearest chair, mopped at his steamy face with a crumpled handkerchief, dabbed ineffectually at a small, bright, and obviously new scratch on the back of his hand. He bellowed for someone to fetch him a fresh drink and finally said, wearily, to Melville Fairr, "Just who the hell are you and what do you make of this mess?"

"I don't know what to make of it," Melville Fairr said, not quite truthfully. "Do you?"

"I know I ought to run her off the premises," Bart Cannon said.

"Well," Melville Fairr said very quietly, "why don't you?"

"Because she married me for my money," Bart Cannon said. "Look, Mr. Whoever–you–are, I'm a rather simple guy. When I pay for something, I like to get what I pay for. Whether it's a block of stock, a parcel of land — or a wife. And when I've paid for something, I don't like to lose it." He was gazing in the direction of Tony Gay's farm. "I may give away something I've paid for, as a gift, or I might sell it at a profit. But I hate to lose things or throw them away. In fact, I think I'd rather have something taken from me by force than to lose it through carelessness. Even my life."

He looked it Melville Fairr, laughed harshly, and said, "You think I'm a drunken fool, don't you? Only half of that is correct. He lurched toward the house and bellowed, "Where the hell is my drink? Have I got to get it myself?" Then he disappeared into the house.

Little Mr. Melville Fairr sat gazing at the lawn until the first shadows of twilight began to turn it into a mysterious pool. In the distance the trees framed a post–sunset sky of green, violet, and rose. But he was scarcely conscious of what he watched. He was wondering if anyone besides himself knew that Tony Gay had not left but had hidden himself behind the bushes beside the house.

It seemed to him that he waited there a long time. Actually, it was not much more than a quarter of an hour before the screen door opened softly and Jesse Cattermole came out.

"Mr. Fairr," Jesse Cattermole said, "I've made up my mind. I'm going to take Lucia away from here immediately. I'm not going to let anyone or anything stop me. I'll manage somehow as far as the money is concerned. There are still a few books I can sell, and I can surely find some kind of an engagement. Anything to get her away from here before something does happen. You saw — this after-noon."

Melville Fairr nodded. "You're quite right," he said, "if she can be persuaded to go."

At that moment they heard the shot.

Melville Fairr, sunk deep in the canvas deck chair, was at a disadvantage in getting to his feet. Jesse Cattermole reached the front door a good thirty seconds ahead of him. Melville had just reached the entrance to the big shadowy hall when he heard the second shot.

For just an instant he stood there confused. It was a strange house and its lights had not yet been turned on. Then he saw a rectangle of light at the end of the hall and ran toward it.

The room was evidently a kind of combination office and library. Melville Fairr's first quick glance took in a desk, an enormous fireplace, shelves of new looking books and a pale beige rug. Lucia Cannon was crumpled on the rug in a faint, a revolver lying near her hand. Bart Cannon was sprawled in front of his desk. He looked dead.

Melville Fairr said, "Don't touch anything."

"Why not?" a voice said behind him. "Why not touch things? Because of germs? Is the germ of murder something one of us could take in merely by touching his filthy dead body? And would it infect us to go on to other murders?"

Melville Fairr turned around, saw Tony Gay's pale face, and said very quietly, "That will be enough from you, young man."

Jesse Cattermole sobbed "*Lucia* — "

"Don't touch anything," Melville Fairr repeated, "and I'll call the police."

By the time he'd called them and been assured that the sheriff's car would be speeding on its way through the twilight, Lucia was opening her eyes, and Jesse Cattermole, regardless of Melville Fairr's orders, had determined that the man *was* dead.

They lifted Lucia from the floor and carried her to a couch in the next room. They rubbed her hands and put a hot water bottle at her feet, and held a glass of brandy against her pale lips, until at last she stared at them, smiled that sweet and rather silly smile, and said, "Hello!"

"Lucia!" Jesse Cattermole said. Tears streamed down his cheeks.

Little Mr. Melville Fairr pulled a warm blanket over her and said, "Shock.

She'll be all right." He rubbed her hands again and said, "Tell me, my dear. What happened?"

Her eyes were wide, childlike. "What happened — where?"

"Your husband is dead," Melville Fairr said. "He's been killed."

At that moment the police came, in time to see her lovely eyes widen with shocked surprise.

"Poor Bart," she said. "Who killed him?"

The young sheriff, Harry Olsen, gave Melville Fairr a questioning look. Melville Fairr nodded. There was sympathy and understanding in the young sheriff's eyes.

"My dear girl," Melville Fairr said gently, "don't you remember?"

It seemed for a moment that she was trying to remember. The she shook her head.

"Did you shoot him?" Harry Olsen asked. He was blond, pleasant–faced, and obviously uneasy in this situation.

She stared at him for a moment and then said, "Don't be silly."

"For the love of Heaven," Jesse Cattermole said, "don't torture the child. Can't you see that she's ill?"

"Mr. Fairr," Tony Gay said, "can't you do *something*?"

Young Harry Olsen said, "Just what happened, Mrs. Cannon?"

"Bart was angry with me." She frowned slightly. "I don't remember what he was angry about. Something. I'm always forgetting things. Bart keeps scolding me because I forget things. But I do try to remember. I remembered about the new cleaning woman, but Bart didn't seem to care — he was angry anyway. He always seems to be angry."

"Not any more," Melville Fairr said softly. "He's dead."

"That's right," she whispered. "You told me. Poor Bart. It seems rather a shame. I think he really did enjoy living." Her eyes closed; she breathed slowly and regularly. She seemed to have fallen asleep.

Melville Fairr took the young sheriff by the arm and steered him in the direction of the murdered man's library.

"That poor kid," Harry Olsen said. He took out a bright–bordered handkerchief and wiped his brow. "Everybody thought he'd drive her crazy, just like he did his first wife. *She* went clear off her head and jumped in the creek down yonder. Nobody thought so much of it at the time. She was one of the Gay family, and they always was a trifle flighty." He shook his blond head and sighed. "Oh, well, this poor kid, she's alive and she won't need to go to jail, and nut hospitals ain't such bad places these days. Well, I guess we better go look at the remains, Mr. Fairr."

"Just a minute," Melville Fairr. "I'm debating a problem of ethics." He paused as he reached the library door. "*Are* there circumstances under which a murderer should be allowed to go free?"

"Mister," Harry Olsen said, "I'm the law. My business is to catch murderers, not to let 'em go. But just between us, if I'd seen someone shoot Bart Cannon down in cold blood, I'd have been inclined to give him a good running start before I started catching him. And so would anybody who ever knew Bart Cannon."

"Just the same," Melville Fairr said, almost as though to himself, "*she* said — 'he really did enjoy living.' And you *are* the law, and that implies — certain duties."

"I don't get this," Harry Olsen said, scowling.

"You will," Melville Fairr told him, pushing open the library door. "I'd like to draw your attention to a few things. One, that there were two shots. One bullet went through Mr. Cannon's brain. Very nearly, right between the eyes. The other went wild. You can see where it lodged in the plaster, about two feet from where Mr. Cannon must have been standing. The *second* of the two shots was the one that killed him. There wouldn't have been any point in firing again after he was dead."

The young man's eyes narrowed. "How close together were the two shots?"

"About half a minute," Melville Fairr told him. "And I'm a fairly good judge of time."

"I think I know what you're getting at," Harry Olsen said. "Go on."

"From where she fell, when she fainted," Melville Fairr went on, "she was standing only a few feet from him. Yet there's not a trace of a powder burn around the wound."

As though instinctively, Harry Olsen turned and looked at the open doorway into the hall, through the matching doorway into the room beyond, and at the wide–open French windows at the far side of the room.

"I suggest," Melville Fairr said quietly, "that we go back in the other room and take the revolver with us. And that you let me ask several questions."

"Mister," Harry Olsen said, admiration in his voice, "I'm the sheriff of this county and you're just a private dick from the big city, but I'll play along with you." He whipped out his handkerchief and picked up the revolver as tenderly as though it were a sick child.

Lucia's eyes were still closed, her face as expressionless as that of a sleeping child. Melville Fairr sat down beside her and took her hand.

"My dear child," he said, "I must annoy you with one question. Nearsighted as you are, why don't you wear glasses?"

Her eyelids flew open and she stared at him. For a long moment her gaze and his carried on a silent but important conversation.

"Vanity, I guess," she whispered. "No woman ever really likes to wear glasses."

"And tell me," he said, "How many times in your life have you fired a gun?"

"Once." She gasped. "I mean — "

"Never mind," Melville Fairr said, "I know what you mean. You're near–sighted, you'd never fired a gun before, no wonder you had poor aim." He turned to Tony Gay. "You habitually carry a gun?"

"Yes. I thought that sometime I might have a chance to shoot him and get away with it. Here, take the damned thing." He drew the small revolver from his pocket and handed it to Harry Olsen.

The young sheriff looked at both guns. He looked at Jesse Cattermole and at Tony Gay. He turned to Melville Fairr and said, bewildered, "Which?"

"The *second* shot killed Bart Cannon," Melville Fairr said. "One of two things happened. But first, one thing we know happened. Mrs. Cannon fired a gun, once. Either from deliberate intent, or because she has poor eyesight and had never fired a gun before, she missed. And then — "

"Now just a minute, Mr. Fairr," Tony Gay said angrily.

"Shut up, you," the sheriff said.

"Then," the little man in gray continued, "someone watching through the French windows and seeing the tableau could have drawn his revolver and fired. If he happened to be a country–bred boy who probably had shot squirrels at the age of ten, he would undoubtedly have been able to bring down Mr. Cannon with a shot right between the eyes. Or — "

"Just a minute, Mr. Fairr," Jessie Cattermole began.

"And you shut up, too," the sheriff told him.

"Or," Melville Fairr continued, wishing with all his heart that people would not go around murdering each other, thereby creating problems for the next–of–kin, the authorities, and himself, "someone rushed into the room, saw that Lucia had fired, missed, and fainted, grabbed her gun, killed Bart Cannon, hastily wiped off the fingerprints from the gun, and dropped it on the floor near her hand."

Lucia opened her eyes and said, "Well?"

"I suggest," Melville Fairr said, "that a ballistics expert examine both bullets and both guns. I also suggest that the gun found in the murder room be examined for fingerprints. If there *are* none, since Lucia was not wearing gloves — "

"He *deserved* to be killed," Jesse Cattermole said. His voice was hoarse. There was a strange glitter in his eye.

"Why, Jesse!" Lucia said. She laughed, that tinkling little laugh like drops of water falling into a silver basin. "Why, Jesse, you're *crazy*! You've always been a little crazy, but now you're *really* crazy!"

He drew himself up proudly. "That's what *he* was always saying. It is not so. That's why I killed him." He struck a Shakespearean pose. "*I am very proud, revengeful, ambitious, with more offenses at my back than I have thoughts to put them in, imagination to give them shape, or time to act them in. What should such fellows as I do crawling between earth and Heaven — *"

"I kind of remember that speech," Harry Olsen said. "My folks used to take me to the theater when I was a kid. Saw Mr. Cattermole, too. Golly, he was good." He drew a long, sighing breath. "Glad this guy will never have to face a jury. Just a bunch of these psychiatrist Joes." He turned, smiled, and said, "Come along with us, Mr. Cattermole."

Jesse Cattermole struck another pose. He said, in the golden voice so many still remembered, "*It will be short: the interim is mine; And no man's life no more than to say, one.*"

"That's all, brother," Harry Olsen said. "Come along!"

"You'd better," Melville Fairr told him gently. "If you don't go with him you'll be late to the theater and you've got to put on a special show tonight."

"A benefit performance," Jesse Cattermole said, grinning foolishly. He walked away quietly with Harry Olsen.

"He *is* a ham," Melville Fairr said at last. "But I think he'll be able to get through this one role."

Lucia stared at him. Her lips parted, formed one word silently, "Jesse — "

"Don't worry about him," Melville Fairr said. "He'll have a wonderful time acting. And he'll have a good audience. No audience can be much better than one composed of doctors." He smiled down at her. "That was what he wanted, you know. An audience. That's why he encouraged you to marry Bartley Cannon, because he thought Cannon would back a Shakespearean tour for his father-in-law."

Melville Fairr turned, walked to the window and stared across the broad lawn, white–blue with moonlight. "He knew he had to murder Bartley Cannon," he said very softly, "for two reasons. One, he needed his money. The other, Cannon was cruel to you."

"He *would* have driven her crazy," Tony Gay cried out. "Gloria — his first wife — my cousin — it wasn't insanity he drove her to, it was despair. There never was any insanity in the Gay family."

"There would have been insanity in the Cannon family," Melville Fairr said, "if Jesse Cattermole's plan had succeeded. It was necessary for him to kill Bart Cannon. It was just as necessary for him to provide the police with a murderer, and at the same time make sure that he would handle the Cannon fortune — as he would have done with Bart Cannon dead and Bart Cannon's wife declared insane."

"Wouldn't it have been simpler," Tony Gay asked harshly, "to have murdered Cannon, framed Lucia, and let her hang? Then he'd have had the money and no questions asked."

"You forget," Melville Fairr said, "he loved Lucia. That's why he was planning her defense even while he was planning Bart Cannon's murder."

Tony Gay looked down at Lucia with a warm tenderness in his face that made Melville Fairr turn his eyes away. "He — Jesse — damn near talked you into insanity, at that. If this chap hadn't come along — " He turned to Melville Fairr. "I still don't understand, though," he said, "about the shots — "

"She'll explain that to you some day," Melville Fairr said, smiling.

There was nothing more for him to do. He found his hat and topcoat and walked to the untended door, pausing there for a moment to gaze at the broad lawn and the trees beyond. Everything was all right now. Jesse Cattermole would be happy and well cared for. In time Lucia would marry Tony Gay and they would live happily on what had once been Tony's father's farm. The moonlight seemed brighter now, and somehow warmer. Then he heard soft whispering footsteps in the hall behind him and he turned.

She stood in the doorway, a small silvery smiling shadow. Melville Fairr, picked up her cool, pale hand and, kissed it, "Congratulations on a magnificent performance. Your mother was a great actress, too. I remember her as Juliet."

Her eyes shone at him. "You know then?" she whispered.

"It's my business to know things," Melville Fairr told her. "Such as that *you* knew what Jesse Cattermole was planning, and because you were so fond of him, and so grateful, were trying to help. That you were pretending a kind of madness. That you were making unsuccessful attempts at murdering Cannon, so that when the actual murder did come — " He paused. "I think, though, it turned out better this way."

"Wait a minute," she whispered. "You said I was a good actress. *How* did you know?"

"Because of a quotation," Melville Fairr said. "Shakespeare, I think, though I can't be sure. I can't quote it and I've no idea what it's from. In fact, it may not be from Shakespeare at all — "

He heard Tony Gay call her name, saw her go back into the house. He turned and walked away across the moonlit lawn that now seemed, somehow, to be as bright as day.

This short story made more money for Craig than any of her others — not because she continued to sell it, but because she used the story as collateral for her loans from wealthy mystery aficionado Ned Guymon. The collector was fascinated by the story, which he described as the only one where the victim is "f***ed [sic] to death." Fred Dannay demurred at publishing the story, concerned about sending what some might consider pornography through the mail. When Craig wanted to sell the story to a magazine, she tidied up the end and added sleuth Melville Fairr. -JM

Death in the Moonlight

That night, pure moonlight turned the meadow of softly waving grass into a pale, ripping sea. Beyond, tall dark trees moved silently against the sky.

"She's dead, isn't she," the young man said in a hushed whisper.

"Yes," little Mr. Melville Fairr said gently. He drew a long, slow breath, "Yes, I'm afraid so." He stood like a small gray shadow in the moonlight, looking down.

She was still as beautiful as audiences of twenty years ago would have remembered her, a little wisp of a woman, so delicately formed as to seem almost brittle, like some rare and exquisite carving. The tall, soft grass brushed against her face, as though with love. Her pale, moon–colored hair mingled with the grass, blowing softly in the light wind.

There was a smile on her slightly parted lips. Her wide–open lovely eyes gazed upward toward the moon. Mr. Melville Fairr knelt and looked at her closely, as though be were trying to read some secret in those eyes.

"She should never have tried to walk so far alone," the young man said.

"If she was alone." The small gray man looked around him. The gentle wind that continually stirred the grass would have quickly erased the marks of anyone who passed that way. It had already obliterated their own. "We'd better go back to the house, Lance," he said, "and tell the others."

Lance Kane frowned. "And leave her here alone?"

"She has the moon for company," Melville Fairr said. He paused one more moment, looking down at the body of Rosalie Kane. A half–smile crossed his face.

Who gazed into the starlight; and were slain.
Who lay eyes up in moonlight, and were drowned...

104

"What's that?" Lance Kane asked.

"Nothing. Just some lines from a poem I happened to remember." He took the young man's arm. "We'll be getting back now."

They had gone through the little gate in the hedge and were halfway across the lawn before either spoke.

"*If* she was alone," Lance Kane repeated. "I don't understand. Surely if anyone had been with her — " He paused.

"Your mother has never gone anywhere alone, even to walk in the garden, for nearly five years," Melville Fairr reminded him.

They went on into the house, through the wide, shadowy hall, into the pleasantly lighted library.

"Did you find her?"

"Yes," Melville Fairr said. "Yes, we found her."

There was a little silence. Melville Fairr looked around him and wished he could be anywhere else in the world. There was something frightening in the quiet room. He didn't quite know what it was, but he could feel it. Warm midsummer air poured in through the wide open French windows, yet he was conscious of sudden cold.

Perhaps it was because there was too much beauty. Out there, the exquisite dead face, the moonlight, and the softly rippling grass. Here, the sheer perfection of every detail in the paneled library, even to the pale yellow roses that floated in a crystal bowl on the table.

The people in the room. The twins, Lance and Laura Kane, both with Rosalie's delicate coloring. Lance, tall, lithe, and slender, with a face which, though strongly masculine, had to be called beautiful. Laura, small and lovely, like a moonbeam. Only nineteen. Nineteen seemed terribly young to Mr. Melville Fairr.

Tony Melrose, Rosalie's husband. Widower, now. Curious that no one had ever thought of her as Rosalie Melrose, only as Rosalie Kane. He was almost, but not quite, too handsome. Dark and muscular and magnificently graceful. A dancer once, Melville Fairr remembered. Ten years younger than Rosalie. That would make him twenty–nine.

Dr. Arnold Fletcher, Rosalie Kane's physician and devoted friend, who never let one day pass without a visit. A man somewhere in his early fifties, Melville Fairr guessed. Another kind of beauty there, thick white hair that waved back from his forehead, dark, friendly eyes, a strong face, deeply lined.

It was Dr. Fletcher who spoke first. "It was her heart, of course." There was no surprise in his voice.

Little Mr. Melville Fairr said nothing.

Lance said, a shade resentfully, "Mr. Fairr seems to think there is something strange about her death."

Everyone looked at him and then at Melville Fairr.

Laura Kane's face seemed to have turned a shade more pale. "Mr. Fairr, who are you? Why are you here?"

"I am here at your mother's invitation," he told her, smiling a little. No reason to tell them now that he was a private detective. No reason to frighten any of them.

"We've all known for years that it could happen at any time, any moment," Dr. Fletcher said almost angrily. "The slightest shock, the slightest exertion. We worried even about Lance's coming, though we knew it would be a happy surprise. We were amazed when she told us you were to arrive, Mr. Fairr. She's lived in such strict seclusion since we brought her home from the hospital nearly five years ago. No visitors, no excitement."

He drew a, long breath and went on. "Even so, someone was always near her in case of a sudden attack. All of us carried these, every minute of the day." He held up a little gleaning capsule that he fished from his pocket.

"That," Melville Fairr said, "is what is so strange." They stared at him. "Why was she alone tonight?" he asked gently. "And if she was not alone — why was no capsule used to save her life?"

This time the silence was a long one.

There was no sign of shock, no actual grief on any of their faces, no tears in Laura's eyes, Melville Fairr observed. It could have been because they had known for so long that it was coming.

At last the doctor, said, "Will you come with me, Mr. Fairr?" He started toward the door. "The rest of you had better wait here."

As they went down the long path across the lawn, he said, "I wish to heaven I knew, just what you were driving at, Mr. Fairr." He added, "You see, I know who you are, and what your profession is. I wish you'd tell me why Rosalie sent for you."

"I can tell you that better," Melville Fairr said, "when we know how she met her death."

"Her heart," Dr. 'Fletcher began. "Any shock, any excitement."

"Yes, I know," Melville Fairr said. "The exertion of walking so far?"

The doctor said, "She was accustomed to walking. Slowly, of course, and not too far, and never alone." He repeated thoughtfully, "Never alone." He frowned. "Which of us could have been with her and failed to save her life?"

"After dinner," Melville Fairr said, "she was lying down on the couch on the terrace. She wanted to watch the moonlight. Tony was in the library reading. Lance had gone to his room to write a letter. Laura was having a conference with the cook about tomorrow's menus, and then went to her room to change into something cooler."

"You are very observing," the doctor said.

"It is my profession," the little detective said modestly. He added, "Then you arrived, and we discovered that she was missing from the house."

"And I," Dr. Fletcher said, "could actually have been here much earlier and only pretended to arrive when I did. But I never would have harmed her. I've adored her for more than twenty years." He turned to look at Melville Fairr. "How much do you know about her?"

"First," Melville Fairr said, "that she was the loveliest and most popular singing and dancing star of her time. When she was nineteen she met and married Kane, an unsuccessful actor who as quite a bit older than she was. A year later; the twins were born. But she was a tremendous success, and he was a bitter and hopeless failure. They quarreled, parted, and divorced. Laura stayed with her mother, Lance was given to his father, and Rosalie did not see him again."

"Until last week," the doctor said.

Melville Fairr nodded. "Later, when she was in her early thirties, and at the very top of her career, she married Tony Melrose. But her heart — "

"It was the day of their marriage," Dr. Fletcher said. "And the closing performance of *Moonglow*. They were married just before the performance and immediately afterward they were to leave on their honeymoon. Tony and I watched from the audience. After it, when we went back to her dressing room, we found her on the floor." He stopped walking for a moment, his eyes closed. "For a minute, we thought she was dead."

Now they had reached the little gate. Before them stretched the ocean of moonlight.

"For five years, Tony has been devotion itself, waiting on her, nursing her, keeping her amused and happy, always knowing that she would never be any better and that this might happen at any moment." He walked on into the meadow. "I still wish I knew what you are driving at, Mr. Fairr."

Melville Fairr said nothing.

The doctor went on, "Not long ago, Kane died, somewhere in California. Lance wrote that he was coming to see the mother he could not remember and last week he arrived. Then you came. And now, this happens." He shook his head. "I can't understand it at all."

They reached the spot where Rosalie Kane's body lay cradled in the soft grass.

After a while, Melville Fairr said, "There is no need for the law and nothing that we could tell them. As her physician you can, of course, sign the death certificate, and that will be the end of it."

Dr. Fletcher nodded his head. "I agree with you."

"But," Melville Fairr said softly, "it still was murder."

The big house was very quiet, though lights still showed in its windows, and everyone in it was awake. Melville Fairr walked slowly up and down the terrace, watching the moon that had slipped down now to the very tops of the tall trees and was about to disappear behind them.

Suddenly he heard a sigh, so long and so deep as to be almost a moan. He turned and saw Tony Melrose on one of the terrace chairs, his chin resting on his hands. At the sound of footsteps, the young man looked up. His dark, expressive eyes were bright with tears.

"I'm terribly sorry," Melville Fairr said, starting to turn away.

"Please don't go," Tony said. "I'd like to talk to you."

Melville Fairr sat down in the shadows.

"No one would have harmed Rosalie. Everyone loved her. I worshiped her. I've known all along this would happen some day, but — " There was a little silence, then he said suddenly, "I want to tell you something. It's a confession, in a way. Funny, I never met you before today, but — "

Melville Fairr sat silent, waiting. Many others had said the same thing to him in his lifetime.

"A situation like this — people talk. Especially since we have lived such a secluded life. People love to speculate. Rosalie, ten years older than I and a helpless invalid. Laura, nineteen, and lovely. The three of us, shut up here together."

He caught his breath. "The hell of it is, it's half true. No one knows it but me — and now, you. Dr. Fletcher told me, very confidentially, that there had been talk. All of a sudden I realized — Mr. Fairr," he said passionately, "I adored Rosalie. I would have, done anything for her. I would have died for her. I could hardly believe it when she said she'd marry me. But I'm in love with Laura. I guess I have been for a long time."

Melville Fairr went on listening silently.

"Naturally I've never let Laura even guess. Naturally I never will."

The moon finally slipped behind the trees, and a shadow crossed the terrace.

"Thanks," Tony whispered at last. Then, "I guess I would like to be alone for a bit."

Melville Fairr went away quietly.

Only one lamp was lighted in the big library, where Laura Kane sat curled in a big chair, her chin resting on her fist, her face white in the shadows. She looked up sharply as Melville Fairr came in.

"My dear Miss Kane — " he began.

"Thanks," she interrupted, "but I don't want sympathy. I don't need it. But I wish you'd sit down. I want to tell you the truth."

Again Melville Fairr listened and waited.

"I've got to tell somebody," she said almost defensively. In a moment she went on in a rush of words, "I couldn't have stood it any longer. I think I would have run away. You don't know — Mr. Fairr, I've been cooped up here since I was fourteen. No one here would have understood. Tony — Dr. Fletcher — and then Lance — they all adored her. But, Mr. Fairr, invalids can be terribly difficult, and cross, and demanding. Especially, spoiled invalids. And she'd made her first success when she was so very young, and everyone had spoiled her ever since."

Melville Fairr said nothing. He would never tell anyone that Laura's opinion of Rosalie coincided with his own, formed though it was on only a few hours with her.

"I'm young. I want some fun out of life. I hate being here, being a hermit. And besides, I'm so in love with Tony — "

She jumped to her feet. "I didn't mean to tell you that! I don't know why I did. It's true, though. I was crazy about him when I first met him. That was just after mother was taken ill and I was called home from school. It was just teen–age stuff then. But now I'm grown up, and it's different."

She stood there, looking at him. "I've had to be so careful not to let anyone guess. Dr. Fletcher warned me that in a situation like this there was bound to be talk. And I've had to be extra careful not to let Tony know. I've never told anybody except you and I never will."

Suddenly she started for the door. "I'm going to tell Molly to make a pot of coffee," and she was gone.

This time, it was Melville Fairr who sighed.

In a little while there were footsteps in the hall, and Lance appeared in the doorway. His face was pale, almost haggard.

"All this business — " he burst out. "Rosalie dead. People saying it's murder. It seems so senseless. Why? Do they think somebody poisoned her?"

"No," Melville Fairr said. "Nobody thinks that.

"I just don't get it at all," the young man said. He plumped down in the nearest chair. "Damn! I can't believe it. Why, only this afternoon we were sitting right in this room talking. About whether I'd ever be any good on the stage. About her experiences in the theater. About the schools I'd gone to. We were really getting acquainted."

A wry smile crossed his face. "That sounds funny, doesn't it. Getting acquainted with one's own mother. But that's what we've been doing ever since the day I arrived here."

He frowned. "Mr. Fairr, I want to tell you something. I wish you wouldn't tell Laura, or Tony or anybody."

Melville Fairr listened.

Lance said, "I told everyone that I'd come here because of a life–long devotion to a mother I'd never seen. Someone I'd worshiped in my dreams. Everyone believed it. Even she believed it. But it wasn't that at all."

Melville Fairr sat still as a shadow, waiting for him to go on.

"It was half curiosity," Lance said slowly.

"I wanted to see if she was as much a — a monster — as my father described her. He hated her so. He never would speak her name, he always called her 'that woman.' I know, now it was because he was a failure and she — she was Rosalie!"

The young man looked down at the floor. "The other reason, Mr. Fairr — you see, we were always poor. Not hungry, nor homeless, but — poor. In my father's last weeks, when he knew he was dying, he told me over and over to come to her, to get my share of the money she had made, because, after all, I was her son. You see?"

Melville Fairr did not so much as nod.

There was a sudden knock. Dr. Fletcher stood in the open doorway. There was a shiny little gun in his hand. Melville Fairr moved silently across the room to his side.

"I just took this away from Tony," the doctor said. "I don't blame him for wanting to be with her. I do myself." He slipped the gun in his pocket and said, "I'd like a word with you, Mr. Fairr."

The two men walked through the shadows of the wide hall to the deeper shadows of the terrace.

"If anyone had a reason for murdering Rosalie," the doctor said, "I did."

Little Mr. Fairr shuddered. Murder. He didn't like the word. He looked up at the sky, from which the moon had fled. A few stars were there, not paying any attention, minding their own mysterious business.

"You might as well know it. You're an easy man to talk to, Fairr. Don't know why I trust you, but I do. Well, here it is. We all knew the terms of her will. Her fortune is to be divided equally among the four of us — Laura, Tony, Lance and myself. She made the will, signed it, and told us about it at dinner only a few days ago."

He went on. "No one knows, except yourself now, Mr. Fairr, that I am, not only deeply in debt, but — " he seemed to be forcing the words through a choking throat — "please understand — trying to build a hospital — money entrusted to me — needed more — undoubtedly I could be sent to prison — undoubtedly should be — now Rosalie's death solves all that — " His voice broke off sharply.

Melville Fairr stood in the shadows and said nothing.

"I'd even thought of murdering her. It would have been so easy. So very easy. Without her suffering. Being alive didn't matter to her any more. It was as though she had died that night on the floor of her dressing room. And it would have happened soon in any case. Yes, I meant to do it. But then — suddenly she seemed so happy. Happier than she had been in years. Why? I don't know. I suppose I'll never know, now. But how, when she was so happy, could I let her die?"

The heady odor of magnolia blossoms came up from the gardens.

"Someone else, perhaps," the doctor whispered. "Anyone else. But not Rosalie. Not *Rosalie!*"

Somewhere, in some far–off time, a nightbird was singing its heart out to the stars.

Melville Fairr walked to the edge of the terrace and stood looking over the darkened gardens and the darker trees. Again the sudden chill crept over him, in spite, of the warm and sweetly scented wind.

Such a few hours ago he had been talking with Rosalie. *Rosalie.* On this same terrace, with the sunset rimming the far–off trees with fire; and again, later, with the first moonlight of the evening moving timidly across the lawn.

"I like you, Mr. Fairr. I'm sorry I brought you up here on a false alarm." The voice of Rosalie, forever unforgettable. "But it's nice having you here. You're the sort of person I can talk to."

He'd sat there, quiet, listening to her.

"Mr. Fairr, I know I'm going to die very soon, and everyone will be tremen–dously sorry. Tony and Laura will console each other — oh yes, I've watched it all along. They'll tell each other about love and end up making each other very happy. Lance will have everything he came here for. His career he'll do well by it. Arnold will have his precious hospital and pay off the debts that have been driving him out of his mind."

Her laugh was as quick and silvery as a falling star.

"Oh yes. Mr. Fairr, I know all about everything. I don't know why I sent for a private detective. I haven't done too badly myself."

The stars had been coming out shyly, one by one.

"To be happy," she had whispered, not to Melville Fairr. "I'd forgotten what it was."

He remembered the smile on her cold lips, so pitifully short a time later.

Suddenly he turned and walked into the library. They were all there, but the room was silent. Too silent. Melville Fairr picked up his cup of coffee, sipped it, and put it down again.

"I'd like to play a kind of game," he said. "A silly kind of game. Let's try to recreate everything we talked about at dinner tonight."

People talked to little Mr. Melville Fairr; they also listened to him. Almost always they did whatever he suggested.

There was a brief silence and then Tony said, "Well, baseball. I'd been listening to the broadcast."

"And I was pretty stupid," Lance said, "because I never learned much about baseball."

"And, oh," Laura said, "Mother began talking about some Army–Navy game she'd seen and she didn't know any more about it than Lance did about baseball. Then somehow we got to talking about our ages."

She laughed, and it was the same silvery little sound that Melville Fairr had heard earlier that night on the terrace.

"Mother said it was lucky we twins were born in 1933, because she had been born in 1913, and she could always figure out how old we were.

"That makes no sense," Tony said.

"Neither did Mother's arithmetic," Laura told him. "She just always figured we were twenty years younger than she was."

Suddenly it was the dinner table conversation come to life again. Melville Fairr closed his eyes. Talk had gone on to the stage and screen, Lance confessed to having wanted to be an actor from the age of five. Laura remembered her first visit to the movies. Tony raved about the first talkie he'd seen.

Rosalie had remembered, too. Mary Pickford as Cinderella. Chu Chin Chow. Sally, Irene and Mary.

Lance had said, "Will you ever forget Clifton Webb in *The Little Show*? I was a ten–year–old kid, in New York on my Christmas vacation — "

Suddenly the spell that had taken them back to the dinner table was broken. Laura cried out, "But what does all this have to do with Mother?"

Everyone looked at Melville Fairr.

"She was murdered," Melville Fairr told them softly, "by the strangest weapon I have ever encountered. She was murdered by — an excess of happiness."

Again the odor of magnolias swept through the room on the warm wind.

Laura whispered, "I don't know what you mean."

"I'll tell you exactly what I mean," Melville Fairr said. "Happiness. It killed her with a smile on her lips and her face turned upward to the moon — just as surely as if it had been a knife."

Again he closed his eyes for an instant.

"You have been wondering why I was here, why she sent for me. It was because of certain doubts in her mind. But those doubts were settled tonight at dinner, not by myself but by the man who killed her. He did so by accident, but the result would have been the same as regards her knowing. Because I had made certain inquiries."

He turned to the blond young man. "You remembered seeing Clifton Webb in *The Little Show*. But *The Little Show* closed in 1929. Four years before you were born — if you were Lance Kane!"

He went on quickly to the others: "I had learned that the real Lance Kane died a year ago. This Lance Kane had his general build and coloring, and remember, he is an actor. It has not been too difficult for him to play the role of a nineteen–year–old–lost son."

"And Rosalie?" Dr. Fletcher asked. "She engaged you to find out?"

"Yes," Melville Fairr said, "but not for the reason you think. She wanted it to be this way. She had sensed it from the very beginning. I had not had a chance to tell her what I had learned, but our conversation at dinner convinced her. She remembered the same show — and when it closed. She knew then that her heart had been right — that he was not her son but could be her lover. So she walked with him through the moonlight in the meadow of waving grass, told him, and died smiling at him. Her heart broke with happiness."

Lance rose from his chair. "All right. You've got it almost pat. I meant just to stick around until she kicked off. But then you turned up, and I had to do something fast. I took her for a walk in the meadow, and told her I loved her. That was that."

He turned to face them all. "What are you going to do about it? My story will be that I planned to impersonate her long–lost son, but soon as I met her I fell for her and couldn't go through with it. I didn't know she had a bum heart. I told her the truth, and the shock of it killed her. Do you think a coroner's inquest is going to give me even a slight scowl? To say nothing of a jury!"

He was right, and Melville Fairr knew he was right.

"There are juries and juries," Dr. Fletcher said.

The gun was fired almost before Melville Fairr realized it was out of the doctor's pocket. The young man fell, shock and surprise on his handsome face. Laura cried out softly and clutched at Tony, who put a protecting arm around her. Dr. Fletcher stood, still holding the gun.

"But not Rosalie," the doctor said very softly. "Not *Rosalie*."

Melville Fairr said, "I've already had my bag sent down to the station, and it's a very short walk from here, so you don't need to bother sending for a taxi."

He turned to Dr. Fletcher, who was standing in the doorway. "You can do one of several things. You can wipe off that gun, squeeze the young man's hand around it, call the police and tell how, in front of witnesses, he shot himself because of the sudden — and natural — death of the mother he had only known a short time. Or you can tell the whole truth, and involve yourselves and Rosalie's memory — in a lot of unpleasantness."

Dr. Fletcher interrupted him with a gesture. "Rosalie always hated un–pleasantness." He smiled at them all as he walked out the door. It was a moment later that they heard the shot.

Outside, the moon was long since gone and the night was very still.

Fred Dannay dubbed this story as Craig's finest ever when it was appeared in Ellery Queen's Mystery Magazine. As Craig continued to write at the Meredith agency, her work showed marked improvement. It was an obvious step in the right direction when she titled a story from a quote by Keats's "Endymion." Not only that, but Craig's peculiar brand of naming conventions is back with characters like Dr. Martin Martin.
-JM

Beyond the Shadow of a Dream

"I know a lot of lawyers who could use a good psychiatrist," John J. Malone said, "but this is the first time I know of a psychiatrist needing a good lawyer."

Dr. Martin A. Martin said, "That's very funny, Malone." He didn't laugh. "But you have needed me a few times at that." His handsome face managed to crack itself into something faintly resembling a smile. "The Gifford case, for instance."

"You handled the Gifford case very nicely," Malone conceded, "and I defended him very brilliantly, if I may say so. Though both of us know that the guy was as sane as a hoot owl." That didn't sound right, so he tried it again. "The guy was as hoot as a sane owl." He tried a few more variations, then gave up. He started to say, "Of course, you're a terrific ham in front of a jury," but he caught himself just in time. After all, it was Dr. Martin A. Martin who was paying for the drinks at Joe the Angel's City Hall Bar.

"But this situation isn't funny," the doctor said. He noticed the condition of Malone's glass and waved at the bartender. "I need advice, and I need help."

"If it's a traffic ticket," Malone said, "or — "

"It's murder," Dr. Martin A. Martin said. "*My* murder."

The drinks arrived. Malone picked them up and said to Joe the Angel, "My friend and I have things to discuss in the backroom. Bring us two more of these in about five minutes — and leave out the water."

A minute later he slid into a booth in the backroom and looked at his new client: Dr. Martin Alexander Martin, tall and athletic, dark hair graying at the temples, right now a little pale under his healthy tan.

"Who do you plan to murder?" the little lawyer asked cheerfully. "Anyone I know?"

"It's a difficult situation," the doctor said.

"Murder often is," Malone said. "Go on."

114

"I have a patient. I can't tell you who he is — " the famous psychiatrist paused, drew a quick breath and went on, "Oh, hell, Malone, you'll nose around and find out anyway. It's John Evarts."

Malone said, "Well?" This was no time to make comments. Evidently Dr. Martin A. Martin's clients were in the millionaire class these days. He wondered how much he could decently ask for giving a little free advice.

"Not long ago, Evarts came to me," the doctor went on. "I knew him — as a friend, not as a patient. Been at his home a number of times. He came to me because he'd been dreaming."

"Most people do," Malone said. "Dream, I mean."

"He's going to murder *me*." Dr. Martin A. Martin said.

Joe the Angel arrived just then with two pairs of straight shots and a lone glass of water which he set in the exact center of the table.

The psychiatrist gulped one drink and said, "He's been dreaming of having committed horrible — indescribable — crimes. Of waking in the morning, feeling exhausted, as though he hadn't slept."

"If he's building up an insanity defense in advance," Malone said, "in case he wants to murder his wife or one of his rich uncles, I'd say he was on the right track."

Dr. Martin A. Martin chased his second drink by lighting a cigarette and saying, "But the thing is, he has committed murders." He reached for the check with one hand and his wallet with the other. "If you can spare a few minutes, I'd like you to look at the notes in my office."

Malone downed both his drinks and said, "Fine."

Dr. Martin's office, on Lake Shore Drive, was exactly what Malone had imagined: an elevator boy with West Point manners; a waiting room in dove gray, with comfortable chairs, conveniently placed ashtrays, the latest in light fiction on modernistic tables, and a receptionist whose dress matched the pale gray carpet, whose long sleek hair matched the maple furniture, and whose eyes said she would match pennies with anybody.

"Why, Mr. Malone!" she said. "How nice to see you again!"

Malone blinked and tried to remember.

Dr. Martin laughed mirthlessly and said, "Miss Adams never forgets a face or a name. She took notes for me at the trial of Alswell McJackson, whom you defended so brilliantly."

"With your help," Malone said modestly.

"Miss Adams," the doctor said, opening a door, "I have gone for the day."

Dr. Martin A. Martin's private office made the reception room look like a broken–down hut in the slums of Old Delhi. It was subdued, restful, and as expensive as a second mortgage on the Hope diamond. Malone repressed an impulse to lie down on the two–inch–thick pale–green rug and confess to everything from the Custer Massacre to the kidnaping of Charley Ross.

"No one, not even Miss Adams, has ever seen these notes," Dr. Martin A. Martin said. His crisp professional tone suddenly made the room seem like any other doctor's office, anywhere. "Mr. Evarts consulted me for the first time on April 13. At that time his dream did not seem to have any significance. However — "

He opened a folder and began to read aloud. "Dated, April 13. 'I dreamed that I rose from bed, dressed myself, left the house and took an El train to the south side. I entered an apartment about half a block from 63rd street. The apartment was locked, but I broke open the door. There was a horrible old woman lying on the bed. I cut her throat with a knife I found in her kitchen. I ransacked the apartment, but found nothing of value. Then in an excess of rage, I set fire to the apartment and fled. The dream ended there but I woke in my own bed, sweating and exhausted.' "

The doctor put the folder down and said, "Dreams of that type are not uncommon. And I was not surprised at John Evarts consulting me so privately — without any notes being taken except my own, which I made rather hastily after he left." He looked up. "The notes are mine, but the story is his. He told me his dream on April 13th. His dream had taken place the night before — April 12th. I found this in the newspaper, quite by accident."

The clipping he handed Malone was dated April 13. It told of the brutal murder of an old woman. Malone felt a small chill run up and, down his back. The body of an old woman had been found in the ruins of her ransacked and half–burned tenement apartment. Her throat had been cut with a knife from her own kitchen.

"Of course it could have been mere coincidence," the doctor said. "But later he had another dream. In that one he broke into the kitchenette apartment of a young woman in the Wilson Avenue district, stabbed her with a paring knife he found beside the kitchen sink, slashed at her dying body savagely, and, again, fled."

Malone reached out his hand for the clipping that told of the brutal stabbing and mutilation of a young stenographer.

"He dreamed it," Dr. Martin A. Martin said, "on May 7th."

The clipping was dated May 8th. The story it told was not pretty.

"There are two others," the doctor went on, "pretty much along the same line. A dream of a girl picked up at a bar, stabbed with a nail file that she carried in her purse. That dream was the night of June 2nd." He handed over another clipping, dated June 3rd. "And another dream of a — well, you'd better read it for yourself. He dreamed about it on the night of June 25th; it actually happened that night, just before midnight."

Malone read the fourth clipping, then pushed it aside and waited.

"Now," Dr. Martin A. Martin said, "he's going to murder *me*."

Malone said, "You don't want a lawyer, you want a bodyguard." It seemed to him that his voice sounded a little hoarse and shrill. He tried to laugh, and failed.

The psychiatrist didn't seem to notice. He shoved the notes in his desk drawer and continued: "Last night he dreamed that he came here, late at night. He dreamed that he rang the night bell, and I admitted him. You see, this is not only my office but my home. I have a bedroom, a bath, and a kitchen beyond this office, but the only entrance is through the reception room."

"Go on," Malone said.

"He dreamed that we came into the consulting room, where we are now. I sat down behind my desk. Suddenly he lunged at me across the desk, and stabbed me with a knife taken from my own kitchen."

There was a little silence. The pleasant room seemed unpleasantly cold.

"Did you live?" Malone inquired, very casually.

"No," the doctor said, just as casually. He rose and asked quietly, "Would you like a drink?"

"You're damned right I would," Malone said. He watched Dr. Martin A. Martin walk through the door that led to the kitchen. Then he closed his eyes and tried to imagine John Evarts, millionaire sportsman, in this same room, telling his frightening story. He tried to imagine how Dr. Martin A. Martin's bedroom was decorated, judging from the reception room and consultation room, opened his eyes fast, and hoped a blush didn't show on his face.

"Thanks," he said, accepting a glass. "Now, what kind of advice do you want? Move away, buy a gun, or call the cops?"

"I may be foolish," the doctor said, "but I've already bought a gun. I don't want to move away. And since it is John Evarts, I don't think I ought to discuss this with the police."

"Having taken your own advice," Malone told him, "what the hell did you call me for?"

Dr. Martin A. Martin laughed slightly and said, "I thought you might like to hear an interesting story and have a drink with me." He refilled Malone's glass.

"Nice of you," Malone said. "But since you expect to be murdered any hour now, you'd better make out a check for my consultation fee. Beyond that, any advice I give you is strictly on the house."

Dr. Martin grinned and pushed a button on his desk. A lovely voice from the box said, "Yes — ?"

"Make out a check to John J. Malone for legal services," the doctor said. "Make it for five hundred dollars, and mail it to his office."

Malone wanted to say he'd be glad to take it with him and save the doctor the price of a stamp; but he changed his mind and said nothing.

The doctor smiled wryly at him and said, "If I'm still alive tomorrow, I'll stop payment on the check."

On his way back to the office, Malone paused at Joe the Angel's. There were a few things he wanted to think about. At the top of the list was the luscious and long–eyelashed Miss Adams. There surely must be some way of making a date with her. Next to the top was the matter of the man who dreamed he was a murderer.

After two ryes and a little meditation, he told Joe the Angel the story, translating it into something that had happened to a friend of his while vacationing in Haiti. Joe listened, and told Malone of a similar occurrence that had been told to him by his aunt from the old country. A Hungarian janitor from the City Hall, attracted by the conversation, bought a round of beers and told the sad story of what had once happened to the nephew of his second cousin. By that time a reporter from the *Tribune* horned in with, "Say, let me tell you what happened to a friend of mine while he was driving past a cemetery in Nebraska — "

Malone decided it was time to go back to his office.

"There'll be a check for five hundred dollars in the mail tomorrow morning," he told Maggie. "So see if you can cash a check for a hundred bucks at the liquor store on Washington Street. If they won't do it, try that bookie over on Clark. And pay yourself some back salary. But when that check comes in, get it into the bank *fast.*"

"Why?" Maggie asked, reaching for her hat. "Is the guy going to change his mind?"

Malone said, "No, but I doubt if he'll live till morning. Wear your coat, it's colder than an old maid's elbow outside."

Maggie put on her coat. "The rent is due," she said reproachfully, "but you need a hundred dollars. Cash, that is."

"I think I have a date," Malone told her, "and don't ask questions."

He went into his private office and sat for a long time, thinking things over. Finally he looked up John Evarts' telephone number in his very personal telephone book, dialed, and when a dignified male voice answered, he came back with twice as much dignity and said, "This is Mr. O'Leary's office calling. Mr. O'Leary was to meet Mr. Evarts this evening and has mislaid the address — "

A moment later he wrote down on a tattered envelope the fact that John Evarts would be at The Blue Casino sometime after nine.

He thought for another minute, then dialed Dr. Martin A. Martin's number. "Miss Adams? This is Mr. Malone. No, I don't want to talk to Dr. Martin. I want to talk to you. Yes, yes, I do. Why? Because you're a very lovely person, and I really want to know you better. How about dinner tonight?"

After several minutes of coaxing, which he suspected was basically un–necessary, he said, "Wonderful! Now where do I call for you?"

She would have to live in Rogers Park, Malone reflected bitterly as he hung up.

While he dressed and shaved, he considered bringing her an orchid, then gave up the idea. Miss Adams gave him the definite impression that all he needed was a friendly smile and a bag of popcorn. Or perhaps, a square meal and an evening at The Blue Casino. Besides, he reminded himself, it was really only information he was after.

Thinking back, he wondered if she picked out her own clothes. She was "definitely what the well–dressed receptionist should wear." It was certainly smart of Dr. Martin A. Martin to let her skip those starched white uniforms usually seen in doctors' reception rooms. Her soft gray dress with the little pink frill at the throat would either take a patient's mind off his worries, or make him think up some new ones.

When he picked up Miss Adams at the Rogers Park address, he decided that she did choose her own clothes. Dr. Martin A. Martin might have thought of the soft gray dress with the pink frill, but he could never have been responsible for the fur coat that nestled against Malone's shoulder like a lonesome kitten. Malone expected it to purr, any minute. And it did.

"It was so sweet of you to phone me, Mr. Malone."

"It was so sweet of you to answer, Miss Adams." He wondered what she was wearing, under the fur coat.

It turned out to be a rose-red strapless affair, exactly the same shade as her lipstick. He decided once and for all that she did pick out her own clothes. Even an eminent psychiatrist like Dr. Martin A. Martin couldn't be that smart.

Then he found himself wondering how she could afford a dress like that on a receptionist's salary.

She smiled at him across the table and cooed, "I made it myself."

Malone blinked. He hoped he wasn't blushing. He said, "So, in addition to all your other talents, you also do mind–reading."

She laughed. "I didn't have to be a mind–reader. I saw you looking very thoughtfully at my dress. Naturally, you were trying to figure out how I could be an honest woman, and still buy a dress like this on the salary I earn. Now you have the answer. Including everything, down to the last spool of thread, it cost nineteen dollars and twelve cents."

"If I'd met a girl like you twenty years ago," Malone said, "I'd be a rich man today." His eyes narrowed. "I suppose you keep a pair of minks locked up in a cage, and every now and then they provide you with a new fur coat."

"Not only that," she said cheerfully, "but I keep a pair of silver foxes and a pair of chinchillas, in case I get tired of wearing mink." She laughed again. "Mr. Malone, you'd be surprised what you can buy for ten dollars down and ten dollars a week. Any year now, and the coat will be mine."

"Curiously," Malone said, "I have the damnedest notion that you're telling the truth."

Dinner, six drinks, and two dances later, he had learned a number of things. There was only one entrance to Dr. Martin A. Martin's office. She preferred double bacardis to any other drink. Yes, she did have an almost photographic memory. Dr. Martin A. Martin was wonderful. All his women patients adored him. Yes, most of his patients were women.

No, Malone told himself, it would take more than a mink coat or a diamond bracelet — unless it *was* a bag of popcorn, or one more bacardi.

"There's one of his patients now," Miss Adams said suddenly.

Malone looked up quickly. John Evarts had just come into The Blue Casino. The little lawyer scowled. Evarts certainly didn't look like a man who needed a psychiatrist. A diet and a good gymnasium, perhaps, but no more.

The millionaire sportsman was a big man, over six feet, heavily built, with fat just beginning to overlay the muscles. His broad, friendly face was pinkish. He looked as though he got a lot of fun out of just being alive.

The woman beside him — Malone blinked, and took a second look.

She looked like a very well bred and very well groomed horse. High strung as a racing filly, but better controlled. Malone had a feeling that she was brown all over. Her smooth brown hair was beautifully dressed, as sleek as though it had been curried. Her angular face was tanned to just the correct shade. Her dress, too, was brown, obviously expensive, from just the right shop, and just as obviously not from Paris.

Miss Adams muttered something under her breath.

Malone jumped at least an inch. "Someone you know?" he asked politely.

"That woman," Miss Adams said. "Mrs. John Evarts. One of Dr. Martin's patients. I don't know why the doctor puts up with her. I know it's fashionable to consult Dr. Martin, but she could have had a better excuse than dreaming she was married to a jockey."

The little lawyer hastily choked back half a dozen things he was on the verge of saying. "Is that her husband with her?"

"I hope it is," Miss Adams said. "She — she needs a good psychiatrist like — like I need another bacardi."

"She probably does need a good psychiatrist," Malone said gallantly. He waved at the passing waiter.

It was some hours later that he sat on the edge of his bed and debated whether or not it would be simpler to take his clothes off now, or sleep in them and change in the morning. It was a long and serious debate, and just as he had decided to flip a coin, the telephone rang.

He determined not to answer it. Telephones, at this hour of the night, usually meant trouble, and he was tired. But he reached for the receiver — trouble or not, he was curious.

It was Dr. Martin A. Martin. His voice was tense, and he was talking fast.

"He's on his way here, Malone."

"Nonsense," Malone yawned. "You'd better see a good psychiatrist." He realized that was the wrong thing to say and added hastily, "You can relax. From the condition Evarts was in when he left The Blue Casino, it'll be twenty–four hours before he can hit the broad side of a barn with a hand axe. Lock the door and go to bed."

"Malone," Dr. Martin said desperately, *"he's at the door!"*

"Shoot him," Malone said wearily.

"Malone. My gun — "

There was a sound Malone couldn't quite identify, and then silence. The little lawyer sat on the edge of his bed for a few minutes, trying to think things over. Finally he told himself that he could sleep anytime, and put in a call for Captain von Flanagan, of the Homicide Squad.

At last a sleepy and indignant von Flanagan mumbled, "You're drunk."

"That may be," Malone said, "but I know a murder when I hear one. And I can tell you all about this one, so you'd better pick me up in front of my hotel in fifteen minutes."

The car, sirens screeching, actually arrived in slightly over ten minutes. In the back seat, von Flanagan was still tucking his shirt in and adjusting his tie. Malone got in fast, and gave the Lake Shore Drive address. Then he settled back and told von Flanagan the whole story.

"Dr. Martin Martin!" von Flanagan interrupted once. It was a gasp.

"John Evarts!" he interrupted a second time. "Why, the guy must be nuts!"

"That seems to be the general idea," Malone said calmly. He wished he were asleep.

Nobody answered Dr. Martin's bell. Nobody answered repeated poundings on the door. Malone felt a few small chills running up and down his spine, like small mice with cold wet feet.

It took a little time to rouse the janitor to open the door with his passkey. The reception room was dark and empty, but a light showed around the door to the inner office. Von Flanagan pushed the door open, took one quick look, and grabbed the nearest telephone to call his office for everything and everybody that would be needed.

"Don't touch anything," Malone said weakly, forgetting that von Flanagan was head of homicide.

Before von Flanagan's boys had arrived, he and Malone had determined a few things.

The most important one was that there was no other living person in the apartment with the exception of themselves.

The knife that had cut Dr. Martin A. Martin's throat had come from the little kitchenette back of his office.

The gun in Dr. Martin A. Martin's hand was an Iver Johnson .32. It had recently been fired.

Miss Adams had told the truth; there was only one entrance to the combination office–apartment, and that was through the reception room.

As soon as the first arrivals had taken over their official duties, Malone drew von Flanagan aside.

"They know what to do. We'd better get going."

Von Flanagan growled that this was not time to go out for a drink.

"John Evarts," Malone reminded him. "The doc must of missed with that peashooter of his, and according to the doc's notes, Evarts must have gone home."

The police officer got the idea right away, left a few instructions, and got going. Reporters were already coming into the lobby downstairs.

"I'll have an arrest before morning," von Flanagan promised them.

Somehow Malone wished he hadn't said that.

The police car drew up quietly in front of the building where John Evarts lived. A self–service elevator took them up to the penthouse.

Again, pounding on the door and repeated rings on the bell drew no results. Not for a long time, at least. Finally a voice through the door said, very sleepily, "Who is it?"

"Police," von Flanagan bellowed.

The door opened an inch, secured on the other side by a bolt and chain. Von Flanagan shoved his credentials through the crack. The bolt and chain rattled and the door opened.

Mrs. Evarts had very obviously been wakened from a sound sleep. Her hair was becomingly mussed, her face naked of make–up. She had put on a deep–rose velvet robe.

"Oh, dear," she said, "I hope Albert — the chauffeur — isn't in trouble again. He does get into trouble on his nights off, but he's a good boy, really." She smothered a yawn and said, "Sorry. Sorry I took so long to answer the door, but I was sound asleep, and it's the maid's night out too."

"I've got to see your husband," von Flanagan said.

She smiled wanly. "You can see him, but I don't think you can talk to him. I poured him into bed when we came home, and I doubt if he'll stir for hours. But you can try."

She led the way down the hall. There was a huge living room whose decor would still be called ultramodern in 1966, and beyond it Malone could glimpse other rooms. There was a wide corridor hung with Oriental prints and which seemed to have doors opening off in all directions. Mrs. Evarts paused at one of the doors and knocked.

Von Flanagan had evidently grown tired of knocking on doors and getting no answers. He reached for the knob.

"He's probably sleeping like the dead," Mrs. Evarts said apologetically.

She was almost right. John Evarts wasn't sleeping, but he was dead.

He was curled up in bed, the covers comfortably tucked around him. One arm, in a flamboyant striped pajama sleeve, was outside the covers. The sleeve was made even more colorful by the blood that had run down from the bullet hole in his forehead.

Mrs. Evarts let loose with a well–bred scream.

Malone said hoarsely, "If it turns out that he was shot with an Iver Johnson .32 — and somehow I think it will — "

"I am not superstitious," Malone said firmly. "It's that I know how to let well enough alone." He downed his drink in one gulp and waved at Joe the Angel.

"But Malone," von Flanagan said in a plaintive voice, "I promised an arrest before morning."

"It's morning right now," Malone said, "unless you call half–past 5 yesterday." He scowled. "Yesterday. That's what I've been trying to remember. Because of yesterday being tomorrow."

"Malone," Joe the Angel said, leaning on the bar, "go home. You need a good night's steep." ·

"Tomorrow," Malone mused, "and by tomorrow it may be yesterday. Give my friend here another drink and charge it to me."

"Tomorrow," Joe the Angel said, "tomorrow you pay the bill." He moved down the bar.

"I'm not superstitious either," Captain von Flanagan said. "But it's a damned funny thing to think about. Here's this guy, dreams about committing murders. Tells this high–class psychiatrist about it. Turns out, though, the murders *were* committed. Only he never left no fingerprints, he was never seen, and nobody thinks he even left his apartment." He scowled. "How could he have murdered people in his sleep, without ever leaving the place where he was sleeping?"

Joe the Angel shoved two drinks across the bar and said, "Something almost like that happened in the town where my aunt lived in the old country — "

"Go away," von Flanagan said. Absent–mindedly he paid for the drinks. "Then he dreams he killed the doctor. He goes to bed, sound asleep. Maybe he dreams again… "

Malone had a notion that small cold mice were now running up and down von Flanagan's back.

"He stabs the doctor. The doctor shoots *him*. And the two of them eight blocks away from each other all the time! Who dreamed what? And what kinda report am I going to make?"

The Hungarian janitor from the City Hall moved up and said, "In my country we have a belief that — "

"Go away," Malone said.

"And," von Flanagan added unhappily, "I promised an arrest by morning."

Malone finished his drink, slid off the stool, and said, "It won't be morning till the sun comes up. Let's go and make the arrest right now."

The sun was on the verge of coming up when they arrived at the apartment. This time the door was opened promptly by a tired–eyed young woman who said, "Well?"

Before von Flanagan could speak, Malone announced, "I thought you ought to know. As a defense lawyer, I've never lost a patient yet. I'll see you after the arrest, and you'd better bring your check book along, so you can give me a retainer."

She stared at him.

Von Flanagan said, "Mrs. Evarts, it is my duty to arrest you on suspicion of the murder of your husband, John Evarts, and the murder of Dr. Martin A. Martin. And I think you'd better take Mr. Malone's advice."

The sun was up and so was Joe the Angel. Von Flanagan growled at him across the double–sized coffee royal he was holding, "Don't you ever go to sleep?"

"Not when my friend Malone don't go to sleep," Joe the Angel said proudly. "Then I stay up all night and wait." He'd already heard the bare outline of what had happened. Mrs. John Evarts had broken down and admitted everything. She had engaged Malone as her attorney and he was already planning an insanity defense — after all, she had been consulting a psychiatrist for months. Malone now had a second five-hundred-dollar check to deposit as soon as the bank opened.

"Malone, you pay the bar bill any time," Joe said happily, "also the twenty dollars you owe me." He added to von Flanagan, "I bet you the twenty dollars he gets her off."

Von Flanagan sighed. "I'd have been in a fine spot if she'd denied everything. Now, Malone, how did you know?"

"Tomorrow and yesterday," Malone said. "Yesterday and tomorrow."

"He's drunk," Joe the Angel said, this time with purely professional pride. "Von Flanagan, you pay attention to what he says."

"To consult the doctor," Malone said, "Evarts would have had to come through the reception room. Yet Miss Adams, who really has a phenomenal memory, didn't recognize him when she saw him at The Blue Casino. She did recognize Mrs. Evarts as one of the many women patients who had fallen in love with her psychiatrist." He took a swallow of the coffee and said, "I will never know why women fall in love with psychiatrists, when they could just as well fall in love with a good lawyer, and for much less money."

"Go on," von Flanaaan said in a peevish voice.

"Dr. Martin figured out a lovely way of murdering John Evarts, so that he could marry Mrs. Evarts and the Evarts millions," Malone continued. "Every time there was a particularly brutal murder, of a particular type, in the newspapers, he would sit down and write a set of notes, presumably the result of an interview with John Evarts. Of course, Evarts never consulted Martin — the doc made it all up, including the dreams. And when he had notes on enough murders, he confided the whole story to me." Malone added, "Of course, I knew right away it was phony."

"How did you know?" demanded von Flanagan.

Malone drew a long breath. "The deal was, Mrs. Evarts was to get her husband up to the doctor's office, late at night. The doctor, after notifying me, was to shoot him. A knife from the doctor's kitchen was to be planted in Evarts's hand. Of course the doctor forgot one item in this set–up, which von Flanagan brilliantly realized at once."

Von Flanagan blinked, said nothing, and waited.

"To get the knife," Malone said, "Evarts would have had to cross the office into the kitchenette, take the knife, and come back — all in plain view of Dr. Martin A. Martin, who was presumably wide–awake and waiting for him, with a gun in his hand and a phone call in for me."

There was a little silence and then von Flanagan said, "Sure, I saw that right away."

"It was perfect for the doc except for one thing," Malone said. "Mrs. Evarts changed her mind. Maybe she decided she could do better than a psychiatrist. A lawyer, for instance. Or maybe she found out the doctor was two–timing her. Or maybe she just wanted all that money for herself." Malone paused. "For the love of Michael, Joe, make some more coffee! I've got to be in court at 10 in the morning, and it's almost 9 now."

"And you need a shave and a bath," Joe said sympathetically; "but talk loud so I can hear too." He moved away.

"I had figured out the set–up," Malone said, "up to the point where Dr. Martin A. Martin called me on the phone. I even knew — I was pretty sure I knew — what he was going to say. But just before the line, and he, both went dead, the doc said, 'Malone. My gun— ' And I thought he sounded shocked and surprised."

Joe called from the back room: "Louder Malone."

"I know now," Malone said, "that he was shocked and surprised because his gun wasn't there in his desk, and because he'd expected a drunken or drugged Evarts to be shoved through the door by his future widow. Instead, he saw Mrs. Evarts, with the previously agreed–upon knife in her hand. He was so shocked and surprised that he dropped the telephone and just sat there. Whereupon she stuck the knife neatly in his throat, stuck the gun with which she'd already killed her husband in the doctor's hand, and went quietly home to bed like a good girl to sleep the peaceful sleep of the innocent — until we crude and horrid people banged on the door and waked her up."

"But how did she expect to get away with it?" von Flanagan asked.

"She probably would have," Malone said, "if it hadn't been for — " he caught himself just in time " — you."

Joe came in with fresh coffee, and poured brandy into each cup.

"She probably planned originally to get Evarts into Dr. Martin's office, let the doctor shoot him, managed to stab the doctor, and then let the police decide who did what first," Malone said. "But Evarts spoiled her plan by getting good and drunk. She couldn't very well carry him for eight blocks. So she changed her plan and did it this way."

"But Malone," von Flanagan said, "How did she have the gun?"

"Mrs. Evarts is a smart babe," Malone told him. "She wasn't taking any chances on things going wrong, and she wanted the ammunition to be on her side. She probably got the gun from Dr. Martin's office sometime during the afternoon and carried it around with her, just in case."

After a little silence, von Flanagan asked, "One more thing, Malone. You said you knew right off that the doc's story was a phony?"

"Yesterday and tomorrow," Malone said again, with rising pride. "Dr. Martin's notes — remember, he wrote them himself. According to the doc's notes, Evarts had these dreams of murder, woke up limp as a bar rag, and every time it turned out that the murder had been committed. Each murder and each alleged dream of it took place at the same time. But then he dreamed he was *going* to commit murder; in the doc's case, Evarts dreamed a murder *before* it happened." Malone yawned and waved his cup at Joe the Angel. "If the doc's murder had been real," Malone said fuzzily, "it would have happened like the others — at the time Evarts was dreaming." Malone raised his head suddenly. "Or maybe it's the other way around... I'm going home."

It was twenty minutes to 10 when Malone walked into his office, shaved, showered, and put on the neat doublebreasted gray suit that he liked best for courtroom wear. His cheeks were pink and his eyes were bright.

Maggie stared at him.

"It's wonderful," Malone said, "what a good night's sleep will do."

"Court," Maggie reminded, still staring. "Ten o'clock."

Malone reached for the brief case she was handing him. With his other hand he tossed the check on her desk.

"Get this through the bank fast," he told her. "Pay yourself some salary, and save me a hundred dollars. I think I have a date tonight." He started toward the door, paused, and pulled out a crumpled envelope with a name and address scrawled on the back.

"And while you're out, I want you to send something to Miss Adams, at this address," he said. "A bag of popcorn — and have it wrapped as a gift."

Craig loved to include her own past careers as fodder for her mysteries, and killing off a true crime writer hits fairly close to home as Craig wrote for the Hearst syndicate for six months before being unceremoniously dumped for getting too involved in the cases. Her coverage of the Heirens case made more headlines for her and less for the accused murderer. -JM

One More Clue

The girl was very beautiful. She sat across the desk from John J. Malone and dabbed at her eyes with a silly–looking lace handkerchief. "I don't care what the police say," she told him. "Alvin didn't commit suicide. He didn't have any reason to commit suicide."

The little lawyer leaned back in his chair and regarded her benignly. "Suppose you start from the beginning, Miss Connell, and tell me all about it."

The girl brushed long black hair away from her face, hair as black, Malone thought, as the inside of a coal–cellar. But with attractions no coal–cellar had ever had for him before, he added silently. She was dressed in a light tan suit, a plain white blouse and a tiny tan hat, and Malone was sure that the outfit would never look quite so perfect on anyone else, ever. The man who'd come with her, Malone thought, didn't seem to be her type.

"Now, now," the man said. Malone glared at him. He glared back. "As Miss Connell's close friend," he said, "I advised her not to come here. I fail to see how a lawyer can do any good at all — "

"But he's John J. Malone," the girl said. "Really, Casper, we argued this through — " She looked at Malone and seemed ready to begin sniffling again.

"Your name is Helen Connell," Malone prompted her, "and you were born on — "

"July fourth, nineteen–thirty–five," she said, and stopped, and almost smiled.

"And my name is Casper Jorgenson," the man said, "and I was born on December eighth, nineteen–twenty–four, and I fail to see what any of this has to do with Alvin and what's — what's happened."

"My question exactly," Malone said smoothly. "What's happened?"

"It's all so horrible," the girl said. "Alvin couldn't possibly have killed himself. He had everything to live for. He and I were — " She stopped again and dabbed at her eyes. Casper Jorgenson and Malone simultaneously reached for hand–kerchiefs; Helen Connell took Malone's, said: "Thank you," without looking up, and began to cry in earnest.

"Here, here," Malone said helplessly. "Laugh and the world laughs with you, cry and you're all wet. And if you cry, you can't tell me what happened so I can help you. This Alvin was your fiancé?"

She looked up. "How did you know?" she said, and there was wonder in her voice.

Malone reflected that it would be nice if someone else — say, von Flanagan, or even Casper Jorgenson — would be so easily impressed by his marvelous deductive powers. Aloud, he only said: "See? I can help you, if you'll only tell me what happened."

"Helen, I seriously advise against this," Casper Jorgenson said. "The police know their job. If they say — "

But he couldn't have killed himself," the girl said. "Malone, listen. Last night, I was going to meet Alvin at his apartment. Alvin Breck. He had work to do, and I was supposed to pick him up at ten–thirty; we were going out to a movie. He — when I got there, Malone, he was dead. And now the police say he committed suicide."

"What makes them think that?" Malone said after a second.

"Just because the gas was turned on, and all the windows were closed and locked, and he was all alone in the room, the police say he — killed himself. Malone, he always worked with the windows and door shut and locked. He said fresh air was a soporific. Malone, he couldn't have killed himself."

The little lawyer thought of several possible answers, and selected one with care. "The police usually know what they're doing."

"But Alvin — he and I were engaged. We were going to be married. Every—thing was so wonderful."

Helen Connell had a point, Malone reflected. He couldn't imagine someone engaged to this girl committing suicide. "Maybe he had money problems," he suggested after a second.

"Everything was going so well," the girl said mournfully. "He had a new assignment, and it looked as if he was going to start making real money. Malone, he wouldn't have any money problems."

"Assignment?" Malone said.

"He was a writer. He wrote about — about crimes, Malone. And now he's dead and somebody killed him, and they say it's suicide and they won't listen to me and... "

"Now, now," Malone said quickly. "Now, now. Remember I'm going to help you. He tried to look comforting and dependable. "You think that Alvin Breck was murdered," he said. "Who do you think murdered him?"

Helen Connell looked up with surprise written all over her lovely face. "Oh, Malone," she said, "how would I know?"

Half an hour later, Malone was seated in a booth at Joe the Angel's City Hall Bar. In the opposite seat of the same booth, Captain Daniel von Flanagan scowled at a boilermaker, picked it up, drank half of it off, and said: "All I want to know is why you got me down here, Malone. What's your ulterior motive?"

"Just a friendly little chat," the lawyer said, brushing cigar ashes off his vest. "For old times' sake."

"And what," von Flanagan said suspiciously, "would you want to chat about? Except the old lady who shot her husband last week, there hasn't even been a murder in Chicago in a month. And don't tell me you're defending the old lady. It's an open and shut case, Malone, and I won't have you coming in and messing it up for me. I... "

"All I know is what I read in the papers," Malone said disarmingly. "I don't even want to hear about your old lady. I mean the one who shot her husband." Malone took a sip of his own drink, waited a second, and said: "No murders? I'll bet there must have been a couple of interesting suicides, though."

"Nothing much," von Flanagan said.

"Oh, I don't know," Malone said. "There was that writer, just yesterday. I must have read about it somewhere. Died in a gas-filled room, all the windows and the door locked from the inside."

"Nothing new about that," von Flanagan said, "except maybe the pigeon, and we got an explanation for the pigeon."

"Pigeon?"

Von Flanagan looked up. "Malone, are you working on that?" he said. "That's a suicide, and let me tell you it's open and shut. I've got enough troubles without you making them any worse, mixing up nice simple suicides for me. Let me tell you... "

Malone listened patiently through a recital of von Flanagan's troubles for some minutes. At last he said: "I sympathize with you. Believe me, I do. And who said I was working on the suicide? What would I want to do that for?"

"I wouldn't know," von Flanagan said. "But I suspect the worst."

"You just have a nasty mind," Malone said. "I'm just interested. Isn't there some way of turning on the gas from outside a room? I mean, the police would naturally think of that first."

"Sure we did," von Flanagan said, "and there isn't. You have to turn the handle on the oven, right there in the kitchen. Open and shut."

"What did the suicide note say?" Malone asked.

"No note."

"A writer, and he didn't leave a suicide note?"

Von Flanagan shrugged. "Why should he write one? He wasn't getting paid for it. He was one of those true–crime writers. Did a story on me once — good story, too. I gave him a lot of material."

"Very nice," Malone said. "You must show me the story some day. Didn't he have any motive for suicide?"

"You're asking a lot of questions, Malone," von Flanagan said.

The little lawyer tried to look supremely innocent. "I'm just interested," he said. "I'm curious, that's all."

"Curiosity," said von Flanagan oracularly, "killed the cat. But about motive: sure, he must have had a motive. Maybe he was losing on the horses."

"I didn't know he played the horses," Malone said.

"We found betting slips, racing forms, in his apartment."

"Oh." Malone waited a minute, and took another drink. "About that pigeon — " he said.

"The pigeon interests you, right, Malone?" Von Flanagan almost grinned. "This Breck, he had a friend who kept pigeons. Some of this other guy's pigeons were sick, so he gave Breck one pigeon to keep, kind of so that pigeon wouldn't get the disease."

"What was his name?" Malone said.

"The pigeon?"

"The man who owned the pigeons," Malone, said wearily.

"What do you want to know for?" von Flanagan said. "But after all, Malone, if you are working on this, what harm can you do me? It's an open and shut case. Casper Jorgenson — little guy with glasses. He keeps pigeons."

"Casper Jorgenson," Malone said thoughtfully. "Anybody else connected with this?"

Von Flanagan put down his empty glass. "Malone, the next time I trust your word — the next time you tell me you just want a friendly talk — "

"I'm just curious," the lawyer said defensively.

"Sure," von Flanagan agreed. "You're just curious, and you're out to make my work harder for me than it is already. You haven't got sympathy for an old friend. You want to get everything all mixed up. Well, Malone, I'll tell you every– thing I know, because this time you've put your foot in it. This time you're not going to get anywhere. This case is all filed away. It's an open and shut — as open and shut as — "

"As the Black Dahlia murders," Malone contributed.

"Sure," von Flanagan said. He blinked. "Now look here, Malone — "

"Just a little joke," Malone said. "A harmless little joke. That's all."

"Fine thing," von Flanagan said. "Old friends stabbing you in the back... " He appeared to be thinking for a minute. Then he smiled. "But this time, Malone, you've put your foot in it. And I'm going to help you get yourself in dutch. Any information you want, you can have."

"How about other people involved?" Malone said. "So far, there's Casper Jorgenson, who keeps pigeons, and Alvin Breck."

"The suicide," von Flanagan said with relish. "Suicide, and don't you forget I warned you. There's Breck's fiancée, a nice kid — her name's Helen Connell —

and there's a nut. He was downstairs in the apartment building where this Breck lived when we got there, said he was going to see Breck, so we got his name and asked him a couple of questions. His name's Alfonso the Great."

"Alfonso the Great?"

"He's a magician," von Flanagan said. "Good luck, Malone. And don't worry — when you get into trouble I'll be right there to put you into a nice, safe jail."

A little later, after a few more questions and a session with the Chicago telephone directory, Malone had a plan of action. Alvin Breck, the medical examiner had said, had died between eight–thirty and nine–thirty, and the gas had been turned on perhaps a little before eight. The first thing to do, Malone told himself, is to check alibis. He wondered about all those betting slips and racing forms. Perhaps he'd better go and see Max Hook before he did anything else; Max would be able to tell him about Alvin Breck, if Breck had been a big horse player.

But when he called Max Hook's number, the line was busy, and stayed busy for ten minutes. "Oh, well," Malone said. "There's always time for everything." He wondered briefly what he meant by that, and decided not to think about it. Instead, he flagged a cab outside his office building, and gave directions to the Bright Theater.

"No matinees today, Malone," the cabbie said.

"I know," the little lawyer told him. "I've got to see a man about a room."

"A room, Malone?" the cabbie said. "In the Bright Theater?"

"This is a magician," Malone told him, "and the room is a locked room."

There was silence for the rest of the ride. At the theater, Malone, thankful that he'd found time for a poker game a few nights before, took out a roll of bills, paid the cabbie, and went around to the stage entrance. An old, old man in a rusty blue suit barred the door.

"You looking for somebody?" he said.

"Alfonso the Great," Malone said, feeling just a little silly.

"Around back," said the ancient man. "Third door on your left."

He stepped aside and Malone went through, into a long dingy corridor. Green paint was flaking from the walls, and one naked electric bulb hung in the center of the ceiling. He counted doors carefully, came to the third, and knocked.

A voice inside said: "Who's there? Who is there?"

It was a woman's voice. Malone said: "I'm looking for Alfonso the Great."

"Just a minute," the woman said. Malone stood outside the door and waited, and at last he heard a latch click, and the door opened. "Perhaps you are a reporter?" the woman said. Her accent sounded French to Malone, but it was hard to tell. It was hard, Malone realized, to think of anything while the woman stood in the doorway watching him.

She was, he imagined, well over six feet tall. She was built like a Greek wrestler, and her square face, topped by a froth of brass-blonde hair, stared down at him disapprovingly. "Well?" she said.

Perhaps, Malone thought, she had misunderstood him and this was the wrong dressing room. "I'm looking for Alfonso the Great," he said.

"So you say," the woman, muttered. "You say nothing else? I am Madame. I am his wife. We are at work on a new effect. He has gone out to a lunch, to bring back lunch for us, and he will be back. You will come in and wait? Perhaps you are a reporter to write a story about Alfonso the Great?"

"I just want to ask him some questions," Malone said modestly. "My name is Malone."

"Ah," the woman said slowly. "Melon. Come in, then, Mr. Melon."

Malone said: "Malone," realized it wasn't going to do any good, and went through the doorway behind the enormous woman. He found himself in a tiny room which contained a large mirror on one wall, a shelf–like table set against the mirror, and three chairs. He sat down in one of the chairs and watched the enormous woman lower herself to another. "You know the other reporter who was here, perhaps?" the woman said, smiling at him horribly.

"The other reporter?"

"His name was — " The woman thought. "Alvin Breck. The police told my husband all about how Mr. Breck had committed suicide. That is the way you say it?"

"That," Malone said, "is the way you say it. You could say I'm a friend of his."

"He, too, was writing a story about Alfonso the Great."

Malone said: "Really?"

"Oh, yes," the woman said, and nodded heavily.

There was a silence that lasted for several seconds. Then the door opened and a small, mustached man came in carrying a steaming paper bag. The enormous woman managed to stand up in the dressing room. "Alfonso, she said, "this is Mr. Melon, who is a friend of Mr. Alvin Breck, and he is going to write a story about you."

Alfonso the Great put down the paper bag and turned to Malone. "Ah," he said. "I'm so happy to meet you." His accent was also clearly distinguishable, but he spoke English with a little more ease. "Perhaps you'd like a bite of lunch?" he said.

Malone said: "No, thanks. I only want to ask you a couple of questions."

Alfonso nodded and took the third chair. His wife began removing things from the paper bag: sandwiches, paper cups and utensils. She spread them on the shelf–like table. Alfonso said: "I was born in nineteen–twelve in Alsace–Lorraine. I come from a family of magicians. My greatest illusion, Walking Through A Wall, I conceived in nineteen–twenty–four, when I was but twelve years old. I... "

"I only want to ask a couple of questions," Malone said. "Walking through a wall?"

"It is the illusion that has made me famous," Alfonso said. "Perhaps you prefer my Appearance Of Eagles?"

This didn't seem the time, Malone reflected, to admit that a) he wasn't going to write any articles about Alfonso, and b) he'd never seen the magician's act. He merely nodded. "The Walking Through A Wall illusion interests me, though," he said. "You could escape from a locked, sealed room that way, couldn't you? Just walk through a wall into the corridor."

Alfonso laughed as if Malone had said something hysterically funny. His wife joined in, shaking the room with great gasps of sound. Finally Alfonso got enough breath back to say: "Of course I could if the wall were specially prepared."

"Well," Malone said, "the wall in Alvin Breck's apartment, for instance."

Afonso nodded. "I was in the apartment," he said. "Early this morning. Then I had to come back here; we are at work, my wife and I, on a new illusion."

"How about walking through that wall?" Malone said. "I mean the wall in Alvin Breck's apartment."

"You are joking," Alfonso said.

"Sure," Malone said. "I'm joking." He brushed cigar ashes off his vest and tried to think of some more questions. "How long did you know Alvin Breck?" he said.

"Only a few days," Alfonso said. "He was going to write a story about my illusions — as you are going to do."

Malone thought. Alvin Breck had been a true crime writer. Why would he have bothered with a story about magic and magicians? Unless there had been some crime involved...

Well, it never did any harm to ask, he told himself.

"He was going to write about them from the criminal point of view, of course," he said.

Alfonso stood up. "Get out, Mr. Melon."

"But — "

Alfonso said: "Get out," again and his enormous wife stood up.

"Leave us," she said. "Why do you pretend to be his friend?"

"I'm his friend," Malone said. "I only meant — "

"We know too well what you meant," she said. "It is all over now. Do not dig it up again."

She came toward him. Malone backed to the door and opened it. "Listen a minute," he said, and stepped out into the hall. "Listen, I — "

The door slammed shut behind him.

That, Malone thought, was a dirty shame. There'd been at least one more important question he'd wanted to ask. Well, there wasn't any time to lose if he was going to get everything done, and he still had to call Max Hook and talk to Helen Connell again, and then see a man about a pigeon.

He left the theater, saying a polite: "Goodbye," to the ancient man at the stage door, and found a drugstore phone nearby. He called Max Hook.

This time the line was free, and in a few seconds he was talking to the gangster. "What can I do for you, Malone?"

"I just wanted to ask you a question or two," Malone said. "Ever hear of Alvin Breck?"

"Breck?" Hook waited a minute. "Malone, what's this about?"

"I understand the guy played the horses quite a bit," Malone started.

Hook interrupted him. "Played the horses? Something happen to the guy?"

"He's dead," Malone told him. "Turned on the gas in his room last night."

The telephone was silent.

"You still there?" Malone said.

"I'm here," Max Hook said. "I was a little surprised, that's all. The guy owed me a couple of G's. I suppose it's not important now, but I didn't figure him to welch. He wasn't that kind."

"What can you tell me about him?" Malone said.

"I — " Hook paused. "Hold on a minute, will you, Malone?"

The little lawyer rested against the wall of the telephone booth. He could hear a whispered conversation in the background, between Hook and some voice he couldn't identify. After a minute the conversation stopped, and Hook came back to the receiver. But his tone had changed.

"You listen to me, Malone," he said. "We've been friends for a long time. I've done you a lot of favors, Malone. But that's all over. When you start in framing me for some murder you can't do anything about, Malone, we're through. I want to talk to you — alone. I'm sending my boys down... "

Malone thought fast. "I don't know what you're talking about," he said, "but wait for an hour. I'm going down to my office. Tell your boys to come down there in an hour."

"Malone, I'm not ready for any fooling around. Trying to frame me, Malone — I don't like that."

When Max Hook didn't like something, Malone thought, the consequences were liable to be drastic. "Wait an hour," he said. "For old times' sake."

"You're a fine one to be talking about old times," the gangster said. "Listen, Malone, I want to see you. Up here. Alone."

"In an hour," Malone said. "I'll be in my office. Would I try to pull anything on you?"

"You tried to frame me... "

"I did no such thing," Malone said. "One hour."

He waited a second. Finally Max Hook said: "One hour, Malone. And you better have a good explanation. I don't like this at all, Malone, not at all."

You've got nothing on me, Malone thought as he hung up the receiver. Some fast thinking was called for, and he didn't have any facts to work with.

He only knew one thing for sure: Alvin Breck had *not* committed suicide.

Back in his office, he found a stack of messages. Maggie had gone out for a bite of lunch, she'd written, but there had been a lot of calls.

Malone leafed through the papers. Von Flanagan had called. And the tele—phone company (about the bill). Von Flanagan. Von Flanagan. Max Hook. Von Flanagan. Von Flanagan. Von Flanagan. Helen Connell. Von Flanagan.

This, Malone told himself, means trouble. If von Flanagan wanted him so insistently, von Flanagan wasn't happy. And if von Flanagan was mad at him…

That's all I need, Malone thought. The police and Max Hook.

He wondered if perhaps finding a nice hole to hide in wouldn't be the smartest thing for him to do. After all, if the police were satisfied that Alvin Breck had committed suicide, who was he to argue with them?"

Even if he knew that Breck hadn't committed suicide at all…

Somebody was vitally interested in getting Malone off the case, he realized. The somebody who'd called Max Hook and told him that Malone was trying to frame him, Hook, for the murder. The somebody who had probably gotten von Flanagan mad at him.

Malone wondered about Alfonso the Great. How he had managed to get into the Breck apartment that morning? Maybe Helen Connell had let him in, Malone thought. And he ought to call Helen Connell anyhow; she'd left her name, and maybe she had some news for him.

What he really ought to do, he told himself, was go home and start all over again. Maybe if he got some sleep and avoided his office for a few days things would brighten up. But he'd promised Max Hook that he'd meet Hook's man there in the office in an hour — and by that time he had to have the case sewed up. No other explanation was going to be good enough, Malone knew.

He put his head in his hands for a second and sighed. Then he straightened up, lit a fresh cigar, and picked up the phone.

Helen Connell, said: "Hello?"

"Miss Connell, this is John J. Malone"

"Oh… have you… "

"There's nothing definite yet," he said, feeling that, things were a little too definite to suit him. "But I want to know if anyone was in the — your fiancé's apartment this morning. Did you take anyone there?"

She hesitated a moment. Malone pictured the black hair, the wonderful face and figure, and almost felt resigned to going on with the job. At last she said: "Before I came to see you… the police were finished anyway, and I thought that — talking, to them, perhaps I could see who had killed — killed Alvin. He'd given me his key… "

"Of course," Malone said. "Who was there in the room with you, this morning?"

"That magician," she said, "and Casper Jorgenson — he gave Alvin a pigeon, and the pigeon was in the apartment when — it happened, and so the pigeon was dead, too, and Casper was very mad about it. And — a man named Fingers, who said he worked for a friend of Alvin's. Malone, that was strange."

"What was strange?"

"He said… somebody called him and told him to be there. Somebody called his boss, I mean."

"Who's his boss?" Malone said, telling himself that the answer he knew was coming couldn't possibly come.

"A man named Hook," Helen Connell said. "Max Hook."

After a few seconds, Malone hung up very carefully. Strange, he thought, was not the word for this case. Not only did he have the police on his neck, and Max Hook on his neck, but he had a locked–room murder to deal with.

And a magician, he told himself savagely. A magician whose specialty is walking through walls. That, Malone thought, would come in handy for locked rooms.

Von Flanagan, Max Hook, Alfonso the Great, and a locked room. And, of course, a pigeon. Malone wished that he could stop thinking that the case had given him the bird. He got up and found a bottle of rye in the Emergency drawer of the filing cabinet, and he poured himself a long drink.

How would anybody get in and out of a locked, sealed room to turn on an oven? And why would Alvin Breck — who had everything to live for — let someone do it? Maybe the someone was a person Breck had trusted, Malone thought. But that would leave him with only Helen Connell as a suspect, as far as he knew — or maybe Casper Jorgenson, and wouldn't the bird–fancier have taken his pigeon out before turning on the gas?

The pigeon reminded him that he still had calls to make, and he was searching through the telephone directory again when Maggie arrived. Relieved, he let her do the searching and call Casper Jorgenson. There were still a lot of questions to ask, and he had most of an hour to ask them in.

That, Malone told himself without any conviction at all, was plenty of time.

C asper Jorgenson was perfectly free, and would be glad to come right down to Mr. Malone's office. The ride should take little more than five minutes, he said in a pleased, slightly oiled voice, and if Mr. Malone would wait until he had finished feeding his birds.

Mr. Malone, lighting a fresh cigar, said he would be glad to wait. There was no hurry at all, Mr. Malone thought, hanging up. Mr. Malone scowled horribly.

Motive, he thought, was something nobody had thought of. Of course, motive was easy. There was Max Hook's motive, although he knew he'd better stop thinking about that. He was in enough hot water. But if Breck had owed Max Hook money, murder was a perfectly possible result. Of course, Hook said that he hadn't worried about Breck's debts, and that he expected Breck to pay him back. But what else would Hook say if he'd actually killed Breck?

Not that Malone believed it for a minute, he reminded himself thankfully. If Hook had killed Alvin Breck, he'd have hired someone to do it, and arranged a couple of neatly unbreakable alibis. Locked rooms weren't Max Hook's style.

They weren't anybody's style, that Malone knew of.

How, he asked himself for the hundredth time, would someone manage to get into a locked and sealed room, turn on the gas, and leave?

At that point the telephone rang.

Maggie, in the outer office, picked it up. Her voice sounded strained. After a few seconds she put her hand over the receiver and called in: "Malone, it's for you."

"I died yesterday," Malone said.

"It's Captain von Flanagan," Maggie said. "He sounds terrible."

"He is terrible," Malone said. "Leave me alone."

"He says he has to talk to you."

"I — " Nothing was going to be gained by avoiding the inevitable. Von Flanagan could have what was left, anyhow, after Max Hook was through.

Malone nodded and picked up the telephone. "This is John J. Malone," he announced, and held the receiver away from his ear, waiting for the screams of von Flanagan's wrath.

Surprisingly, the voice was mild and soothing. "I just thought you'd like to know how bad you put your foot in it, Malone," von Flanagan said.

"What?"

"We sent a man up to that Breck apartment just a little while ago, and he found a suicide note. Typewritten — but Breck did everything on his typewriter, his fiancée told us. Do you want me to read it to you?"

"You might as well," Malone said.

Von Flanagan cleared his throat. " 'I have nothing more to live for,' " he said. " 'I am taking the easy way out. Goodbye.' What do you think of that, Malone?"

"I feel sorry for you," Malone said.

"What? Now listen — " von Flanagan stopped, and then went on, "I shouldn't get mad at you, Malone. Everybody's entitled to one little mistake. And if you happened to make a big mistake, well, Malone, I won't say I told you so. I'll be just as friendly as if it had never happened, Malone. I — "

"When did you find the note?" Malone said.

"A man went up just a little while ago," von Flanagan said. "He found it in the living room, on a chair."

"You'd searched the apartment last night?"

"Well," von Flanagan said, "yes, but — after all, Malone, you could have missed it yourself... "

"Lying there on a chair," Malone said.

"That's right," von Flanagan said. "Now don't go getting fancy on me, Malone — "

"Why did you send a man up today?" Malone asked.

"We got a telephone call," von Flanagan said. "We got a tip. Now you listen to me, Malone. This is an open and shut case. There's no sense fooling around with it. It's nice and simple and don't I have enough troubles, Malone? I never wanted to be a cop at all except my old man owed a favor to the alderman and... "

"Don't worry about it, von Flanagan," Malone said. "After all, anybody can make one little mistake. Even a Homicide Squad Captain." He hung up gently.

Then he leaned back in his chair. He was beginning to feel a lot better. The suicide note, he told himself, explained everything. There was no doubt at all in his mind that Alvin Breck had been murdered, and he even knew who had murdered him.

Of course, Malone told himself, there were little details. He might be shot dead at any time. But that wasn't really anything to worry about.

The door opened and Helen Connell came in, with Casper Jorgenson behind her.

"Well, Miss Connell," Malone said, shifting mental gears in a hurry. Behind her, Jorgenson looked small, pale and helpless. He smiled hesitatingly at Malone. "And Mr. Jorgenson," Malone said.

"I met him downstairs," Helen Connell said. "I was coming to see you. After you called — I got to thinking that maybe there was something I could do."

"You just sit quietly," Malone said. "There's nothing to worry about. I've got to go outside and see about something. I'll only be a minute."

"Of course," Jorgenson said.

"I'll wait," Helen Connell said.

Malone slipped into the outer office. "Call von Flanagan," be told Maggie. "Tell him to be down here right away." He was about to go back to his clients when the door opened again. A gigantic woman and a small, mustached man confronted him.

"Aha," the woman said.

Malone said: "Aha?"

"We find out about you from the doorman at the theater," the woman said. "He knows your face. John J. Melon. The lawyer. We wonder why it is a lawyer pretending to be a story writer. Then we think of Alvin Breck, and we think you are suspecting my husband of killing the man Breck."

"Suspecting?" Malone said.

Everything, he thought, was happening much too quickly.

"This is not a nice thing to do, suspect Alfonso the Great," the woman said.

"Not nice at all," Alfonso added.

Malone took a deep breath. After all this was over, he promised himself, he was going to spend about a week in Joe the Angel's City Hall Bar, just recuperating. Perhaps be could move into Joe the Angel's back room, and live there. The idea sounded very peaceful.

But now: "Come into my office," he said quietly. "I think we can straighten everything out very simply."

Suspiciously, they followed him. Malone's small inner office was crowded with the four people in it, not counting Malone himself, who went behind his desk, sat down and regarded everybody with an impersonal benevolence.

"We'll only have a few minutes to wait," he said. "I'm expecting another visitor or two any minute."

Von Flanagan's arrival was the signal for everybody to look around and start whispering. That, Malone thought, was only natural. They'd all seen the Homicide Squad Captain before, and they were all wondering what he was doing in Malone's offices.

"Mysterious telephone calls!" von Flanagan said, shutting the door behind him. "I'm telling you, Malone, if it wasn't for our long–standing friendship — "

Malone quieted him with a single motion of his hand. Everybody turned round again, this time to look at the little lawyer. He took his time about lighting a cigar, and rapidly filled the small office with blue smoke. Then he cleared his throat.

"I guess you're wondering why I called you all here" he said. That wasn't quite true — he hadn't called Helen Connell, for one, or Alfonso and his wife, for at least two more — but it was such a fine opening it seemed a shame not to use it. "I heard about the death of Alvin Breck this morning. I'm now prepared to say that it wasn't suicide, but murder, and that I know who committed the murder."

Von Flanagan said: "One of these days, Malone — "

"Wait," Malone said. "Think about that suicide note for a minute. Everybody was in Alvin Breck's apartment this morning. Isn't it possible — considering that the police usually do at least a fair job of searching an apartment — that one of the people who was there this morning left that note?"

"But Malone — "

"And then, the person who'd left the note called the police and told them about it, just to make sure it was found? Just to make sure that Alvin Breck's death was definitely labeled a suicide?"

"This case was open and shut, Malone!" von Flanagan roared.

"Everybody," Malone said, "assumed this was suicide because they couldn't figure out how the murderer got in and out of the locked room. Well — he didn't get out."

Von Flanagan's face was a deep, glowing purple. "Please, Malone," he said in a piteous voice. "Tell me what you're talking about."

"The pigeon," Malone said.

There was a scuffle, a thump, several cries and a thud. Von Flanagan had hold of Casper Jorgenson by the neck. "You come with me," von Flanagan said in his best official tones.

Malone called after him: "Don't worry about a thing. And don't admit anything. I'm your lawyer — remember that."

Just before they got to the outer office, Jorgenson managed to twist around in von Flanagan's grip. "Okay, Malone," he said, with surprising cheerfulness.

The door slammed.

Helen Connell said: "What's this all about?"

Alfonso and his wife added: "What is it going on?"

"Simple," Malone said. "The way I see it — and this is confidential, remember — Casper Jorgenson had some secret in his past and he was afraid that Alvin Breck, in his criminal researches, had dug that secret up. He had to kill Breck, and he worked out an ingenious method of doing it.

"What does the pigeon have to do with — "

"You can train pigeons to do almost anything," Malone said. "Look at carrier pigeons. Smart birds. All Casper had to do was train one bird to open a gas jet — which the pigeon could probably do with one claw tied behind its back — and then give Alvin Breck the bird. Breck kept the doors and windows closed while he worked — "

"That's right, Malone," Helen Connell said.

" — and the rest was easy," Malone said. "The pigeon was the real killer."

"But how did you — "

"How did I think of it?" Malone said. "The suicide note. It meant that somebody who wanted the death to look like suicide had forgotten a detail, and was desperately trying to patch it up. The note, I guess, reminded me of carrier pigeons carrying important notes from place to place. And the pigeon — it's all in the subconscious," he said vaguely. "Massa's in the cold, cold subconscious."

"My goodness," Helen Connell said.

Alfonso said: "But — "

"Oh, yes," Malone said. "Alvin Breck's digging up some old facts on you, Alfonso, reminded me that he could dig up facts on anybody — even Casper Jorgenson. The facts he found out about you — well, it was probably in Alsace-Lorraine, and it was a long time ago, and if you ever get in trouble call a good lawyer."

The enormous Madame said: "Mr. Melon?"

"What I mean is," Malone said slowly, "I don't care what he dug up. Or what you might have still hidden. Just remember the name — John J. Melon. Lawyer."

"We will remember," the enormous woman said.

The door was thrown open again.

"Well, well," Malone said. "So you came down yourself, Max?"

"It's the least I can do for an old pal," Max Hook said. "Even if he turns out to be a rat — "

"But I'm not a rat," Malone said cheerfully. He turned to the others. "You'll excuse me — a previous appointment. He got up and took Max Hook's arm, heading him for the door. "I'll explain everything," he told the gangster. "It's all very simple if you remember the pigeon — "

Everything, Malone knew, was going to be all right.

When Rodney Melcher consults Malone over a series of accidents that could have turned fatal, Malone doesn't suspect that someone else in the Melcher household will end up dead. This was one of the final stories Craig wrote before her death in 1957 and one of her better stories as well. -JM

They're Trying to Kill Me

John J. Malone looked sourly at the young man across the desk.

"There's nothing I can do about it," he said. "Hire yourself a bodyguard. Or a bloodhound. I used to know a wonderful bloodhound... " He sighed deeply and took a puff of his cigar. "That's another story," he went on. "But there's absolutely nothing I can do."

"I don't know where else to turn," the young man said. He was dressed in a light gray suit, a white–on–white shirt and a light gray Countess Mara tie. He wore thick–rimmed glasses and his hair stood up in a black, bristly crew–cut. He looked about twenty–two years old and he could have come straight from Madison Avenue, New York.

"Well, don't turn here," Malone said peevishly. "I've got troubles of my own. And bodyguarding isn't my business. Now, if I could find that bloodhound for you — "

"A bloodhound isn't going to do me any good," the young man said. "Malone, somebody's trying to kill me."

"It isn't me," Malone said.

"But you don't understand," the young man said. "They're trying to kill me. And I need help."

Malone sighed and brushed at his vest. It was early afternoon, he'd been in his office for several hours. There weren't any cases that needed any work, and he hadn't even been bothered by bill collectors. All in all, the day had been a dull one. Now it seemed to be turning into an irritating one, too.

Maybe, he thought sadly, if I convince this man he doesn't need me, he'll go away and I can go home and get some sleep. He told himself that he needed sleep badly. He had a very important date set for later in the evening, and he wanted to be at his very best.

"Who's trying to kill you?" he said at last.

The young man shrugged. "How would I know?" he said.

"But you told me — "

"I just know somebody's trying to kill me," the young man said. "Strange things have been happening. Last week I nearly took poison by mistake."

"That," Malone said, "sounds like carelessness."

"I had a headache, so I went to the medicine cabinet to take some aspirin. Only the pills in the bottle were just a little too large for aspirin. I stopped just in time."

"So you sent them away to be analyzed," Malone began.

"Not then," the young man said. "I only sent them away after the radio fell."

"Oh," Malone said. "Radio." This wasn't working out exactly as he'd planned it. But he couldn't think of any way to stop things from going on. Soon, he promised himself, the young man would be gone and he could go home and sleep.

"I keep a radio on the shelf above my bathtub," the young man said. "The other day I noticed it beginning to teeter. I got out of the tub just in time. If the radio had fallen while I was in the tub, Malone, I'd have been electrocuted."

"Accident," the little lawyer said, hiding himself behind a cloud of smoke. "Happens all the time."

The young man grimaced. "And I suppose that wooden shelves in bathrooms are being sawn halfway through all the time, too," he said. "Because that's what happened to my shelf. I realized then that somebody was trying to kill me, and I thought of the pills and sent them away to a chemist I know. He told me they contained white arsenic. Malone, I could have been poisoned."

"Or electrocuted," Malone said judiciously. "What else has happened?"

"Nothing," the young man said. "But I don't want to wait for something else to happen. I've been lucky twice. The next time I might not be so lucky. So, you see, I need your help."

"What do you want me to do?" Malone said sadly.

"I want you to find out who's trying to kill me," the young man said. "Once I know that I can take care of things. Whoever it is — there must be some kind of settlement. I'm not a hard man to get along with."

"Somebody seems to think differently," Malone offered. "But I'm not the man you want. Why don't you go to the police?"

"I'm afraid to," the young man said.

Malone puffed at his cigar. "Afraid?" he said.

"That's right," the young man said. "If the police started asking questions, the person who's trying to kill me might get panicky. And he might just shoot me or get a blunt instrument from somewhere, or something."

Malone tried once more. "I'm very busy," he began.

"I can make it worth your while," the young man said. "I'm Rodney Melcher."

The little lawyer wondered where he'd heard the name before. After a second he had it. Rodney Melcher had inherited his father's jewelry business the year before, when old Cotton Melcher had died of complications resulting from indigestion. The business was estimated to be worth somewhere between two and three million dollars. Malone remembered reading about it in the *Examiner*.

"It's not a matter of money," Malone started to say, and then thought better of it. Money would come awfully handy for his important engagement. "Well," he said at last, "suppose you tell me about some of the people you know who *might* be trying to kill you."

"That's easy," the young man said. "There are only three of them. There's my wife, and my mistress, and my brother."

A nice, friendly little family, Malone thought. "Which one of them might have had the opportunity to substitute pills, or to saw through that bathroom shelf?" he said after a second.

"All of them," the young man said. "You see, Malone, we all live in the same house."

Malone tried to imagine a household consisting of a man, his brother, his wife and his mistress. His imagination boggled, and for a long second he couldn't think of anything to say. He covered the pause by lighting another cigar.

"Will you help me, Malone?" Rodney Melcher said at last.

Malone sighed and blew out smoke. "I'll start first thing tomorrow," he promised. That would give him the time to keep his engagement that night. "But I'll need a retainer," he added quickly, thinking about the engagement.

"Let's say five hundred now, then," Rodney Melcher said. He withdrew his wallet from the inside pocket of his light–gray jacket and counted out five hundred–dollar bills. Malone looked at them, lying gently on the top of his desk. "Is that all right?" Rodney Melcher said.

"That's fine," Malone said. "That's fine."

"And here's my address." From the same wallet he picked a printed card. "I'll look for you tomorrow morning."

Malone stared at the card. The address was in Lake Forest. "You mean you want me to go out there?" he said.

"Of course, Malone," the young man said. "You'll have to meet everybody, and look for clues, and things. I'll just introduce you as a friend, or something like that. So nobody knows you're investigating for me — "

"And so the killer doesn't get nervous and bump you off in a hurry," Malone said.

The young man nodded. "That's right," he said. "I'll see you tomorrow."

"I'll be there," Malone promised. Privately, he wondered how he was going to get up at all the next morning, let alone find his way to Lake Forest. But, somehow, he knew, things would work out."

"I'm glad you decided to help me out, Malone," Rodney Melcher said.

"So am I," Malone said dismally.

The afternoon went by, but no more clients appeared. Malone filled his ashtray with cigar butts and wondered how he had ever let himself get hired by Rodney

Melcher, and at last it was five o'clock. He put out his final cigar, emptied the ashtray neatly into the wastebasket, and brushed off his vest for the last time. He stood up with a great sigh of relief.

In the outer office, the phone rang.

Let it ring, Malone decided. If it doesn't want to ring during office hours, why should I cater to its whims? He got his hat and coat from the closet.

Maggie's voice called in: "Malone, it's Captain von Flanagan."

"Tell him I died last week," Malone said pleasantly.

"But he's very excited," Maggie said. "He says you're involved in something terrible and he has to talk to you. He said to tell you it was about Rodney Melcher."

Malone stopped. "Rodney Melcher?" he said. "Is he dead yet?"

Maybe the young man had been killed, he thought, while I sat here doing nothing. I should have gone out and helped him right away, he told himself. Now he's dead and it's my fault. I should have known...

"He's not dead," Maggie said. "He's been accused of murder and he says you're his lawyer."

It took a long time for that to sink in. At last Malone sighed and sat down at his desk again. "You'd better put von Flanagan on," he told Maggie in a resigned voice.

When he picked up his phone, the police captain was already talking, "— and you listen to me, Malone," von Flanagan said. "If there's any funny business about this — Rodney Melcher claiming you're his lawyer — "

"I am his lawyer," Malone said mildly.

"— and raising a fuss about — Malone, *are* you his lawyer? You're not kidding me?"

"I'm not kidding you, von Flanagan," Malone said. "He came to see me this afternoon."

Von Flanagan took a deep, hissing breath. It sounded as if he were in pain. "So that's it," he said. "He came to see you and told you about what he was planning to do, and you told it was okay, that you'd get him off no matter who he murdered. But it won't work Malone. It won't work. It won't — "

"Tap the needle," Malone said. "It's stuck."

"Now, Malone — "

"Rodney Melcher didn't tell me about any murder, and I didn't guarantee him that if he did commit one I could get him off," Malone said. "Really. Would I do a thing like that?"

Von Flanagan didn't hesitate. "Yes," he said. "And what's more — "

"Well, I didn't do it," Malone said. "And that's that."

"Oh, no, it isn't," von Flanagan said quickly. "I want you to come down here right away. I want to get this whole thing straightened out. When I think of the favors I've done you — "

"I can't come down right away," Malone said. "I've got a date."

"Break it," von Flanagan said. "I want you down here. And that's an order."

"But von Flanagan — "

"Don't but me," the police captain shouted. "Just get down here!"

Malone sighed. "All right," he said. "Where?"

"*Where?*" Von Flanagan sounded as if he were about to have a stroke. "Rodney Melcher's house! You know where that is, don't you?"

"I know," Malone said, fingering the card in his pocket. "Right away?"

"*Right away*," von Flanagan said.

"All right," the little lawyer said despairingly. He hung up.

After a second he reached for the phone again, to cancel his date.

Rodney Melcher's home was a big white square in the early evening. It stood alone in a grove of trees. Malone walked up the white gravel path to the big front door, found the bell–push and leaned on it.

Somewhere behind him, an owl hooted. At least, Malone thought it was an owl. It sounded like a lost soul complaining about Hell. He tried not to listen to it. After a second he pushed the bell again.

This time the door opened slowly and noiselessly. Malone found himself staring into the oldest face he had ever seen.

"Yes?" said the death's head. The face was covered with wrinkles, and, in the hall light, it was the color of old dried cheese. Under the face was a body as thin as a stick, wearing a dark–blue uniform.

"I'm John J. Malone," Malone said, wondering if he was. If this place wasn't the House of Usher, he thought, it would do nicely for a substitute. He tried to imagine Rodney Melcher, in his Madison Avenue suit, living in this Chamber of Horrors, with his brother, his wife, and his mistress. He felt his imagination beginning to boggle again and stepped inside the doorway.

One of those three people was dead, he realized. But which one? Rodney Melcher could have killed his wife — or his mistress could have killed his wife — or else his wife could have killed his mistress. No matter how you looked at it, Malone thought, it didn't make any sense.

"The police officer is expecting you, Mr. Malone," said the ancient butler. "Please come this way."

He turned and started down the hall. Malone followed him past an umbrella–stand and two faded pictures, turned to the left and found himself in a brilliantly lit living room. The furnishings were ancient, polished, and solid. At the far end of the room was the largest fireplace Malone had ever seen, and seated near it, in   carven chairs, were four people: von Flanagan, Rodney Melcher, and two women.

"You took your time about getting here," von Flanagan said.

"Waste not, want not," Malone said at random. "Does somebody want to explain all this to me? I don't understand any of it."

Rodney Melcher said, "Come over here and sit down, Malone. It's very simple. My brother — "

"He knows about it already," von Flanagan growled. "You told him this afternoon."

"How could I?" Melcher said. "I didn't know it myself, at the time."

"But you — "

"Let him explain it to me, von Flanagan," Malone said. "Humor me. Pretend I never heard about it before." After a second he added: "Which I haven't."

Von Flanagan snorted. Rodney Melcher said: "It's my brother, Malone. He's dead. And the police think I killed him."

"Did you?" Malone said.

Melcher stared. "Of course not. I wouldn't — Malone, he was my brother. Maybe we weren't very close. But I wouldn't kill him. Not my brother."

"You weren't very close," Malone said, "but you lived in the same house."

One of the women said: "That's the way things are." She was about twenty-five, Malone thought, a tall, pale blonde dressed in an ice–green sheath. The other woman was a redhead in sports clothes. Which, the little lawyer wondered, was the wife? For that matter, which was the mistress?

"I'm sorry," Rodney Melcher put in. "I should have introduced you." He nodded toward the women. "This is my wife Carla." The blonde gave Malone the smallest smile he had ever seen on a human face. Carla was apparently not disposed to be friendly.

"And this is Margery Dawes," Melcher said. The red–head nodded at Malone.

"You're the famous lawyer, aren't you?" she said. "I've always wanted to meet you. You look cute."

Malone had no answer at all for that one. He took an empty chair next to Rodney Melcher, facing von Flanagan, with the women at his left. "So the police think you killed your brother," he said conversationally.

"We don't think anything yet," von Flanagan said. "We're waiting for the evidence."

"That's nice," Malone said. "Then why bring me all the way out here and accuse me of things you haven't got any evidence for?"

"Malone," von Flanagan said, "for you, I don't need any evidence."

Malone sighed. "I didn't do a thing, von Flanagan," he said; "I have no intention of doing anything; and I resent your suspicious nature."

"I didn't do anything either," Rodney Melcher put in. "Malone, you've got to help me."

Malone looked around the room, fished a cigar from his pocket and lit it. He took a few puffs, wreathing himself in smoke, before he spoke. "Who found the body?" he said.

"You're not here to investigate anything," von Flanagan said.

"I don't know what I am here for," Malone said cheerfully, " and neither does anybody else. I might as well find out who did kill Rodney Melcher's brother — it doesn't look as if anybody else is going to. Because it wasn't me, and it wasn't Rodney Melcher."

"How do you know it wasn't?" von Flanagan snapped.

"Because," Malone said simply, "he's my client."

After a second Rodney Melcher said: "I found him. I went upstairs to change for dinner — and he was there, in my room. Stabbed."

"Let's go upstairs," Malone said. He started to stand up.

"Nobody's allowed up there," von Flanagan said. "We closed the room off as soon as we arrived."

"As soon as I saw what had happened," Rodney Melcher said, "I called the police. Then I locked the door of the room myself. Nobody else has been up there. It's — horrible." He shuddered.

Malone nodded quietly. "I'll have to talk to everybody, one at a time," he said. "Where can we be alone?"

Rodney Melcher said: "There's a little alcove right off this room. I'll show you, Malone."

The little lawyer stood up, brushing ashes from his vest. He followed Rodney Melcher across the great living room to a smaller room beyond a paneled door. It was dimly lit and the walls looked as if they were deciding to close in. There were only two chairs and a small table in the room. Malone sat in one of the chairs.

Rodney Melcher turned to go.

"Wait a minute," Malone said. "I might as well talk to you first. After all, you're the only one who's seen the body, except for the police. When did you find him?"

Rodney Melcher sat down opposite Malone, across the table. "I told you," he said. "I went up to dress for dinner. It must have been about four–thirty. He was lying there… "

"All right," Malone said softly. "Now, who had any reason to kill your brother?"

Rodney Melcher thought. "I suppose I did," he said. "He and Margery… well, maybe it wasn't such a good idea to have all of us living in the same house. It seemed sensible at the time, but when Margery and poor George began… I suppose I was jealous, Malone."

"Margery's your mistress," Malone said.

"That's right," Rodney Melcher said. "But it looked as if she was going to be George's mistress before long. Or his wife; George wasn't married."

"That gives you a motive," Malone said after a second. "But what about somebody else? After all, you didn't do the killing."

Rodney Melcher grimaced. He pushed a hand through his crewcut hair. "No. That's right," he said. "Well — George really didn't get along too well with anybody. Even the servants seemed to dislike him. But that isn't much of a motive for murder, is it?"

"I knew a murder once," Malone said, "that was committed solely because of a brown fur teddy bear. But that's another story." He thought for a second. "Ask von Flanagan to come in here, will you?" he said.

"Von Flanagan?"

"The police officer," Malone said.

Rodney nodded and left. In a few seconds the little door of the room opened again. "Who do you think you are, Malone?" von Flanagan roared. "Coming in and just — taking over as if you were a police captain yourself — "

"Calm down, von Flanagan," Malone said crossly. "How are you going to answer my questions if you don't calm down?"

"Answer your questions?" Von Flanagan was beginning to turn cerise.

Malone lowered his voice. "Or maybe you'd like your wife to know about the five hundred dollars you won at Judge Touralchuck's poker game," he said pleasantly.

Von Flanagan took a deep breath. "That's not fair Malone," he said. "You were at the poker game too."

"Do you think your wife would mind if I played poker?" Malone asked.

There was a long silence.

"All right, Malone," von Flanagan said at last. "Go ahead. I suppose I've got to play along with you. But all I'm going to do is answer questions, remember. Don't try to get me to do something else."

"I won't have to," Malone said with a confidence he wished he felt. He sneaked a look at his watch. It was after six. Oh, well, maybe she'd meet him tomorrow, he thought. But she'd sounded a little peeved on the telephone.

"When did George Melcher die?" he said.

Von Flanagan shook his head. "Coroner was here, but he didn't say anything definite. Between three and four–thirty, when his brother found him."

"What killed him?" Malone said.

"He was stabbed in the back with a knife from the kitchen," von Flanagan said. "Listen, Malone. If Rodney Melcher didn't come to you about the killing — and I'm not saying I believe that — but, if he didn't, what did he want to see you about?"

"He thought he was going to be murdered," Malone said truthfully, "and he wanted a bodyguard."

Von Flanagan turned cerise again, then purple. "If you think I'm going to believe a story like that — " he started.

Malone looked for an ashtray, didn't find one, and sprinkled cigar ash liberally on the polished floor. "Anyhow," he said helpfully, "this time I'm asking the questions. Did you find anything in the room?"

"Nothing except what was supposed to be there," von Flanagan said. "I haven't even started questioning those two women myself Malone. You — "

"The poker game," Malone muttered.

Von Flanagan said: "All right. All right. But I'm warning you, Malone. If you don't come up with something I'm going to take care of you for good. I'm going to lock you in a cell and throw away the key. I'm going to put you where you'll never bother me any more. I'm going to build you a new jail, seventy feet under the ground, just for you, Malone. I — "

"But I will come up with something," Malone said. "Just watch. He smiled with what he hoped was a confident air. "On your way out, ask one of the women to come in, will you?" he said.

"Which one?" von Flanagan said.

Malone shrugged. "It doesn't matter," he said. "Pick one at random."

When the door opened Carla Melcher stood staring at Malone, her mouth in a firm line, he hands clenched at the sides of her ice green gown. "You wanted to see me," she said.

Malone thought back. "You're Rodney Melcher's wife," he said.

"That's right," she said. "And I don't see what all this fuss is about."

Malone said: "Come in, sit down, and shut the door." When the woman was seated opposite him, he went on: "George Melcher is dead."

"Oh, I know that," Carla Melcher said. "But I didn't do it. Don't blame me. I don't see why I should be bothered."

"Where were you between three and four–thirty this afternoon?" Malone said.

"I was in my room," Carla said, "working on a crossword puzzle. I do a lot of crossword puzzles. There isn't much to do."

"But — "

"Rodney and his wonderful ideas!" Carla went on, as if she hadn't heard the little lawyer at all. "Inviting his brother to stay with us — and then — that woman? I suppose it was more — convenient for him. Having her right here in the house."

"You mean Margery Dawes," Malone said helpfully.

"Of course I do," Carla said. "The cheap little slut — spending half her time in the servant's quarters. She's nothing but a — "

"Did anyone see you while you were in the room?" Malone said smoothly.

"See me?" Carla thought. "I rang for Max once, about three–thirty, I suppose it was, to bring me a drink."

"Max?"

"The butler. He let you in this afternoon."

Malone thought of the ancient death's head and shivered. "Oh, yes," he said. "Max."

"There wasn't anybody else," Carla said. "I was alone. I'm usually alone." She stood up. "Do you want to ask me anything more?" she said.

"A couple of questions," Malone said. "It won't take me long." Reluctantly,

Carla Melcher sat down again. "Did you know about the previous attempts at murder?"

"Previous attempts?" Carla said. "What previous attempts?"

"I guess you didn't," Malone said.

"But you've got to tell me," Carla said. "You mean — somebody tried to kill George?"

"Somebody succeeded," Malone said. "Before that, there were a couple of unsuccessful attempts. Rodney walked into them, and thought they were meant for him."

Carla laughed. Her voice was strained. "For Rodney?" she said. "Now, who would want to kill Rodney?"

"Would you?" Malone said softly.

"Malone," Carla said, "I may be a little bitter, and I may be disappointed. But I don't go around murdering people." She paused, then said: "Are there any more questions?"

"Just one," the little lawyer said. "Who do you think might have murdered George Melcher?"

Carla shook her head. "George was all right," she said. "He was — well, overbearing at times. A little difficult to get along with. But I can't imagine anyone wanting to kill him."

"Well," Malone said, "how did George and his brother get along, for instance?"

"Nothing special," Carla said. "Rodney had the money, you see, and that made for a little friction — but he was generous enough. George never really needed money. Rodney gave him whatever he asked for.

"I see," Malone said helplessly. After a second he added: "I guess that's about all."

Carla nodded. She stood up and went to the door of the dim little room. Malone crossed the room and opened it for her.

"Von Flanagan!" he bawled.

"What now?" the police captain's voice called back.

"See if you can find that butler — Max. I want to see him right away."

Probably, Malone thought dismally, nothing at all would happen. Carla's alibi would check out, and where would that leave things? Just where they had been. Carla could easily have stepped out before Max came in, or after he'd gone. How long did it take to stab somebody?

But there didn't seem to be anything else to do, Malone realized. He'd told von Flanagan he'd find the answer — and, if he didn't, Rodney Melcher wouldn't be the only one in trouble. Von Flanagan was just waiting for Malone to make one little mistake.

Malone thought he'd probably make the mistake already. He'd probably made it when he got out of bed that morning.

Being alone in a small, dim room with a man who looked like something out of an old horror movie was not, Malone discovered, the most pleasant thing in the world. He tried to smile at the butler, but his voice came out in a kind of whispered croak.

"You're Max," he said. "You're the butler."

"That's right, sir," the ancient horror said. "You wished to see me?"

"Did you go up to Mrs. Melcher's room with a drink this afternoon about three–thirty?"

Max wasn't sitting down. He stood over the table, looming like Boris Karloff. "She asked me to bring her a drink," he said in a neutral tone. "I did so. The time must have been approximately three–thirty. Is that all, sir?"

Well, Malone thought, he might as well go through the whole series of questions. "Where were you from three o'clock until four–thirty?" he said.

"It was four–thirty when Mr. George was discovered stabbed in the back?"

"That's right."

"A terrible thing," Max said, with something like relish. "Terrible." He seemed to recall himself to Malone's question. "I was downstairs, sir, washing–up the lunch dishes, and helping Cook prepare supper. I'm afraid that Cook could not provide me with an — alibi. I believe that is the word —?"

"That's the word," Malone said.

"Thank you, sir," Max said. "I'm afraid that Cook could not provide me with an alibi for that time; we were not constantly in each other's sight."

"Oh," Malone said. He prepared his second question. "Do you know anyone who might have wanted to kill George Melcher?" he asked.

"Mr. George was a gentleman," Max said.

That seemed to be that. After a second Malone said: "That's all, Max. Thank you. Would you ask Miss Dawes to step in?"

"Certainly, sir," Max said, and left silently. His departure seemed to make the room a more cheerful place. Malone was almost relaxed when the door opened again and Margery Dawes came in without invitation, sat herself down opposite him.

"I'll do anything I can," she said. "I think this whole thing is just terrible."

Her voice was flat and honest, like that of a little girl. Malone thought that sports clothes fit her; he tried to imagine her in Carla Melcher's green sheath and failed. "I'd like to know where you were between three and four–thirty this afternoon," he said, wondering how often he'd heard himself ask the same question.

"Between three and four–thirty?" she said. "I was out. I just got back — I found that poor George had been stabbed, and the police were already here."

"Stabbed in the back," Malone muttered.

"In the back?" Margery said. "How horrible!" She drew in her breath. "I was out shopping," she said.

"Any witnesses?" Malone asked.

Margery nodded. "Of course there are. Salesgirls — I can tell you where I went, if you like."

"Make up a list, and I'll go over it later," Malone said. But there wouldn't be any time, later, he knew. He had to come up with something now. "How did you and Rodney Melcher meet?" he said. Maybe there's something in Rodney's background, he thought. But that was silly; it hadn't been Rodney who'd been murdered. Even the murder attempts hadn't been meant for Rodney. That had all been a mistake.

"I came to the house one day by mistake," Margery said.

"By mistake?" Malone puffed on his cigar.

"I was looking for someone else. Someone who doesn't live here at all, but I thought they did. I talked to Rodney and he was very nice about it, and — well, after a few dates I suggested staying here, in the house, and Rodney thought that was a good idea. That was about two months ago."

"And you've been staying here ever since," Malone said.

"That's right," Margery said. "Poor Rodney — with that wife of his. He needs me, Malone."

Malone didn't comment on that. Instead, he said: "How about George? How did you feel about George?"

"I hate to speak ill of the dead," Margery said, and proceeded to do so. George, it seemed, was a slimy, loathsome beast, of dubious patronage and shocking habits. George was everything that Rodney, thank God, was not and never could be. "I'm afraid we just didn't get along," Margery finished.

"I'll say you didn't," Malone murmured admiringly. "Do you know anyone who might have wanted to murder him?"

"I'd have don't it myself," Margery said, "except that I didn't of course. He was mean to the servants, he treated Rodney with nothing but contempt, in spite of the fact that Rodney gave him money, and he was just cold and distant to Carla — though I can understand that. Carla is such a cold person herself."

Malone said: "Umm." He tried to think of another question to ask, and realized there wasn't one. "That's all," he said at last, and followed her out of the little room into the bright living room where everyone was waiting.

"You're just making a mystery out of this to confuse me," von Flanagan said. "You question everybody and get nowhere because there isn't anywhere to get. Rodney Melcher murdered his brother, and you know it because he told you he was going to do just that, when he saw you. And if you think all this mystery's going to work, Malone, you'd better get your head examined. Because I'm taking Rodney Melcher in right now. And you're coming with him."

"Wait," Malone said desperately. "Rodney didn't kill his brother."

"How do you know?" von Flanagan said. "And if he didn't, who did?"

"Rodney," Malone said, "where were you from three to four–thirty?"

"I was right here, Malone," Rodney said. "Sitting in the living room, reading.

I was all alone."

"There," Malone said triumphantly. "You see?"

"See what?" von Flanagan growled. "I see that you're trying to mix me up again, Malone. But it won't work. It won't work."

"You're stuck again," Malone offered helpfully. Before von Flanagan could say anything more he went on: "If Rodney Melcher had come to me, I'd have told him to fix up a good alibi. He'd have been somewhere else, with witnesses to swear to it. But he hasn't got an alibi. Therefore, he didn't come to me, and he didn't kill his brother." In his best courtroom manner, he continued: "It's obvious from that fact alone that you'll be making a terrible mistake, von Flanagan, if you arrest this poor man — "

"Then I'll make the terrible mistake," von Flanagan said. "Klutchesky!" he called.

The big patrolman appeared in the doorway. "I was talking to the servants," he said. "None of them knows a thing."

"Klutchesky," von Flanagan said, "I want you to take Malone in. He's gone nuts. He thinks he's a great detective."

"Malone?" Klutchesky said. "If you say so — "

Suddenly the little lawyer said: "Hold it." He tossed his cigar inaccurately at the fireplace and waved his arms for silence. "Great detective — that's it!"

"Completely mad," von Flanagan said. "Take him away."

"No, wait," Malone said. "I know who killed George Melcher — and I can prove it." He turned to Margery Dawes. "Dawes isn't your real name is it?" he asked.

"Of course it is," she said.

"We can check that," Malone told her.

She seemed to sag a little in her chair. "All right," she said at last. "So what if it isn't? I tell you I didn't kill George Melcher."

"I know you didn't," Malone said. "And now that I know your name isn't Margery Dawes, I know why you didn't. I mean I know why the real killer did."

"Malone," von Flanagan said, "are you putting on an act? Because temporary insanity isn't going to get you anywhere."

"I'm not insane," Malone said cheerfully. "I've just solved your case. It all happened because Rodney had the money."

"But Rodney isn't dead," von Flanagan said.

"That's right," Malone said. "George had to take an allowance from his brother, and he didn't like it. So he thought of a way to get money from somewhere else. If Rodney hadn't been rich, it would never have worked."

"Rodney?" Von Flanagan shook his head. "Malone, are you trying to tell me something?"

"I'm trying to tell you the name of the murderer," Malone said, "but you'll have to listen to me and hear me. *Is* that what I mean?"

"I don't know, Malone," von Flanagan said. Klutchesky stood on one foot and then he stood on the other one.

"Do you want me to arrest him?" he said.

"Never mind that," Malone said. "Margery Dawes isn't her real name. See?"

"See what?" von Flanagan said in spite of himself. Then he added: "This doesn't make any sense, Malone."

"It will," Malone said. "Be patient." He took a deep breath. Everything was perfectly clear in his mind, now. "George Melcher found out who Margery Dawes was, and he was blackmailing her. So he was killed."

"But you said Margery Dawes didn't kill him," von Flanagan said.

"She didn't," Malone said. "Her father did. He mentioned that George Melcher had been stabbed in the back. How did he know that?"

"Her *father?*" Rodney Melcher was on his feet.

"George knew that Margery would be ashamed of her father's being a butler in your house," Malone told him. "She probably came to live here — at her suggestion, remember — on her father's request. Maybe they thought they could get away with money or valuables if they both worked here as a team. Margery didn't want her connection with her father known, anyhow — so when George tried to blackmail her she went to her father, and her father killed him."

"Malone, what — " von Flanagan started to say.

"Watch Max!" Malone screamed. The butler came out swinging — but Klutchesky was right there, and it was all over.

"I can't thank you enough," Carla Melcher said. "I knew there was something wrong with that woman from the start."

"Sure," Rodney said disconsolately. "She was no good. Knew it right along. I was just waiting for the right time to make my move."

Carla looked at him. But there was less coldness in that look, now. There was understanding, and perhaps a little love. "Of course, darling," she said. "I understand."

"You do?" Rodney said. His face was amazed.

"Of course I do," Carla said.

Malone cleared his throat. "Maybe I'd better get back to the city," he said.

"Don't go back before I pay you," Rodney Melcher said. He brought out his billfold. "I gave you five hundred this afternoon, didn't I?"

Malone nodded. Rodney Melcher drew out another sheaf of bills. "Here's another five hundred," he said and handed it to Malone.

The little lawyer took the money silently. It would come in handy — when he finally got in touch with his important date. Suddenly he looked at his watch.

It was seven–twenty. Maybe she was still home.

He decided to find out.

We get a rare second glimpse at a Malone date in the person of Dolly Dove, whom Craig describes as "the mouse who built a better man-trap." Unlike the cool beauty of Helene Jusus from the Malone novels, Dolly is a more earthy woman who seems to have eyes just for Malone. Dolly attracts almost as much trouble as Malone himself, no easy feat. Von Flanagan never stands a chance against the two of them. -JM

No, Not Like Yesterday

Behind the big black hearse and the open convertibles banked with floral wreaths, the line of mourners' cars stretched for two miles, flanked by newsreel and television trucks, motorcycle police, and the reporters and photographers in press cars.

Up the broad avenue the procession moved at a pace that seemed, to Malone, a bit hasty for a funeral. Evidently the police detail which was leading the cortege up ahead had orders to get it done and over with as quickly as possible, before anything happened to mar the solemn obsequies.

For the city was alive with rumors. This was the first time in years an important gangland death had occurred, and the newspapers were giving it the full treatment. Not so much because of the status of the deceased, but because of potentially deadly differences of opinion over who was going to inherit his empire. 'GANG WAR MAY FLARE, 10 TOP HOODS MARKED FOR DEATH?' and 'GUNS BARK AGAIN IN GANG FEUD' were some of the page one headlines.

It was like old times again, the fellow mourner on John J. Malone's right remarked, and Malone nodded, and exchanged a nostalgic smile with Joe the Angel who sat beside him in the big black limousine rolling just behind the flowers and the chief mourners. Joe's cousin, Rico di Angelo, was the officiating mortician, which accounted for the up–front position of their car, a favor that was as eagerly coveted as a low–figure license plate or ringside seats at a heavyweight world championship bout. For the guest of honor was none other than Alvin (the Pike) Peake, one–time war boss and racket king, reportedly in retirement and now making his first public appearance in years — and his last.

Not that John J. Malone would not have rated a high up–front position in the funeral cortege in any case, as a friend of the deceased and as an honorary member of the Oblong Matching Society. But Joe the Angel had seen to it that the little lawyer, his friend and chief patron of Joe the Angel's City Hall Bar, should ride up front as near to the head man of the parade as funeral etiquette permitted.

156

"It's like old times again," the man on Malone's right repeated with a sigh, and mopped his bald head with a black–bordered handkerchief. This was the tenth time he had said it since he slipped into the seat beside him when they left the funeral chapel, and for the tenth time Malone bowed his head reverently.

The man's face looked familiar. One wouldn't be likely to overlook that combination of bald head and bushy red eyebrows. But Malone had failed to catch his name and now, after the fifth helping from the bottle that Joe the Angel had thoughtfully brought along to assuage his grief and that of his fellow mourners, Malone wasn't even sure introductions had been exchanged at all. He was on the point of correcting this oversight when Joe the Angel broke in with the opinion that it really wasn't like old times.

"Big Jim, he had twenty–seven cars with flowers. O'Banion, nineteen cars with flowers. I count them myself. All the time, less and less." Joe the Angel shook his head sadly. "No, not like old times."

Malone glanced at the man on his right to see if there would be any argument coming to the contrary, but the stranger was looking glumly out the window, seemingly lost in thought. Anyway, Joe was right, he reflected. Even moving three abreast behind the hearse there couldn't have been more than twelve convertibles full of flowers, quite a come–down from the old days when a gangster funeral resembled nothing so much as the Pasadena Festival of Roses followed by a Fourth of July parade, and gangland picked up the tab for fifty grand or more.

Even so, Alvin (the Pike) Peake was getting a send–off that a Senator might have envied. Bronze casket, silver handles, and a roster of honorary pallbearers that read like a combination of the City–Hall Elevator Board and the FBI's Most Wanted list. The works, with television — something that the old days didn't have. It added to the glow of sweet nostalgia that Joe the Angel's medicinal offering had already given him to think how his old friend the Pike would have loved it. Especially the occasional ticker tape and baskets of waste paper that office workers were tossing from the windows, evidently under the impression that what was passing down below was a reception for a returning channel swimmer or a visiting foreign dignitary.

But arriving at the cemetery, Malone was again struck by the unceremonious haste with which the rites were being rushed to completion. The air seemed to be filled with tension, as if everybody on this hot day — the city was in the fourth day of a sweltering heat wave — expected a storm to break at any minute, not from the elements of nature but what the newspaper editorial writers like to call the "city's criminal elements" — a phrase that the little lawyer had once defined to a jury as anybody who failed to make the customary arrangements and connections before embarking on a life of border–line business ventures. Police were everywhere and plain–clothesmen mingled with the crowd, keeping a sharp eye on every bulge that might indicate concealed artillery. Malone spotted von Flanagan, of Homicide, and signalled to him.

"What goes on, von Flanagan?"

"You tell me," von Flanagan grunted. "These are your friends." His nerves seemed to be on edge too.

Malone moved a little closer and said, "I shouldn't tell you this, von Flanagan, but if you hear of anybody being murdered tonight with an African throwing–spear, don't say I didn't warn you."

The big police officer grunted and moved off into the crowd. It was obvious that he was in no mood for chit–chat.

The unseemly haste finally resulted in everything getting tangled up with everything else. Pallbearers got lost and replacements had to be hastily recruited from the crowd, the hearse approached the grave wrong end to and had to be backed around, nearly running down half a dozen of the chief mourners. The fife and drum corps of the Oblong Marching Society, which was supposed to give something like drum–roll military finish to the final rite — someone had dis–covered that the Pike had been a World War I vet — never did show up at the graveside and was found afterwards wandering disconsolately around the edge of the crowd, trying to collect its members.

In the scramble for the returning limousines, Malone ran into the stranger with the red eyebrows once more. He was going back to town with friends in their car, he explained, but could he have a word with Malone privately? He looked scared.

"I planned to talk to you on the way up in the car, that's why I slipped in with you. But too many people around. You see, Malone, I expect trouble — " He looked around him apprehensively. "If something should happen to me — "

Someone in the crowd yelled "Come on, Smitty, let's go!" and the man with the red eyebrows started. He had the look of a strayed housecat hearing an angry bark. "If anything should happen to me — " he began again, "Call Maywood 9 — "

Again his friends called to him to come, and this time be broke off and ran back to them, disappearing in the crowd. But not before he had stuffed an envelope into Malone's coat pocket. When he got into the limousine Malone put his hand in his pocket and felt the envelope. It was sealed, but even through the paper he could detect the crisp feel of folding money. He decided not to open it in the presence of the oddly assorted strangers who had crowded into the car with him.

All during the uneventful but hurried ride back to town he worried about the stranger. Or was he a stranger? He did look familiar, but then, so did a lot of people. Most people, to Malone. He finally relegated the stranger to the classifi–cation of people he'd seen around somewhere, and waited until he was safely back in his office before opening the envelope. It contained ten crisp new hundred dollar bills.

Maggie, Malone's secretary, looked at the money and then looked across the desk at Malone.

"It's a retainer," Malone explained. "Deposit it. Break one first and bring it back in fives and tens. I've got a date tonight."

Maggie said, "What is it for?"

Malone took a cigar from his pocket and went about the business of slipping off the cellophane wrapper slowly and methodically. He needed a little time to think this one over.

Finally he said, "I told you. It's a retainer."

"Yes, but who's it from?"

"A client," Malone said unhappily. "A new client."

"What's his name?"

The little lawyer fished around in his pockets for a match.

"They're on the desk," Maggie said coldly. She handed them to him. "Now, what's his name? This new client?"

Malone said, "I don't know."

Maggie eyed him suspiciously. "What do you mean, you don't know?"

Malone took a few long puffs on his cigar before replying, like a destroyer laying down a defensive smoke screen. "Well, in a way, I mean, I don't know. His name is Smitty and he lives in Maywood." He paused, looked at Maggie and saw that she wasn't satisfied either. "He's got red eyebrows," he added, as if that explained everything. "Bushy red eyebrows."

Maggie looked at him and said absolutely nothing. At last Malone picked up the money and replaced it in the envelope. "Oh, all right. Put this into the safe. It stays there until I know who it's from and what it's for." He sighed deeply, "There is such a thing as professional ethics."

He spent what was left of the day worrying about a purely personal problem, and was no closer to solving it early in the evening when he sat in Joe the Angel's City Hall Bar, watching Joe the Angel polish up some glasses while he reminisced sadly about the late departed, about funerals in general, about his cousin Rico's dismay at the way the cops had loused up this funeral, and how the big rush of business that always followed such funerals at his bar had failed to materialize, owing, he lamented, to the newspaper headlines which had thrown everybody into a panic and sent them scurrying for cover. And all because Alvin (the Pike) Peake had finally died, in a quiet gentlemanly way, of a ruptured appendix. Which only went to show the way things were these days.

Malone said nothing for a while. In spite of the fact, that an appendix had done the job instead of a burst of machine–gun fire, the Pike had left a few heirs to his highly lucrative business operations who were bound to settle the estate the hard and noisy way. There was sound reasoning behind the newspaper headlines and the general disquiet in the atmosphere.

At last, to change the subject, Malone told Joe the Angel about the stranger in the limousine — he and Joe the Angel had lost each other in the crowd — laying particular emphasis on the thousand dollar cash retainer.

Joe the Angel beamed. "That's just fine." He reached behind the cash register for a grimy slip of paper. "Seventeen dollars and forty–five cents, even. Okay, make it seventeen even. And your drinks today–on the house, account of the Pike's funeral."

Malone shook his head.

Joe the Angel said, "Wat's a matter? You got a grand, no?"

"I got a grand, yes," Malone said. "But I can't touch it, not yet."

"What do you mean, you can't touch?"

Malone said, "I don't know who the client is, or what he's done, or if he even needs the services of a lawyer." He drew himself up with an impressive show of dignity. "There's such a thing as professional ethics." He waited to see what effect this noble sentiment would have on Joe the Angel. "There is one thing you can do for me," he said. "I've got a date tonight — "

Joe the Angel started automatically to shake his head. Then he said, "The brunette with the blue sedan, or the blonde with the yellow sportscar?"

"It's a green convertible, lime green, and the lady's name is Dolly Dove. A double sawbuck ought to do it, just for the incidentals. I've always got credit at the Chez."

Joe the Angel went on polishing his glasses, thinking things over.

Finally he went to the cash register, rang up No Sale, and handed over a twenty dollar bill. "The lady, what did you say her name is?"

"Dolly Dove," Malone said.

"She's the mouse who invented a better man–trap and now everybody is beating a path to her door."

Credit having been established and everything on a friendly and firm footing again, Joe the Angel poured another rye and beer on the house. Then he went into the back room and returned a moment later with a huge bunch of flowers. "Rico saved them for me," he explained. He stripped off the *Rest In Peace* ribbons and handed the bouquet to Malone. "For the lady," he said gallantly.

Malone thanked him, went out and hailed a cab. The driver eyed the bouquet and grinned. "Where to, Malone?"

"Sherman Hotel," Malone said. "The Style Show."

He settled back on the cushions before the driver could think of any remarks about Malone's choice of destinations. No reason for explaining that Dolly Dove was appearing as a model at the show that was the feature of the testimonial dinner for Robert P. Swale, and also a benefit for one of the philanthropist's favorite charities.

He sent the flowers around backstage to Dolly Dove and sat down at the rear of the ballroom to wait. The style show was just ending, and he noticed happily that Dolly was making her exit gracefully in a one piece bathing suit amid a round of applause. He looked around him and was struck at once by the number of men standing around that nobody, even without the experienced eye of the little lawyer, could possibly mistake for waiters, hotel attendants or guests. He wondered what new rumors or police tips might account for this detail of plainclothesmen at a charity testimonial dinner to one of the city's leading citizens. He knew Robert P. Swale as a business man and philanthropist, who had his finger in any number of financial pies, and he found himself wondering if these might still include certain interests which had once linked the name of Robert P. Swale with various politicians and assorted higher–ups of the old South Side boys.

"What's up, Malone?" Dolly Dove asked when she joined him in the lobby. "Backstage is crawling with cops. Somebody aiming for Mr. Big, maybe?"

Malone said, "Anything can happen, anytime, anywhere," and followed Dolly Dove to where her car was parked, in a special private parking lot reserved for officials, distinguished guests, and people like Dolly Dove. The attendant in charge insisted on unparking the car and held the door for her with fascinated attention as she ankled into it. Malone climbed into the front seat beside her and, pulling out the dashboard ashtray, safely deposited an inch of ash that he had been carefully juggling on the way. This was a rare show of neatness on his part, out of deference to Dolly Dove and the new lime green convertible. Normally the ashes would have been allowed to cascade down his vest and onto the floor.

"I haven't any idea who might be aiming for, or even at, Robert P. Swale," Malone said, as Dolly Dove made a hair–pin turn into traffic, with just a hair between them and disaster. He waited a minute to catch his breath before going on. "Maybe it's just the general scare. It's years since Bob Swale was mixed up in anything. You remember the Twenty–second street affair, the one the newspapers called the Chinatown Massacre — " He paused and looked at Dolly Dove. The honey–gold hair, the baby–bloom complexion. "No," he said decisively, "you wouldn't remember."

He laid a protective hand on the tiny one that was zig–zagging the convertible through the early–evening Loop traffic. "It's really before my time too," he said, mostly to reassure himself. Dolly Dove didn't seem to hear a word he was saying. "But, I've heard tell that in those days Bob Swale had a piece of nearly everything. On the South Side, that is. North of the Loop the North Side boys had it all their own way. That is, before the war started. I mean the one in Chicago, not the one in Europe. Of course, that was before Bob Swale married into the Horwell millions. The big headache powder people. Lilli Horwell. Lilli's put on a lot of weight since those days. You must have seen her sitting up there at the head table, the ones with the diamonds in her hair."

Maybe it was the mention of diamonds, but for the first time Dolly Dove took an interest in the conversation. "See her! Lilli was all over the place. Back stage, trying to run the whole style show. She drove everybody crazy. Maybe she's the one they're after," Dolly Dove finished wistfully.

He could sympathize with Dolly's feelings, Malone reflected. Lilli might have been a lively one in her salad days — she must have been, or she wouldn't have gone in for a marriage that was so far off–beat for a Blue–Book bride. The salad had wilted long ago, but the lettuce was still holding up pretty well, or Lilli wouldn't be able to afford such worthy — and well–publicized — philanthropies including a home for wayward girls, ping–pong and sweet–talk centers, for the rehabilitation of juvenile delinquents, and the personal sponsorship of an arts magazine. For most of these — except the arts magazine — Robert P. Swale was taking the public bows, and Malone couldn't help wondering how Lilli was taking that, what with that "driving, dynamic personality" the newspapers were always referring to.

He wondered what Robert P. Swale was up to lately, after all those years as a leading citizen and a philanthropist, for the police to be bothered about him.

The lime green convertible pulled up in front of the *Chez Paree* with the spine–snapping lurch that was standard landing procedure whenever Dolly Dove was at the wheel. Then she swept through the door a step ahead of Malone, smiled dazzlingly at everybody in sight and especially at the waiters, sat down gracefully at their reserved table and announced that she was so hungry she could eat the favorite at Tanforan, hide and all.

Malone looked across the table and what met his eyes drove all reminiscences of gang wars and rumors of murders out of his mind. Whatever magic she had done to her hair, it brought out the spun–gold tones in a lustrous halo, just like they said in the singing commercials. The lipstick she wore was something between rosy hope and purple promise, and her voice had a touch of both in it. He noticed that the corsage she wore was a tasteful selection from the flowers that Joe the Angel had so thoughtfully salvaged from Rico's funeral parlor.

That brought his thoughts back to the funeral and while they waited for their drinks he recounted the events of the day, the confusion at the cemetery, the police swarming all over the place and only adding to the feeling of terror and suspense that the newspapers had succeeded in whipping up all over town.

"But let's forget about it," he said reassuringly, as the waiter arrived. "It's nothing that's going to interfere with our lovely evening — "

He'd seldom been quite so wrong in his life.

They'd barely reached the stage of ordering supper when von Flanagan appeared at the edge of the room, looking over the crowd, and Malone immediately felt an unpleasantly cold finger of apprehension poking along his spine. The *Chez* was not one of the big police officer's regular visiting spots and furthermore, Klutchetsky was with him, which gave it the appearance of an official call.

He kept his aplomb however even as von Flanagan spotted him and strode purposefully over to his table.

"Sorry to bust up your evening," von Flanagan said, "but you've got some explaining to do. You've got a lot of explaining to do."

"Now look here — " Malone began in what was a feeble and, he knew, futile protest.

"Look here, nothing," von Flanagan said briskly. "Kiss your date goodbye and come along and start explaining how you knew, ahead of time, how Bob Swale was going to be murdered."

Malone blinked. "The last time I saw Robert P. Swale, he was enjoying the best of health. At least, almost the best."

"Well, he ain't now," von Flanagan said. "Not even almost. And you not only knew it ahead of time but what's more, you knew he was going to get it with an African throwing–spear." Before Malone could catch his breath he added, "So let's go downtown and talk this over, and not make a nasty scene in this nice, quiet nightclub."

"But I've been planning this date for a long time," Malone protested unhappily.

"And maybe some of your clients had been planning to murder Bob Swale for a long time," von Flanagan said. "The little lady can wait."

It always happened that way, the little lawyer thought bitterly. The long and perfect buildup, even to a corsage — and then something like this.

Dolly Dove rose to the occasion. "The little lady is coming with you," she said briskly.

"Oh no, you're not," von Flanagan began.

"Oh yes, I am," Dolly Dove told him. "I was around Mr. Swale this evening. In fact, he even made a pass at me. And I made one right back at him, with the flat of my hand, the plastered bum."

"Plastered?" von Flanagan said.

Dolly Dove said, "He was so pie–eyed, his crust was showing. So I probably know as much about this as Malone does, and I'm coming right along."

It may have been the firm finality in her voice, or it may have been just one good, long look at Dolly Dove, but von Flanagan growled an assent, nodded to Klutchetsky, and began elbowing a path to the exit. Malone seized an opportunity to squeeze Dolly Dove's hand and whisper, "You didn't need to do this, you know."

"I know," she whispered back, "but I don't like being left stranded at the *Chez* or anywhere. Besides, I was curious."

In spite of the warm glow that her presence gave him, Malone felt the sense of apprehension grow and envelope him. Something had gone on and was going on that he couldn't understand at all, perhaps didn't even want to understand. It was dark and obscure and mysterious, and it frightened him.

It didn't make him feel any better to walk into von Flanagan's office and see the throwing–stick itself lying on top of the big flat–topped desk, a slender, delicate, but deadly looking weapon with a wicked looking spear–head and a feather tail. He looked at it, at the dark blood still congealing on the needle–sharp point of it, and shuddered.

"Lab's through with it," Gadenski said, getting up.

Malone looked at the skinny, black–haired police detective and said, "Who's missing? Thought he was dead."

"Borrowed Gadenski from Missing Persons," von Flanagan said. He sat down heavily. "Account of, he's an expert on these things." He indicated the throwing–stick.

Malone raised a questioning eyebrow. Gadenski nodded. "Have been, ever since somebody gave my nephew Stanley a bow and arrow. Got to be a hobby of mine. Read all about this stuff."

The lawyer waved Dolly Dove to the most comfortable chair and kept on with Gadenski, still stalling for thinking time. "What's some more about it?"

"Well," Gadenski said, brightly and happily, "it's real name is assegai. Because the wood comes from the assegai tree." He went on, reciting rapidly, "Botanically named the Curtisia faginea, a relative of the dogwood tree, with big white and pinkish flowers. It's the favorite weapon of the Zulu warrior who can drive it clear through a gazelle a hundred yards away. Notice how delicately balanced it is, and how sharp the point is. The feather tail is to make it fly faster." Gadenski paused, smiled patronizingly. "Eagle feathers, naturally. To make it fly faster than chicken feathers would."

"I suppose horse feathers would make it fly even faster," Malone said nastily, "if they came from Nashua."

Von Flanagan snorted. "Shut up, Malone. It's nice to know what this African throwing–stick is all about, but what I want to know is, how Malone had the information on how it was going to be used, and had it early today."

Gadenski looked hurt, and sat down again. Malone looked innocent.

"I didn't know anything about it," he said weakly. "I just — said that." He hoped that was the truth. Because there was only one other possible solution he could see, and he didn't like the prospect of it. Though, he reminded himself, while there was no Welsh grandmother in his ancestry, there had been times when his premonitions had come uncomfortably and terrifyingly close to second sight.

"Why did you say it?" von Flanagan demanded, in a voice like thunder.

Malone thought frantically and miserably. "I don't know."

Von Flanagan snorted again, and glared at him.

Dolly Dove came to his rescue and changed the subject by asking, "Where did you find it?"

"In Robert P. Swale's back," von Flanagan said. "And Robert P. Swale was flat on his face in the private parking lot by the hotel." He turned back to Malone. "And you — "

"Were there any Zulus around?" Dolly Dove asked hastily.

Von Flanagan glared at her instead. Malone felt a rush of gratitude that included thoughts of a certain pearl grey chiffon negligee, straight from Paris, he'd noticed only a few days before in a Michigan Avenue shop.

"No, there weren't any Zulus around," von Flanagan said, "and you keep out of this."

"Wouldn't have to be a Zulu," Malone said quickly, picking it up. "What about a javelin thrower, like in the Olympic games? That thing can't be easily thrown."

The subject seemed to be successfully changed, at least for the moment. Von Flanagan nodded, slowly. "Could be."

Klutchetsky stirred his huge bulk and spoke for the first, and probably only time that evening. "Pitcher," he said.

Von Flanagan nodded again. "Could also be a baseball pitcher." He looked at Gadenski. "You're the expert."

"Well," Gadenski said dubiously, "of course, it would be an entirely different kind of windup, but — "

There was a little silence, for which Malone thanked providence. "So all I've got to do," von Flanagan roared at last, "is find a javelin thrower outa the Olympic games maybe, or a baseball player with a funny wind–up who didn't like Robert P. Swale *and who knows Malone!*"

This time, the silence was a deathly one.

And this time, it was Malone who succeeded in switching the subject. "Just how could this javelin thrower, or big–league baseball player, throw that thing a hundred yards — like Gadenski said — across the parking lot, without attracting anybody's attention?"

It worked. Von Flanagan looked through some papers on his desk and said, "At that time, which must have been around eleven–fifteen, there wasn't nobody in the parking lot except the attendant. And I say it must have been around eleven–fifteen, on account of, the attendant was gone, for about ten minutes maybe, about that time. This attendant, whose name is," — he looked closely — "Willie R. Henkin, states he left the parking lot for approximately ten minutes beginning at eleven–fifteen to sneak out and catch the girl act in the floor–show next door which goes on at that hour. "And the body of Robert P. Swale was discovered at eleven–forty–five and hadn't been dead long." He looked up. "And there wasn't anybody else around as far as he knows. Now Malone — "

"Who found him?" Malone asked.

"Mrs. Swale. Lilli Swale. He'd wandered off someplace after the big doings, and after the last act in the show she and some friend of hers, name of Mawson Satterlee, went looking for him and found him dead by his car in the parking lot. So that's what we know, and we know what the name of this thing is, and what kind of wood it was made of, and an Olympic games javelin thrower or a baseball pitcher could have, but not necessarily did throw it, and that's all we know, except — "

"Where did it come from?" Malone said, catching at what he suspected would be his last straw. "How did it get all the way to Chicago from Africa?"

Gadenski cleared his throat. "I can make a good guess," he offered. "It came from a little shop in Maywood, full of all kinds of funny junk. Old books, and second–hand furniture, and just plain junk, and also a lot of old firearms and funny old weapons of all kinds. The guy's a collector of 'em. I go out there sometimes, and he had a couple of these hung up on the wall."

A premonition that was more than second–sight began to grow in Malone's mind.

"Crazy little guy," Gadenski went on. "Reads everything he can about gangsters, the real old time stuff, so much he thinks he's one himself. Hangs around the bad boys all the time. They usually brush him off, but he gives 'em laughs." He added, "Little guy, Walter Schmidt. Bald as an ostrich egg, bushy red eyebrows."

The premonition had become a certainty. The cold poking finger of apprehension had grown and become a fist now, and it was choking him breathless.

"We'll pick him up," Von Flanagan said, making a note, and nodding to Klutchetsky to get going. "All right, Malone — "

"Von Flanagan," the little lawyer begged miserably, "Think something."

Von Flanagan stared at him balefully. "Think *what?*"

"I don't care," Malone said. "Think anything. You pick it. Just *think* something."

There was another silence, a puzzled one. After a time von Flanagan said, "All right, I am thinking something, I'm thinking you'd better quit stalling and tell me some facts."

"I know that," Malone said, waving that idea away. "You don't understand." He drew a long breath. "Von Flanagan, I want you to think about something. Don't tell me what it is. You pick it out. Just think it. I want to see if I know what it is."

"You mean, you — " Von Flanagan blinked. Then he nodded. "Okay, here goes." He looked hard at Malone and turned fairly purple in the face with concentration. After a full minute he said, "All right, I was thinking."

Malone shook his head. "I didn't get it." There was a little relief in his tone, but puzzlement too. "What was it?"

"I was thinking about my mother–in–law's birthday party a week ago yesterday night," von Flanagan said, "and how my cousin Al — " He checked himself. "Malone, are you sure you feel real well?"

"No," Malone said in an unhappy voice, "no, I don't feel well at all."

"Malone," Dolly Dove said, fascinated, "do you mean you've turned out to be one of those people who can read other people's minds?" She gasped. "Like telling what's on playing cards other people are looking at?"

"If I could tell that," Malone assured her, "I'd be a much better–off man today. But — "

Von Flanagan was still staring at Malone. "Maybe you ought to go somewhere and lie down for a while."

"Maybe I should," Malone said. He wanted a little peace and quiet in which to do some thinking of his own. All he knew now was that whatever was happening to him was something he didn't like at all.

"Malone," von Flanagan said suspiciously, "you wouldn't lie to me, would you?"

"I would not," Malone said. He added, "Certainly, not about a thing like this. I told you, I didn't know why I said that about the African throwing–stick this afternoon, and I was telling the absolute truth. I'm telling the absolute truth now when I tell you that I'm positive somebody near me was thinking about murdering somebody with an African throwing–stick, and the thought got into my mind." He reflected that in the strictest interest of absolute truth he should go on and explain about Smitty, but that would be carrying honesty just a little too far.

"I never met anything like this in my life!" von Flanagan said, with unmixed awe as he looked at Malone. A light came into his eyes. "Malone, maybe if you get near this person again and he thinks something else, you'll be able to identify him."

"It's a chance," Malone said. He added, "though I doubt if it would hold up in front of a jury — "

Von Flanagan shrugged his shoulders and remarked that juries were the district attorney's worry, and not his. "Maybe this person will even be so obliging as to think why he did it, and save us a lot of trouble all around. If anyone needed any particular reason for murdering this guy."

Malone nodded at that. The late Robert P. Swale had been a man who attracted enemies as naturally as candy attracted babies.

"He was still mixed up in a lot of stuff," von Flanagan said. "For a public–spirited guy, that is. Tangled with Max Hook lately. Though the Max Hook boys don't go much for African throwing–sticks." He grinned unpleasantly.

Malone reminded his old friend of the business rivalry that was reputed to be springing up since the recent natural death of Alvin (the Pike) Peake.

"That would fit in too," von Flanagan said. He added suddenly, "So his widow says. Want to meet her? She's in the next room with this Satterlee guy, waiting to sign her statement." He told Gadenski to invite the lady in.

Malone looked up curiously as the former Lilli Horwell swept into the room with all the aplomb of a once–famous beauty who hasn't been told yet that age can wither. The headache powder heiress still had the blazing red hair for which she'd been justly admired and, it seemed to Malone, it had grown even redder with the years. There was a lot more of Lilli Horwell, now Swale, than there had been, too, but he had to admit that she carried it with considerable dash.

Her companion was a pallid, frail man with a slightly receding chin, pale hair and eyes, and a dress shirt that, to Malone's shuddering horror, was a light, delicate blue.

She seemed to feel that some explanation of him was necessary, and introduced him to Malone as editor of *Dynamic!* the new literary publication she was sponsoring. Malone nodded to him and reflected that while dynamic was certainly the word for Lilli, the only word for Mawson Satterlee was delicate.

He wondered why she'd been brought to police headquarters. Certainly the so recently made widow of Robert P. Swale deserved all the red carpet treatment that could be rolled out. Then on immediate second thought, he realized that it was the other way around. She hadn't been brought here, she'd come here. Lilli Swale was going to want to know what was going on in the investigation every inch of the way, and von Flanagan was going to be fortunate if she gave him time to go home and shave.

He watched while she and her little editor signed statements regarding the discovery of the body, having come out to the parking lot in search of the late Mr. Swale after the last act of the floor show at which they had a ringside table. Or rather, she had discovered it and gone in search of Mawson Satterlee, informing him, the police, the parking lot attendant and, as near as Malone could figure out, everybody within earshot. She had very little else to say, except adding that naturally Mr. Swale had enemies, especially among the lower elements of the city, giving Malone a cool look as she added the description. And was the police department doing anything about it?

Von Flanagan hastened to assure her that they were doing everything about it, but Lilli Swale showed every indication of remaining right where she was until her husband's murderer was not only found, but quite probably convicted and executed. And it was getting later by the minute.

Malone stepped up with the smile and manner which had, more than once, reduced the feminine members of a jury to complete and moist-eyed harmony and fellow feeling, and said, "My dear lady — let me assure you, you haven't a thing to concern yourself about. The affair couldn't be in more capable hands and believe me, I've known Captain von Flanagan for years and years."

He did everything but pat her hand as he went on, "Why, he even has a suspect right now, a very hot suspect. Has his name, his address, his description — everything. And there's a man out after him right now."

Lilli Swale looked at von Flanagan. "Well?"

"That's right," von Flanagan said. "Absolutely right."

"Why," Malone assured her warmly, "he'll probably have the arrest made and everything settled by the time you wake up in the morning, dear lady. I promise it."

This time she said it. "Well — ", and after only a few more minutes, and many more reassurances from Malone, she was on her way.

Von Flanagan mopped his brow and said, "Well, I owe you for that, anyway. So go on with your date — but be here in the morning!" He scowled. "And we'd better have that guy Schmidt here in the morning, too, if I know that red–haired dame's temper."

Malone remembered that the missing Schmidt was, in a manner of speaking, his client, and called himself several names, including Judas. But it was too late now.

"Tell me," von Flanagan said suddenly, "while she was here — Malone, was she thinking anything?"

Malone shook his head. "Not a thing, as far as I know."

Dolly Dove sniffed. "She probably was keeping her mind a blank, if she has a mind, and if it isn't blank all the time anyway. Because she probably killed the guy herself."

"It would make everything very simple if she had," Malone said, "but she was watching the floor show. And anyway, why?"

"Oh, stuff like this fool editor and that fool magazine."

Hardly a motive for murder, Malone thought, but he knew what she meant. Causes were all in line with Bob Swale's manner of life, but they were causes like free milk for voters' babies, and benefit funds for Christmas baskets. He and the insipid little Mawson Satterlee came from very different sides of the tracks. Malone had seen one issue of *Dynamic!* and reflected that it — made up of writers writing about other writers, at no cents per word — was hardly reading matter that would have appealed to the once gusty and lusty Robert P. Swale. But maybe the great man had changed.

"And he was a chaser," Dolly Dove said. "Not the kind that pinches girls in elevators, the kind that thinks about pinching them."

The little lawyer cluck–clucked, reminded her not to speak ill of the dead, steered her hastily out of the office before von Flanagan could change his mind, out to the sidewalk and into a taxicab.

There was, he decided, no point in trying to pick up the lost gossamer threads of the evening now. Dolly Dove was still at his side, but the build–up was a total loss. And it was too late to go back to the *Chez* anyway.

And Joe the Angel's was the only place where he still had credit. A back booth in Joe the Angel's was no place to start a romantic build–up over again, but at least he could buy a drink.

Joe the Angel had heard all about the murder of Robert P. Swale, and looked hopefully at Malone. In a case like this, there was always the possibility of a profitable client. He hailed them as they came in the door and waved them to seats at the bar. Malone abandoned his idea of the booth, Joe the Angel might have some helpful hints, and tomorrow was always another night.

The owner, manager, bartender and janitor of Joe the Angel's City Hall Bar beamed approvingly at Dolly Dove and said to Malone, "Who killed him, Malone?"

"I don't know," Malone said. "I'll probably read all about that in the newspapers."

Joe the Angel thought that was very funny. He poured two drinks and said to Dolly Dove, "That Malone, he knows everything."

Dolly Dove nodded solemnly and said, "What's more, he even knows what people think. He reads minds."

Joe the Angel stared at her incredulously. "You mean he can tell what you think? And what I think?"

"What everybody thinks," Dolly Dove said. "He even knew what the murderer was thinking, only he doesn't know who it was?"

Now Joe the Angel stared at Malone.

"It's true," Malone said. He went on to tell his old friend what had happened that afternoon at the cemetery and its sequel that evening, omitting the minor detail of Smitty and the retainer. That was still nobody's business but his own.

Joe the Angel crossed himself hastily, then poured another drink. The Polish janitor from the City Hall, who had been brooding silently into his beer, rose, walked to the door, looked at Malone and began, "Back in my country — " Then he went out.

"In his country," Dolly Dove said, "you'd probably have been burned as a witch."

And quite possibly rightly, Malone thought dismally. He didn't like this business, he didn't like any part of it, and yet there it was. Facts were facts, and there was no getting around these. It gave him an unhappy, haunted feeling.

"Try it again," Dolly Dove said. She looked at Joe the Angel. "You think something."

"Malone, he knows what I am thinking," Joe the Angel said dourly.

"I do," Malone said, finishing his drink, and pushing the glass back for a refill, "and you'll be paid in the morning, and let's change the subject."

"Let's not," Dolly Dove said. "I'll think something."

"That wouldn't be fair," Malone objected. "If I did get it right, I'd probably just be wishing."

She sighed. "All right. Suppose we try it in reverse. You think something and I'll try to get it."

Malone paused, his glass in mid–air, and stared at her. "Just a minute. You've got something there — "

Before he could go on, the telephone rang. Joe the Angel came out of the booth and announced that it was for Malone.

Walter Schmidt had been found. He had been found, riddled with bullets, as the morning papers would put it, in an alley near Chicago Avenue. But he was alive, and he was calling for Malone. And von Flanagan was being very difficult, and suspicious over the phone.

The little lawyer finished his drink, waved goodbye to Joe the Angel and went out to the lime green convertible with Dolly Dove. On the breathtaking drive to the hospital he was strangely silent, brooding.

Parked at the entrance he grabbed her hand and said, "Wait for me, don't leave me."

"I'll be here," she promised.

"I need you for something. An experiment. I don't know exactly what it is yet, but I know I'm going to need you."

He hurried up the steps. An indignant and red–faced von Flanagan was waiting for him in the lobby.

"Second sight," he snarled, "and I fell for it! I might have known better. After all these years, Malone — "

"I told you the truth," Malone said earnestly, "and I'm telling it to you again right now. And besides," he added, "it isn't second sight, it's mind reading."

Von Flanagan shrugged his shoulders to indicate what he thought of the difference. "The guy's asking for you. I suppose that's second sight too. Or mind reading."

"I don't know what it is," Malone said. "And what happened?"

"Just what I told you," von Flanagan said. "Little guy was found in an alley. Won't talk. Won't say anything except ask for you." He glared at Malone, then suddenly softened. "Malone — old friend. Maybe he'll talk to you."

Malone started to say something, changed his mind and said instead, with a wan smile, "Maybe he will." And maybe what he had to say would be for Malone's ears alone.

He noticed a few reporters hovering in the corridor and among them, Ned McKoen, reporter, columnist, commentator and occasionally, friend. That meant Smitty's little mishap was considered on the important side. He made a mental note to see McKoen on his way out and find out just what the social standing of this murder was.

Smitty had nothing to say, and he was saying it with grim determination. His lips, as the saying goes, were sealed. But his waxy face brightened a little at the sight of Malone.

"Here you are," von Flanagan said with forced brightness. "See, I got Malone for you. Now will you be a good boy and tell me who shot you up?"

Smitty's eyes told von Flanagan he'd happily see him in hell first.

"Now," von Flanagan said gently and reprovingly. "That's no way to be. That's no way to cooperate. We're your friends." He cleared his throat, deli–cately. "Suppose you don't make it, Smitty. We want to punish the guys who done it. We want to stop them from doing the same thing to somebody else. You want us to do that, don't you?" He looked at the injured man hopefully and anxiously.

"No," Smitty said flatly.

Malone sighed. "Leave me alone with him."

This time von Flanagan said, "No," flatly.

Malone sighed again. He looked at Smitty. "Am I your lawyer?"

"Yes," Smitty said.

"Good." Malone looked at von Flanagan. "Privileged communications. Lawyer and client. Beat it. Scram. *Scat!*"

Von Flanagan muttered something highly inappropriate for a sick–room and the presence of a possibly dying man, and went away shaking his head gloomily.

"Now," Malone said, sitting down by the bed. "You can talk to me. Who shot you?"

But Smitty still said, "No."

He argued the point for a wasted fifteen minutes and gave up. Smitty's lips were not only sealed, they were padlocked.

"Oh all right," he said wearily at last, "have it your own way. What do you want me to do for you?"

"Somebody — " Smitty whispered, "trying to — frame me — for a murder." His round blue eyes were frightened.

"Happens all the time," Malone assured him comfortingly. "Who? Whose murder? Why?"

Smitty shook his head weakly. "Know lotsa — the guys. Knew the Pike. Went to see him when he was sick. He give me box of papers to keep for him. Locked box. Said his partner would want them if he — died."

Malone rolled a cigar around between his fingers. "And his partner was — ?"

"Don't know. But — somebody stole the box." His eyes held Malone's imploringly. "And — somebody stole — assegai — throwing–stick — "

"I know that," Malone said. "Now look, Smitty, this is important — this morning — "

But Smitty's eyes were closed. Malone looked at him for a moment, then fled into the corridor and howled for the doctor.

Smitty was all right, the doctor announced a few minutes later, in fact in time he was going to be as good as new. But right now he was dead to the world and likely to stay that way for a long time.

Malone and von Flanagan looked at each other, two tired and defeated men. "Somebody was trying to frame him for murder," Malone said at last.

"That," von Flanagan snapped, "is what they always say. He owned a bunch of these African throwing–sticks. So he probably knew how to throw one. He'll probably come up with an alibi for the fifteen minutes the attendant was out of the parking lot" — he gave Malone a shriveling glance — "if I know his lawyer, but I've broken alibis before."

"And then somebody shot him in a purely playful mood," the little lawyer said.

"I'll find out about that too," von Flanagan said wrathfully. "In the meantime, he can't get away from here. And," he added with a final glare, "I always know where to find you when I want you." He strode off purposefully.

Malone and Ned McKoen headed for each other simultaneously. The lawyer said, "What brings you here, McKoen?" and the columnist said, "What's the score, Malone?" in one breath. It was Malone who stared down the other and was answered first.

"Bob Swale was done to death, as I like to put it, with an African throwing–stick," Ned McKoen said. "This little guy was known to be a dealer in such odd and fanciful weapons. And according to my Little Gem Lightening Pocket Calculator, two and two make news."

"Good as far as it goes," Malone said sourly, "and that *is* as far as it goes." He was damned if he'd let the news of his sudden discovery of mental telepathy get all over Chicago. There wouldn't be a soul left in town to play poker with.

"Bob Swale," the columnist said, "was tied in very closely with some of the late Alvin Peake's less salubrious interests. Or so the story goes. Or rather so the story would have gone."

Malone managed to look just interested enough and no more so, with a faint touch of skepticism added in.

"With Alvin Peake's sad and untimely end," Ned McKoen said, "there was about to be an investigation, and there would have been one hell of a big stink and one hell of a big story. Now, with Bob Swale dead, nobody cares, including me, and my paper. But where, Malone, does this Schmidt guy fit in?"

"If I knew," Malone said, "I just might tell you. But I don't. And," he added thoughtfully, "somehow I don't think he knows much either."

"Old pal," Ned McKoen said, "have you anything to say to an old pal?"

"Just this," Malone stated sententiously, "that Walter Schmidt, in keeping with the best old–time gangland tradition lies with sealed lips tonight, refusing to name his would–be assassins."

He went on out to the car and Dolly Dove, climbed in wearily and slammed the door.

"I waited for you," Dolly Dove said softly.

He squeezed her hand. "Don't go away," he said miserably.

Her smile promised him that she wouldn't. "Where to, Malone?"

He shook his head and lifted his shoulders.

"Let's go up to my place for a nightcap?"

It was a remark he'd been working towards now for days. And any other time during the long build–up he'd have welcomed it effusively. Now, he simply nodded.

He'd learned a few things but right now, none of them seemed to be important. Robert P. Swale and Alvin (the Pike) Peake had been hand in glove and glove in hand, that was news, but not exactly surprising. Alvin Pike had left a locked box probably full of information about Robert P. Swale with the little junk dealer and would–be gangster, Walter Schmidt. The box had disappeared and an explosive investigation into Robert P. Swale's connection had been imminent. Obviously, Malone reflected, some enterprising American reporter had swiped the box. But American reporters didn't go around murdering prominent citizens, even reprehensible ones.

Now Robert P. Swale was dead and so was the investigation and the story, which was unfortunate from the viewpoint of the investigators, the newspapers, and Robert P. Swale himself. Somebody had made off with an African throwing-stick from Smitty's collection and thrown it with deadly accuracy at Robert P. Swale. Now someone had taken a bunch of pot shots at Smitty himself.

That was that, and none of it seemed the least important. The important thing, Malone thought, important and terrible and frightening, was that somehow, he'd known about it in advance.

He shivered.

Dolly Dove looked at him consolingly and said, "A drink will fix you up."

It did, and it didn't. It warmed him and comforted him a little, as did the brightness and cheerfulness of Dolly Dove's gay little living room, but it failed to lighten his spirits nor drive away the terrors that oppressed him.

She pushed a hassock over by his feet, sat down, clasped her lovely hands around her lovelier knees and looked up at him. "Tell me, Malone. That little man. While you were in the room with him — did he think anything?"

Malone scowled in thought. He shook his head. "Not that I noticed." He paused. "And, damn it, he didn't say much, either. Just that he was being framed for murder. I assume he meant this one. There haven't been any other conspicuous murders lately, not that I know of."

"I suppose there's no doubt at all about Alvin Peake?"

"None whatsoever," he assured her. "Everybody made very sure of that at the time." He scowled again. "Unless he means a murder that hasn't been committed yet, and somehow I don't think that he does."

"Anyway," she said thoughtfully, "you'd know if it were that, wouldn't you?"

He looked at her unhappily. There it was again, the thing he didn't like to think about. Somehow, he had to put it out of his mind, and right now.

Here he was, he reminded himself, in Dolly Dove's little apartment, a drink in his hand, Dolly Dove looking up at him with that sweet, gentle smile of hers. It was a situation he'd been working hard at creating and for a long time. Now he was here. But it was also four in the morning after a long, hard, full day.

After a few minutes of futile struggle, Malone put down his glass and his cigar, yawned once, and slept.

He woke a few hours later to the cheering odor of coffee and the bubbly sound of it perking away in the kitchen. Sun was streaming in through the chintz-curtained windows. Malone yawned and stretched. Somehow, nothing seemed quite as bad as it had a few hours before.

Dolly Dove came in with a tray of coffee and her brightest smile. The little lawyer lighted his first cigar of the day and smiled at her affectionately.

"And now," Dolly Dove said, passing him a cup, "as you were saying a little while ago — "

The problems of the day came back to him in a rush, but so did something else. Last night he'd been on the verge of a very important discovery when he'd been rudely interrupted by von Flanagan's call, and it came back to him now.

"Dolly," he said earnestly. "Remember last night, in Joe the Angel's — you said — "

She nodded. "I said — suppose you try it in reverse. You think and I'll try to know what it is." She giggled. "And don't make me slap your face."

He stared at her. "That's it," Malone said. "I've got it now." He rose. "And I'm going right down to von Flanagan's office, right this minute."

"Right the next minute," she corrected him. "I'm going with you, but not in a hostess gown. You don't think I'd miss any of this now, do you?"

He had barely time to get his first cigar of the day under way before she reappeared, ready to go. One look at his rapt face informed her that this was no time for asking questions, and the drive in the lime–green convertible was made with velocity and in silence.

Von Flanagan looked up from his desk gloomily. "I didn't expect you to show your face around here right away," he said in a heavy, unhappy voice. He added, "But I suppose you know everything about everything."

"I don't know anything about anything," Malone said, waving Dolly Dove to a chair. "But I think — "

Von Flanagan glared at him. "Don't mention that word around here, now, or ever," he said firmly. He went on, "Your little pal Smitty is in the clear. At the time Robert P. Swale was having an African throwing–stick thrown into him, Walter Schmidt was arguing out a traffic ticket with an Oak Park cop."

"I'm not surprised," Malone said smoothly and serenely. "I always expect my clients to be innocent. And" — this time, a little smugly — "I'm not even confused. You see, von Flanagan — "

He paused, lit a cigar, smiled and said, "Now on the subject of thinking — "

Von Flanagan groaned.

"We just had it backwards," Malone said. "I didn't know what anyone was thinking. Never could and never did. As my dear friend Dolly Dove pointed out to me, it was just the other way."

"You mean, you thought something?" von Flanagan asked.

"No," Malone told him, "I said something."

There was a little silence. Von Flanagan scowled at Malone, rubbed his ear, and finally said "I don't exactly get it."

"It's just as I told you," Malone went on. "I said something to you about not being surprised if somebody was murdered with an African throwing–stick. Now what put that in my head?"

"I've sometimes wondered," von Flanagan said acidly, "just what puts anything in your head."

Malone ignored him. "All the way out, I'd been wondering who Smitty was, and where I'd seen him. Well, I remember now. I'd met him right at his own place, that fantastic little junk shop of his. Judge Touralchuck and I stopped there one night in Maywood on our way to a — a meeting."

Von Flanagan snorted skeptically.

"I saw the African throwing–sticks. Seeing Smitty again put them in my mind. When I spoke to you, I simply said the first thing that came into my head, and that was it."

"Logical enough," von Flanagan said. "I'll go along with you that far."

"And," Malone said, "somebody heard me." He paused for dramatic effect. "Somebody had the murdering of Robert P. Swale already in mind and thought that I'd made a fine suggestion. As I had. Somebody who knew Smitty and that he had the things in his shop. Somebody who figured, rightly, that it would throw the police department into no end of confusion by making my prediction come true. As it did. It even," he added with due humility, "confused me."

Von Flanagan nodded slowly. "All right. I'll keep right on going along with you. Who was there, in earshot?"

Malone frowned, trying to remember. "Not so many. You were. Smitty was. Joe the Angel's cousin Frankie, driving the car. Judge Touralchuck. And" — he frowned — "Robert P. Swale."

Von Flanagan rubbed the other ear. "Judge Touralchuck is out. He's deaf enough he probably didn't even hear you, and besides — " He paused. "And Robert P. Swale would hardly go around throwing African throwing–sticks at himself even if he could have done it."

"No," Malone said, "but he could have mentioned the remark to someone else."

There was silence while they both considered that.

"His wife, for instance," Dolly Dove said suddenly. "I bet he's the kind of guy who tells everything to his wife. Or was," she amended hastily.

They thought that over, too. "She was watching the floor show at the only time the attendant was away from the parking lot," von Flanagan objected. "Grant that Lilli Swale had reasons for wanting to murder her husband."

"Including," Malone put in, "the fact that a big scale investigation was about to bust loose, which would raise particular hell with the Swale social and other standing. Lilli would much rather have seen her husband dead than investigated."

"I'll take that, too," von Flanagan said. "And she probably could have thrown that thing the length of the parking lot and landed it right where she wanted it. But she couldn't have done it without the attendant seeing it, and the fact remains that the only time — " He paused, grabbed the telephone and said, "I'll check."

Fifteen minutes later they faced the fact that during the brief interval the attendant, Willie R. Henkin, had been away, Lilli Swale had been at a floor–side table watching the last act of the floor show, and had been seen by, apparently, half the city of Chicago.

They sat and considered that in another long, gloomy silence.

"Cheer up, Malone," Dolly Dove said at last., "Nobody can be right all the time." She took out a cigarette and said, "Toss me a match."

He handed it to her instead —- or started to. Instead he stared at her, lighted match in hand, burnt his fingers, dropped the match, beamed at her, hugged her enthusiastically and turned to von Flanagan, who inquired politely if he'd suddenly gone mad.

"Look!" the little lawyer said. "Because the damned thing is called an African throwing–stick, we've all blithely assumed it had to be thrown. Which, naturally, would have attracted the attention of the parking lot attendant. But she could have come along a little later, slipped up behind him, stabbed him with the spear — "

"Malone — " von Flanagan said, his face brightening.

"And," Malone went on, when you point that out to her — you can also point out that Walter Schmidt is recovering, and can identify the party who swiped his African throwing–stick, likewise the party who shot him up — that he can, and he will — " He crossed his fingers and hoped that the luck which had never deserted him before would not desert him now.

Von Flanagan's big red face fairly shone.

"Furthermore," Malone finished, "when it's all over and she's broken down and admitted it — which she will — she's bound to need a good defense lawyer, and — "

"I'll mention your name," von Flanagan said, reaching for the phone.

Events proved that Malone was right on all points but one. After it was all over, and after he'd visited Lilli Swale in the county jail, accepted her retainer and warned her to say nothing to anyone unless her lawyer was present, he decided to call on the recuperating Smitty. Furthermore, he decided to return the little man's thousand dollar retainer. Reviewing what had happened, it had occurred to him that, for the thousand dollars, all he'd done for his client was to get him robbed, accused of murder, and finally, shot.

"But now," he said, "you can go ahead and tell who shot you. She's confessed."

But Smitty shook his head.

"Look," Malone said. "There's no reason not to talk now. There's no code, of gangland ethics involved any more."

"Gangland ethics hell," Smitty said, opening his eyes wide. "The only reason I didn't tell last night, was because I didn't know."

Oh well, Malone told himself as he went away, it wasn't going to matter to von Flanagan anymore anyway. He went on happily to keep a new date with Dolly Dove, but first to do a little shopping and properly express his gratitude to her.

It was nearly four the next morning when he sat in Joe the Angel's bar, thinking things over. He looked almost as disreputable as he could get, his eyes red–rimmed from lack of sleep, his face unshaven, his hair mussed and his tie under one ear. And he was puzzled.

"It's not at all like the old days," he complained to Joe the Angel, twirling his glass of rye in his hand. "A negligee from Saks. Paris import. She didn't want it. A bracelet. A wrist watch. No. Turned them both down."

Joe the Angel yawned and went on polishing the bar. "And what did she want, Malone?"

"She wanted," Malone said, "a supercharger for her car." He downed his rye, and sighed.

"Times," he said wearily, "have changed."

Vaguely reminiscent of her novel The Fourth Postman, *Craig bumps off a series of door–to–door salesmen in this story. Craig's fourth husband, Hank DeMott, was a vacuum cleaner salesman, but who are we to say where she got her inspiration? Malone is in the rare position of being flush and trying to avoid taking any new cases. Quite the novelty for our intrepid little lawyer. -JM*

Hard Sell

"Malone," the voice said, "you've got to help me."

The little lawyer waggled a finger at Joe the Angel and sat impassive while the bartender poured another double shot of rye. Then he swallowed the rye, reflecting thoughtfully that clients were always turning up when you needed them the least. "I don't have to help you," he said without bothering to turn around. "My office rent is paid a month in advance. My secretary is paid a week in advance. My bar tab is paid several drinks in advance. So go away."

"Money," said the voice, "is no object."

"That's what I've been trying to tell you," Malone said. "Besides, if you want me, why don't you call me at my office?"

"I tried," the voice admitted. "I talked to a girl named Maggie. She said *this* was your office."

Malone turned around, deciding firmly that Maggie would never again be paid anything in advance. He found himself looking at a large man with iron–gray hair, blue eyes, and a prominent chin. The man looked so healthy that Malone wanted to turn away again. "Go ahead," he said. "Tell me about it."

"Can't we go someplace private?"

"This is my office," Malone reminded him. "How private can you get?"

The man looked around vacantly, then back at Malone. "My name is Gunderson," he said. "Frank Gunderson. Mean anything to you?"

"Nothing," Malone said. "So far."

"I sell magazine subscriptions," Gunderson announced.

"That's nice," Malone said pleasantly. "Working your way through college?"

Gunderson looked very unhappy. "I don't exactly sell them," he explained. "I employ salesmen. Gunderson Sales, Inc. Door–to–door sales of leading magazines. A customer buys one or two magazines and gets another free. It's a very attractive offer."

179

"I'm sure it is," the little lawyer agreed. "But I can't read. So you're wasting my time."

"You don't understand," Gunderson said. "It's like this, Malone. Somebody's been killing my salesmen. One after the other, day after day, my men have been murdered."

"By prospective customers?"

"By a friend," Gunderson said. "First Joe Tallmer, struck down brutally by a hit–and–run driver. That was a week ago. Then, two days later, Leon Prince was pushed into an empty elevator shaft. The very next day, Howie Kirschmeyer was shoved from an elevated platform and mangled by an oncoming train. And — "

Malone help up a hand, both to silence Gunderson and to summon Joe the Angel. He downed the double rye that Joe poured and fixed sad eyes on Gunderson.

"Accidents," he said soberly, "can happen."

"But, Malone — "

"Three accidents," he went on. "The first one got hit by a car. The second one was too dumb to wait for the elevator. The third one tried to walk across the tracks. It figures, in a way. Anyone dumb enough to sell magazines for a living — "

"You don't understand," Gunderson cut in. "There was a fourth one. Just this morning."

"What happened to him?"

"He was shot through the head with a .45," Gunderson said. "He's dead," he added unnecessarily.

John J. Malone suddenly felt very tired. "Sounds like murder," he admitted. "But I'm sure the police can take care of it."

"I don't see how," Gunderson said. "The man's name was Henry Littleton. He was sitting over coffee while his wife was upstairs making the beds or something. Somebody came in, shot him, and left."

"The gun?"

"It was on the breakfast–room table. No prints, no registration."

"Hmmmm," Malone said.

"You see," Gunderson continued, "the police can do nothing. Littleton wasn't murdered by someone who knew him. He was murdered for the same reason as Tallmer and Prince and Kirschmeyer."

"And why were *they* murdered?"

"I wish I knew," Gunderson said. "I wish I knew."

Malone paused to light a cigar. "Come, now," he said gently. "You must have some idea. Otherwise you wouldn't be here annoying me."

Gunderson hesitated. "Malone," he said, "I don't want to sound paranoid. But I think someone is trying to ruin me, Malone. Killing my men one after the other. Crippling my sales force. Two of my men quit me today, Malone. Left me cold. Told me they couldn't take the chance of working for me. One of 'em said he had a wife and kid. Hell, *I've* got a wife and kid. Two kids, as a matter of fact. And — "

"Shut up for a minute," the little lawyer said absently. "Who would want to cripple your sales force? You have any competition in this little con game of yours?"

Gunderson colored. "It's not a con game. But I do have a competitor."

"Does he have a name?"

"Tru–Val Subscriptions," Gunderson said.

Malone sighed. "That's a strange name for a man," he remarked. "What do they call him for short? Troovie?"

"That's the company name, Malone. The man's name is Harold Cowperthwaite."

Malone looked around vacantly. He could understand the murder of door–to–door salesmen, especially if such murder were performed by dissident customers. But he didn't *want* to understand, not now. He didn't want the case at all.

"Malone? Here's a check. Twenty–five hundred dollars. I'll have another check for twenty–five hundred for you when you clear this up. Plus expenses, of course. Will that be sufficient?"

Malone took the check and found a place for it in his wallet. He nodded pleasantly at Gunderson and watched the man leave the City Hall Bar, walking with a firm stride, arms swinging, chest out. Then he looked around until he found Joe the Angel again and pointed to his empty glass. It was, he decided, time to begin piling up expenses for Gunderson.

Harold Cowperthwaite was not helpful. He looked as sickly as Gunderson looked vigorous, and was just about as much fun to be with. Malone decided that he disliked them both equally.

"— incredible accusation!" Cowperthwaite had just finished shouting. "A couple of his doorbell punchers keel over and he blames me for it! Blames me for everything! Ought to sue him for libel! Serve him right!"

Malone sighed, wishing the little man wouldn't talk exclusively in exclamation points. "Then you didn't kill them," he suggested.

"Kill them!" boomed Cowperthwaite. "Course I didn't kill them! I wanted to kill anybody I'd kill Gunderson! Know what I think, Malone?"

Malone was totally unprepared for the question mark. "Hmmm," he said, "what *do* you think?"

"Think he killed 'em himself!" Cowperthwaite shouted. "Throw suspicion on me! Make trouble for me! People bothering me all the time!"

"Oh," said Malone. "No, he couldn't have done that."

"No?"

"Of course not," Malone said. "He's my client."

Cowperthwaite's words followed the lawyer out of the door marked *Tru–Val Subscriptions*. Malone managed to close the door before the man reached the last exclamation point. It was, he decided, a day for small triumphs.

"The way I see it," von Flanagan said, "we wait until he kills another one. Then maybe he leaves a clue."

"He?" Malone said, lost. "Who he?"

"The killer," the big cop said. "The bird who killed Littleton and the others without leaving a trace. Pretty soon he'll find another magazine salesman and kill him. Maybe we get lucky and catch him in the act. Wouldn't that be nice?"

"For everybody but the magazine salesman," Malone agreed. "You don't seem to be taking much of an interest in this one. Something wrong?"

"Plenty," von Flanagan said. "For one thing, it's an impossible one to solve. For another, I don't want to solve it."

"Why not?"

Von Flanagan shook his head wearily. "Malone?" he said, "have you ever had a run–in with a magazine salesman? Have you ever had one of those little monsters stick his foot in your door and tell you how much you needed his rotten magazines? Have you, Malone?"

Malone nodded.

"They should kill every last one of them," von Flanagan said. "I mean it, Malone. Anybody kills a magazine salesman he deserves a medal."

Malone sighed. "The case," he reminded von Flanagan. "Let's talk about the case. Tell me all about it. Everything."

"There's not much to tell, von Flanagan said, relaxing into a chair. "This Littleton is thirty–three years old, has a wife and two kids. One is a boy and the other — "

" — is a girl," Malone guessed.

"You know the story? Then why bother me?"

"I'm sorry," Malone said. "Please go on."

"He's a hustler," said von Flanagan. "Holds down two jobs at once. Works real hard. Sells magazines evenings for this Gunderson character and works nine to five in a garage. Hasn't got any money, though. He's had a tough run of luck lately. Doctor bills, things going wrong with the kids, you know. But he's not in debt either. A good, steady guy. A guy you might like if he wasn't a magazine salesman."

"The crime," Malone said gently.

"Murder," von Flanagan said. "Not by the wife, either. I thought of that, Malone. I didn't want to because she's such a sweet little woman. A doll. But she was upstairs with the kids at the time. The kids said so. They wouldn't lie. Too young to lie."

Malone lit a cigar. "He was shot by somebody inside the house?"

Von Flanagan nodded. "At close range," he said. "It almost looked as though the killer wanted to make it look like suicide. But he didn't try very hard. No powder burns, for one thing, and the gun was lying near Littleton's left hand. And he was right-handed. We checked."

"Clever of you," the lawyer said. "So it was murder, and not by the wife. How about the other salesmen? Tallmer and Prince and Kirkenberger?"

"Kirschmeyer," von Flanagan corrected. "That's the funny part of it. Tallmer was a typical hit-and-run. Prince and Kirschmeyer look more like accidents than most accidents. But with them all coming together like this — "

"I know," Malone said gloomily. "Did Littleton have any insurance?"

"Insurance?" von Flanagan looked lost. "Oh," he said. "Littleton, insurance. Yeah. A big policy. But that's out, Malone. The wife is the only beneficiary and she's clear. So that's out."

"Thanks," Malone said. "So am I."

"So are you what?"

"Out," Malone said. "For a drink."

With two double ryes under his belt and a pair of beer chasers keeping them company, Malone felt in condition to use the phone. He called Charlie Stein, a useful little man who served as Dun and Bradstreet for a world far removed from Wall Street, running credit checks for gamblers and similarly unsavory elements.

"Take your time on this one," he told Stein. "Nothing urgent. I want to find out if there's anything around on a man named Henry Littleton. And," he added sadly, "there probably isn't."

"You're wrong," Stein said. "There is."

Malone came back to life. "Go on," he said. "Talk to me."

"Henry Littleton," Stein said. "He's into Max Hook for seventy-five grand. That all you want to know?"

"That's impossible," Malone said. "I mean — "

"Impossible but true."

"Oh," Malone said. "Well, you better cross him off, Charlie. Somebody shot him in the head."

Malone hung up quickly, then lifted the receiver again and put through a call to Max Hook. The gambler picked up the phone almost at once. "Malone, Max," Malone said cheerfully. "You didn't order a hit for a guy named Henry Littleton, did you?"

"Littleton? That's the fink who owes me seventy-five grand. Seventy-five grand he owes me and a nickel at a time he pays me. That guy." There was a pause. Then, with the air of someone just now hearing what Malone said in the first place, Hook said: "You saying somebody chilled him?"

"This morning. It wasn't you, was it?"

"Of course not," Hook said. "Why kill somebody who owes me money?

That doesn't make sense, Malone."

"I didn't think it did," Malone said pleasantly. "Just checking, Max." He put the receiver on the hook and made his way back to the bar.

"You don't look so hot," Joe the Angel said thoughtfully. "You want me to leave the bottle?"

Malone sighed. "Don't be ridiculous," he said. "Then I wouldn't have anybody to talk to." He closed his eyes and tried to think. This Littleton had been hard–working, honest, and seventy–five thousand dollars in debt. Hook hadn't killed him, and Cowperthwaite hadn't killed him, and his wife hadn't killed him, and he hadn't committed suicide. The whole thing was terrifying.

"I'm glad I found you," von Flanagan was saying. "You're drunk, but I'm still glad I found you. I want to tell you you've been wasting your time. We thought there was a connection between the salesmen. But there isn't."

"You're wrong," Malone said magnificently. "But go on anyway."

"Tallmer," von Flanagan said, ignoring the interruption. "The first one. A guy walked into the station–house and said he was the hitter–and–runner. Conscience was bothering him. And there was no connection between him and the rest. Accidents. Like we figured."

"Wrong," said Malone sadly. "Completely wrong."

"Huh?"

"I'll explain," said Malone. "I will tell all. I sort of thought something like this would happen." He sighed. "Tallmer was a typical hit–and–run. That much you know."

"That much I told you."

Malone nodded. "Prince and Kirschenblum — "

"Kirschmeyer."

"To hell with it," said Malone. "Anyway, the two of them were murdered. By the same person who killed Littleton."

"If you're so smart," said von Flanagan, "then you can tell me that person's name. The one who killed them all."

"Simple," said Malone. "The name is Littleton."

He explained while von Flanagan sat there gaping. "Littleton was in debt," he said. "Seventy–five grand in debt. With no way out. The Tallmer got hit by a car."

"Precisely," said von Flanagan.

"And Littleton got an idea," he said. "He wanted to kill himself but he didn't want his wife to lose the insurance. So he killed himself and made it look like a murder."

Malone lit a fresh cigar. "He set up a chain," he went on. "Chucked Prince down an elevator shaft and heaved Kirschengruber in front of the elevated."

"Kirschmeyer."

"You know who I mean. Anyway, Littleton did this, and set up a chain. A subtle chain. Then he shot himself."

"Left–handed?" From a distance?"

"Of course," Malone said. "If you wanted to make it look like a murder, would you use your right hand and put the gun in your mouth? See?"

Von Flanagan thought it over. "So it's suicide," he said. "And we write it off as murder and suicide, with Littleton the murderer. Right?"

"Wrong," Malone said. "You write Prince and Kicklebutton off as accidents and Littleton as murder by person or persons unknown. If he went to all that trouble there's no sense in conning the wife and kids out of the insurance. Besides, you'd never get a suicide verdict. Not unless I persuaded the coroner's inquest. And I won't."

Von Flanagan shrugged. "How are you going to collect your fee?"

"I'll tell Gunderson his salesmen are safe," Malone said. "I'll offer to repay the fee in full if another one gets murdered. And if that's not enough for him, he can keep the twenty–five hundred he owes me. Remember, I didn't want this case in the first place."

The title of this story (which also appeared under the name "Murder Marches On") was one of Craig's jokes. Who better to know about death and murder than an undertaker? Craig loved to use undertakers in her work. In one mystery, she had a corpse disappear from the back of a hearse on the way to the morgue. One of my personal favorites, Malone not only participates in a funeral procession, he also takes a trip down memory lane with references to characters from several of his earlier exploits including mentions of Hercules, the bloodhound, Joshua Gumbril, and a few cases that Craig didn't live to record. -JM

The Dead Undertaker

The parade started late, as all parades do. There was the usual confusion, with bands mustering on the wrong street corners, floats getting stuck in the traffic jam, and drum majorettes detained at the last minute by snap and elastic failures in strategic areas. There was the customary mix–up in the line of marching orders, with division captains running up and down waving their arms and blowing whistles, and the parade marshal sweating it out in his limousine and scowling at his wristwatch. And there was the usual search for visiting dignitaries, finally discovered in a nearby saloon. That was why John J. Malone was able to catch up with the parade after it had progressed only a block or two from its starting point at Michigan Boulevard and Roosevelt Road.

For the little lawyer, too, had been detained. Finding a rental outfit that would trust him for a frock coat, a high hat and a pair of patent leather shoes without the formality of a cash deposit was not easy on such short notice. That was the formal regalia of the Oblong Marching Society and to have appeared in anything else would have made him look conspicuous. Somewhere along the line of march one of the marchers was to slip him a list of names and one thousand dollars in cash.

"What do I have to do for the money?" Malone had asked Rico de Angelo. Rico was an undertaker, a relative of Joe of Joe the Angel's City Hall Bar. "You don't have to do anything," Rico had told him on the telephone. "All you have to do is keep this guy's name out of the newspapers."

"Why?" Malone said.

Rico hesitated. Then he said, "Remember the Gerasi murder? Well, this friend of mine, he was a friend of Gerasi's too. And Gerasi gave him this list of names before he was killed. Gerasi wanted him to give the list to the cops. But when Gerasi got killed, my friend got scared. He wants *you* to take the list and give

186

it to the cops, Malone. He wants to stay out of it."

Simple. Just a shade *too* simple, Malone told himself as he hung up the receiver. The newspapers had been running black headlines for weeks about ballot box frauds in the spring elections. Ghost voters. Names taken from the cemeteries. The cops had figured that Gerasi's Funeral Home had been supplying the names for the fraud. But Gerasi had turned honest, and passed the list on before he'd been killed. Now Malone had to get the list to the cops. But it had to be on the q.t. If the gang found out about it Malone, and Rico's friend, might both be Rico's customers.

His friends on the papers would thank him for a list like that, Malone knew, but he also knew that gangsters and crooked politicians took a dim view of informers. He would only be taking the heat off Rico's friend and putting it on himself. Still, a thousand dollars was a thousand dollars. He had a date with a blonde that night. There was also the office rent, three months overdue, with the landlord breathing down his neck. A thousand dollars would very nicely take care of both emergencies. He could depend on the boys at the city desks to keep his own name out of the papers, he assured himself. Besides, there was his duty as a lawyer to help the innocent, and this guy was an innocent party to the fraud — he hoped.

Third row from the front, fourth guy from the left, facing front, the guy with the red face and the gold tooth. That was how Rico had identified the client. Now, what with the hot Chicago sun beating down from above and the sizzling asphalt giving him the hotfoot from below, the instructions were getting a bit fuzzy in his mind. Fourth row from the front, third guy down from the left, or was it third row from the left, fourth guy from the front — no that couldn't be it. Something about facing front. He had been following the contingent. The thing to do was to hurry up ahead of it and count facing it. Malone hated walking, anywhere, any time, for any reason. Maybe he shouldn't have reinforced himself quite so much from the bottle in the emergency file in his office before leaving. Under forced march he managed to get up ahead of the marchers and, turning around to face them, walking backwards, he scanned the lines. Yes, that was it. Third guy from the front facing left — Oh, the hell with it. One thing he *did* remember. Somewhere in that weaving line of faces was a red–faced guy with a gold tooth and one thousand dollars. Never look a gift horse in the mouth, Malone reminded himself. Especially one with a gold tooth.

The girls' band from Bloomington struck up with a deafening rendition of John Philip Sousa's *Washington Post March*. The particularly curvaceous drum majorette doing cartwheels momentarily took Malone's mind off his work. A visiting dignitary hurrying to catch up with his place in the line of march shook Malone's hand and disappeared. Walking backwards was beginning to make him dizzy. He was about to give the whole thing up when he spied the flash of a gold tooth and quickly fell in line beside the red–faced guy, a maneuver that brought a polite "Pardon me" from the jolly little fat man he had bumped out of place, and an oath from the big, sad–faced man who reminded Malone of the hound dog Hercules he had once befriended up in Jackson County, Wisconsin, the one whose feet hurt him.

Now there was only one thing left to do. Wait for the red–faced guy on his right to slip him the fraudulent voting list and the one thousand bucks. That was to happen when the close order drill band of the Oblong Marching Society struck up, "How much wood could a woodchuck chuck if a woodchuck could chuck wood," Rico de Angelo had informed him on the telephone. That was to be the signal for him to edge over to the guy with the gold tooth and receive the list and the money.

Keeping up with the steady tread of the marchers, face front, Malone stole a look out of the corner of his eye at the man with the red face. He looked the way any respectable undertaker would be expected to look. His frock coat was well tailored with an expensive Capper and Capper cut to it. His top hat was of the glossiest silk and sat well on his well–groomed head. The expression on his face was the one every undertaker wears when the last notes of the organ music are dying away and he steps up to the coffin to invite the mourners to file past for a last look at the remains.

Solemn. Serious. But nervous. You could tell he was nervous by the too–rigid way he kept his eyes fixed ahead of him, afraid to look either to the right or to the left. Afraid to betray by so much as the flicker of an eyelash that he was even aware of Malone's sudden and unceremonious appearance in the line beside him. The sweat that glistened on his forehead might have been from the heat, but it stood out in shiny explosive little beads — fear sweat. Yes, he was scared. The red–faced man with the gold tooth was scared stiff. And he wasn't the only one. There was a feeling of tension all around him, Malone felt. It showed itself when, during a lull in the band music, the jolly little fat man on his left gave out with the first six notes of "Donna E Mobile." The big sad–faced Hercules behind him promptly squashed him with a "Shet–up!" and the red–faced guy winced all over like a spastic.

Yes, there was tension in the ranks. But definitely, Malone told himself. It set him to thinking. What assurance did he have, after all, that he and the red–faced man with the gold tooth were the *only* ones in the line who knew about the incriminating list of names and the money that was about to be passed. The red–faced guy was sticking his neck out a mile, playing informer on the voting fraud gang. Where there was a neck that long there was probably an ax *somewhere* in the vicinity, waiting for a chance to strike. A cute little Colt automatic in the pocket, maybe, with the safety off. Or a shiny Smith & Wesson .38 with a sawed–off barrel, under one of those respectable frock coats. And they could be aimed straight at the red–faced guy, ready to fire the minute he made one suspicious move. Or aimed at *him*, Malone reminded himself ruefully. Either/or — or both.

You don't pick up a hot list of names and a thousand bucks easy money without putting yourself in jeopardy, the little lawyer reflected, and wiped the sweat from his brow. Who was the jeopard? The little fat guy on his left? He didn't look it, but appearances could be deceptive. Malone remembered the jolly little man in the Hanson ax–murder case on the South Side. He turned out to be the coldest, most murderous killer he had ever tangled with. Could it be the hound–faced Hercules who was marching directly behind him? There was something sad, even gentle, in the pouchy droop of his eyes. When he said, "Shet up!" to the jolly guy who wanted to sing "Donna E Mobile" it was more in sorrow than in anger. A tired, weary, beaten–down "Shet up!" rather than an angry one. Just the same it could be either one of them. You couldn't tell about people.

No, and you couldn't tell about places, either. The middle of a street parade didn't seem like the kind of a place a gangster would pick to commit a murder. But neither did the corner of State and Madison, 'the world's busiest street corner,' and yet that was where death had caught up with snuffy little Joshua Gumbrill. Right in the middle of the noon–hour rush, too. And the killer had made a clean getaway in the milling crowd.

Yes, it could happen here. And it could happen to him.

He had come away from the office unarmed, with nothing deadlier on him than a half pint of whiskey in his hip pocket. Not that he ever used it — a gun, that is — but it was always comforting to know it was there if you needed it. For that matter, the same could be said for the half pint, Malone reminded himself. He wondered if it was strictly according to the manual of close order drill or the by–laws of the Oblong Marching Society to summon liquid reinforcement in the line of march. Just then a woman fainted from the heat in the watching crowd on the sidewalk and, while all eyes were on the scene of the accident, he raised the bottle to his lips with a quick, practiced gesture that had long ago made his most celebrated elbow at Joe the Angel's City Hall Bar.

It was a good thing he had fortified himself in time, for it wasn't two minutes later, at the intersection of Michigan Boulevard and Randolph Street to be exact, that the band leader of the Oblong Marching Society blew a shrill blast on this whistle and the band struck up:

"How much wood could a
    woodchuck chuck
If a woodchuck could
    chuck wood."

Malone sidled over slowly toward the red–faced guy on his right, ready for the pass that was to deliver the list of names and the money into his hand. Then something happened that wasn't on the program. The girls' band from Bloomington just behind them gave out simultaneously with:

"Oh, the monkey wrapped his talk
    around the flagpole."

The resulting disharmony and din threw the whole column out of step. Everybody stopped and turned to scowl at the bunglers. Instinctively Malone turned too. When he turned back again the red–faced man was no longer beside him. For a second Malone stared about him, bewildered. Then he looked down and saw that the man had collapsed on the street.

He lay on his back and he was gasping for breath. Immediately the marchers closed around him.

"Give him air," somebody shouted. "Can't you see the man's fainted?"

The parade came to a dead stop as the marchers carried their fellow member off the street, through the crowd and into the lobby of the corner building. He was still gasping for breath as they laid him down on the floor, fanning him with their top hats and debating excitedly about the best way to handle a case of sunstroke. By the time the police shouldered their way through the crowd he had stopped fighting for breath and lay quite still. Too still, Malone thought. He knelt down and reached for the man's wrist to feel his pulse. As he did so he heard a familiar voice behind him.

It was Captain Daniel von Flanagan of the Homicide Division.

"Well, if it isn't John J. Malone, attorney and counselor at law. And since when, may I ask, have the undertakers been taking lawyers into membership?"

"*Honorary* membership," Malone began lamely, and then, "Don't ask foolish questions, von Flanagan. A man's fainted from the heat and we've got to get him into an ambulance."

Von Flanagan bent down and felt the man's pulse. Then he turned.

"Fainted, did you say? Fainted from the heat? Malone, this man is dead."

"Heart failure," someone in the crowd said, and for a moment Malone was almost prepared to believe it. That red face. The way he had gasped for breath.

Von Flanagan turned the man over on his stomach. A wet patch was spreading over the black broadcloth of this frock coat. The stone floor where he had lain was wet too. And bright red. Von Flanagan pulled the coat up over the dead man's head and ripped off his shirt. In the middle of his back below the shoulder blades and a little to the left was a neat bullet hole.

"Drilled through the heart," von Flanagan said. He rose and looked around him at the frock–coated brethren.

"Didn't anyone hear a shot?" he demanded.

The looked at on another in dumb amazement, shaking their heads.

"I was right next to him," Malone said. "I didn't hear any shot."

But this time the lobby was crawling with cops.

"Nobody leaves here till I say the word," von Flanagan called out to them. "And you, Malone, I want to have a word with you. In private."

Malone followed von Flanagan to the storeroom behind the lobby cigar counter. The Captain's face was red with a hot Irish anger. His eyes narrowed as he looked down at the little lawyer.

"Malone, what do *you* know about this? I'm putting you all under arrest. You and this whole Oblong Marching outfit. I'll sweat it out of you if I have to — "

"If you'll take the advice of an old friend," Malone said, "you'll let the parade proceed as scheduled, without another minute's delay. You'll order every member of the Oblong Marching Society to take his place in line just exactly where he was before this thing happened. First though, I want your permission to go through the dead man's pockets."

"What for?"

"I've got my reasons, but I can't tell you now," Malone said. "There isn't time. You want to catch the killer, don't you?"

"Somebody drilled him from behind," von Flanagan said. "All I want to know is, who was marching directly behind this guy? What I can't figure is why didn't anybody hear the shot?"

"The noise," Malone said. "The bands got their signals mixed and two of them started up the same time. You could have shot off a cannon and everybody would have thought it was part of the program. Now, if you'll order the members back into some sort of formation — "

"Maybe you've got something there," von Flanagan said. "And the minute I see who the guy is that was marching behind the murdered man I'll order him searched and put under arrest at once."

Malone said, "Listen to me, von Flanagan. You won't do anything of the kind. If he committed one murder he won't hesitate to commit a second murder — this time to wipe out the evidence of the first murder. He'll try to shoot his way out — and innocent people are going to get hurt."

"Wait a minute, Malone."

"I'll point some guy out to you," Malone said. "You'll put the guy under arrest in full view of the whole crowd. Then you'll order the rest of them back into line and let the parade go on. After you take the suspect into custody you and your boys will do a fake vanishing act. Stay out of sight but not too far out of reach. I might need your help. When the killer starts shooting... "

The captain's face lighted up with its first faint ray of understanding. Then he shook his head. "No. No, Malone I can't let you do it. No friend of mine is going to make a clay pigeon out of himself."

But the Captain quickly let the little lawyer talk him into it. Too quickly, for such a devoted friend, Malone thought afterwards.

Back in the lobby again Malone went through the dead man's pockets looking for the hot list and the money. There wasn't a sign of anything like a list anywhere on his person. The only money was a few crumpled bills in his pants pocket. Could it be that the killer had murdered the wrong man? Or had the red–faced guy been scared out of the deal at the last minute?

He rose to his feet, hiding his disappointment and confusion behind a mask of smiling confidence.

"There's your man," he told von Flanagan, and pointed to a bewildered, professional guy in the crowd. The others fell back in amazement as von Flanagan's cops clapped handcuffs on the man and went off with him.

Von Flanagan addressed the crowd.

"Now I want everyone of you to fall in line again, just the way you were before this happened."

They filed out of the lobby and took their places in the parade again. Malone noted that his high hat lay on the street, a battered mess, where the marchers had trampled it underfoot in the excitement. He wondered how much that was going to set him back with the rental people. Beside it lay the dead man's hat. It had miraculously escaped being stepped on. Malone picked it up and put it gingerly on his head. It didn't quite fit, but he figured it would have to do. He wondered if the rental people would accept the substitution.

At a signal from von Flanagan the band leader blew his whistle and the band struck up "The Stars and Stripes Forever." The parade began to move once more up Michigan Avenue. Murder marches on, Malone muttered to himself as he looked uneasily to his right at the vacant spot where only a little while before the red–faced man with the gold tooth had been marching beside him.

He stole a backward glance at the man who was marching behind the vacant spot, and wondered why he hadn't noticed him before. Then the reason dawned on him. Who would figure the fat man for a killer? A jolly little guy singing "Donna E Mobile." That was why the gang had picked him, Malone realized — he looked like anything but a killer. But if the little fat guy had committed the crime it was going to be hard to convince a jury of it, unless he was taken *in flagrante delicto* with the murder weapon still smoking in his hand.

That was precisely what he had let himself in for, the little lawyer reflected ruefully. A sitting — or rather, a marching — duck. A waddling duck — his feet were killing him, and the dead man's hat sat on his head like a tin can on a post. A perfect target for a pot shot, if the fat man happened to miss this time. If he didn't miss, if his aim was as good on the second try as it was on the first, then he, John J. Malone, attorney and counselor at law, was a dead duck.

It was a sobering thought and the last thing he wanted just now was sobering thoughts. He reached into his hip pocket and brought out the reinforcing fluid. Let the members of the Oblong Marching Society, and the million spectators along the line of march, too, for that matter, think what they pleased of an undertaker taking a drop of liquid nourishment in public. He was damned if he was going to die of thirst just to uphold the reputation of the undertaking profession.

The band struck up a Sousa march and Malone, in an effort to add further support to his drooping spirits, raised his voice in song.

> *"Be kind to your flatfooted friends,*
> *For a duck may be somebody's mother,*

They live in deep marshes and fens,
Where it's damp — "

"Shet up!" said the sad–eyed Hercules behind him.

"What's the matter with my singing?" Malone replied without turning around.

"It stinks," said the sad–eyed man.

Malone decided that the man had no ear for music.

The Oblong Marching Society. The name was probably meant to suggest the shape of a hearse. Or was it a coffin? He dismissed the thought from his mind. This was no time to be thinking of hearses or coffins.

When was it going to happen? Was the killer going to fall for the decoy? He was probably weighing his chances right now. He had killed one man and he probably had the murder weapon on him this very minute. What would he have to lose if he killed a second man? They couldn't kill *him* twice. And there was always the chance that he could make a get–away in the excitement. So far as *he* knew the incriminating list was now on the person of John J. Malone, who had searched the dead man. Malone had even taken the precaution to "palm" the papers as he was searching the red–faced guy, just in case the killer was watching him, which he probably was. In short, he had done everything he could to put himself on the spot for anybody intent on obtaining possession of the hot list.

If that was what the killer was after — and what else could it be? — he was certainly a desperate man to be taking such chances right out in the open. Only one thing could explain it. He was one of the gang of racketeers who had muscled into the Oblong Marching Society as a source of cemetery names with which to help the crooked politicians stuff the ballot boxes. They were probably using the Society, too, as a respectable front for plenty of other rackets. Obviously the killer had been hand–picked by the mob as the fall guy for this dangerous assignment. His orders were "Get those papers, or else." He was right smack between the blue–barreled service automatics of von Flanagan's boys and the sawed–off shotguns of the mob.

Malone was almost sorry for the guy. He was even a bit sorry for himself. Where *were* von Flanagan's boys? He had warned the Captain to keep his men out of sight but not out of reach. Marching with measured tread to the music of the band — a bit unsteadily now, to be sure — he was listening for the reassuring purr of police motorcycles. He told himself he could hear them, ever so faintly, in the distance. He hoped, not too far distant.

He was lost in these reveries when suddenly the drum and bugle corps of V.F.W. Post No. 9 just up ahead and broke into:

"How much wood could a
   woodchuck chuck
If a woodchuck could
   chuck wood."

This is it! Malone told himself. The next instant he felt himself pushed from behind and when he looked up from the asphalt the scene that met his eyes was one of pure pandemonium, uncut and unrefined. The jolly little fat man was struggling in the grip of a dozen arms and von Flanagan's cops were converging on all sides with sirens moaning, cut–outs blasting the air like jet fighters. In less time than it takes to tell it the culprit was in handcuffs and being led away to the waiting squad cars.

"You did it," von Flanagan told Malone. "You did it and the department owes you an apology for ever suspecting — "

"The department owes me more than an apology," Malone said. He examined the silk topper. It had a bullet hole on each side of it. "How much," he asked, "do you think it's going to cost me to replace one of these things?"

Von Flanagan shrugged and, after a congratulatory handshake, took his departure with the squad car. Malone was left holding the hat. He looked up at the sad–eyed Hercules whose shove from behind had pushed him in the nick of time out of harm's way.

"I owe my life to you," he said. "Do you mind if I buy you a drink?"

Ten minutes later at Joe the Angel's City Hall Bar, the little lawyer sat brooding, head in hand, on the turn of events that had left him with nothing to show for his pains but a bullet–pierced high silk hat that he would have to pay for when he returned the outfit to the rental people. No hot list. No thousand dollars. Two tired feet that felt like half–raw, quick–fried beef in the tight patent–leather rented shoes. And a headache from the dead man's ill–fitting hat.

The sad–eyed guy wasn't proving to be much of a help either, sitting there and staring moodily into his beer. Malone ordered up another double rye. He turned to the sad–eyed one and said for the dozenth time, "I owe my life to you. Can I buy you another beer?"

The dour one shook his head.

"You don't owe me nothin'," he said sourly.

This was a hell of a note. A guy saves your life and when you offer to buy him a drink he insults you by ordering one beer and refusing a refill. This was one more frustration in a day that had been nothing but frustrations. This was the last straw.

"Bring this guy a double rye," he said to Joe the Angel. "Give him *two* double ryes, Joe. And a beer chaser."

"In your hat," said the sad–eyed one.

"Nobody talks like this to my friend Malone," Joe the Angel said.

Malone said, "You keep out of this, Joe. I owe my life to this man. The least I can do is buy him a drink."

"Then let him drink up," Joe the Angel said. He sat down two glasses on the bar and poured two double ryes. And a beer chaser.

"Down the hatch," Malone said, raising his own glass.

"In your hat," said Hercules.

Joe the Angel reached for the bung–starter, but Malone stopped him with an imperious wave of the hand.

"An insult is an insult, friend or no friend," he said to the dour one. He was beginning to feel the heartening effects of the rye. "Now, if you'll oblige me by stepping outside we can settle this thing like gentlemen."

The sad–eyed one lifted himself off the bar stool and started for the door. Malone donned the silk topper and followed him outside.

At the first passage of arms Malone found himself sprawling on the sidewalk. Beside him lay the silk hat, a shapeless mess.

"In your hat," said the dour one, and stalked off.

Before Malone could get to his feet the sad–eyed Hercules had disappeared in the sidewalk crowd.

Malone picked up the battered topper and as he did so his fingers encountered something bulging in the hat–band. He reached in and pulled out a sheaf of carefully folded sheets. They were covered on both sides with close–packed single–space names. He dived into the hat–band and this time he came up with a little sheaf of crisp hundred dollar bills. He counted them. Ten.

For a second, it didn't register. Then he got it. Hercules had been a friend of the murdered man. Hercules had known where it had been hidden. He'd known about Malone, too, and he had been telling Malone everything the lawyer needed to know about the list and the money. It was all cleared up now.

Malone considered chasing the sad–eyed man, but decided against it. Hercules would want no publicity, and very probably no thanks. The way he'd look at it, he'd only have been doing his job. Helping out a friend.

Besides, Malone told himself, Hercules would be too far away by now.

The little lawyer shrugged. He'd had the money with him all the time — and never known it.

"In your hat," Malone told himself. He put the crumpled topper on his head, and went back to the bar.

Sources

"Wry Highball," *Ellery Queen's Mystery Magazine*, March 1959

"The Frightened Millionaire," *The Saint*, April 1956

"Shot in the Dark," *Manhunt*, August 1955

"Say It With Flowers," *Manhunt*, September 1957

"How Now, Ophelia," as by Michael Venning, *Ellery Queen's Mystery Magazine,* June
   1947

"Death in the Moonlight," *Popular Detective*, March 1953

"Beyond the Shadow of a Dream," *Ellery Queen's Mystery Magazine*, February 1955

"One More Clue," *Manhunt*, April 1958

"They're Trying to Kill Me," *The Saint*, February 1959

"No, Not Like Yesterday," *The Saint*, February 1956

"Hard Sell," *Ed McBain's Mystery Book 1*, 1960

"The Dead Undertaker," *Manhunt*, December 1953, as "Murder Marches On"

Murder, Mystery and Malone

Murder, Mystery and Malone by Craig Rice, and edited by Jeffrey A. Marks, is set in 11–point Garamond font and printed on 60 pound natural shade opaque acid–free paper. The cover illustration is by Gail Cross, and the 'Lost Classics' series design is by Deborah Miller. The first edition comprises 200 copies in trade paper and 200 copies in cloth. *Murder, Mystery and Malone* was published in March 2002 by Crippen & Landru, Publishers, Norfolk, Virginia.

Printed in the United States
4676